FINDING
Hemingway

KEN DORTZBACH

CLOISTER INN PUBLISHING
Brookfield, WI

Published by Cloister Inn Publishing, Brookfield, WI.

Finding Hemingway is partially inspired by and written in homage to *The Sun Also Rises* by Ernest Hemingway. All language and content in *Finding Hemingway* complies with the fair use doctrine and other applicable legal authority, including but not limited to by providing credit for short quotations in-text where necessary.

Cover Design by Elizabeth Lane Designs
Editing & Proofreading by Erika's Editing
Publishing Support by Books Fluent and its affiliates

Publisher's Cataloging-in-Publication Data
Names: Dortzbach, Ken, 1969, author.
Title: Finding Hemingway / Ken Dortzbach.
Description: Brookfield, WI : Cloister Inn Publishing, 2020. | Summary: Petulant Callie McGraw has six months between jobs and a hefty severance check when she is literally called to Spain by Ernest Hemingway, the author of her very favorite book The Sun Also Rises. Along the way Callie learns about life, love, and herself—and how to run with the bulls in Pamplona.
Identifiers: LCCN 2020903964 | ISBN 9781733624701 (pbk.) | ISBN 9781733624718 (epub) | ISBN 9781733624725 (Kindle)
Subjects: LCSH: Hemingway, Ernest, 1899-1961--Fiction. | Man-woman relationships--Fiction. | Self-actualization (Psychology) in women--Fiction. | Women lawyers--Fiction. | Spain--Fiction. | BISAC: FICTION / Women. | FICTION / Romance / Historical / 20th Century.
Classification: LCC PS3604.O78 F56 2020| DDC 813/.3--dc23
LC record available at https://lccn.loc.gov/2020903964

For Jennie

CONTENTS

New York City | 1

Chapter 1: Two Calls 3

Barcelona | 13

Chapter 2: Transported to Places Far Away. 15

Chapter 3: Interning for an Intern 22

Chapter 4: Like Stones Skipping Along the Water 28

Chapter 5: The Callie McGraw I Could Never Be in New York 34

Chapter 6: The Mountain Monastery. 43

Chapter 7: Picasso Was a Friend of Mine 50

Madrid | 59

Chapter 8: Sexy as Hell 61

Chapter 9: Enter Spain Man 67

Chapter 10: Murdering Tomatoes 78

Chapter 11: A Spanish Kiss 89

Chapter 12: Drippy Clocks and a Hidden Bull 97

Chapter 13: Fuzzy Sharks and a Hairband 107

Chapter 14: Hell Hath No Fury Like a Woman Scorned 115

Chapter 15: The Sage and *Un Niño* 125

Chapter 16: A Frenchman and a Tartiflette. 135

Chapter 17: A Theatrical Detour 147

Chapter 18: When Everything Was Dying 157

Chapter 19: Claiming My Strong. 166

Chapter 20: A Canadian in Madrid 175

Chapter 21: Sex Never Changes Anything(Situational Irony) 188

Chapter 22: Difficult Truths. 198

Chapter 23: The Ultimatum. 207
Chapter 24: A Matador Emerges 219

Pamplona | 229

Chapter 25: Viva San Fermín! 231
Chapter 26: Until We Shared One Skin 241
Chapter 27: Callie's Perfect Day. 249
Chapter 28: Nightmares & New York 260
Chapter 29: A Special Circle of Hell. 271
Chapter 30: Mr. Hemingway, I Presume 284
Chapter 31: A Fever of the Blood. 293
Chapter 32: Living All the Way Up 302

Madrid (*Más*) | 313

Chapter 33: Ten Mornings from Now 315
Chapter 34: The Greatest Plan Ever 322
Chapter 35: Almost Like a Truce 335
Chapter 36: A Colorful Goodbye. 343
Chapter 37: No Need for Leftovers 355
Chapter 38: Three Types of Red Lights. 362

San Francisco | 375

Epilogue: California Company. 377
Acknowledgments 381
About the Author. 382

New York City

Chapter 1

Two Calls

See that woman over there? The one lounging around in yoga pants and a university sweatshirt in the middle of the day? That's me—Callie McGraw, an unemployed thirty-something with a law degree from an Ivy League institution. I won't mention my school's name because I don't want to brag, but it rhymes with "snail."

Perhaps it's misleading to say I'm "unemployed," but I'm definitely between jobs—and I was definitely fired. "Laid off" is the nicer term. Pretty much everyone in my department was laid off after the acquisition. Which is too bad for the folks who took over, because I'm a damn good lawyer. A damn good lawyer who could find another position anywhere.

Straight out of law school, I became a hotshot young corporate attorney at a hotshot New York law firm. I worked long hours, to the point where I relied heavily on the "perks" of corporate America to cram in time for my personal stuff. For one thing, the firm had its own twenty-four-hour, state-of-the-art gym. I could take a break from my merger agreements and get my cardio in at ten in the evening. I did that most nights, and it got me in shape—I actually lost the weight I gained in law school—but it also made me very drowsy all the time, which only made my days seem that much longer. I made damn good money and was on an accelerated partnership track, but eventually I realized all I was doing was working, exercising, sleeping… and working some more. The sleep deprivation finally won, and I decided I didn't want to be a partner after all.

I left the firm for an in-house attorney role with one of our clients. I rose through the ranks quickly there. My days were still demanding and frenzied, but a least I could manage some decent sleep—a significant lifestyle upgrade. The company was large, and although I didn't quite make it to the executive echelon, I got close. Then came the merger, the slashing-and-burning of the legal department. And so, as of last week, I learned the reality of the word *severance*.

My severance package wasn't enough to make me rich-rich, but it was a lot of money—enough to fund a job search for a while, even in New York, without touching my savings. That was a smart move on the new company's part—if you're going to ax the lawyers, you'd better make us happy enough that we won't sue. Because, trust me, I know how to sue.

The money softened the blow, but the sting was still there. Which brings me back to me in my yoga pants, keeping company with the empty box of Pop-Tarts on my kitchen island and the mostly empty pot of coffee next to it. My "breakfast of unemployed champions."

To put it mildly, I was bored, listless. But not the sort of bored I actually wanted to do anything about. The sort of bored where the only cure is doing a whole lot of nothing. The "nothing" I was doing was watching *The Sun Also Rises*, the movie version of my favorite book. For a film made in the 1950s, I guess it came close enough to the novel, but at the same time it wasn't what the Spain Hemingway had crafted, the Spain that had rescued me time and time again over the years.

I was midway through the film when my smartphone rang. I jumped. I thought I'd put the damn thing in silent mode, because I've always hated being interrupted in the middle of a movie. I snatched my phone from the coffee table and was about to hit "Ignore" when I noticed the caller info. It was Matt, from my law school days. Matt, who I hadn't talked to in two years… and never at eleven on a weekday morning. The timing was intriguing enough to make me pause the film.

Matt and I had slipped into a friendship early in law school. I was nice to him because I'm nice to everyone—or at least I was in those days, when I had the patience for that sort of thing. Back then, I made an effort. Matt was a somewhat-dumpy kid who didn't have many friends, but as it turned out, he was really funny. Believe me when I say every laugh in law school *counts*—without a good chuckle every now and again, stress-induced insanity was a real threat.

His family had money. Lots of it. So much money that Matt wasn't in law school to get a job, he was there for the "educational experience." Normally I hated people like that because I'd worked damn hard—if only out of spite for my parents—to get where I was, but Matt's humor was his saving grace, and he made an art out of insouciance. By our last year of school, though, he realized he had to do *something* next, so he got his act together. When we graduated, he went to work for his aunt's investment firm in California. We more or less lost touch, just as I did with most of my friends.

"Callie here," I said, answering the call. That was my standard power greeting. I wasn't in a position of power at the moment, but Matt didn't need to know that, and no one called an old friend wanting to hear the world's smallest violin.

We made small talk for a few minutes. It was nice to hear his voice, I'll admit that much, but as we talked, I could tell Matt wanted something. He had that "scratch my back and I'll scratch yours" tone that only the very wealthy could pull off. What he could possibly want from me was a mystery, because Matt always asked for small favors outright. Beating around the bush meant something important was on his mind.

I was right. Not two minutes later, he said, "Look, Callie, I know this is short notice, but I'm in New York right now. Are you free for lunch? I have an idea you'll be interested in."

"In New York now?! That's great," I replied, pulling my hair out of its low ponytail as if suddenly Matt could see me. I surveyed the disaster that was my apartment, noticed a fresh coffee stain on my sweatshirt, and calculated how much time was left in my movie—I wasn't leaving before the big bullfight, not even for Matt. That scene was the only part of the film more enthralling than the book: bulls were the creatures of my nightmares—an unfortunate childhood incident at a local farm had seen to that. Despite the twenty-something intervening years, I was still astonished anyone would willingly face such a beast.

"Yeah, I'd love to," I continued, "but you'll have to come to me. I'm in the Village."

"The Village. So bohemian."

"Yeah, sure. Bohemian lawyer," I retorted. He laughed too hard at my joke. Yep, Matt definitely wanted something.

I met him at an Italian restaurant, an old standby of mine a few blocks from my building. He already had a table, and I almost didn't recognize him as he stood to give me a hug. Matt was very put together; no more dumpiness, no air of insouciance, a real adult in a real suit. I, however, looked like someone who was unemployed—I'd changed out of my stained sweatshirt, but my yoga pants were my friend for the day. Which was okay, actually, because a heaping plate of pasta was in my near future.

Matt did most of the talking until our food came. Turned out, investing wasn't his thing, and he'd finally worked up the courage to tell his aunt as much. Hey, that only took the better part of a decade, but good for him.

Our food arrived, and then it was my turn to do "my life in five minutes" thing. Maybe it wasn't the most interesting life, but up until last week it was a life I was damn proud of, and I didn't feel the need to hide it. I'd clawed my way up the corporate ladder by my own wits and sweat; one pink slip didn't change that.

"That's why I'm here, Callie," Matt jumped in as I shoveled a well-timed forkful of pasta primavera into my mouth. I was about to get to the severance portion of my story and was buying myself some time. "Susan Thompson said you might be in the market for a new job."

Susan was one of our classmates. She'd made partnership track at one of the other hotshot New York law firms, yet she still managed to keep tabs on everyone from our class. She took it as a point of pride to broadcast everyone's business, like a living, breathing alumni newsletter.

"You have a job offer?" I asked, confused.

"I'm in tech now. I started my own company."

I bit into my garlic bread to hide my amazement. I didn't think Matt had it in him. He had the skills, that much I knew, but founding a tech company... that took ambition, drive, focus. Was this really Matt, *my* Matt?

"And I need a general counsel," he continued. "Sort of."

"A general counsel? And what does 'sort of' mean? What do you even need a lawyer for?" My questions came out unfiltered, in rapid succession.

"For my company," he said proudly. "Honestly, we're not much of a company yet, but I laid out the start-up capital. The paperwork is filed, and I have a few staff. We're cutting-edge tech with a groundbreaking product in early development. Very cool."

"Matt, are you sure I'm right for this? I don't know much about technology and I don't know much about general counseling."

"But you do, Callie. Have you seen your résumé?! Two big players, promotions like clockwork. In New York, no less. You've seen it all, you'd be perfect." He took a sip of his wine as if his argument was irrefutable.

"Matt... I..."

"And I trust you."

It was hard to argue with basic trust, so I listened as he explained further. Strong business model, a new tech niche, game-changing innovation. It sounded good. Damn good.

"There's one catch, though. The position doesn't begin for a while," he said, suddenly looking a bit sheepish. "You see, I'm still raising funds. I have tons of letters of intent, but I need about six months to nail down investors before I can start paying a general counsel."

"I understand." Six months wasn't *that* far off. Not far enough for me to jump ship this early in the conversation, and I certainly wasn't in any rush to get back to my empty box of Pop-Tarts.

"It's a funny thing, Callie. I have to go investor by investor, look each of them in the eye and ask for millions of dollars." Matt's gaze locked onto mine with a practiced power-look that suited him surprisingly well. "And they all know there's a decent chance they'll never see those millions again. But, if things break the right way, their return on investment could be tenfold—that's the gamble I'm selling." He paused, but his power-look didn't waiver. "I always need to make that final ask: Will you give me millions of dollars?" He paused again and his eyes intensified. "Please?"

Damn. I was ready to give him millions of dollars right there. I didn't have that kind of money, of course, but I had my severance, and I had my savings. I offered some of it. Matt said not to worry. He had so many letters of intent that even if two or three investors fell through, he'd still have enough capital. Not a bad position to be in.

We chatted a bit more, with Matt eagerly answering my many questions. I put the screws to him, yet not one single answer raised an alarm, and I was one-hundred percent sure he wasn't bullshitting. Matt, not bullshitting—that alone held my attention.

He scooped a forkful of broccoli rabe into his mouth, chewing it quickly. "And of course we'll cover your relocation costs."

That hit hard. "Leave New York?" I blurted out. He should've led with that—a cross-continental move wasn't exactly a small ask.

"We're in San Francisco. Northern California is *the* tech hub for this kind of thing." He looked apologetic as he added, "But my offer also includes three months of housing, with an option for a long-term lease."

I thought about it for a minute, pushing the last of my pasta around my plate. Why did I want to stay in New York? I didn't have family here—my parents, now divorced, were still back in Illinois. Friends?

No one close, no one I'd stay put for. Men? *Definitely* no one I'd stay put for.

I sipped my wine, buying myself a few more seconds to think. I'd done all the shots I wanted to drink in New York bars. Actually, I didn't drink that many shots. The women I knew drank all the shots they wanted, and I'd lived vicariously through them. I'd also slept with all the New York men I wanted to sleep with. Actually, I didn't sleep with many New York men; relationships weren't really my thing, and the women I knew slept with all the men they wanted—I'd lived vicariously through them in this respect as well. And the "culture?" My one true non-vicarious exploit was art—museums and galleries. But I'd been in the city for so long, I'd been to them all multiple times. The decision suddenly seemed easy.

"Matt, count me in!" I shook his hand in a formal, deal-closing kind of way. He then pulled out his phone, tapped the screen a few times, and I heard the *swoosh* sound of a sent email. He looked up at me with a smile that was both relieved and confident as my own phone beeped.

"What was that?" I asked.

"Paperwork, company background, financial stats. The whole package. All the good-faith stuff, plus the offer. I had my assistant put it together for you."

Of course, it was. Having a prepped package ready was the way anyone who'd spent three years in law school would handle things. Anyone but the Matt I'd known. Obviously, "new Matt" was going to take some getting used to.

I sat there with my mouth hanging open while the waitress cleared our plates. "Any thoughts on your next six months?" he asked, changing the subject and winding down the conversation.

"Dessert," I replied.

"Dessert?"

"Yeah, I just landed a fantastic new job. That calls for a celebration. Lava cake, I think."

Matt laughed. "A brilliant strategy! I can't stay, though… I have a three-thirty on Wall Street. But don't let that stop you."

He called the waitress back over. I ordered my cake, he paid the bill. I didn't argue about his paying. I wasn't exactly unemployed anymore, but I wasn't exactly employed, either. Now what would I do?

⤚

I didn't feel like going home after a lunch like that. Relishing the lava cake kept me on a high for a little while, but as soon as I'd finished my last bite, I'd started reeling. Matt's offer was basically my dream job, but how often do dreams come true? What the hell had I just committed to?

I wandered around the Village, finding myself on a bench in Christopher Park. I sat down and began reviewing Matt's documents on my phone. All was just as he'd pitched it—I couldn't find a single misrepresentation or loophole. Yet an ominous, six-month black hole was reading over my shoulder the whole time.

I was at a loss as I started meandering around again, sort of heading home but sort of *not* heading home at the same time. As I passed a Spanish restaurant on Seventh Ave., I caught the scent of beef cooking in some marvelous combination of spices. The aroma stopped me in my tracks. I let myself melt into the heavenly scent, the dervish of the city spinning around me. The mid-winter sun was already slanting toward sunset, its rays casting a golden brightness. The glow, devoid of warmth, contrasted with the powerful, heady spices, and I lost myself in the discord. Enthralled and distracted, I didn't bother looking at the caller ID when my phone rang. In fact, I'm surprised I answered it at all, since the world was spinning so deliciously around me.

"Callie, it's me," came the voice. A confident voice, pragmatic and straightforward, but with a touch of gentleness in its timbre. A voice I'd heard somewhere before, like on an old-fashioned newsreel. A voice I couldn't quite place.

"Who is this? Do I know you?"

"The sun also rises in Spain, Callie." My stomach lurched.

"What kind of prank is this?" I snapped. Who'd given this lunatic my number?

"It's me, Callie, I can assure you."

I don't know what about the voice rang true, but some part of me trusted it. An implicit trust that wafted through me, dissolving my skepticism.

"Hemingway? Mr. Ernest Hemingway?" The words fell from my mouth cautiously yet free of doubt.

"Yes, that's correct."

"The Pulitzer Prize winner? The Nobel Prize author?"

"Once again, correct. Well done," he said.

"The *deceased* Ernest Hemingway?"

"Death is but a small detail. Pay it no mind."

I had no comeback for that, so I remained quiet. Death didn't seem like a small detail to me, but I was too intrigued to argue.

"Callie, the sun also rises in Spain," he repeated. "Come find me, I'm waiting for you. You must find me."

The line went dead.

I looked up, perplexed and trying to reorient myself. I was still on Seventh Ave., but now the city was transformed. It all looked so bleak. I'd lived here for more years than I cared to count; New York was still magical, but that magic was long over for me. I'd done well here, sure, but that wasn't reason enough to stay. Not anymore.

I needed sun. I needed wine. I needed tapas. I needed a universe of old-world tradition imbued with modern vivacity. Every part of me felt refocused, as if I'd locked onto a new target, and that target was Spain. And most of all, I needed to find Earnest Hemingway.

That was it for me. I ran home and accepted Matt's offer as-is and pulled my suitcases out of storage. The next morning, I bought a one-way ticket across the Atlantic, and in the afternoon, I started calling long-distance movers and San Francisco storage facilities. The day after that, I researched a few of the finer points of housing law and bullied my landlord into letting me out of my lease. With that locked down, I started packing my worldly possessions. I found it kind of pitiful that I didn't have many worldly possessions after so many years here, but that heaviness only further convinced me this was the right moment to leave the city, possibly for good. I was on my way to Spain.

To Hemingway. I only had six months to find him.

BARCELONA

CHAPTER 2

TRANSPORTED TO PLACES FAR AWAY

I first read *The Sun Also Rises* in middle school, when my parents' marriage was circling the drain. I was already dealing with all the insecurities and inadequacies that germinate during those horrible in-between years, and then my parents laid their issues—and ultimately their divorce—on top of it. Wonderful. Like growing breasts hadn't been difficult enough.

I'd always loved to read, and with my parents at each other's throats, fiction became my one true escape. It transported me to places far away, places without my mother and father and their incessant battling. Places where I didn't feel *guilty* about their incessant battling. Fiction brought me to worlds where I could be the Callie McGraw I wanted to be.

I bought my first copy of *The Sun Also Rises* for no good reason except that the cool kids were reading it—and in middle school, anything the cool kids were doing *was* a good reason. I was in a bookstore searching for an author. I don't remember which author I was looking for, but I know I was in the *J* section. Two super-cool high-school girls were a couple of cases over, in the *H* section. I moved in closer, pretending to browse.

"Ugh, I have to read this for class," one said, pointing to a book on the shelf.

"It's not so bad. I read it last year. There's some cool stuff in it," the other replied. "Hemingway isn't nearly as awful as the other authors they torture us with."

"He wrote a lot of other stuff too, right? Like that fish book?"

"You mean *Moby Dick*?"

"No, like about an old guy… and a fish…. *Moby Dick* is about a whale. Whales are mammals. Everyone knows that."

"Whatever. What's this one about?"

"Living in Europe, I guess. Pay attention to the cities, because Theobald's quizzes are *hard*."

I listened intently to every word. I wanted to be like them, to read what they read. One of them, the girl who knew *Moby Dick* was a whale, pulled a book off the shelf before they walked away. I grabbed the second copy of that book before they made it to the register. I felt an odd twinge as I read the back cover: Hemingway had entered my soul.

When I started reading the novel, I couldn't put it down. The pages flew by as the characters careened from the cafés of Paris to the wilds of Spain. Their lives seemed blissfully free and easy. Of course, my middle-school mind didn't pick up on the heavier themes—I only saw lives free from pain or deep connections. Any pain the characters did feel was apparently washed away by the next bottle of wine. Oh, God, the wine. Bottle after bottle. Could you do that? They did. The characters managed to transcend their lack of connections in a way my young mind mistook as an ongoing party.

Moby Dick girl and her friend were wrong. *The Sun Also Rises* isn't a book about "living in Europe." It's about people drifting, although I didn't figure that out until I was older. American veteran Jake Barnes joins the throngs of expatriate youth in post-World War I Europe. Jake loves Lady Brett Ashley, but the war left him impotent, and while she longs for him too, they can't make a relationship work. Almost all the male characters in the book also idolize Lady Brett Ashley, ranging from the wealthy American writer Robert Cohn to the dashing Spanish bullfighter Pedro Romero, which creates a lot of tension. Everyone in the novel is looking for something, although they don't really know it. They overcompensate by living it up in various locales in France and Spain, filling their days with food and wine as they fend off the void they share inside. It's a heavy book, replete with themes and metaphors. I've read it dozens of times, yet I always found something new each time I picked it up.

≪≒

I didn't sleep on the plane to Barcelona. I should've slept—I was exhausted after two whirlwind weeks of packing and planning—but I was beginning my adventure and my eyelids wouldn't stay closed. Instead, I watched the two in-flight movies, since I'd wanted to see both but had missed them in theaters. The two very different movies shared one thing: underneath the special effects and plot twists, they were both the kind of film where the premise is really good and the first seventy-five percent is really good, but—as if the screenwriters suddenly ran out of ideas—the last twenty-five percent is predictable and boring. Wholly disappointing, when predictable and boring were *not* what I needed.

We landed with a hard jolt, the type that made me suspect the pilot almost botched the landing. Yet I was thrilled to touch ground. Barcelona wasn't in *The Sun Also Rises*; in fact, much of the book is set in Paris. But I'd been to Paris many times, so much so that my French had become pretty solid. I had no interest in elbowing past tourists in the City of Lights for months; I knew from experience that even if I found a place off the beaten path, I would still be haunted by the feeling I was traversing a well-worn trail.

Besides, Hemingway told me to find him in *Spain*. He obviously had plans for me on the Iberian Peninsula, and he clearly wanted me to do something exciting and new. So, because I'd never been to Barcelona before, I'd decided to start my journey in a fresh city. Hey, literature is about interpretation, so why couldn't take I some liberties?

After claiming my luggage (a large backpack and two suitcases), I caught a taxi to my downtown hotel. I didn't speak Spanish, really, but my driver could manage a few words of bad English in the same way I could manage a few words of bad Spanish. When he dropped me off, I was pleased to see my hotel was just what I'd expected. Simple. Clean. Nice.

That night I had a dinner of sausages and cheese at a nearby café—really good Spanish sausages and even better Spanish cheese. I also had a bottle of red wine. I wasn't sure exactly what type I was drinking, but the suave older waiter (in beautifully accented English) had recommended it, saying it was "authentically Spanish." Initially, he'd asked if I wanted a half-carafe or maybe just a glass. But I was looking for Hemingway: I needed the whole bottle.

I took in my meal in alternating bites—one meat, one cheese, one meat, one cheese, big sip of wine—savoring the flavors quietly and feeling as if I'd achieved a Spanish-culinary-Zen on my palate. I remained in Zen-bliss until I felt myself being watched.

It wasn't unusual for me to get lecherous looks from men, and I'd learned to tune them out, but I could always still *sense* when someone's interest fell on me. I zeroed in on the culprit—some guy at a standing table a few feet away. His look wasn't a lecherous look, though, it was just a "noticing" look. I gave a noticing look back—just a glance before turning back to my plate. But I'm a lawyer, I'm trained to take in a ton of details quickly. I caught the basics: the guy was young-ish like me. Sort of skinny. A little on the tall side. Short hair, a light brown beard, not Spanish. Definitely someone who knew how to travel on a budget.

He lobbed across the short divide between our tables. "American?" he asked, politely enough.

"Mmmmhh?" My mouth was full.

"You're American, right?"

Annoyed at having to rush through the last of my cheese, I replied, "Uh, yes. And it sounds like you are as well."

"I am, and I can usually spot other Americans. There aren't many of us here right now. Most are in Madrid, or they don't come to Spain at all. They go to Paris."

I nodded in understanding. I felt like I had passed some initial test of his, but at the same time I felt somewhat denigrated—the last thing I wanted was to look like a typical American tourist. Because I wasn't typical: I was on a mission.

"I'm not a tourist, I'm a visitor." I shot him a glance that clearly said, "There's a difference between the two. It was the same look countless New York "visitors" had given me over the years. I cocked my head slightly. "And you're...?"

"Sorry, my name is Trevor. I guess I'm a visitor, too." He paused. "Are you going to finish that?" He pointed at my bottle of wine with the fork he was still holding.

"Probably." I nodded again, more slowly this time.

"I didn't mean to intrude. It's just I've been on my own for a while, and I haven't seen a lot of Americans lately." I sized him up quickly as he spoke. He seemed harmless. Something about him and his brown-green eyes said, "puppy dog."

"I'm Callie. I flew in this afternoon, and I plan to stay in Spain awhile. And you?"

"I'm... sort of passing through. Not quickly, though. I'm back-packing, and I've been on the road for three months already." When I didn't answer immediately, he volunteered more. "I spent two months in France, and then I was in Mallorca for a while—I just came over to the mainland last week. I guess you could say I'm seeing the world. Or at least this part of it."

I pointed to the open chair at my table. "Well, you're welcome to see this part of it," I said, then gave him a stern look. "But bring your own wine." Trevor smiled as he stretched between our tables and picked up his not-quite-empty glass.

The lone mouthful of red wine looked sad in his glass. I acquiesced. "Well, maybe I can share a little." I added some of my wine to his. I didn't know what he was drinking, but he didn't seem to care about mixing reds.

He launched into his tale as we drank my bottle (and then started on another one). He was a graduate student—a PhD candidate in Comparative Literature—but was taking some time off. Typical, I thought. But then, not everyone could have instructions from Hemingway himself.

Trevor told me about wanting to see all kinds of places. Germany. Denmark. Hungary. The list went on—I think he was lonely. He managed to keep talking without saying much, occasionally stammering in a sort of non-language when he seemed unsure of what to say next. I mostly listened and nodded agreeably, throwing in a "Yes," or "That's so true," here or there. It got a little monotonous after a while. Honestly though, I think he simply enjoyed speaking English to another native speaker—it had probably been a while since he hadn't had to deal with a language barrier.

As the wine did its work, we agreed to experience some of Barcelona together. Trevor was staying at a small hotel in another part of town. He recommended a place that was somewhere in between his hotel and mine to meet for breakfast. He didn't make a single innuendo the whole night, and we parted ways with a handshake. Yep, harmless enough.

The next afternoon, we signed up for an English-language walking tour of Barcelona's medieval quarter. Our tour guide said there were four major phases of Barcelona's history, which was interesting. But what got me was when she said one period—a period of great Barcelonan wealth and power—ended with the "discovery" of America. She explained that because Barcelona was on the Mediterranean coast, it had been a major center of commerce for countless generations.

However, once Europeans figured out their cartographers had missed two whole continents, most eyes turned to the potential spoils of the Americas. Cities like Seville that were near the Atlantic coast rose to prominence, essentially leaving Barcelona in the dust.

This tour guide slathered on a lot of contempt whenever she said the word *America*. I could only let that go on for so long. When I couldn't take it anymore, I jumped in with a scathing, "We didn't want to be found." She stopped the tour and turned to me, displeasure on her face. That didn't stop me. "We didn't need discovering, you know. You guys came looking. You colonized us." She cocked her head, lips pursed. Surely, she fielded questions and comments all the time, but this was not one she expected.

"I do not understand," she replied. I knew she was lying; I could see it in her eyes. "*Señorita*, we found you. This is fact."

"The Americas were a world of indigenous peoples," I shot, "who were perfectly happy minding their own business. For millennia before the Spanish financed Columbus. And, actually, he flubbed the whole thing up—he never found his trade route to India, even after four tries." The group around me tensed, and Trevor started chuckling nervously as I cut the woman down. "Europeans could've left the 'New World' peacefully, but instead you decided America—north and south—was yours for the taking. And you took and *took*." The crowd began grumbling, eager to get back to the tour, so I wrapped up. "So, don't blame Americans for what we are today. You guys created us."

I nodded sharply to close my case. Trevor fist-bumped me victoriously. I wanted to "drop the mic" and walk off, but there was still more of the tour left. The guide grunted a defeated "humph" before leading us forward. Later, she declined, none too politely, to offer me restaurant recommendations, which prompted another fist-bump from Trevor. Right then, I knew I'd found the right traveling companion.

CHAPTER 3

INTERNING FOR AN INTERN

Perhaps *friendship* wasn't the right word for my relationship with Trevor. It was more of an alliance. We spent hours taking in the streets of Barcelona, but we weren't always together. Sometimes he'd go off and do God-only-knows-what on his own, and I was happy to let him have his space, because I needed my space, too. Thirty minutes later he'd pop up again, by my side, as if he'd never wandered away.

We learned a lot about Barcelona, about the Catalonian region and the Catalan people. Something would spark my curiosity, and I'd look it up on my phone and read the text aloud to him. Or vice versa. We'd say things like, "Wow," or "Cool," or "No way," a rudimentary language that kept us from having to actually converse. When we did achieve polysyllabic communication, Trevor always managed to say a lot of nothing—no clever anecdotes, sparse personal details—and I did a fine job of holding him at arm's length, myself. It was enough to pass the time, but that was pretty much all we were doing—passing the time.

Catalans are known for being businesslike and somewhat serious. If there's a blanket adjective to describe them, I'd say it's the word *prag-matic*. I liked these people. Their region, in the country's northeast, is the most prosperous in Spain. The Catalans feel they make the money that keeps the country running. The rest of Spain disagrees.

The Catalan language is markedly different from, and generally more formal than, Spanish, and a lot of people still speak it. Catalan food is usually not spicy, and the traditional regional dance is the Sardana, a slow circle-dance. The dancers often hold hands as they create an economy of movement—nothing flashy. Much of the time they keep their hands low, down near their sides, as they step gingerly in time to the drawling, brassy music. When the dancers really get going, they raise their joined hands—but not above shoulder height, unless things are getting crazy. Sometimes they hop to the music, but the jumps are very restrained—ankle-height at best. It's a serious dance for a serious people, although Trevor thought the Sardana would be a great dance for underachievers and stoners.

The Catalan tradition I loved the most was their two breakfasts—an early one that's mostly coffee, and a more robust one later in the morning. Trevor and I immediately adopted this. We joked that with first breakfast and second breakfast we were "eating like hobbits" as Tolkien described. I even called Trevor "Bilbo Baggins" a few times. He didn't object, but I could tell he didn't care for that at all.

In fact, Trevor didn't object too much, and he seemed content following my lead. I'll admit I enjoyed that. When you're a woman in a male-dominated field, leading isn't handed to you—I'd had to fight for it. Not so with Trevor. When I announced, after a week or so of floating through the city, that it was time to venture beyond the confines of Barcelona, he eagerly agreed to a day trip.

We could've taken the thirty-minute express train to Tarragona, but since we weren't in a rush, we opted for the local train. The slower train took well over twice as long—maybe three times as long because something on the tracks kept us stuck in place for a while. We never learned what caused the delay, and we largely didn't care. We luxuriated in the one thing most people don't have: time.

Tarragona's Roman ruins were magnificent, and February's sun warmed us as we made our way around the famed Amphitheatre. I read the various plaques and markers aloud, and Trevor made his typical non-comments. Yet today was different from our mornings in Barcelona—and not just because the ruins were so engrossing that we forgot about second breakfast. For the first time, we felt as if we'd accomplished something.

We decided to reward ourselves by rolling straight into lunch, and we found a nice café near the center of town. Normally we would've asked for a table inside, but we found a sunny spot alee from the breeze. The waiter almost certainly would've preferred our being inside, but we'd made our choice. He put up with it. Grudgingly.

We stuffed ourselves with seafood; everything tasted off the boat fresh, especially the shrimp. I was feeling decadent, so we got dessert, which gave me a sugar high but made Trevor sleepy. I'd been increasingly curious about my travel companion, and with his guard now down, I pounced. I wanted more than just bare-bones basics—I was after whole sentences and real words, and an actual personal detail or two.

Using my spoon as a microphone, I did my best impression of a hard-hitting reporter. "So, Trevor, my boy. What brought you from the distant shores of America? You've given us the fundamentals, but why are you *really* here?"

"I told you, Callie. I'm taking time off from grad school."

"Yes, we all know your *official* line, but what are you *really* doing? The world wants to know."

He paused, giving me a blank look. "I don't know," he admitted. Angst crept into his face.

"Have a sip of liquid courage." I motioned to his wine. He brought the glass to his lips and took a big sip. "There, that's better." I shifted personas and transformed into a cross-examining trial lawyer. "Now answer. You're under oath."

Trevor was shocked, but that shock was enough to get him to

reply. "I guess... I guess I wasn't happy where I was." He pulled on his beard anxiously.

"Elaborate, please." I motioned to his glass again. Few things can bring out honestly like a bottle of wine at lunch.

"Maybe I wasn't happy with where I was going." He shrugged, as if he'd just wrapped his entire life story up with a neat little bow.

"Permission to treat the witness as hostile, your honor."

"Okay, okay. Geez, Callie. Not happy with teaching, or whatever I was headed for with a Comp Lit degree. I mean, I like the literature part, but I *don't* like teaching. It's the students. They're kind of stupid."

I eased off, dropping my act. "Not liking students is a big problem for a teacher, I can see that."

He looked away, down the street. "It was more than that. I took out so many student loans, all for a career I wasn't sure I wanted. My area was Prussian Lit. With a degree like that, the *best* I could hope for was a professorship. Forty years of students!" He looked at me again, his eyes meeting mine. "I was all turned around and just wanted to let go. So I did."

"That's fair enough," I said, letting a hint of sympathy into my voice.

"I thought I might find something out here, something I was missing in school." He leaned back in his chair. "I don't know. Maybe I should've kept going. I was really far into grad school."

"How close were you to your degree?"

Trevor purposefully avoided my eyes, which were glaring at him. "One semester—two at most. I had half my dissertation written." I glared even harder. He felt it. "Yeah, Callie," he said, turning to me again. "I know. I basically blew it."

I took a deep breath. "Why didn't you just go back home? Get your bearings?" Trevor winced just slightly as I said the word *home*.

"Because I'm not really from *anywhere*. It's just a small town in the middle. Not a destination for anything. Everything is brown. The buildings are brown. The trees are brown, and the grass is usually brown. We ate brown food with brown gravy."

"I like brown food with brown gravy. It's food you can depend on."

"The only part that wasn't brown were the people. They were gray." He looked wistfully down the street again; I joined him in looking down the street. "I needed color. So here I am, in Spain."

"Here you are in Spain." We sat watching the quiet bustle of Tarragona and letting the silence settle comfortably between us.

"Callie, did you always want to be a lawyer?" he asked after a few moments.

"No, but I soon saw the light," I answered. My professional life was one of the many things I *hadn't* told Trevor much about. I'd convinced myself I didn't want to bore him, although the truth was I simply didn't want to think about work for a while. Now that I'd put him through the wringer, though, I figured he deserved a few answers of his own. I braced myself for the onslaught.

"That takes a lot of time and commitment. Law school, I mean."

"Yeah, but once you're far enough down the road, a certain inertia takes over." It was true. Semester after semester of chasing the next *A* in the Ivy League had a way of normalizing the madness; once that happened, things got easier.

"Do you like it? Being a lawyer?"

"Honestly, it can be really fun. Parts of it at least. There's a certain… gravitas to it that suits me."

Trevor thought for a minute, then asked, "What else did you want to be? Before law school?"

I bristled—too many questions—but I forced myself to answer. "My first passion was art. Impressionism. I wanted to work in a museum. Maybe even run one, eventually."

He furrowed his brow. "Then why didn't you work in an art museum?"

"I did, sort of. Right out of undergrad, I had my sights set on a job at the Metropolitan Museum of Art. Of course, they weren't hiring anyone entry-level—the economy was a disaster back then—but they had internships. Cool internships, the ones that make you *feel* like you have a job. And the MET's so prestigious. An internship there can get your parents' hopes up about you."

He perked up, like the exciting part of the story was coming. "And you landed one of those?"

I slumped my head. "No, though not for lack of trying." Trevor looked confused, so I continued without prompting. "I volunteered as an intern's assistant."

He suppressed a chuckle. "You were an intern... for an intern?"

"When you put it that way, it sounds so... pathetic. But I was young—I had pluck, moxie, drive!" I slapped my hand against the table as if I were defending myself. "I was making a difference for art!"

"Sounds like you were making coffee runs for the people who were supposed to make coffee runs."

"Yeah, that too," I admitted sheepishly. "Six months of coffee runs."

"I'm sorry, Callie. That's the bottom rung of the ladder—minus a rung. You did that for six whole months?"

I gazed at the table. However inadvertently, Trevor had uncovered a bitter pill. Surviving in New York without a steady, paying job hadn't been easy. My father sent the occasional check, which had helped pull me through. That wasn't the type of attention I'd wanted from him. I'd wanted him to be excited about my art career. I'd wanted to show him around the MET on a Monday, when it was closed to the general public but open to employees and their guests. Yet he never came to visit me, not even once.

I'd shared enough personal details for one afternoon, so I simply sighed again and wrapped things up with, "I wasn't making good choices at the time."

Trevor nodded—a knowing nod of "poor choices" solidarity. We finished the wine in our glasses, which finished up the bottle itself. When we were done, we meandered back to the station. We tried not to think about the future for a while. The local train to Barcelona left late and arrived even later than scheduled. Trevor and I barely noticed. We could spare the time.

CHAPTER 4

LIKE STONES SKIPPING ALONG THE WATER

Trevor moved to a closer hotel. He didn't want to move into my hotel (even though my hotel was awesome); he said that would be weird. I didn't see it that way, but I wasn't going to deny him his space. In any case, having him in the neighborhood made things that much easier. Meaning, of course, we could get sloppy-buzzed without having to worry too much about it. Any evening, after we finished our exploring and people-watching, we could sit and enjoy our wine until the world took on a fuzzy, warm, crimson-touched glow.

More and more, Trevor was becoming my perfect traveling companion. He validated me and my choices nicely, and he didn't question my motives at all—and half the time he seemed tuned into another world. We watched Barcelona go by without having to truly participate in it, and that was how we wanted things. We were like stones skipping along the water, stones that didn't sink. We swept along the surface but never went deep.

Well, almost never. Once in a while, one of us abutted the realities we'd left behind a little too closely. This typically happened well after dinner. Usually, we would feel the discomfort rising silently between us, then one of us would have the good sense to call it a night. But not always.

"Yeah, it's a good book. I really liked it."

"You liked it? Just *liked* it?" I asked, mockingly—but also truly—aghast.

"It was a good read. I'd read it again." Trevor replied, not noticing my distress. "Actually, now that I think of it, I've read it twice."

"*The Sun Also Rises* isn't a book you read *twice*. It's a book you read over and over. Throughout a lifetime." I swirled my wine to emphasize my point.

"So, you've read it a lot, I take it?" He eyed me as if I were a stalker whose obsession had been revealed.

"Many times. More than many times. But it's not like I'm a—"

"—A Hemingway nut? We have those in grad school, you know. Hemingway the magnificent. Hemingway the demi-god."

"No, not a Hemingway nut," I retorted, pushing the thought of my Seventh Avenue call from my mind. "I've read a couple of his other books, but they didn't *speak* to me in the same way."

Trevor started analyzing my beloved novel in a way that really pissed me off. He picked it apart bit-by-bit, with all his comp lit training backing him up. Piece by piece, element by element. He even scribbled the character list on a napkin as he spoke.

"Stop!" I finally cried, forcefully and drunkenly. I felt analyzed, put under a microscope. What right did he have to judge?

"What?" he asked, a goofy, overly academic look on his face. "I love the novel too."

"Not the way I do."

"Just because I didn't read it a hundred times doesn't mean—"

"—Just stop, okay?" He paused his assault but still seemed puzzled. "Look, Trevor, I just love it. There's no other word for it. There's this whole aspect of independence and freedom."

"Is that what the novel means to you?"

"There you go again!" I slammed down the rest of my wine like a shot of whiskey.

"I didn't mean… I'm sorry," he mumbled. Lowering his eyes, his lap suddenly becoming the most interesting thing in the café.

"You have to understand, Trevor. I've always loved it, and I still love it. I don't want you psychoanalyzing me or deconstructing it! When I read it, I drink it in. It takes me away from wherever I am. That's why it was important to me… that's why it *is* important." I felt like storming out, but my legs were a bit wobbly from the wine.

He relented and refilled our glasses as a sort of olive branch. "Are you going to follow the book? The locations?"

"No. Maybe some, the Spanish ones. I don't know. I don't want any complicated plans right now." A call from a deceased author was complication enough.

"Yeah. I know the feeling." He held his wine up to the light, gazing at the burgundy glow and sighing. He lowered his focus and looked me apologetically in the eye. "I get it, Callie, it's okay. Some books are sacred, and we all need an escape."

❦

Barcelonan marketplaces became a favorite of ours. Trevor and I would stroll slowly through the aisles as the midmorning sun climbed over our heads. We marveled at the piles of food—literally a movable feast. We would pick over this pepper or examine that tomato, remarking on freshness or color. Trevor was really into the colors, identifying each specifically; "red" was "crimson," and "cherry" "maroon." We'd often split up until one of us stumbled upon something interesting. "Hey, look at this!" or, "Come over here for a minute!" we'd shout. Of course, this led nowhere. Neither of us had a kitchen in our hotel, and neither of us knew how to cook. But what did it matter? We were content playing pretend.

One morning we found ourselves at the seafood market—fish,

shrimp, crabs, all laid out on great piles of ice. Trevor loved it. He would get close to the fish and stick his nose *right up against them*, practically staring them down, before inhaling their salty scent like they were a bouquet of flowers. Gross.

I was watching him delight in the aroma of a large and very-dead fish when we heard English for the first time in weeks. We instinctively looked down the row: There stood two women, both a little younger than me. One had long blonde hair, while the other, a brunette with black hair, sported a pixie cut. She was pointing at something, and the blonde was shaking her head in disagreement. Now that they'd caught our attention, we had no trouble hearing their conversation.

"That's the wrong one," the blonde insisted.

"You don't know what you're talking about," the brunette replied, making a face.

"Fine, you pick this time, but next time I choose."

"Deal." The brunette said something in Spanish to the man in the stall, and he jumped into action.

"You're Americans!" I called out, almost without realizing it. Both women turned at the same time.

The brunette spoke first. "Yes," she replied over the market's din. Her eyes screamed, "What of it?"

"We are too! I just… you don't see a lot of Americans here this time of year." I felt dumb after such a clichéd comment. Trevor could've jumped in at this point, but of course he was no help.

The blonde saved me. "No, you don't. Americans are rare enough." Her face brightened as she walked over. "I'm Susan, and this is Jane." She glanced at her companion, who smiled. It seemed we had garnered Susan's initial seal of approval, so Jane had decided we were okay to talk to. She waved as the man in the stall handed her a bag of something fishy.

Susan's handshake was lively and firm. Trevor smiled and shook hands as well; Jane came over to join us. Her hands were full, so she half-waved instead of shaking.

"I didn't mean to intrude," I continued. "We make a habit of saying hello to Americans we see." This was a lie; we hadn't seen any Americans.

"You're a rarity then!" exclaimed Susan. That was probably an exaggeration, but I took it as a compliment.

I pointed at Jane's full basket. "Looks like you're on a shopping spree." She had herbs, a couple bottles of something that definitely wasn't alcohol, and the weighted bag she'd just been handed.

"We're making mussels tonight," she explained. "What are you guys buying? You're empty-handed."

"Nothing," Trevor broke in. It was his first contribution to the conversation. A useless contribution, but at least he was making an effort.

"We don't cook." I felt a little pathetic, so I elaborated. "We don't have kitchens." A solid excuse. Expatriates didn't always have kitchens, did they?

Susan caught Jane's eye for a split second, and then she turned back to me. "Then you'll *have* to join us for dinner tonight."

"Oh, I don't know…" I hesitated out of politeness. Those mussels sounded delicious.

"We don't want to impose," added Trevor, finally achieving something socially acceptable.

"It'll be fun! We love to entertain," encouraged Susan. She turned to Jane. "Don't we?"

"It's true. And doubling the recipe is easy enough, it doesn't take any extra time."

They were sincere; I accepted. Trevor didn't seem to mind. Even if he did mind, I didn't care. A home-cooked meal after weeks of restaurant food sounded fantastic.

"Nine o'clock for cocktails, dinner at ten!" Susan said, handing me their address. Given that Trevor and I had nothing scheduled, ever, that worked perfectly.

I convinced Trevor to leave the market as soon as we parted ways with our new friends. I was afraid if we stayed, we would keep bumping into them—with those socially awkward after-smiles and repeated waves—and they'd reconsider their invitation. To my own surprise, I was already looking forward to the evening. I'd never felt the need for American company so keenly. Was I homesick already? When I hadn't even found a trace of Hemingway yet?

CHAPTER 5

THE CALLIE MCGRAW
I COULD NEVER BE
IN NEW YORK

Jane examined the bottle in my hand, and right away I knew we'd chosen poorly. When it came to wine, I was more of a drinker than a picker. I knew good wine when I drank it, and I knew bad wine when I tasted it, but other than throwing an absurd amount of money at a bottle, I didn't know the first thing about selecting a quality wine. Money can resolve a lot of issues, but in this case it led to another problem: when giving wine as a gift, I felt "throwing money at it" was a capitulation—a complete abdication of a guest's responsibilities. Since Trevor wasn't exactly a wine connoisseur either, I'd tried to find a decent pairing for seafood at a decent price. Apparently, I'd failed.

Jane's face betrayed her disappointment for only a split second. In the next instant, she smiled warmly and ushered us inside. Susan bounded over and welcomed us as well, her long blonde hair flowing from her shoulders. She looked at the bottle. "That's one of our favorites!" she fibbed. She didn't flinch at all; she was a better liar than her girlfriend. She immediately escorted the offending selection into the kitchen, where I'm sure she hid it away with any other "Don't Drink These" gifts they'd collected from other guests.

Few cities have smaller apartments than New York, and by that standard, Susan and Jane's apartment was a palace. It was small but not cramped, with a cozy, functional dining area off the kitchen. The living room was the largest space (or at least I assumed so, since I didn't see the bedroom), and our hosts had clearly put some effort into decorating. Although none of their furnishings were all that expensive, they'd taken care to coordinate nicely. There was a lot of wicker.

"You're right on time," chuckled Jane as we moved into the kitchen. It smelled marvelous; I started salivating instantly. "Nobody is on time in Spain."

"Isn't that the truth?" Susan agreed, putting a plate of salami and cheese on the counter where we could all reach it. "There's no real sense of urgency here. We joke that Spain's national word is *mañana*."

"Tomorrow," translated Trevor. "Or sometimes, 'later,' depending on the context."

"You're truly a boy genius," I quipped, nodding in his general direction. Who translated a language they didn't speak? God, he was weird.

"We're starting with sangria!" Jane pointed to a glass pitcher full of a deep red liquid and chunks of floating fruit. "We made it this afternoon. Please help yourselves." I poured Trevor's glass for him, then my own.

The flavors exploded in my mouth—fresh, fruity, wine-soaked flavors. I'd had sangria before, but it was always the cheap stuff. Stuff from overpriced New York bars pushing an "authentic" Spanish experience. Tonight, however, was the real thing. Now that I knew the difference, I decided I liked sangria.

Our conversation flowed easily. Susan was a freelance journalist who'd lived in four countries already. Jane had majored in Spanish and was native-speaker fluent; she now consulted for Spanish businesses that had American clients. Listening to them talk, I felt as if they were both much more interesting than I was.

Oddly enough, the pair had met in Milwaukee during one of Susan's US stints. Jane had just finished her degree, but her job hunt was going nowhere. One thing led to the next, and… *voilà*! Lovebirds in Barcelona.

Well, no, not exactly *voilà*! Nothing is ever that simple.

"The trouble was, there was really no 'wrong' Spanish city for us," Jane said. "Pros and cons, yes, but overall… we just couldn't choose. Weeks went by, yet we still hadn't made a decision."

"*Jane* hadn't made a decision," corrected Susan. "I could live anywhere in the country, really."

"So what'd you do?" asked Trevor, nibbling on a bit of salami. "Draw cities out of a hat?"

"We did one better than that!" exclaimed Susan with surprising enthusiasm. "Darts and a map!"

"What?" I couldn't hold in my surprise: who moves across the Atlantic so capriciously? Then I remembered: Callie McGraw, that's who.

"Only problem was, I really suck at darts," she continued.

"Yep, that's true, no question." Jane nodded in hearty agreement as she popped a cube of cheese into her mouth.

"My first throw didn't even hit the map."

"Made a nice hole in the wall, though."

"Darts tend to do that, sweetie," Susan chided. "My second throw hit the middle of the map, but it didn't stick."

Jane linked arms with her girlfriend warmly. "She managed to defy the laws of physics. She hit the map with the *side* of the dart."

Susan chuckled. "My third throw… that was a disaster too. It landed in Portugal."

"And I was *not* moving to Portugal!" cried Jane. "I didn't take all those years of Spanish to move to a Portuguese-speaking country. So, all we got out of that throw was another hole in the wall."

"My fourth try put us somewhere in the Atlantic Ocean. Which was not ideal."

"I can see that," I joked as I refilled my sangria. "It's hard to get good wine in the middle of the ocean." I immediately felt like an idiot—why had I mentioned wine when I'd brought such a crappy bottle?

Fortunately, Jane stayed right on track and saved me from my own embarrassment. "That was it. I couldn't take it anymore! I grabbed the dart and threw."

The pair looked at each other lovingly, then exclaimed in unison, "Barcelona!"

I couldn't help but laugh. Trever did too. Well, almost laughed. New companions in a new setting was a bit much for him. I suspected he'd be better when the sangria kicked in.

"Barcelona-bound, and a security deposit that was a good bit lighter," Jane said. "For all the holes in the wall."

"A small price to pay," Susan joked. "That landlord was a jerk, anyway."

I knew my turn to explain how I landed in Barcelona was coming, but I really would've rather listened to Susan and Jane. I was envious, I guess; here they were in Spain, living the life they wanted to live, a life on their own terms, while I was only *pretending* to live life on my own terms. In a few months I'd be facing a slew of new responsibilities in San Francisco, and between now and then I had a mission to complete. I wasn't calling my own shots, not in the same way they were.

I talked about New York living as much as I could. I didn't want to sound like I was whining about my new, too-good-to-be-true job, and I certainly couldn't tell my perfectly nice and reasonably sane hosts that Hemingway had phoned me from beyond the grave. Instead, I filled them in on my legal work, gushed about the Guggenheim and the Whitney, mentioned the few Broadway shows I'd seen over the years. Nothing too deep. I embellished a little. Okay, I embellished a lot, in the way New Yorkers tend to. Even if I wasn't exactly a New Yorker anymore.

Our hosts thought it was "so cool" to have "made it" in New York—at one point, Susan even started singing Sinatra. I didn't think making it in the city was all that impressive, I'd done what literally millions of others had. I didn't say as much, though—I let my new friends go on thinking I was an interesting person.

When Trevor's turn came, he did his typical thing—a lot of words, very few details. I added the part about his not liking students. He shot me an over-anxious look for that, like I'd given away his great secret. Maybe I had—that's a real possibility—and Susan and Jane agreed that Trevor was facing a real conundrum as a future teacher, and they began offering alternate options for his life-path.

I could almost see the idea form in Jane's mind. "I know!" She raised her finger excitedly. "You could join the Army, Trevor. They're always looking for new recruits."

He shuddered slightly, his eyes widening. I couldn't resist torturing him and added, "Right, in the paratrooper division. Jumping out of planes!"

His eyes became even wider. "Callie, I'm afraid of heights!"

Without missing a beat, Susan picked up where I'd left off. "Oh, you don't need to jump, if that's the issue. The person behind you can push you out. Gravity will do the rest." Jane and I nodded in agreement.

"Yes, just don't forget to pull your rip cord," Jane advised. Otherwise... *splat*."

Trevor went pale. I could see him frantically searching his inner self, almost like we were trampling upon a dream of his. I felt bad about that and resolved to change the subject, but our hosts kept things going.

"Wait, I know! You could join the French Foreign Legion!" Jane continued, the sangria having loosened her up. "They'll take anyone!"

Susan forced a straight face, looking Trevor in the eye. "Okay, that's the plan. Unless you come up with a better one, Trevor, we'll escort you to the nearest enlistment depot. I don't see any other option for you. *Esprit de corps* and all that."

"Callie, you could get him into fighting shape," Jane offered. "You obviously work out."

I seized the opportunity to steer the conversation elsewhere before Trevor melted into a puddle of horrified embarrassment. "I don't work out in Spain, but I did back in the city. Usually in the gym, but whenever I could find the time, I would jog the four miles from my apartment to the Reservoir in Central Park. Then I'd run around the lake, watching the melting pot that is New York City."

"Like all the different ethnicities and cultures?" Jane asked. "I visited Manhattan a few times—people from everywhere!"

"No, not exactly. More like Upper-West-Side-culture meeting Upper-East-Side-culture. It was like an anthropology course. Intellectualism versus old money."

Clearly relieved to be out of the spotlight, Trevor asked timidly, "Callie, I want to know what you listened to when you ran?"

"Mostly house music. Fast stuff. But sometimes, when I was feeling especially masochistic, I put on old Soviet marches."

"Since when do you speak Russian?" he asked. He eyed me as if I were leading a double life as a communist spy.

"I don't! For all I know, they were pledging life and limb to the Red Army, but I made up my own words." I shifted into my best Russian accent. "Geet mooveeng! Run fahster, you capeetilist peeg."

That got a chuckle from everyone in the room, so I took things one step further. "But sometimes I didn't listen to anything when I ran. That way I could hear the Upper East Siders approaching from behind."

Jane took the bait. "How could you tell when the Upper East Siders were catching up to you?"

"I could hear their jewelry rattling."

The kitchen exploded in laughter; I felt accomplished and interesting. Callie McGraw, life of the party.

My mussels were soaking in a rich, magnificent broth. The scents of white wine, shallots, and a hint of curry filled my nostrils; I couldn't wait for my first bite. Yet Trevor was frowning into his bowl as if someone had served him a science experiment.

"Anything wrong, Trevor?" Susan asked.

"No, it's just… I've never had mussels before."

"They're not hard to eat," she offered helpfully. "The shells open up as the mussels cook. The meat comes out easily."

"But don't eat the ones with unopened shells," Jane added. "Some don't want to open up."

"Maybe they just aren't ready yet?" I interjected, my head full of sangria and delicious scents. "Maybe they want to open up, but they need more time?" I raised one eyebrow like I was making a brilliant point, but the joke fell flat. I felt like a dud; Jane stared at me in bewilderment.

"Too bad for them, then," she groaned. "If they don't open up, they go in the garbage."

"Is that a metaphor?" asked Trevor, even more puzzled.

"No, they literally go in the garbage," Jane responded. "They might not be cooked through properly."

"And don't forget the broth," I said, recouping and focusing on Trevor. "When you dip your bread in, it becomes a yummy broth-sponge." In the interest of leading by example, I dunked in my own hunk of bread, then took a big bite.

"A yummy broth-sponge? Is that a technical term, Callie?" Susan joked. "Clearly, you haven't drunk enough this evening. Let's fix that." She refilled my glass—with a wine that we *hadn't* brought.

"How long have you two been a couple?" Jane asked, changing the subject. Honestly, I was a bit surprised she hadn't brought it up earlier.

"A couple?" I laughed. "We're not a couple." I glanced at my shrinking-in-his-seat travel companion and realized I'd laughed too hard. "No offense, Trevor."

"None taken." He smiled a big easy smile, which surprised me. He turned to Jane. "We only met a few weeks ago."

"We didn't mean to assume," Susan said. "It's just... you two have a certain... *banter*, I guess."

"It's okay, assume all you want," Trevor replied, smiling even more widely. I wondered what that was about.

Four wonderfully full stomachs and two more bottles of wine later, we topped the evening off with the only true way to end a Barcelonan dinner party: the Sardana. We formed a circle in the living room—all holding hands at waist level. Jane, who was streaming the music through her phone, hit "play," and we began following the time-honored steps. There was much aggressive small hopping—mild hopping, but aggressive nonetheless.

When the music got all the way up to a full-on medium pace, we raised our hands high and began circling less slowly. I saw Trevor's foot reach halfway up his shin, then I began twisting my hips. At that point, all decorum broke down and the four of us started twirling around and flinging our joined hands up and down. I bumped into the loveseat more than once, and Trevor became overly familiar with the coordinating chair. Susan kicked as if she were punting a football badly. Jane gave her a "tsk tsk" look before we settled down and finished our dance in the traditional style. None of us broke a sweat.

As we collapsed, laughing and content, I noticed that the wicker living room set had slipped out of place. Wicker is great, but it *will* slide—especially when taking liberties with the Sardana. I was about to offer to straighten it, but just then, Trevor asked, "What time is it?"

"It's *mañana.*" Susan answered, pretending to look at her watch. "Definitely *mañana* o-clock."

Jane mentioned she had to go to the office tomorrow, but she urged us not to rush off: her colleagues dedicated the first hour or two of any given workday to discussing *fútbol* matches. No one would miss her if she slept in.

It was indeed late, though, so I started winding things down. The evening was such a success that we all agreed to meet on Saturday, with our hosts promising to bring us on a "must see" day trip. They wouldn't specify further, but a day out of the city sounded like a nice change.

The sharp winter air of the night combatted the sluggishness of our gluttonous evening. We were halfway to our hotels when Trevor started laughing for no apparent reason—he was way too buzzed. Then he got a bad case of the hiccups, which only made him laugh more. I started laughing too, hard yet easy. After such a fantastic evening, the nighttime streets imbued me with an invincibility. I was the Callie McGraw I could never be in New York. Maybe that's why Hemingway had sent me here?

CHAPTER 6

THE MOUNTAIN MONASTERY

The fresh coffee in my stomach sloshed violently as Jane made a hard right. It was a sunny morning, and we were heading out for our day trip, but with Jane in full-on Formula 1 racing mode, I was beginning to suspect this would be my *last* day trip ever. We weren't even three minutes from my hotel, and already I was clutching my seatbelt for dear life.

"Callie, help," Trevor cried. "It's not working. It won't click." His expression conveyed the desperation of a man trying to fit a square peg into a round hole. Susan glanced over her shoulder from the front seat and shrugged—she was probably used to Jane's driving. I grabbed Trevor's buckle and slammed it into its slot. He sighed in relief at the reassuring *click*.

It was early in the day—too early. We'd barely managed to have first breakfast before meeting our new friends in front of our hotel at eight o'clock. Jane had borrowed a very yellow, very compact car from one of her coworkers. The teeny thing didn't look like it had more than a single horse of horsepower, but Jane was proving my assessment wrong.

"We're only going about forty-five miles away," Susan said. "We're heading northwest once we're out of the city."

"Okay, but where are we going?" Trevor asked. "All you said was to bring a sweater." He pinched his cardigan and pulled it forward, almost as if he was expecting a smiley-face sticker for following directions.

"Up!" exclaimed Susan. "We're going up!"

"North being 'up' is a Eurocentric concept," Trevor quipped, trying—and failing—to channel his inner comedian. I glared at him in defeated amazement as the car flew around another corner.

"No, we're literally going up!" cried Jane. "About four thousand feet into the mountains. We'll tour a winery or two in the afternoon, but there's something we want to show you first."

She didn't elaborate, and although I wondered what the pair had in store for us, I didn't ask. They seemed content keeping it a secret, while I was content keeping my full focus on surviving the ride.

We began our ascent. The route was a lengthy series of winding roads and hairpin turns, all alarmingly adjacent to the mountain's precipitous drop-off. I fought back my nausea, and Trevor was literally starting to turn green—although I didn't know if his new hue was caused by his fear of heights or the speed. Susan and Jane, having a grand old time, chatted away in the front seat, while we—their prisoners—held on for dear life, utterly unable to appreciate the natural beauty surrounding us.

At long last, we turned one last hairpin. "There it is, Montserrat Abbey!" exclaimed Susan, pointing up the road. As I peered through the windshield, I was amazed to see a collection of buildings, almost like a village, tucked into the mountain. A few higher peaks loomed above, while the buildings themselves clung to the side of the cliff, looking as if they'd tumble down if they ever loosened their grip. "A true Catalan gem. I can't wait for you two to see it."

Jane screeched us to a halt in a parking space. We prisoners immediately scrambled out of the cramped backseat and planted our feet on terra firma—I don't think we could've moved any faster even if there were an actual "eject" button to propel us.

"Come this way first." Jane guided us toward the cliff's edge, mere yards away. We were high, higher than I'd thought. We could see for miles below, almost like we were in an airplane. Poor Trevor looked like he might faint at any second.

"Cool, huh?" Jane smiled and nodded as she surveyed the valley below. "We'll tour the abbey later, but let's do pictures first. While we still have the morning light."

Trevor obviously needed the fresh air, and honestly I did too, so I didn't argue as she led us to a trail along the edge. Every once in a while, I would turn around and marvel at the abbey. How did something so immense get built so far up this mountain?

We walked for about an hour, stopping frequently for "edge of the cliff" pictures. Trying not to succumb to the gorgeous scenery around us—or to become victims of the great fall below us—some combination of our group would precariously pick our way to a particular rock formation to mug for the camera.

Held back by his fear of heights, Trevor took most of the photos. He had a particular knack for snapping pictures when one of us was blinking or looking away—we needed three or four takes just to get one decent shot. Thank God for digital cameras; we never could've hauled that much film with us.

"Nope. No good. Susan, your eyes were closed in that one."

"Shit! Okay, take it again. But give us some warning, Trevor. A 'one-two-three' or something."

Click.

"Uh-uh, that one's no good either. Callie, look at the camera, not at your toes."

"Trevor, you suck at this. Like Susan said, you have to give us warning."

"But then it won't be spontaneous! You'll seem posed!"

I argued several times that our pictures would always seem posed—

no one casually hangs out on a rock face. It didn't register; Trevor envisioned us as mountaineers, and nothing short of a live-action snap would do. And so, our photo shoot went on, intermittently, until I never wanted to see a camera again. For all that effort, we only got one frame-worthy shot.

After we'd reversed course, Susan explained, "Montserrat is really a whole complex. A monastery, an art museum, the cloisters. But it's the cathedral we really want you to see. It's amazing, my favorite spot in all of Spain."

A coolness greeted us when stepped inside the dim basilica. The aroma of burning wicks and melting wax filled my nostrils. My mouth fell open instinctively as I turned my head to the ceiling. Golden images lined the dome, and the stonework itself was art. My head swirled. I snuck a look at Trevor; he was even more awed than I was.

A glowing ray of sunlight, streaming in from a small window in the dome, created a welcoming, warm circle on the stone floor. All four of us were drawn to its radiance, willing moths to a flame. There we stood, transfixed, spinning in slow circles and relishing the beauty and artisanship surrounding us.

Susan turned to me. "It's like God is looking down on us. Like God is all around us in here."

"Yeah," I lied. I was thrilled by the sculptures, the stained glass, the sweeping domed ceiling. But God? No, I felt nothing on that score.

"This place is cool," said Trevor, overstating the obvious in his usual way. "Like a world within a world. I could get used to it here."

We didn't speak again in the basilica. A reverential hush descended over us, and we split up without discussing it—Trevor doing his thing, me doing mine, and the lovebirds strolling around arm-in-arm. I soaked up the gilded and grand wonders around me. Sixteenth-century iconography was a little out of my wheelhouse, but I appreciated the patience and craft the artists brought to their works.

At some point the four of us sort of bumped into each other, and—without saying a word—we all acknowledged it was time to go. When we stepped outside, it took us a few minutes to adjust to the sunshine. Despite being perfectly sober, we stumbled like stupefied fools in the bright light. The other visitors, spare though they were, gawked at us on our way back to the car.

Jane finally broke our collective silence. "Lunchtime!"

"Now you're talking." Trevor seemed relieved—and hungry. Just then, I realized we'd skipped second breakfast. My stomach growled in objection.

"Lunch and then wine," Susan added. "Or lunch *with* wine, and more wine to come."

Our Formula 1 driver only seemed emboldened by the downward slope. Trevor turned green again, but I think the promise of the winery tour steeled his nerves a measure. Halfway down the mountain, we found a rustic restaurant in one of the villages, where we partook in chicken, seafood, vegetables, and bread. So much bread. We washed it all down with local wine.

We moved on to the winery; fortunately, it was in the same village, granting us a merciful stay from Jane's driving. Our passes were all-inclusive, and we sampled and sampled. Our new friends would remark that this wine tasted like something, or that that wine tasted like something else, but for me, the flavors all ran together. We were supposed to cleanse our palates between wines by eating bits of cheese, but I was full and didn't bother. Trevor didn't bother either, the expression on his face grew goofier with each sample. He didn't know what he was drinking, nor did he care. Whatever world Trevor inhabited was, at that moment, a happy one.

Somewhere around our five-hundredth glass, Susan and Jane trained their full attention on me, much like the three of us had done to Trevor a few nights ago. Only it was a lot less fun now, since I was the one in their sites. I was beginning to wonder if "circle and attack" was their trademark move as a couple.

"Callie, you're obsessed!"

"Jane! Just because she's read the book a thousand times doesn't mean anythi—"

"—O-b-s-s-e... No, wait. O-b-e-s... Ugh!"

"Have another one, Jane," I mumbled. I really didn't feel like being picked apart, especially since I still wasn't clear on how I could possibly track down a dead author in a foreign country. For now, I simply wanted to enjoy my afternoon, which seemed much more difficult with Jane having killed my buzz.

"We know why Trevor's here—he's joining the Foreign Legion," Susan said, a devilish grin on her lips. "But you came all the way across the ocean because of a *book*. Maybe you're not obsessed, but you're definitely more than a fan."

"I'm not joining the Foreign Legion!" Trevor objected, more tenacious in his tone than I'd thought possible. "I'm not!" He gestured grandiosely in a way that didn't quite match his words.

Ignoring him completely, I shot back defensively, "I didn't come all the way here just for the book. I came for me." I gulped my wine, contemplating whether to reveal my true motives now that I knew the pair better. That was the wine talking, though—I caught myself and mentally backtracked. "I came because I could. Because I'll probably never have six months to myself again. Is that so hard to believe?"

Jane scoffed, but she backed off a little. "Don't get me wrong, Callie. We love hanging out with you guys. We're just trying to figure you out, that's all."

"I've never done well with psychoanalysis," I replied, intentionally keeping my voice calm and light. I took a breath and forced a smile; I didn't want to get worked up and march away, especially since Jane was my ride. "I am who I am," I added more firmly, although I took pains to smile as I said it.

"Hear, hear!" cried Susan boisterously. "Don't let us pick on you. And *never* after the fifth glass."

A touch of contriteness in her voice, Jane agreed. "Really, don't. We're just having some fun."

Seeing an opening to get our afternoon back on course, I raised my glass in a toast. "Here's to fun."

"Here's to fun!" Susan and Jane chimed, their glasses meeting mine. Trevor was late on the uptake and only got out the word *fun*, but his glass managed to arrive just in time to *clink* in harmony with ours.

We spent another hour or so at the winery, and I did manage to get my buzz back. But as we were leaving—and even after some good, strong coffee—Jane said she was still too tipsy to drive. She handed the keys to Susan in the parking lot. "You take it from here, sweetie." I was overjoyed to hear those six words.

It was dark but still not late by the time we achieved sea level. We'd all had a long day and a good number of laughs, but one more meal together today would've been too much. That fact went unspoken but was unanimous.

They dropped us off at my hotel. Jane took the wheel again and sped away, whipping her borrowed yellow deathtrap around the corner. Once they were out of sight, Trevor eyed me expectantly, as if asking, "Where next?"

"Nowhere. Nowhere is next," I answered. "Bed is next."

"On a Saturday night? Callie, are you feeling okay?"

"I'm feeling like I need some alone time. And maybe a good book." A gleam I'd never seen before lit Trevor's eyes, as if he knew my deepest, darkest secrets. "Okay, boss," he began slowly, "the sun also rises tomorrow."

CHAPTER 7

PICASSO WAS A
FRIEND OF MINE

The drizzle pattered against the windowpane of our usual first breakfast café. It wasn't a heavy rain, just enough to make the streets slick.

"Trevor, let's go to a museum today." I dipped my baguette into my steaming coffee. "There are so many here in Barcelona."

"Ok… but we've been to museums before." He seemed doubtful. Or maybe he was just groggy—sometimes it was hard to tell.

"No, we haven't. Not really. We go to the *lobbies* of museums, but we always wind up in the gift shop or café. Let's *really* go this time. Get headsets and everything. *Learn* something for a change."

"Callie, where's this coming from?" For an academic, Trevor seemed perpetually unconcerned with education.

"There was a whole museum at the top of that mountain the other day, but we didn't even step inside. The Montserrat Museum has some great pieces—even a Dalí. We should've at least seen that."

He considered this, watching the morning rain. "Okay, we'll do a museum today. As long as you don't ask me to write a five-page paper when we're done."

"God, no," I replied. "Three pages will be fine." He chuckled sleepily.

We settled on the *Museo Picasso de Barcelona*, and for once I convinced Trevor to take a cab. I blamed the rain, but I just wanted to get there as quickly as possible. Now that an entire day of art lay ahead of me, I was surprised by my own enthusiasm. I tried not to let it show.

The museum itself was five joined townhouses, with all exhibits on the upper level. I bought our tickets since the visit was my idea, then Trevor dutifully got our headsets for the audio tour. He then dutifully exchanged them when we discovered he'd picked up the Swedish version.

I proceeded to lead our march around the museum—stopping at every work, whether it was part of the audio tour or not. I concentrated on each piece and attempted to discern Picasso's intent. I studied his form, tried to figure out which paintings had new techniques in them versus those which relied on tried-and-true methods. I dredged my memory of art history. It felt magnificent.

Trevor was into it initially—for the first thirty minutes. Then he got antsy. His eyes began wandering around the room, then *he* began wandering around the room. Then he started wandering into other rooms, only to drift back ten minutes later to see if I was ready to move on. I wasn't.

After almost an hour of this, Trevor was annoying me to death. A grown man, acting like a puppy at my ankles, yipping. I told him he could go do something else for the day if he liked. He said he wanted to stay; I told him he needed to behave. He promised to behave. He lied.

I suffered through his bad jokes. "Did Picasso paint anything red in his Blue Period?" or "Cubism? Was the man a total square?" When I couldn't take it anymore, I instructed Trevor to keep two full rooms away from me at all times. He looked a little hurt, but I didn't care. I wanted my art.

The museum was small enough that a normal person could've

browsed through it in two hours or so, but I was in no mood for that kind of thing. I was hungry for this. I continued going piece-by-piece, relishing each work and taking my sweet time. Occasionally, I thought about Trevor wandering around unchaperoned, but mostly I got lost in the colors and brushstrokes, examining each work from every perspective I could think of. The paintings whirled around me, much like they had when I'd first moved to New York; I felt like I was in my twenties again.

The audio tour had long since ended by the time I started on the last room. When I finished, I pulled out my museum map to make sure I hadn't missed anything. I had. I'd somehow skipped rooms six and seven, which, when I thought back on it, roughly lined up with the moment when I'd banished Trevor. I knew he'd been distracting me, I just didn't realize by how much.

Room seven was the larger of the two adjoining, skipped, rooms and the first off the hallway. A whole gallery devoted to Picasso's post-impressionist work—I spent forty-five minutes in pure bliss.

But when I stepped into room six, my heart nearly stopped. Hanging above me was a young couple painted in dark yet vibrant pastels. The city night surrounded them as they melded into each other in a passionate, perfectly tender, embrace. As if the two were intertwining into one whole, as if so consumed by each other that they formed a universe unto themselves.

I forced my feet to move forward, the painting calling to me. I scanned the plaque below for the English translation. "Embrace in the Street, 1900." New passion at the dawn of a new century. Emboldened, unapologetic, amorous passion. Public passion for a pastel city.

I stood there for a long, long while, swallowed whole by this masterpiece and not fighting the tears welling in my eyes. What was it about this couple that made me feel so empty, so lost, so isolated and alone?

The void inside of me swelled when the realization hit: I'd been hugged and kissed and touched, I'd had flings now and again, and a handful of a few one-night stands, but no one had ever *embraced* me, not like this. No guy had ever engulfed me in his arms—I'd never *let* any guy get close enough to engulf me. I'd never trusted anyone in the way these lovers trusted each other, never shared my life with anyone in any real way.

Another patron entered the small room and stood beside me, utterly breaking the spell. "*Les amants dans la rue*," she said, as much to herself as to me. I didn't know how to respond—and I was far more concerned with pulling myself together than niceties—so I repeated the phrase back to her in English. "Lovers in the street." That sounded kind of dumb, so I added, "*Mucha pasión*." I resented her intrusion and forced myself move away casually, as if I were simply moving onto the next room.

The last thing I wanted was Trevor asking if I'd been crying, so I fled to the nearest restroom where I splashed some cold water on my face. I hadn't been crying, not really—just a few tears—but my eyes were puffy, nonetheless. I tried taking some deep calming breaths, but there was nothing calming about the aroma of a public bathroom.

I made a beeline for the lobby, intending to text Trevor from there. But when I stepped off the elevator, I found him sitting in a corner next to a potted tree, a shell-shocked look on his face. As if Picasso had just rocked *his* world, not mine.

"I guess you really *are* into this art stuff," he said, looking at his watch as if we had somewhere to be. I made amends by offering to pay for a late lunch. We hadn't had so much as a crumb of second breakfast; I knew Trevor could eat like a horse when that happened, so offering to foot the bill was no small thing.

Trevor had taken a liking to a café not too far away, just off of Las Ramblas—one of the city's longest boulevards. By this time, the lunch-rush crowd had thinned, and we snagged a table by the window. The weather was clearing up; after-the-rain sunshine streamed down from between the dissipating clouds.

We ordered tapas to start—I figured it was the fastest way to get something into Trevor's stomach, and truthfully I was hungry too. Besides, a black-olive tapenade can cure any variety of ills.

"We should do that again. Hard-core museum-going."

Trevor pulled on his beard. "That was a lot, Callie. You were in there for hours."

"Yes, but it was spectacular!" Now that the first bites of my food had reached my stomach, my high from the museum returned—if it ever really left at all.

"Okay, we can do that again, but can we go *faster* next time? Set a timer or something?"

I smirked. "We'll see."

"I don't get it. If you love art so much, why did you stop going to museums? There are tons of them in New York."

"I was much too busy. Do you know how many hours I put in? Like, every week?"

He pushed back just a little. "Come on, Callie. Even I know a cop-out when I hear one." Trevor had been asking more and more questions all the time: I didn't care for it at all, but since we'd now spent so much time together, I guess it was only natural for him to peek out of his shell. I just wished he would focus on his own life, not mine.

"To be truthful, I was never too busy. I could've made the time, if I'd tried. I guess I just... stopped. Left it behind, for some reason."

The conversation hung there. We watched the people outside weaving in and out of each other on the still-damp sidewalk. Sitting there, I felt vulnerable, too exposed, when what I really wanted to do was go sit quietly somewhere with *les amants dans la rue* fresh in my mind. I wanted to be with that couple. I wanted to *know* them, inside and out. I wanted to trust them the way they trusted each other.

With his eyes still trained on the street, Trevor asked quietly, "You regret it, then? Leaving it behind?"

"Yeah," I whispered, defeated. I rallied as I shot back, "Like you regret grad school, Bilbo."

He scrunched up his face, his eyebrows coming dangerously close to touching. Trevor really hated that name, and he wasn't too keen on my mentioning grad school, either. He took a long sip of his cocktail. The ice cascaded against his upper lip and wet his mustache. "We can't change the past, Callie, only the future."

"Yes, and you need to figure out your own future. Seriously, Trevor, pick something and go do it. Pick anything, do that."

"Yeah, just pick something." He scratched his chin, shaking his head as if I were oversimplifying things. "It's not that easy, Callie. Not when you come from a brown town with gray people. Whatever I do next, it has to be in color."

The tone was getting way too heavy, and all I really wanted to do was get out of the café, so I leaned back and quipped, "Don't go all unicorns and rainbows on me, Trevor. Picasso colored his own world, you can too. I'll even buy you the crayons."

He smiled brightly. "Gee, Callie, you're such a good friend." His goofy too-drunk look surfaced on his face, which was strange because we were on our first round. I let it rest—whatever he was thinking, I really didn't want to know.

We sort of split up for the day after that. We still met for dinner, but otherwise we each did our own thing. I needed some time with Picasso's embrace, time to recover from whatever perfect hell that painting had loosened in me. But I didn't want to share any of that with Trevor. I didn't want to share it with anyone, really. I spent the evening in the bathtub, where I always did my best thinking. Trevor said he was going out clubbing, which I noted was a terrific way of *not* thinking at all. Nice work if you can get it, I guess.

I woke up early the next morning. That wasn't normal for me, although I did feel wonderful after my long soak in the tub. Yet I was restless at the same time. I fumbled around in the sheets, the clock on the nightstand blaring its bright red numbers at me. At last, I surrendered to the god of anti-sleep, wondering what to do with myself since Trevor wouldn't be expecting me for almost three hours. I thought about going back to the Embrace in the Street, but the *Museo Picasso* wasn't open this early. *Nothing* in Spain was open this early.

With sleep now impossible and a month of solid eating behind me, a jog had seemed like a good idea. Seemed. Panting and sweating as if I'd never run a single mile before, I paused on a backstreet to catch my breath. I hadn't been jogging since I left New York, and every muscle in my legs was now reminding me of that fact. For a second, I thought I was having a heart attack, and had to remind myself I was too young for a coronary. To calm myself, I grabbed a Valencian orange from a just-opened corner market, then followed the boulevard down to the waterfront.

The city was only now starting to wake up. Things don't move very fast in the morning in Spain, even in industrious Barcelona. Shopkeepers were hosing off their sidewalks, and the wonderful aroma of freshly brewing coffee wafted through the air. A magic filled the streets; since arriving in Spain, I'd never been awake this early, and I wondered if I'd been missing something all along.

On the boardwalk, I peeled my healthy breakfast carefully, the sea air caressing my face. I'd always tried to peel my oranges in one long strip, and I'd always failed. Yet this morning, I managed one long curlicue of skin—my own piece of art. The spiraling rind felt like such a triumph that I had trouble throwing my masterwork away.

My phone rang just as I popped the first juicy section of orange into my mouth. I wasn't sure what time it was now, but I figured it was probably Trevor looking for me. I accepted the call before my phone was even fully out of my pocket.

"Picasso was a friend of mine, Callie," came the voice.

"Mr. Hemingway?"

"I learned from him, and now you have too."

"I'm… I'm not so sure I—"

"—Abolish self-doubt, Callie. You're doing beautifully."

I wasn't about to argue with praise from a dearly-departed Nobel Prize winner, so I stayed silent, waiting for his next words.

"Embrace me in the streets of Madrid, Callie."

"Madrid? I'll find you in Madrid?"

"You will succeed, Callie, if you choose to. You still have five months. Come find me. I'm waiting."

Madrid

CHAPTER 8

SEXY AS HELL

One extremely rushed breakfast. One very confused but generally compliant Trevor. One fast but very hot shower. One whirlwind hour of packing. One additional hour at the station waiting for the next train to Madrid. Zero farewells to Barcelona.

"But Callie, what about Susan and Jane? Shouldn't we have said goodbye?" Trevor asked as we stepped off the train almost three hours later. This constituted his entire objection to my bat-out-of-hell flight from Barcelona. He never asked why we were relocating—or for an explanation of my overwhelming urgency. If I hadn't told him we were headed to Madrid, he probably wouldn't even have asked for a destination. I didn't question his lack of questions, mostly because telling him I was now in semi-regular communication with a demised literary master was unthinkable. Instead, I re-convinced myself that Trevor simply needed a leader; that leader was me, Callie McGraw.

"They knew we'd move on eventually," I replied. "I'll send them a nice message after we get settled, okay? I'll even invite them to come visit us."

"Okay, Callie. So long as we're not being rude." Trevor might've been about as exciting as a marshmallow, but I couldn't deny he had a kind, if somewhat squishy, moral compass.

We made our way onto the main concourse of Madrid's Estación de Atocha. It was one giant open space, the soaring orange-brick walls giving way to a sweeping, arched-glass ceiling. A beautifully light and airy space, even if the station itself was crowded. In the center of it all was a veritable forest, lush with palm trees and greenery. Barely a hint of grease or oil tainted the air; the station smelled fresh, almost tropical, and welcoming.

Trevor wanted a paper map of the city; I told him I would grab one if he stayed with our luggage. I trekked to the information counter on the outskirts of the forest. A young American couple, heavily tattooed and pierced, stood in front of me. Some of their piercings looked painful—like they were still painful. Neither of them seemed overly fond of showers; my nose confirmed this when I stepped too close. Even for all that, I could tell the two shared a bond forged of both transience and resilience.

I craved a window into their life. Nosiness maybe, but I wanted to know what made them tick. I leaned in; it wasn't hard to hear the man because he spoke slowly and clearly, as if over-enunciation would help the woman behind the counter understand his English better.

"Hel-lo. We want to buy tick-ets to the boats."

"*Los botes*? The boats?" the attendant asked.

"Yes. The boats. To ride the canals."

"Canals?" She was perplexed, and I was too. What was this guy talking about?

"Yes. The ca-nals," he repeated, staring her down. "Madrid is the ca-nal city, right?"

The poor woman's face slid from confused to annoyed as she spoke. "No canals in Madrid, *señor*."

A thought popped into my head. It didn't seem possible, but I couldn't resist asking. "Excuse me, are you looking for the city of canals?"

The man turned to me, clearly relieved by my English. "Yeah! With those boat thingies, the… What are they called?" He turned to his girlfriend, hoping she'd fill in the blank.

"Gondolas." Her answer came from an emotionless face.

"Right. Gondolas. I've always wanted to ride in a gondola."

"Venice is the city with the canals—it's a lagoon city, on the coast. This is Madrid. We're pretty far inland here."

"No canals?"

The attendant piped up, trying to put an end to this nonsense. "No canals. No coasts. Only streets. *Calles solamente...*" She continued on in animated aggravation, rattling her words off much too quickly for me to understand. I held back a chuckle.

"Where in Spain is Venice?" he asked me. Clearly geography was not his strong suit.

"Venice isn't in Spain." Trying to be helpful, I added, "You're about a thousand miles off."

"Oh baby, that sucks," his girlfriend weighed in, although the expression on her face hardly changed. She consoled him, rubbing his arm tenderly. "Who knew?" she asked, as if Venice hadn't been founded sixteen-hundred years ago. In Italy.

Playing with his nose ring, the man considered this new information. By the look on his face, he was having trouble processing it. I scoffed. A lack of cognition is one thing, but an abundance of ignorance is quite another—and the two together made for a truly unfortunate combination. A combination that I didn't want to deal with after a three-hour train ride.

"Oh, okay. Thanks." Dejected, he turned back to the attendant. "Then I guess we'll take two bus tickets out of Madrid."

The woman sighed as if she wasn't being paid enough to deal with American stupidity. "Bus tickets over there," she directed, pointing to a giant sign a few yards away. "*Billetes de Autobús*," it read, with translations in several different languages, including English, directly below.

The guy stepped out of line, but he still wanted to talk to me. "You're so nice. Could you loan me a few bucks? For bus fare?"

Astonished and exasperated, I trained my gaze on him, not letting my eye contact waver. "My friend, I just gave you something more powerful than money. I gave you information." I raised an eyebrow and nodded, daring him to ask for a handout again. He paused before nodding back, as if he knew what we were both nodding about. Yet the vapidity in his eyes told another story.

His girlfriend, now somehow even more stone-faced, took his hand and began leading him away. "Come on, baby. We'll find your boats. We'll figure it out together, like we always do." She shot me a glance as if I'd personally exorcised all gondolas from Madrid just to spite the man she loved. Maybe I'd stumbled upon a twenty-first-century *les amants dans la rue*.

❧

My phone pinged as an email from Matt arrived. He'd just landed another investor, and he was writing to offer two options for my housing. I could choose the apartment with a balcony but no dedicated dining space, or the one without a balcony but with a dining area. I took the balcony. I could eat just about anywhere; a view of the bay wasn't nearly as portable.

Part of me appreciated Matt's message—it was reassuring to know things were shaping up as planned—but the rest of me resented it. I didn't want to think about my American life as we navigated with our paper map (and too much luggage) through the city. Trevor and I were on the hunt for new hotels—neither of us had had the good sense to research options from the train. In fact, I hadn't had the good sense to research Madrid at all since arriving in Europe, even though I had known I would end up here sooner or later. I'd told myself I was "living in the moment," but actually I was just being lazy—and loving my laziness for once in my life. My shoulders were paying for it now, though; every possession I owned on this continent was currently in my grasp.

Immediately, Madrid felt like another country—not just another city. While Barcelona had an international flavor to it, with plenty of southern French flourishes, Madrid felt one-hundred percent Spanish. Smack in the middle of Spain, the city is largely insulated from outside European influence, and it takes great pride in being the country's capital.

Even the language here sounded a bit different. The people of Madrid, the *madrileños*, spoke Castilian Spanish, with its clear, robust, pronunciations, and somewhat-formal lilt. They consider it the highest form of Spanish on Earth. Many other parts of Spain, and any number of Latin American countries, believe *madrileños* are linguistically snobby.

Trevor still insisted staying in the same hotel would be awkward. I didn't understand his hang-up, but eventually we stumbled on two hotels that were across the street from each other. Our research—that is, scanning through reviews on our phones—said both were decent places to stay. And just like that, we became expatriates in Madrid.

It was Trevor's idea to spend our first evening at a club. He hardly danced all night though, which—judging from the few moves I saw— was probably for the better. For the most part, he stood by the bar or off in a corner as everyone around him undulated and pulsated, moving to the music as one great mass. Sometimes he'd bob his head or wiggle his hips in time to the music, but that was as wild as he got. Occasionally he'd chat with whoever happened to float by—men and women alike— but then he'd go right back to people-watching. That was fine by me. I myself received no shortage of attention from hot men as I danced. While I probably never would've put up with so much blatant ogling in New York, here in Madrid it felt fantastic. I could be loose and free; every curve on my body felt sexy as hell, and for once I wasn't afraid of showing myself off.

That night we learned something of immense importance: many bars and clubs in the city offered free tapas to patrons. In Barcelona, we never got anything for free. The thought of five months of free tapas more than made up for my unfortunate "welcome to Madrid" encounter at the information booth. This city was full of promise, I was sure of it.

"Callie, I've never seen you dance like that before," Trevor said as we made our way through the night streets to our new digs. It wasn't that late, and we weren't even that drunk, both of which were an accomplishment for us.

"You've never seen me dance in Madrid before," I quipped. "New city, new Callie."

Trevor's eyes grew wide, as if I'd just announced the end of the world as he knew it. "But I liked the old Callie," he whined.

I couldn't imagine why he thought I was being serious, but I didn't want to do him the disservice of killing his buzz. Not on our first night in the heart of Spain, at least.

"Don't worry, Trevor my boy, I'm still here. I'm just *more* here now. More *me*."

"I don't know, Callie. You were a little different at Montserrat, too."

"I was a little carsick at Montserrat. That's not the same thing."

He remained unconvinced. "So, you're not… going to change every time we go to a new city?" The earnestness in his voice worried me. What was eating at him?

"We all change, Trevor," I began gently before flattening my voice into a deadpan worthy of his preposterous question. "But no, there's no geographic link, if that's what you're asking."

"And this new Callie… She… dances more?"

"Maybe, I don't know. Why shouldn't I dance if I feel like dancing?"

"You're a good dancer, Callie. I was watching. Better than the other women."

"I think you have beer goggles on. You'd better go sleep it off, okay? Everything will make more sense tomorrow."

"Okay, Callie. If that's what you think is best." I didn't know what was bothering him, but a prescription for a good night's sleep seemed like a reasonable balm.

I clapped my hand on his shoulder. "And I'll tell you what. We'll find a new first-breakfast café in the morning, okay?"

Mollified and relieved, Trevor grinned widely—so widely his lips seemed to sprawl all the way to his ears. "Yes, breakfast together, Callie. That's a good plan. You always know just what to do. I'll follow you anywhere."

CHAPTER 9

ENTER SPAIN MAN

We'd only been in Madrid for a week, but already Trevor and I had started to settle into a routine. The basic components were sleeping, eating, drinking, and going out at night to do more of the last two. Our routine wasn't that different from our time in Barcelona, except there were more clubs and bars and fewer late-night cafés.

I liked the bars, they were full of life and energy. Some people get stressed by packed bars, but not me. There's something about the din and hum of a crowded, alcohol-infused space that puts me at ease. The commotion brings out a clarity of thought—I can focus on me and only me. That's why I did so well in New York, I think. In a city that's a constant cacophony—shouting and traffic and construction and honking horns—I found it easy, usually, to slip into my own private bubble, a space apart from all else. It wasn't a particularly *happy* space, though I'll say that much; New Yorkers are known for their attitude for a reason.

Limón y Lima (Lemon and Lime) kept showing up on the lists of Madrid's hottest bars, and now, as we stood outside, I could see why. We'd made it a point to show up early—Spanish clubbing early—and even though it was only 11:00 p.m., the large glass windows were already fogging up from the heat of the bodies inside. We passed under the bright, beckoning lights, through the glass doors, and onto a massive porch that ran along the sidewalk. Trevor cringed when I told him to prepare to get a little crazy.

There's an art to getting served at a crowded bar. It's essential to gauge which way the person in front of you is going to move once they grab their order, and timing is important. If they spin counterclockwise and lead away with their left shoulder, to snag the opening, spinning the same way but leading into the vacated space with your right shoulder is the way to go. Also very important is not betraying any anticipation to the others vying for the same opening. Getting served is an art, but there's a remarkably healthy dose of science in play, too.

Trevor had a terrible habit of "counter turning" and running into exiting bar patrons, which always led to a free-for-all for the opening. Watching him was hilarious, so when Trevor asked what I wanted to drink, I told him to surprise me and waited for the show to begin.

After the third bar, space-scuffle broke out, I scanned the room. A local crowd with no tourists to speak of. I did my normal check for good-looking guys and spotted one across the room. He was taller than the average Spanish man, and he had a scruff of a beard. He was probably around my age, probably a couple of years older, but not more. His expression had a certain smolder to it, and his features were striking. Tall, dark, and handsome, he could've been right out of central casting for a telenovela. He didn't merely look Spanish, he somehow seemed like the embodiment of Spain itself. I didn't know his name, of course, so I affectionately deemed him "Spain Man." He looked my way for an instant, but I turned away as Trevor, victorious at last, finally returned.

"Ew!" I cried as I took a sip of the concoction he'd brought me. "What's in this?"

He looked disappointed. "It was a special tonight. It has grapefruit juice in it."

"I hate grapefruit. I told you that."

"No you didn't, Callie. I would've remembered."

"We've eaten every meal together for the last month. This must have come up at some point."

"No, you never said." He was unwavering, so I didn't bother arguing further. I took another sip, which was only marginally better than the first.

"I'm going to the men's room," Trevor announced, a trace of a pout on his face.

The bar was getting even more crowded, but I didn't feel awkward standing there on my own. I took another sip of Trevor's grapefruit nightmare and made a face. When I opened my eyes, I saw Spain Man across the room. We briefly made eye contact—at least I think we did. I took another sip of my drink. The fourth sip was no better. Possibly worse. I surveyed the room again; Spain Man was gone. Vanished, likely out of my life forever. "That's too bad," I said quietly—not that anyone could hear me over the commotion. He'd easily been the most intriguing man in the room.

Five minutes later, Trevor made it back, his drink almost gone. Had he been drinking in the bathroom? That was even more gross than sniffing dead fish. I hoped that somewhere out there, there was a perfect woman for him—a woman who liked the smell of trout.

I abandoned my drink on an empty table. A moment later, I pointed to Trevor's almost-empty glass and made an expression that asked, "Do you want one more?" He nodded, and I spun around a bit too quickly in my haste to get myself a decent drink. I didn't get far. Three wobbly steps in and—*boom!*—I bumped straight into Spain Man.

"Sorry!" I exclaimed, embarrassed. "I didn't mean to—"

"—It was my fault," he said calmly. "I was coming to you. I saw that you did not… enjoy your drink and thought I could be of help." His voice was deep, and although his accent was heavy, his words slid out of his mouth smoothly and effortlessly.

"I think you could." I nodded and desperately tried not to smile like an idiot.

"But you must excuse me, I did not introduce myself. My name is Claudio."

Still putting my energy into not grinning like a fool, I didn't answer immediately. Claudio prompted me. "And your name is…?"

"I'm Callie." Callie McGraw, who absolutely would not start swooning like a teenage girl over this man.

He smiled. "Kauhlie. A very nice name."

Claudio's pronunciation of my name sent a ripple of delight through me. He pronounced the first syllable as if he were saying "cauliflower" and not "California." And he put an extra emphasis on the first syllable—like it was the most important syllable in the world to him.

"A fresh cocktail would be nice. Thank you… Claudio."

Trevor ambled up and cut in. "Can I get one as well, dude?"

Claudio's eyebrows raised ever so slightly in surprise. "Oh, I am sorry, I did not *sense* you were together."

"'Sense' we're together?" asked Trevor, a weird edge to his voice.

"We're not together-together." I explained quickly. "We're just here together."

"Ah, I see." Claudio furrowed his brow, as if he were puzzling out my meaning. "Then let me get a drink for my other new friend as well."

"Trevor," Trevor interjected, clearing the point up.

"Yes, my new friend Trevor," he replied, motioning for us to take a seat at a nearby table. "And then we can all drink together." He smiled again… at me.

"Can I have another one of these?" Trevor asked, pointing to his glass. "The special with the grapefruit juice?"

Claudio looked at him intensely. "No," he pronounced.

"No?"

"No, because you do not want another of those." The man seemed very sure of himself, but not at all in an arrogant way. More of an informed way, like he knew this town well.

"I don't?" Trevor asked, surprised.

"I will get you both something much better. Trust me." With that, he turned to the bar and raised his hand, motioning to the bartender: Our drinks arrived almost instantly and seemingly out of nowhere. I noted that no one else in the bar had table service.

"This is delicious!" I cried in delight. It wasn't the most original sentiment, but it was all I could think to say. Claudio's eyes sparked; clearly, he was pleased by having pleased me.

"It's… okay," Trevor added after taking his first sip.

"I knew you would love it! It is a special, secret recipe. I have shared it with the bartenders here so they can mix it for me anytime."

From there the evening was a whirlwind. A second round of drinks appeared soon, later came a third. Claudio was a Madrid native, although he mentioned having lived in other places as well. He worked in finance, but he didn't elaborate. I didn't push—I hadn't elaborated much about my career in law, either. Fair was fair.

Claudio loved Madrid, loved Spain as a whole. He talked about the wonders of his country—his favorite foods, his favorite soccer teams, his favorite museums. My nickname for him had been apt, he radiated passion for his home city. His fervor for all things Spain somehow made me feel woefully inadequate, although that wasn't his intention at all. He was a marvelous storyteller, and instead of coming off as a conversation-hog, it was clear he was trying to share his zeal with us. With *me*.

By the time he was finished, Limón y Lima was packed well beyond capacity, and so loud it wasn't even worth keeping the conversation going. Our small table was hedged in on all sides by the young and the tipsy, and if any of us moved so much as two inches, we were likely to get an elbow to the face. I liked a crowded bar, sure, but this was ridiculous. I wanted to leave, but I also didn't want Claudio to think I was a wet blanket.

My exasperation must've shown on my face—I was starting to get cranky-drunk, which sometimes happened when I needed some air. Claudio read my expression exactly and rescued me from my own impending funk.

"Enough of this for tonight!" he declared with an excited flourish, shooting up from his chair and half-bumping into the man behind him. "Now I will take my new friends dancing!"

⚜

Claudio turned his head only slightly as he spoke to us from the front seat of the cab. "I tell you, you will love this place. It is the best club for dancing in Madrid. Some clubs are for watching, but we are going to a club for *dancing*!"

"Great!" That was all I could offer. The quick turns of the cab, along with the drinks from Limón y Lima, were making my head swirly—mostly in a good way. By this time, I'd completely lost track of where we were, not that I knew Madrid well enough to recognize much. The night was electric, though, with taxis ushering their passengers to adventures untold. Everyone seemed to be smiling on their ride, as if we were all sharing the same mood of anticipation.

Claudio gave the driver instructions in Spanish. The man nodded, then took a hard right and accelerated. I started to giggle, but nervousness covered Trevor's face; each time the cab swerved, his brow contorted in a new way.

Screech!

The driver slammed on the breaks as a scooter cut us off. The car skidded, missing the bike by just a few inches. Claudio remained motionless, and neither the driver nor the kid seemed fazed at all. It was contagious; I stopped worrying about little things like car wrecks.

Ten minutes later, Claudio exclaimed, "We have arrived!" as we came to an abrupt stop outside an unassuming bar. It wasn't run-down, but it lacked the glitz and glamour of a typical dance club. I wondered if we were in the wrong place.

Claudio sprang out of the front seat and glided to the rear door to open it for me. I shot my legs out of the car, and the rest of me followed. Trevor scooted across the backseat to climb out, and he had to grab the roof of the cab for balance as he stepped onto the sidewalk. We both stared at the building's façade.

"Ah," began Claudio, reading our expressions. "You do not think this club is much to look at? You think perhaps I am…" he paused, finding the right idiom, "taking you on a wild goose chase?"

I shook my head. "No, it's not that. I just thought we were going to another place like Limón y Lima."

"Limón y Lima is for drinking. This is a place for dancing!" Claudio's eyes sparked again, as if he knew I'd be thrilled by what lay inside. "But I must admit I have been keeping a little secret. I am not merely taking my new friends dancing. I am taking you *flamenco* dancing!" He swept his hand through the night air, laughing to himself.

"Of course, you are," muttered Trevor, "What could be more Spanish?"

Claudio reached for the door and grabbed the handle firmly. He froze before turning his head back to us. Still holding the handle, he explained somberly, "This club is called Estocada. The *estocada* is the matador's death-thrust. *Estocada* is the moment when he drives his sword, the *estoque*, behind *el toro's* shoulder blade and pierces the heart."

"That's a strange name for a dance club," I said, mostly because I had to say something. Claudio's eyes were burning into me, and, again, I would not start swooning like a teenager.

"No, Kauhlie. It is a very good name. They say the first time someone truly hears flamenco music it can pierce their heart and capture them forever." He paused for half a second. "We enter!" With that, he threw the door open and ushered us in with a grand, celebratory motion. If anyone else had done that, it would've seemed over-the-top, but Claudio pulled it off like it was the most natural thing in the world.

From the very first moment inside, Trevor and I were entranced by the club's music and energy. Rhythm was the air itself. Claudio led us past the bar, where patrons were drinking and picking at trays of tapas. Up ahead, two guitarists played on a small platform, and the dance-floor was full of people twisting and writhing. Anyone not dancing or eating was clapping their hands to the rhythm. A fiesta unlike any I'd ever seen. Like *Saturday Night Fever* except very Spanish and free of Hollywood cheesiness.

Claudio never broke stride as he caught the attention of the woman behind the bar. Her long black hair shone even in the dim light. When he held up his fingers, ordering three of something, she smiled at him warmly and nodded.

He stopped us abruptly at the dancefloor's edge. Claudio opened his arms and gestured majestically, presenting the crowd to us. Several dancers acknowledged him, and one even shouted a welcoming, "*Bienvenido a Estocada!*" as he whirled by.

"First, we drink!" Claudio announced as three large gin and tonics arrived from behind us. Trevor grabbed his glass as if the cocktail were a lifeline. Having seen his dance moves, I knew why he looked so anxious.

We pushed through the throng to a standing table where we could survey the fiesta and relax into the crowd. For just a split second I felt truly Spanish.

"Flamenco dancing is rich in *el duende*," Claudio announced, clapping along with the music. From his tone, this wasn't a mere comment, it was a statement of fact.

"*El duende?*" I asked. I'd never heard of such a thing. Trevor's disinterested eyes told me he obviously had no clue either. No big surprise there.

"*El duende* is... there's not a good translation. *El duende* is in the soul. The passion inside. *El duende* is the heat, the fire of art and creating. It is the craving, the yearning within. It is the goosebumps on your arm, the thumping of your heart!" He fixed his smoldering eyes on mine. "Kauhlie, *el duende* steals your very breath itself."

"Yes, I think I understand," I replied slowly, feeling almost as if he had stolen my breath with his eyes. I thought of *Embrace in the Street*, the lovers were like *el duende* in pastels. Perhaps I would ask Claudio about that later—when this stupid smile wasn't trying to sneak across my face.

He smiled a mere hint of a smile, then broke eye contact. "Please excuse me, my new friends. I must now say hello to my old friends." He walked over to a group who received him warmly. He might've been a regular here, but his friends acted as if they hadn't seen him in months.

Trevor leaned over his drink and raised an eyebrow. "Callie, if you want my opinion, I think *el duende* is *el* bullshit."

"Noted, but I can do without your opinion on this one, thanks very much."

"I'm just saying, I don't think that's how passion works."

"Trevor, for someone longing for color, you're being very black and white. Passion works the way it works. It doesn't have rules."

"It doesn't?" He scratched his head, sincerely confused. "But doesn't everything have rules? Isn't that why we have imagination—a place with no rules?"

"Passion is beyond rules too. Now loosen up a bit, okay? We're lucky to be here—we never would've found this place on our own."

"Kauhlie, Trevor," Claudio began as he returned to our table. "It is time to experience *el duende*. We dance. Now."

"Now?" Trevor seemed stunned, like he'd forgotten we were in a flamenco club. He pulled on his beard as if bringing himself back to reality.

"Yes, now. We will all dance together, one group. Nobody needs to feel like... the third one?"

"The third wheel," Trevor corrected flatly.

"Right! Nobody needs to feel like the third wheel." Claudio patted Trevor heartily on the shoulder, almost causing my travel companion to spill his drink.

Claudio grabbed my hand, leading me to the dancefloor. I grabbed Trevor's sleeve in turn and dragged him along behind us. He mouthed the words, "Who is this guy?!" but I didn't respond. Because honestly, I didn't care *who* Claudio was. I'd been drawn into his wake.

We walked into the crowd as the guitar players strummed away. The music was louder here, washing over me. Claudio moved into the middle of the floor. I remained a few feet behind him, fighting for a spot. All of a sudden, the music stopped at the exact moment when Claudio did, his back still turned to me. He turned around quickly, then froze in place, staring at me. I felt a little uncomfortable, but it was a good uncomfortable. A *hot* uncomfortable.

The music erupted. The guitarists hammered out a rhythm, and Claudio instantly responded. The other dancers parted, giving him room. He slammed his heels onto the wooden floor again and again, like a pair of jackhammers, with a tantalizing precision. His eyes remained fixed on me. When he spun, it was as if his body rotated on a perfect, controlled, axis; his head didn't turn until the last possible instant, and his eyes only broke from mine for a split second. He maintained his laser-like gaze even as his body became flamenco itself.

Bam! Bam bam bam! Bam! Bam bam bam! I thought his feet would break through the floor. I struggled to keep the rhythm as I raised my arms in the air. I tried to swirl my fingertips in seductive waves like the other women around me, but I probably looked like I was suffering from spasms.

At least I was doing better than Trevor. Out of the corner of my eye, I could see him trying his best, but he was all knees and elbows and looked like he was playing invisible maracas. He'd locked his face into what must've been his approximation of a Spanish-dancer's intensity, but he couldn't pull it off. The poor man looked as if he were in the middle of a surprise prostate exam.

Song after song, the guitar players increased their intensity. Claudio matched their intensity effortlessly. He slammed his heels harder and harder, his movements becoming faster yet no less controlled. I was in awe. His dance was raw emotion—not intensity for the sake of intensity. He was clearly enjoying the crowd's attention, but I could sense he wasn't showing off. Energy and passion oozed from his every movement.

When the guitarists finally played a slower song, all the dancers switched gears, but their intensity didn't waver. Except for Trevor. He'd survived his prostate exam, and he was now very, very relieved.

Before I knew it, Claudio had danced up behind me and nestled in close. He wasn't touching me, but he was so close I could smell him. I took in his scent of fresh perspiration tinged with sandalwood. Turning over my shoulder, I shot him a look that I hoped said both, "Behave yourself, we just met," and, "Come closer."

He again held my gaze in his. "This is how we make the dance," he said. He must've been shouting over the music, but his words felt like a whisper. I finally gave up on not grinning like an idiot.

I reached for Claudio's hands and placed them on my hips. He said nothing as he began guiding me side to side in perfect rhythm with his own movements. I could feel his smoldering eyes—if I turned around, his gaze would reach deep inside mine. I resisted, focusing on the dance. My body began to anticipate the beats, began to anticipate Claudio's movements. As I dissolved into his rhythm, I began to believe in *el duende*.

CHAPTER 10

MURDERING TOMATOES

Trevor's face brightened as I walked through the door of our first-breakfast café. He motioned for me to join him—as if there were any other place I would sit. He'd already ordered, and there was a ton of food on the table. Far more than our usual baguettes and coffee.

He stood up to greet me. "I'm sorry about the grapefruit," he said. It took my un-caffeinated, mildly hungover brain a second to figure out what he meant: last night's grapefruit-cocktail fiasco. "So I ordered something different for us today," he continued. "All your favorites."

I panned the table. He'd outdone himself: bread, cheese, fruit, and my favorite Spanish ham. I was more than ready to indulge. We'd had nothing for dinner last night but tapas, and I was ravenous.

"Wow, Trevor! This is just what I need this morning, thank you."

"But wait, there's more." He thrust his hands into his pockets and pulled out something bulky from each one. "Here," he said, opening his clenched palms and revealing a lemon in one and a lime in the other.

I threw my head back and laughed. "*Limón y lima*. The perfect finishing touch! Very clever!" I was genuinely impressed; he must've gotten up extra early to search for an open market.

Trevor sat back down and cupped his steaming coffee, looking as if he'd scooped up sacred water from the Nile and was about to begin worshiping. A second steaming cup sat by my place setting. It didn't occur to me at the time, but later I wondered what he would've done if I'd been late and the coffee grew cold. Would he have ordered a fresh coffee every fifteen minutes until I showed up? Probably. That would be a very Trevor thing to do.

He took a sip of his coffee, then looked directly at me again. "I know what you like," he said, no small sense of accomplishment in his voice.

"I know you do, Trevor," I answered, again taking in the splendor of his breakfast display. "You're very considerate that way. And there's nothing to apologize for. We try new things... Sometimes we don't like them."

"Yeah, but you *hated* that drink. You didn't even finish it! You abandoned your alcohol, Callie. *Abandoned* it." Trevor said *abandoned* as if he'd caused me to commit the greatest alcohol-sin in human history. A little excessive, maybe, but he did have a point: I hadn't walked away from a buzz since the day we'd met.

"It's okay. It all worked out, anyhow." I picked up a dried date and popped it into my mouth. "These are the simple pleasures. Well done, my friend."

He beamed, clearly pleased by the compliment, then he took my plate and loaded it with tangerine wedges and apple slices. "Start with these," he encouraged, "the fructose will help with your hangover."

I smiled. Even if he was a bit dorky, by now Trevor knew me better than I liked to admit. I didn't fight it. As he smiled back, I replied, "It's just a little hangover, don't worry. A two-too-many hangover, not a fifteen-too-many hangover."

"We did have one heck of a night, Callie. A once in a lifetime thing."

"I hope not," I said earnestly. "We're going to dinner at Claudio's tonight—who knows what'll happen after that?"

"I don't know if we should." He pulled apart his baguette anxiously. "I mean, that guy's a lot, don't you think?"

I thought about it for a second, wondering what he was getting at. "Yes, Claudio's a lot. But a good a lot. An *alive* a lot."

"But really, who *is* he?" Trevor asked, a hint of forcefulness in his voice. Or maybe it just seemed that way—the whole room felt a little too loud. "I mean, seriously?"

"He's Claudio," I offered, as if the answer were obvious.

"Yeah, but what do we really know about him? What's his deal?"

"I don't know. He's nice." I grabbed a roll and took a large bite to signal I didn't really want to talk about it.

"It's like he goes around with a giant *S* on his chest, like Superman."

"Or maybe the *S* stands for 'Spain Man?'" I posited as I chewed. "That's what I called him before I met him. I was checking him out when you were in the restroom."

"You check everyone out, Callie."

"So do you. That's kind of what we do, isn't it?" Hell, sometimes we even checked out people together, women and men alike. People-watching was almost an art with us.

"I guess, but he just seems... larger than life. Like the man we see can't be the man he is. Like he has an alter ego or something." The green in Trevor's eyes scintillated in the strangest way.

Disagreeing, I shook my head—rookie hangover-mistake. "Maybe, but I don't think so. I think he's just... exuberant." I shrugged. "Let's try and have fun tonight, okay? I want to see Spain Man's headquarters."

"You mean his lair?" corrected Trevor.

"No. Villains have lairs. Claudio is a good guy."

"Is he? I bet he has henchmen." From his tone, I couldn't tell if Trevor was joking or not. "Callie, I don't know if I could save you from henchmen. Even if I tried really hard."

This was getting weird—especially for this early in the day. Why was he being so overprotective? And when did I ever ask to be saved? "You're worrying about nothing," I said flatly before leaning into Trevor's weirdness just to indulge him. "I'm sure Claudio doesn't have a single henchman to his name."

"All the super-villains have henchmen. That's how they roll," he countered, speaking as if he'd written a book on the topic. I could almost see a teenage Trevor geeking out over an old-school collection of comic books.

If he was going to embrace the absurd over today's breakfast, I was too. "Okay. I'll grant you that much… but let me ask you this." I wiped my mouth with my napkin in exaggerated seriousness. "Where do super-villains find their henchmen? That has to be a serious problem in their line of work. How do they satisfy their staffing needs?"

Without missing a beat, Trevor deadpanned, "Twitter."

I laughed. "Definitely Twitter."

⋘

Right at nine o'clock, Claudio showed up outside our hotels in a taxi, just as he'd promised. A little odd given the country's general *mañana* philosophy, but when he climbed out of the car, I immediately stopped wondering about silly things: dressed in an immaculately pressed outfit, Claudio looked terrific. His cottony white shirt was unbuttoned one more button than was typical in the States, and his sleek black pants were fitted just enough to show off the definition in his thighs. The night was off to a marvelous start.

"Kauhlie and Trevor!" He held his arms wide open as he approached us. "What fun we are going to have tonight!" He gave me a kiss on each cheek, then shook Trevor's hand warmly. "Come, come," he urged, ushering us into the cab. "Tonight, I will share a very special meal with you. Something very Spanish. We will cook it together, the three of us."

Before long, we pulled up to a beautiful, early-twentieth-century stone building on a quiet street. Despite its age, it was the tallest building on the block. Ever the gentleman, Claudio jumped out of the front passenger seat and opened the rear door for me.

"There's no *S*, Callie," Trevor whispered as we approached the building.

"What?" I couldn't imagine what he was talking about.

"I looked. There's no *S*. Not for Superman *or* Spain Man." He frowned, disappointed. "Maybe he doesn't have an alter ego after all."

"Just behave yourself for once, Trevor. Try hard."

The doorman greeted us when we stepped into the small but ornate marble lobby. In the antique, well-maintained elevator, Trevor glanced at me as if to say, "This guy's loaded!" and we soon discovered that Claudio's place was the only apartment on the top floor.

"Please come in," he said as he unlocked the door and threw it open. "Welcome to my home!"

I walked in first, with Trevor on my heels. He stopped in his tracks once he crossed the threshold. "A *penthouse?*" he gasped under his breath. Again, I was sure only I could hear him.

I turned and whispered, "Some lair, huh?" Even super-villains didn't live like this.

"This apartment has been in my family for many years," Claudio began as we looked around. "It is mine now, but when it came time for renovations, I still had to convince my parents of the necessity. They are traditionalists, they do not embrace change!"

I tried to act casual, as if I walked into multimillion-dollar homes every day. "It's a beautiful space," I offered. That's the sort of thing millionaires said to each other, right?

Modern and clean, the apartment's open-concept layout was beautifully designed—the living room, dining room, and kitchen were all in the same large space, yet were each a separate area. A sliding glass door led to a grand balcony with a view of the city. A hint of orange still colored the night sky even though the sun had long set.

Two black kittens scampered up to Claudio, greeting him. "Oh, and I must introduce you to my furry friends," he said, picking up one kitten in each hand.

"You have kittens?" I asked. I hadn't been expecting that.

"Yes, but only two." He smiled at me as he handed one cat to each of us. "They are very friendly and well-behaved," he promised.

The kitten snuggled into my chest and started purring as if it wanted me to rock it to sleep. Trevor, holding his own kitten, said, "No… way!" He was still agog at the apartment, and now there were adorable kittens too. From the crease of his brow, I was certain he was experiencing sensory overload.

"Trevor, you have the girl. She is Antonia—or Toni. Kauhlie, you have the boy. He is Teodoro—or Teddy."

"Toni and Teddy, that's so cute!" I burst out—the pitch of my voice much too high for a grown woman. Teddy burrowed deeper into the crook of my arm; I bit my lip to keep myself from squealing out any more brilliant remarks.

"They will be your hosts for a moment while I bring the first course."

When it came to tapas, Claudio held nothing back. He'd prepared spareribs in a paprika sauce, goat-cheese tarts, roasted asparagus wrapped in Serrano ham, spicy almonds, and olives with fennel and cumin. He presented the plates as if each were a small masterpiece whose true beauty could only be realized by sharing it.

"The word *tapas* comes from the Spanish word *tapa* which means 'lid,'" Claudio began as he poured our wine. "Many years ago, innkeepers would place slices of bread on top of their patrons' glasses, to keep the fruit flies out of the sherry."

"Yuck," Trevor blurted out. I shot him a glance, begging him to mind his manners. I pointed to the tapas, suggesting we dig in. I couldn't wait another moment; we'd skipped lunch in anticipation of this dinner.

"Then someone came up with the idea to place a small, delicious something on the bread," Claudio continued, "usually a bit of salted ham. This started the evolution of tapas."

"Well, it was a delicious metamorphosis if these are the results," I chimed in, picking up an asparagus stalk.

"I bet he got that off of Wikipedia," Trevor whispered under his breath—again only loud enough for me to hear. I elbowed him as inconspicuously as I could.

"I have also baked some bread," Claudio said casually, pulling his vibrating phone from his pocket. "It is ready now. The timer is going off."

"Of course, you bake too," I said before realizing it. Handsome. Intelligent. Rich. Kitten lover. Chef. Baker. I was dangerously close to declaring him the perfect man.

"Kauhlie, what does this mean, 'Of course, you do?' Do American men not bake bread?"

I sipped my wine to hide my embarrassment. "The bread smells delicious! You'd better pull it out before it burns, though?" I diverted, distracted, obfuscated.

It worked. As he walked into the kitchen, he called over his shoulder, "And after the bread, we will all cook dinner together!"

"We're actually going to cook?" I called back, displaying my elegance and sophistication for the second time in ten seconds. "I thought you were joking," I added quickly.

Claudio turned. "Kauhlie, cooking is not a joke."

Anxiety shot through me. My relationship with the kitchen evidenced a hopeless lack of culinary talent. Who had time for cooking when there were contracts to review? Instead, I developed strong ties to take-out menus, delivery people, and neighborhood restaurants. Almost anyone can get away with that sort of thing in New York, and I'd taken full advantage.

Before I knew what hit me, Trevor and I were in the kitchen decked out in aprons, with Claudio giving us directions to chop this or dice that.

"Kauhlie, pass me that brown bag, please. Inside is something special for our meal."

I peeked inside and shuddered before I could hide my revulsion. "Snails?!"

"Yes! This recipe is Valencian, and snails are a traditional ingredient. They add much delicious flavor. And we must be authentic!"

"But you haven't told us what we're making," Trevor piped up, which was a valid point. I'd been dicing away blindly; I hadn't even thought to ask what our goal was.

"Paella! A dish that is the very heart of my country! And tonight, in honor of the occasion of new friends, we prepare it with snails and rabbit."

"Rabbit?! You mean the hippity-hoppity kind?" I wanted to keep an open mind, but snails and rabbit were a bit of a double whammy.

He laughed. "Indeed. The hippity-hoppity kind." Just then, he noticed the tomato I'd managed to mangle. "Kauhlie, you do not cook so much, do you?"

"No, I don't," I admitted. "My skill in the kitchen is… limited. I like the eating part, but not the making part."

"But food gives us life! If you prepare a meal for someone else, you are giving them life. You are caring for them. When you make an extraordinary dish for someone special, you are *loving* them through food. And when we cook *with* special people, it is *pasión* itself!"

"I never thought about it that way."

"It is true. Would you not like to give life to another?"

"Sure, I guess. But right now I think I've murdered this tomato." I examined the pile of mush I'd created. If I kept this up, I'd be well on my way to ketchup.

"Don't worry, I have many more." He grabbed a fresh tomato and began dicing it with astonishing deftness. He proceeded to the next task, making the work seem effortless. A certain grace to his movements. A certain elegance in his handwork. Complete efficiency, without the slightest bit of rushing. Everything fell into place as if preordained. This was Claudio sharing life right in front of me.

When all else was finished, he picked up a container of uncooked rice. "This is a special moment," he pronounced. He explained that when the rice goes in, the meal is twenty minutes from being done. He stressed that the rice must never be added before all guests are present. "People will wait for rice, but rice will wait for no one!" he concluded.

"An excellent strategy," agreed Trevor. "No one likes over-cooked rice."

Claudio sprinkled the rice in, distributing it slowly evenly. "And now, as is tradition, we must all say, '*Veinte minutos!*' to signal the last twenty minutes," he instructed. "Ready now, on three. *Uno, dos...*"

We called out in unison. Trevor called out a little too loudly. He was warming up to Claudio and relaxing a little. Finally.

A few minutes later, I grabbed a large wooden spoon and offered to stir the rice. For the first time, Claudio became visibly ruffled. "No, no, no, Kauhlie, that is not done. It is an unbreakable rule of paella! We must *never* stir the rice." He eyed me sternly for an instant, as if my very suggestion were sacrilege.

I must've seemed deflated standing there with my spoon raised in the air. His look softened, and the corners of his mouth turned up in a gentle smile. "It is okay. This is your first time making paella."

I didn't reply, but sensing my disappointment, he reached down and scooped up one of his furry companions. Claudio handed his pet to me and said, "Here, have a kitten." I didn't know which kitten it was, but that did the trick.

After our delicious dinner, Claudio brought out a bottle of Orujo, a strong Spanish brandy. We moved to his balcony, into the refreshing, almost-early-spring night. Looking out over the rooftops of Madrid, he said wistfully, "It is good to be back in my native city, but I fear it will not be for long." By this time, we were all very full and just a little bit drunk; his tone was more somber than it had been all night.

"Why?" Trevor asked, continuing his tradition as a stellar conversationalist.

"It seems I am never home for long. Always for sometimes, never for good. Right now I am at what you would call a crossroad."

"Is that why you've been taking time off?" I asked.

"Yes. I am like you, Kauhlie... I am doing nothing right now. For time off. To be in Madrid."

"And you're like me, too, Claudio," Trevor added. "I'm doing nothing too, just like you."

"Yes, my friend Trevor, I am just like you." As Claudio replied, a thought screamed in my head, "Trevor, you're *nothing* like Claudio!" Guilt instantly washed through me; Trevor had pulled together a beautiful meal for me today, too. I immediately apologized to him—also in my head. That orujo was strong stuff.

I refocused quickly. "I don't understand, Claudio," I began with concern. "Why can't you stay in Madrid if this is your home?"

"Ah, Kauhlie, my life... it is not so simple that way. Necessity takes me away from my city—always has and always will. This I must accept."

"But I thought you grew up here?"

"I did, and I did not. As a young child, my parents and I lived here, with summers on the Mediterranean coast. But then came boarding school in Switzerland. A wonderful private school in the mountains. But in the summers, when I came home, we would still go to the sea. So I was not in Madrid so much."

"It sounds like you didn't see your parents much, either. That must've been tough."

He nodded. "My mother and father have a nice marriage. Still do. But my father works very hard, traveling all the time. Ever since I was a boy, he has traveled frequently. My mother came to visit me in Switzerland often, but my father could not."

"What does your father do?" Trevor was getting even more drawn into Claudio's tale than I was.

"He does all sorts of financial things for all sorts of companies. I do too. Or I will again, when I move from this crossroad. It was my father who sent me to university in England to study business, and then to graduate school for finance."

"You couldn't go to the University of Madrid?" Claudio's forlorn tone made me want to fight for a happy ending for him.

"No. My father, he wanted me to live in many different countries, speak many different languages. He said this was good for business-people. And it has been. I have been successful." He smiled just a bit, but it was a sad smile. "I did come home after school for a short while, but then my father's friend offered me a job. And then came another job. And another. Many different cities, many different jobs. But none in Spain."

Trevor, pulling on his beard, pointed out the obvious yet again. "But you're in Spain now."

"Yes, I am! Because I finally said. 'No more!'" Claudio shot up from his chair with surprising speed, his chest heaving. "I am Spanish, no? So, I must be in Spain. I quit my job that very day and moved home within the week! *Dama Fortuna*, she will soon call—and I must answer when she does—but until then, I will be one-hundred percent Spanish again!"

Right then I knew I didn't need to fight for Claudio's happy ending. He'd create it himself—and I was damn happy for him.

CHAPTER 11

A SPANISH KISS

"Trevor, my friend. I need to show Kauhlie something in the park. It is not for you. You will leave us for some time." Claudio said it just like that—very matter of fact.

Over the last week or so, Claudio had made it his personal mission to show us Madrid, and we were now on an extended walk after having stuffed ourselves during an extended lunch. Calling it "Spanish beef," he had sort of tricked Trevor into trying calf's liver (in saffron sauce), which led to Claudio giggling in front of me for the first time. I didn't know he was capable of giggling, but it made him even more attractive. I was now one-hundred-percent ready to take the next step—which, in this case, meant we needed some non-Trevor time. Whatever Claudio wanted to show me in the park, I was all in.

"What's for Callie and not for me?" Trevor asked, surprised and puzzled. "You two are always keeping secrets."

This wasn't exactly true—not that he could've known it. Claudio and I had developed a game, ostensibly to tease Trevor, but really it was flirting at its finest. I would lean into Claudio and whisper something silly like, "The rain in Spain stays mainly on the plain," and he would chuckle conspiratorially. We both knew our game was nothing more than an excuse to get close to each other, but neither of us acknowledged it aloud.

"I will tell you soon, my friend, but for now you must go. You must not spoil this for Kauhlie. You will leave us for some time."

"It's okay, Trevor," I urged gently. "I'm sure it'll only be for a little while."

Trevor eyed each of us in turn before resignation crawled across his face. He took a few hesitant steps away but then froze in his tracks. "What does 'for some time' mean? How much time?" he asked petulantly.

"Kauhlie and I will meet you at the bar down the street in an hour," Claudio insisted. He added more softly, "The three of us will not be parted for long, I promise."

"See you in a bit," I encouraged. Trevor hadn't ever been hesitant to wander off on his own before; what was different today? I promised myself I would check in with him later, more privately, but right now I wanted to know what Claudio was up to.

"Okay, but only for an hour," Trevor consented. "Callie, you have my cell number," he added, as if I hadn't texted him hundreds of times. As he shuffled away, he looked over his shoulder once, like a dog who'd been scolded. My traveling companion was getting weirder and weirder all the time.

"This is Buen Retiro Park, Kauhlie. It is a magnificent park, with beautiful sculptures and gardens. It is a bit like your Central Park, only much smaller."

"Everything is smaller than Central Park," I replied, the New Yorker in me surfacing rebelliously. I surprised myself—I wasn't a New Yorker anymore, and I thought I'd made peace with that. I didn't exactly know *what* I was now, but I knew New York was behind me for good. Claudio, on the other hand, was right in front of me.

"Yes, Central Park is bigger, but El Retiro is no less beautiful. It was, for many generations, the royal gardens. Come." He took my hand

and led me onto a tree-lined path. The spring in Claudio's step was contagious; I began springing alongside him.

As we made our way deeper into the park, I found myself forgetting the city. The noise died away and was replaced by the fresh greenery. Further down the path, a young couple was kissing under a tree, oblivious to everything around them. An old woman walking her dog passed by and greeted us warmly in Spanish. I couldn't translate most of Claudio's reply, but he made her face light up, which made me even happier to be with him.

"It is only a little up ahead, Kauhlie, around that bend. Something beautiful for you to see." His voice twinkled with excitement. Still holding my hand, he caught me off guard as he burst into a jog.

"Dr. Seuss trees!" I squealed, rounding the corner. A grove of beautifully sculpted trees seemed like it had magically sprung up from the ground. Each tree looked like a giant stalk of planted broccoli—or as if Dr. Seuss had drawn it. I could picture these trees populating Whoville itself.

"Doctorsuss trees?" he asked, perplexed. "No, Kauhlie, these are Mediterranean cypresses. See how the gardeners tend to them with such precision and care? It is their guiding love that shapes them."

"Dr. Seuss trees!" I cried again, running toward them. "I love them!" I shouted, reaching up to a branch.

"Kauhlie, what does this mean? They are cypresses. This I know to be true."

"Don't you know who Dr. Seuss is? The author?"

"I do, yes. But I—"

"—Didn't your parents read Dr. Seuss to you as a kid?"

"No, my parents did not read American books to me. Truly, they did not read to me much at all, and then I went off to boarding school. We read to ourselves there."

"So you've never read *Green Eggs and Ham*?"

"No, Kauhlie. Why would I want to eat green eggs and ham? Yuck!"

He scrunched up his face as if he'd bitten into a slice of ham covered in a fuzzy green mold.

"Eating them isn't the point of the story. It's really about trying new things and growing." Claudio seemed unconvinced, like I was making all this up as I went along. The left corner of his mouth curled up as he held back a chuckle.

Trying to keep him with me, I changed course slightly. "How do you say, *Green Eggs and Ham* in Spanish?" I asked.

"Those are very silly words, Kauhlie." Claudio's features turned into a question mark. A cute look for him.

"Yes! Dr. Seuss *is* silly. Intentionally silly. Now come on, translate for me."

"*Huevos verdes y jamón.*"

Uncontrollable giggles bubbled from my mouth. I bounced on the balls of my feet, not even trying to maintain my composure. Giddiness ran through me like liberation itself. I hadn't felt so wondrously free in years.

"What is so funny?" Claudio rolled his eyes, knowing I'd set him up. It was adorable as hell.

"Okay, how do you say, *The Cat in the Hat*?" I asked. "That's the title of a different book," I added for clarity, just in case he thought I'd really gone off my rocker.

"*El Gato Ensombrerado.*"

His earnestness sent me into another spasm of giggles. "*El Gato Ensombrerado!*" I repeated, casting my hand toward the branches for flair. I knocked myself off balance in the process, which caused Claudio to erupt in laughter, too.

"Okay, okay, just one more book. Last one, I promise." I began dancing around him in flowy, loose circles. "Translate, *One Fish, Two Fish, Red Fish, Blue Fish!*"

He spun, trying to keep pace with me. "*Un Pez, Dos Peces, Pez Rojo, Pez Azul.*"

My feet stopped in mid-stride. "That one's… not as good. It doesn't rhyme like it does in English."

"Translations will do that, Kauhlie. They can be sneaky that way." He paused, looking for a way to steer the conversation back to some semblance of normalcy. "But I am glad you like the trees. They are very beautiful, no?" Obviously, our interlude in the park wasn't going at all as he'd expected.

Not to be deterred, I changed the game. "Let's make up Dr. Seuss rhymes!" Without any explanation, I launched into my first attempt.

> "Callie met a guy named Trevor,
> And a beschmuppler called Claudio.
> They thrax and drax each night like zalopers,
> But to the findingler they have yet to go."

His jaw practically dropped. "You are teasing me, Kauhlie," he said slowly. "My English is very, very good—those weren't all real words."

"They're not supposed to be real words," I said through my giggles. You're supposed to make them up. That's part of it!"

"Part of what?"

"Whimsy! Dr. Seuss is all about *whimsy*. Now you try. Go on. Make up a Dr. Seuss rhyme."

"Okay," he said sheepishly. "For you, I will try." He paused, thinking. I watched attentively as he ran his hand through his thick, dark hair.

> "Callie was making Claudio rhyme,
> But it was not really his thing.
> He tried and tried, and he tried some more,
> But it all made his head go *ping-ping*."

"No, Claudio, that was terrible," I laughed. "You're supposed to make up words. It's supposed to be fanciful. You're just rhyming."

"I made up a word. My word is *ping-ping*. Is this not a good word?"

"No, because you repeated a real word. That doesn't count. Your rhyme was a Seussian disaster, my friend." I jabbed my finger playfully into his stomach. His abs were even more muscular than I expected. Nice.

"Then you must show me again. I have read much English poetry, but nothing like this. Perhaps I do not understand. Make up another rhyme for me, maybe then I will do better."

"Fair enough." I scrunched my face in thought as I put together another quatrain.

"Callie came to Spain,
To find her Hemingway.
She cantinkled and canfinkled,
But she hasn't seen him to this day."

Claudio's face changed, his mouth turning down slightly, like he'd suddenly become concerned. Disappointing—I'd thought that rhyme was particularly good for such short notice.

"Kauhlie, I get your made-up words, but what does 'to find her Hemingway' mean?"

My stomach sunk to my feet. Crap, how was I going to explain this one? I'd let my guard too far down, and now I'd said way too much. Damnit.

"Well… um… I guess you could say Hemingway *called* me to Spain," I replied, choosing my words carefully. That didn't seem to cover it, so I launched into my love affair with *The Sun Also Rises*. Under Claudio's attentive gaze, I started spiraling—my sentences came out too fast, my voice too high. Callie McGraw, train wreck in motion.

He listened until I ran out of words. I'd hoped my monologue would more or less steamroll him, but once I'd stopped talking, he cupped my chin in his hand and said gently, "I sense there remains something you are not telling me. What are you holding back, Kauhlie? You need not fear with me."

Looking into his sincere brown eyes, I knew I was done for. I'd been sitting on the biggest secret of my life and I'd been dying to tell someone—and terrified of telling someone. But now I had the chance to pour my heart out to this *el duende* man who might just understand.

After a long, long pause, I admitted, "Hemingway speaks to me, Claudio."

"The great authors can do that!" he replied, zeal shooting through his eyes. "This is true for many of us."

"No, that's not what I mean. Hemingway speaks to me. Literally."

"I do not think you mean literally, Kauhlie."

"Yes, literally. On the phone. Twice."

Claudio stood silently, stroking his scuff of a beard. Me, I was petrified—I would've run away, but my legs suddenly wouldn't work. The ten longest seconds of my life.

"Yes, Kauhlie, Hemingway does this. I have heard he does this."

My knees threatened to buckle. Were random calls from Earnest Hemingway a totally normal thing? "You have?" The question fell from my mouth in a lump.

"I have, yes. It is said he calls those who need him, who share his passion deep down. I thought this was myth, but perhaps it is true."

"You do know Hemingway is dead, right?" I managed, even as relief, amazement, and a touch of disappointment reeled through me. Two thoughts: "I'm not the only one?" and, "Thank God I'm not the only one,"—collided in my head.

"Death is but a small detail, Kauhlie. Pay it no mind. It is a very rare thing, these calls. A very special thing. It is nothing to worry about."

"I think I need to lie down," I muttered through my shock. I felt slightly sick and wished a bench were nearby.

He chuckled softly and kindly as he wrapped his arm around me. "Breathe, Kauhlie. Focus on the trees for a while."

"Oh, right. The trees. Uh-huh." I leaned into him, turning back to the sculpted cypresses. I still didn't trust my legs, for one thing, but more than that, I wanted him to hold me up. Just this once, I wanted someone to hold me up.

We stood silently, with Claudio directing my breathing through his own deep breaths. After a while, he whispered, "You were right, dear one. They are Dr. Seuss trees. Beautiful Dr. Seuss trees."

I leaned into him even more, resting my head on his shoulder. My mind was still reeling, and I couldn't think of anything to say in reply, so for once I stayed quiet. A new type of quiet, safe and comfortable.

"I have one more thing for you today, Kauhlie." With that, Claudio turned me around gently. He leaned down, guiding my chin upward with his free hand. Images of our week together flashed through my head. The world blurred as he pressed his supple lips to mine. I don't know if there's such a thing as a Spanish kiss, but this felt like it. A confident kiss, but not at all pushy. A sensuous, sumptuous kiss. A *complete* kiss, perfectly formed, perfectly whole, perfectly enveloping.

My first embrace in the street.

CHAPTER 12

DRIPPY CLOCKS AND A HIDDEN BULL

"Why yes, I will have more wine!" I thrust my glass forward and Claudio refilled it. The three of us had been going out almost every night for weeks, but now Claudio and I were a "we," and so our group had a new dynamic. Claudio and I sat a little closer at dinner. We kissed clandestinely whenever Trevor turned away—and sometimes we kissed not so clandestinely, too. On nights when I stayed with Claudio, we dropped Trevor off at his hotel first. We laughed a little harder at each other's jokes. Or at least I laughed harder at Claudio's jokes—my jokes were always pretty damn funny, no supplemental laughter required.

There was never a moment when Claudio or I sat down with Trevor and told him about us. He caught on pretty quickly, though, even for him. He took it in stride, like most things. Every once in a while, Trevor would still get strangely overprotective of me like he had the morning after Limón y Lima, but I chalked that up to some new Madrid thing of his. Mostly he was as complacent as ever, maybe even more so. Claudio's energy and charm had won him over.

Our three-person structure might've been awkward to some, but it was natural to us—we'd been a trio right from the start. Sometimes Trevor talked about going off to Germany or maybe Sweden, but that would've required getting organized and taking action. He was far too comfortable for that. All three of us were far too comfortable for that.

Tonight, we were treating ourselves to a hot new restaurant on Madrid's north side. We started with sizzling garlic shrimp; it arrived in a small pan, crackling in hot olive oil. When the Moorish-spiced pork kebabs followed, Claudio pointed out their misleading name. Moors, as Muslims, abstained from all pork—Spanish Christians borrowed the Moors' spice profile and applied it indiscriminately to all meats. Our tomato and garlic soup, served chilled, complemented the spicy appetizers. We finished with braised oxtails in a slow-cooked stew. Somewhere in there, we had a side of oven-roasted wild mushrooms. With garlic in every dish, we were as safe from vampires as any human could possibly be.

"Kauhlie and Trevor, we have so much yet to see in Madrid. What should we do next? Sometimes it is hard to tell what you like." Claudio wasn't addressing me directly, but the question was clearly aimed at me.

"I like lots of things!" I cried, feigning defensiveness.

"You do?" Trevor's eyes flew to me. "Wine doesn't count, Callie," he quipped.

"Yes, I like lots of things. Wine included." He eyed me dubiously. "I *do* like lots of things," I insisted again, meeting Trevor's glare with my own.

"That is good. Kauhlie likes a lot of things," teased Claudio. Then he looked at me as if to ask, "And what are they?"

"If you want to impress Callie," Trevor offered, "take her to a gallery opening or something."

"Art?" asked Claudio, perking up.

Trevor nodded. "But prepare to stay for a while. Bring survival gear."

I couldn't help but laugh at that one. "I take my time," I explained. "Art needs to be *appreciated*."

"Then appreciate it we will!" Claudio exclaimed with even more zeal than usual. "I will take you to the Reina Sofía. It's my favorite museum in Madrid."

"I know of it," I replied. "It is one of the biggest twentieth-century galleries in the world."

"It is our national modern art museum, and full of our greatest artists!" Claudio raised his glass in a toast. Almost automatically, Trevor and I lifted our glasses, too.

"I'm cool with the Sofía," Trevor said. "I want to see those drippy clocks in Dalí's painting."

"The Sofía does not have… drippy clocks for you, Trevor." Claudio laughed gently. "The drippy clocks… they are in New York, in a museum there. But the Sofía has many of Dalí's other works!" He turned to me. "Kauhlie, why did I not know this about you? I, too, am passionate about art."

"Well… I guess because… because I'm not one for volunteering information. How's that for a reason?"

"But Callie *is* very good at volunteering for museums," interjected Trevor, a mischievous smile creeping onto his lips. He jumped into a recap of my intern-for-an-intern experience. Great.

"Kauhlie, you do not give yourself enough credit," Claudio said to the utter mortification on my face. "All jobs are important, even when they are not for pay. So what if you made coffee runs? Coffee is important. I understand it is even important in museums." He paused, but then persisted before I could retort. "Yet I do not understand, why did you not stay until a paying position opened?"

"It was a calculated decision," I replied, suddenly feeling as if I were trying to win a debate. "As in, I *calculated* I needed money. So I decided… to do something different with my life. Something where I could eat *and* put a roof over my head at the same time. I still love art, though—a lot."

"I expect you always will." Claudio sighed wistfully, as if he had given up something once too. All those years away from Spain, perhaps.

"My internship was going nowhere. Some things are good for a while, but they won't last," I explained. "They bring you to a dead end."

I purposely left out the part about my dad not visiting me. Maybe that had been the deadest end of all. I also left out the part about his checks—I'd never *asked* for a single one, but I'd never turned them down, either. Much of my "calculated" decision revolved around never owing my father anything—not financially, not emotionally.

"That is depressing," Claudio began, "but I do see your point. Some things seem like a good idea for a short time, but eventually they lead to something bad."

"Like what?" Trevor asked, sipping his wine.

Claudio looked up, as if the answer were written on the restaurant's tin ceiling. "Gambling is one thing." He paused. "Drinking more than one Bloody Mary at brunch is another, unless you have a fondness for upset stomachs." He thought for a second. "Smoking marijuana is a good example. Marijuana seems fine at first, and maybe it is okay for a while, but one day it will lead to something undesirable. But I do not think loving art is like any of these things."

"No, art isn't like that," I agreed. "But a *career* in art is like being a perpetual stoner. Or at least that's how it felt to me after six months without a paycheck."

"Hey! What's wrong with smoking pot?" cried Trevor. In the clubs, I'd seen him take a hit off a joint if someone offered it, but I'd never once seen him blaze up on his own. But hell, maybe he was a stoner in his American life. That would explain quite a few things, actually.

∽

"Watch out!" Claudio shouted, grabbing Trevor and yanking him out of the path of an oncoming car. "This is no place for carelessness!" he chastised, pointing up the street. "This traffic circle is perhaps the busiest in the city. Few drivers handle it well."

On the verge of a panic attack, Trevor panted, "I owe you one." I stroked his back, calming him. Wandering blindly into traffic was dumb, but I felt for him anyhow. He'd been zoned out since second breakfast, lost in his own little world.

We escorted Trevor across the boulevard, Claudio holding his hand on one side, me holding his hand on the other. In moments like these, I felt like we were Trevor's surrogate parents. How had he functioned without us for so long?

"Ah! There she is!" Claudio exclaimed as we entered a quiet courtyard. "*El Museo Nacional Centro de Arte Reina Sofía.*" Isn't she beautiful?!"

"Who put all that glass around such an old building?" asked Trevor. "It looks weird." The Sofía's original stone building, built in the eighteenth century, was flanked on either end by modern glass towers, each housing elevator banks. Traditional and futuristic all at once.

"My friend Trevor, it is for contrast!" Claudio explained, admiring the façade. "The old collides with the new!"

"Yes, but ultimately, the two live in harmony," I added. "I bet there's a form-meeting-function statement happening too."

"My Kauhlie is correct!" Claudio agreed, his voice full of admiration. "Plus, the style is a preview of what is to come inside. Modern art combines many elements, defying any single category—just like this building itself. The structure is challenging you to open your mind when you enter." More and more, I was counting Claudio's intelligence among my turn-ons.

"Really?" Trevor asked, staring up at the structure. "You got all that from the front of this building?"

"Yes and no," I laughed. "That's *our* interpretation. It could all be bullshit - that's for you to decide. But remember I'm a lawyer. Arguments are like our art."

Once we entered the museum, I was surprised to find that we were practically outside again. The lobby was traditional, but directly beyond sprawled a huge courtyard with tall trees and a fountain in the middle. I hadn't been expecting that at all… maybe I hadn't been bullshitting as hard as I thought.

Claudio then led us to a third, all-glass extension. The addition wasn't like the elevator banks, though; this was a whole building onto itself. With the morning sunshine streaming in through the glass, I felt I was on hallowed ground.

"I don't know much about modern art, or even contemporary stuff," I explained as we entered the first gallery. "I like fields and skies without the heaviness of the twentieth century, and my concentration in college was the nineteenth-century. A class on modern art wasn't required."

Claudio stopped short. "Many of the most wonderful things in this world are not required." He held my gaze for a split second before turning to a painting. I felt diminished somehow. Had I said something wrong?

"I took an art class as an undergrad too, Callie," Trevor piped up, saving me. "A survey of the Northern Renaissance."

I turned to him. "Really? I wouldn't have expected that."

"Yeah, there were a lot of women in art-history courses, so I took one to get dates."

I rolled my eyes. "Well, did it work? Did you get any dates?"

He hung his head. "None at all. But my strategy was sound, don't you think?"

"Pretending to be into something, just to impress the ladies? Not your best move. We know when guys are pulling crap like that."

"You do?" he asked, as if the thought had never occurred to him.

Claudio turned around suddenly. "Trevor, women know many things we do not. Their wisdom is a part of their mystery and allure. Now come, let us enjoy this day of art together. We will speak of women and their beautiful wiles later."

After the first hour, Trevor—having been very good otherwise—started wandering around aimlessly, just like he'd done in Barcelona. Claudio and I took little notice, practically luxuriating in the museum's splendors. He offered insights about the artists, freely shared his thoughts on each piece, explained bits of history for context. We compared the optimism of the pre-WWI years to the post-war "lost generation" disillusionment. We talked about technique, shading, symbolism. Claudio reveled in my interpretations, my "American perspective." All was effortless, completely natural.

Viewing modern art through his eyes transformed it for me. The twentieth century came alive. Claudio explored the depth of each painting, shared his love for each canvas before him. A different Claudio, a deeper Claudio. A Claudio I could… love? Ugh, no—I pushed the thought away as hard as I could. Keep it together, Callie, keep it together.

"Trevor," Claudio called across the gallery. "You must come with us now. It is time!"

Ever obedient, Trevor trotted up to us. "Time for what?"

"Time to take you and my precious Kauhlie to *Guernica*!"

I raised my eyebrow in suspicion, even as Claudio took my hand in his. He was up to something. Trevor didn't ask questions, save for the confused look in his eyes.

"It is in the next gallery. Come!"

A large tour group strolled forward en masse as we entered the room, revealing the enormous painting in full. Claudio sprung forward in a great leap. "This, my friends, is my favorite work in all the world!" he declared. "By Pablo Ruiz Picasso, our greatest Spanish artist! This is *Guernica*!"

"Oh, no," Trevor whispered. "Not more Picasso."

"Hush," I ordered. "Be nice."

"That's… *Guernica*?" he asked. He ran his eyes over the mural-sized, apocalyptic scene. "I thought it would have color. This is all black, whites, and grays!"

"The imagery *is* the color, my friend Trevor. Using actual color would distract."

"How would color distract? I don't get it."

"Distract from the violence, the chaos!" Claudio cried, thrashing his hands wildly. "From the movement on the canvas, the many elements clashing together. One great anguished uproar! Look at the sheer scale! Do you *really* need color, Trevor? Do you?"

"There's a hint of blue over there," he muttered in reply, as if searching for a consolation prize.

I stepped back, hoping to take in the whole piece at once. I couldn't. Picasso's masterwork covered most of the wall and was so powerful I could've been staring into the sun. Here was pain incarnate. Every brushstroke, every figure, every inch screamed agony, carnage.

"Kauhlie, do you know the history behind this piece?"

"The war," I offered meekly. Truth was, I didn't know *which* war, so I took an educated guess and added, "World War II, I think."

"Not exactly. It was the Spanish Civil War, 1936. Spain had little involvement in World War II—we had decimated ourselves too completely by then."

"Fascists versus communist, right?" asked Trevor, surprising me. The man couldn't order a drink in a bar without causing a riot, why did he know the details of Spain's civil war?

"Yes, Trevor, that is mostly correct. For three brutal years, our country was rent apart. Fascist Nationalists supported by Nazi Germany. Republicans backed by the communist Soviet Union. No family was left untouched."

"And Guernica was a battle?" I asked, trying to add something to the conversation. Spanish history was really out of my wheelhouse.

"Not a battle. Look! Picasso painted women and children. He painted horses and bulls. Guernica was not a battle, it was a slaughter! The Germans and their bombers. A massacre!" He swept his hand across the painting as if he were running it across the entire expanse of Spain.

My eyes came to rest on the wailing mother, her baby dead and limp in her arms. "That's... awful. Sickening," I whispered, not finding the words I needed.

"It is, Kauhlie, it is. Some say *Guernica* is the greatest anti-war statement ever created. I believe they are correct."

"You said no family was untouched?" asked Trevor. "What about *your* family?"

Gravity shadowed Claudio's face. "We lost much, but not as much as so many others. We were blessed in this respect. And now, today, there is one Spain again! A nation healed."

I reached out and squeezed Claudio's hand. Something in his tone told me not to pursue the subject further, and I respected that. Trevor must've picked up on this, too, because he pretended to study the canvas further.

We fell silent for a while, gazing at the mural, until Trevor announced, "I don't like it. Too violent."

"You don't have to like a painting about a slaughter, Trevor," I replied a little too harshly.

"Kauhlie is exactly right. You do not have to like it, you need only to *absorb* it. Picasso did not want people overanalyzing this work. Which I find puzzling, since he hid so much within it. The bull most of all."

"He didn't hide it? The bull is there, in the corner," I said, pointing. "Awful creatures."

He recoiled as if I'd shocked him. "Kauhlie, that is the bull you see, not the bull you *experience*." He squatted down until our faces were side-by-side and he was almost whispering in my ear. "The other bull is a hidden figure in the middle." His breath on my earlobe gave me goosebumps.

"Can I see the bull too?" Trevor mocked, positioning his head by my other ear. I elbowed him firmly in the ribs, which had the intended effect of causing him to back off and wander away.

Claudio hardly noticed Trevor's departure. "Gaze deeply, Kauhlie. The bull is below the wounded horse. The horse is the Spanish people, the bull Spain itself. The bull is goring the horse—Spain destroying itself."

I looked as hard as I could, craning my neck and contorting. A solid minute passed; Claudio never once moved from my ear. "I can't see it. Claudio, I don't see it!"

"Stop looking, Kauhlie. *Sense* it. Bring it to life."

I placed both hands over my eyes, pressing on my eyelids firmly to refresh my vision. I took a deep breath, and then another. I couldn't bear the thought of failing this test in front of Claudio. What if I couldn't find it? What would that mean?

The bull leaped off the canvas like a nightmare-memory flashing through my mind. "Holy crap!" I shouted, drawing attention from some patrons. In my shock, I stumbled back a full step. "It *is* there!

Claudio didn't budge but instead gently pulled me toward him. "Ah, now you are *experiencing*," he whispered tenderly. "The soul of Spain has touched you. Now you are changed, Kauhlie. Now you are Spanish, too."

CHAPTER 13

FUZZY SHARKS AND
A HAIRBAND

I woke up next to him. Claudio was still sleeping, breathing with those soft, rhythmic breaths that I'd grown so fond of. I closed my eyes, hoping to again drift into slumber, but then an unfortunate realization came to me: I had to pee.

"Mind over matter, Callie," I thought. "Ignore it. Go back to sleep." Of course, I knew this was futile. Once my mind and bladder started conspiring against slumber, I was doomed. Getting up and taking care of business was my only option.

I didn't want to wake Claudio—he looked so peaceful, so blissfully relaxed. I slowly slid one leg from under the covers and touched my toe to the hardwood floor. I did the same with my other leg, gingerly getting up from the mattress. This led to a second unfortunate realization: I was naked. Not a stitch of clothing on me. I grabbed for the first garment within reach, which was Claudio's white button-down shirt. I slipped into it, finding myself swimming in the soft cotton. I buttoned three buttons so his shirt wouldn't fall off, thinking lustfully of Claudio's three-buttons-left-undone style. I tiptoed into the hallway.

I had five bathrooms to choose from. I'd already ruled out the one off the master bedroom. I'd also ruled out the bathroom in the entryway because that was the one everybody uses, and… well… I wasn't just "everybody." There was a third off of Claudio's office, but that one was just a water closet, with the sink on the outside, adjacent to the built-in minibar. Which left the two spare bedroom suites. The back suite offered the most privacy, so that became my bathroom of choice.

As I made my way past the kitchen, I had the distinct feeling I was being watched. Especially creepy given the early hour. I froze in place before forcing my head to turn toward the "watching." Two pairs of yellow eyes were staring at me from the kitchen island, fixed and unmoving. Toni and Teddy had risen early today, too, it seemed.

"What?" I whispered. "You guys know me by now." In the past month, the pair had grown by leaps and bounds, and they were losing their "baby kittens" look.

Their eyes remained trained on me, like I was up to something.

"What?!" I asked again, shrugging my shoulders. Claudio's shirt slipped down; I pushed it back in place, the cotton heavenly against my skin.

They kept staring.

I stared back. It was no use. One thing I'd learned in my thirty-something years is that it's impossible to win a staring contest with a cat—let alone two cats. By now, my bladder was truly demanding attention, so I resumed my journey across the apartment.

I'd left the bathroom door ajar without a thought—Claudio was still asleep and practically a mile away. As I sat myself down, Toni pushed the door open a crack and slunk inside. Teddy followed her fluidly, as if the two shared one mind. Fuzzy sharks on the prowl.

"I guess this is a group activity?" I asked.

Teddy started doing figure eights around my calves while purring and running his tail along the back of my knees. Toni perched herself on a shelf, a queen surveying her kingdom.

I did what I needed to do, despite the audience. When I washed up, my bedhead shrieked at me in the mirror. The worst kind of bedhead… hair mashed flat on one side, sticking up in limp spikes on the other. I needed a brush, and desperately.

This presented a fantastic opportunity—a valid reason to rifle through the vanity. I hadn't been in this bathroom before, except for a glance when Claudio had given me the full tour. Unexplored territory. With my nosiness leading the way, I started rummaging through the drawers. Everything was organized but generic, typical of a guest bath. I found some mouthwash and was grateful for it—if my hair was this bad, my morning breath was probably worse.

Still no brush, though. As I opened the last drawer on the right, I found a wide-toothed comb, but something else caught my eye, too. I reached down and pulled out a black elastic hairband. I had a million of them, but this one wasn't mine. This was the slightly thicker kind for curly hair; I always bought the skinnier ones.

"Hmmm?" Wrinkling my nose, I held the black loop higher, scrutinizing it. Toni jumped onto the vanity for a proper inspection, although there was really nothing to see. "Whose is this?" I asked her. The silent queen ran her tail along my chin, sending a shiver through me.

I pitched the hairband into the trash can before running the comb through my hair. A thought hit me mid-stroke: was this hers, too? Gross. I dumped the comb into the trash, where it landed with a satisfying thud. Toni, seemingly sharing my disgust, jumped down and strode from the room, tail and head held high. Teddy, although much less indignant, followed.

Claudio was in mid-stretch as I returned, his bare chest and half of his abdomen peeking out from under the covers. "I was wondering where you went," he said, propping himself up on his elbow and winking at me. "I saw your clothes were still here, so I knew you had not gone far."

"I had to pee," I admitted. "And I stole your shirt," I continued, holding the loose fabric out like a dress.

"It fits you perfectly, Kauhlie." After that compliment I decided to leave the shirt on, and I crawled under the covers next to him. He smiled. "But why did you not use the bathroom right here? Do not tell me you are suddenly shy?"

"I didn't want to wake you. You were sleeping so soundly."

"I was probably not sleeping as soundly as you were. You were snoring last night."

"I don't snore!" I snapped coyly. Actually, I had no idea whether I snored or not. No one else had ever told me as much, but I'd been sleeping alone for most of my adult life.

"Snoring like a freight train."

"No!" It generally wasn't advisable to describe me as a freight train, but I let it pass. I needed to bring up the hairband soon, and I didn't want to misdirect any energy into semantics. Not that it stopped me from frowning and pouting a bit.

He kissed me gently. "Let me get my beautiful freight train some coffee. Yes?"

"Woo woo!" I cried, pretending to pull on a train's whistle. Keeping things light was best, and coffee improved just about anything.

Completely naked except for one sock, Claudio rose. He modestly kept his back to me as he reached for his bathrobe. Which was silly—I'd seen both front and back many times. His taut backside was definitely my favorite of the two views, and the crooked scar on the back of his thigh always intrigued me.

I burrowed in deeper under the covers and thought about our agenda for the day. Whenever I spent the night with Claudio, we made it a point to meet Trevor for second breakfast. Beyond that, as far as I knew, we had nothing planned. A beautiful, expansive, empty day to look forward to.

The cappuccino machine whirred in the kitchen. That was a good sign. I rolled onto my side, facing Claudio's pillow. The impression of his head was still there. Without thinking, I leaned over and inhaled deeply, taking in his smell. For an instant, I felt like a creeper, but then I thought, "So what? This is what lovers do, right?" I slid myself over to his half of the bed. It was still warm.

"First you steal my shirt, and now you steal my side of the bed?" Claudio teased, coming back with two steaming cappuccinos. He set the folding tray down on his nightstand and feigned disgust.

"I did, and you're going to have to fight to get it back!" I teased as I kicked my foot high into the air, preparing for battle.

"As you wish, Kauhlie." With that, he tickled my foot. I squealed and scooted a few inches away, moving toward the middle of the mattress. He slipped into the vacant space, but now both of us were sort of on his side of the bed. It was nice.

"See, you are not so tough," he chided. I made a face as he positioned the tray carefully over my legs. "Here, Kauhlie, drink this. I know how you like your cappuccinos. With just a touch of sugar."

Toni crept in and made a little nest for herself by Claudio's knee. Teddy didn't follow and I wondered if he'd gone back to sleep. I could count on one hand the number of times I'd seen one without the other.

"Kauhlie, I must tell you something," Claudio began. "I regret that I cannot be with you and Trevor for second breakfast today."

My thoughts snapped back to the hairband. Did he have a date? Was she coming over? Faking a yawn, I took a breath to calm myself. Ridiculous, Callie, ridiculous. Pull it together.

"I am having lunch with my mother today, on the Skype," he continued. "She is in Greece, an hour ahead. Your second breakfast will end just as we are starting our lunch."

"In Greece?" I asked. "You never mentioned that."

"She wintered there. But now that it is spring, she will likely be coming home soon."

"Just your mother? Is your father there, too?"

"No, Kauhlie, he is in your New York, setting up a business. My mother would not go to New York in the winter. It is bad for her joints." He sipped his cappuccino, a suspicious smile creeping onto his face. "At least that is what she claims. Sometimes I believe the secret to my parents' marriage is the number of countries between them."

"Maybe my parents should've tried that," I said wistfully. Which is more than I meant to say… the caffeine hadn't fully kicked in yet, and I'd been too busy *not* talking about the hairband to watch what I was saying. Crap.

He took my hand in his. "Maybe, Kauhlie, but you once told me that their divorcing was better than staying together."

My eyebrows knit together. I didn't want to talk about this, yet there was no going back now. "Who knows?" I answered. That sounded like too much of a cop-out, so I volunteered an addition. "It was ugly, though—ugly during, ugly afterward. They fought to the point of ignoring me. I wasn't back on their radar until after the divorce, when they started wielding me like a weapon against each other."

"That is… not so good, Kauhlie." Claudio said somberly, sympathy in his voice. "And it is not so good for a teenage girl, either. It is no wonder, then."

"What's no wonder?" I asked, pulling my hand away and forcing my hackles not to raise. Of the many things *not* on my agenda today, psychoanalysis was definitely at the top of my non-list.

"That you have kept so many at arm's length," he said gently. "I think your parents stole something precious from you. Basic trust, perhaps."

"That's not your call to make," I retorted, pulling myself away from him even more. I could feel the strike brewing inside of me—a trapped scorpion always stings. I tried to hold back, but the next thing I knew, the words were flying from my mouth. "And maybe you trust too much!"

Claudio's face changed into an expression I'd never seen before. His eyes blinked. Not quite confused, not quite angry, not quite curious, but definitely not quite kind either.

"What does this mean, 'I trust too much?'"

"I know I'm not the first woman you've had in your home," I said, keeping my tone almost neutral and deflecting the conversation nicely.

He chuckled earnestly but not meanly. "No, definitely not! I am a grown man, Kauhlie, just like you are a grown woman."

I expected his answer but not the exuberance in his voice. It disarmed me, but still I asked, "Who was the last one, before me?"

"Ah. This already. It is okay, my dear one. I have nothing to hide." He sipped his cappuccino and smiled. "She worked for a telecom company here in the city. It was not serious, and we both knew it would not last."

"What about the woman before that?"

He reflected for just an instant. "The one before the last one. She managed a restaurant. She was nice, but that was also not serious. I had only just come home to Madrid then." He smiled at me again, seeming to think his answer was sufficient.

I was a bit stymied. I sipped my cappuccino slowly to buy myself time. Claudio was being eminently reasonable and open, so I decided not to dive any deeper into the dumpster of his past relationships. I wouldn't bring up the hairband—at least not now. I looked at Toni, who had found herself a new spot on the dresser. Her royal highness seemed to be signaling for clemency, and that somehow clinched it for me.

"You're right." I began, resting my head on his shoulder. You're a grown man, and I'm a grown woman. We've both done the things grown men and women do." I lifted my head slowly and kissed him firmly on the mouth.

"We have our futures, too, Kauhlie," he replied, encircling me in his arm. "And perhaps you will share the future of your Madrid-time with me. Just you and me."

My stomach fluttered in excitement even as my brain objected. Now the conversation was getting relationship-y, which I had not seen coming. What was happening to this morning? I deflected again.

"And Trevor," I added as quickly as I could, intentionally deadpanning.

Claudio laughed hard. Relief washed over me. "Yes, Kauhlie. You, me, and… Trevor."

I stretched my neck upward for another kiss. But when Claudio pressed his lips to mine, instead of melting into the fullness of his mouth, a new thought popped into my head: tomorrow, I was going to bring over a bunch of hairbands and hide them in strategic places to mark my territory. Crap, maybe I had bigger trust issues than I thought.

Chapter 14

Hell Hath No Fury Like a Woman Scorned

Sometimes you can see disaster coming before it happens, like an animal standing in the middle of a road—you slam on the breaks, swerve, prepare for impact. Other times, disaster jumps out at you like a deer leaping from the underbrush. Zero warning. Yet you still have to deal with the aftermath, no matter how bloody.

It started innocently enough. The three of us had been out doing what we did best, which was a lot of nothing. Claudio had taken us to the Puente de Toledo, one of the city's iconic, historic, bridges. Going on a Saturday was a mistake—the bridge was crowded and tour-ist-clogged—so we'd made our way down to the riverbank, where we'd found a shaded bench.

The riverbank itself was alive with springtime, and the sun sparkled off the water. We were passing around a margarita-filled thermos when a thought in Claudio's brain rolled out of his mouth, sans filter.

"Kauhlie, tell me, how many men have you slept with?" At this,

Trevor immediately perked up as if this very question had long been in the back of his mind, which aggravated the hell out of me.

"What kind of question is that?" I retorted as my thoughts kicked into high gear. I was trapped. As a woman, there was no good answer to this one. Even in this day and age, some people might say even one partner outside of marriage was taboo. To others, too few partners would make me a prude, while some would believe too many partners made me... I guess *promiscuous* would be the polite word. A no-win all around.

As for my true number? I wasn't going to tell anyone my number— that was mine, and mine alone. Why Claudio thought he had the right to ask, especially here in public, left me annoyed and affronted.

"We have talked about many things—you, me, and Trevor. But we have not talked about this thing," Claudio answered casually. Too casually.

"Yeah, Callie, we haven't talked about this. Inquiring minds want to know," Trevor piped up. He was already too drunk, a goofy grin on his face.

"You're being a bit forward, Claudio."

"I will give you that much, yes. It is a little forward," he answered. Yet he kept his gaze on me, asking the question again with his eyes.

"Enough men," I said bluntly. "I have slept with enough men."

His lips turned up in a tipsy smile. "That is not really an answer. You are evading."

"It *is* an answer. An honest answer." I lowered my voice to a sultry growl. "I've been with enough men to know what I'm doing in bed. You should count your blessings."

"I count them every day, Kauhlie," he replied, gazing up to the cloudless sky, almost as if praying. "My blessings are many, and I am fortunate in this way." He whipped his head downward and trained his smoldering eyes on me again. "But still, you must give me an answer."

"I *must*?" I asked, my anger swelling. I turned the question around on him before he could respond. "What about you, big guy? What's your number? Five thousand?"

"It is not five thousand!" he exclaimed, more amused than annoyed. "That is much too many!"

"Then what's your number? You brought it up, so you have to go first."

"She has you there," Trevor said. "Fair is fair."

Claudio put his hands up in defeat. "Okay, but because you did not answer, I will tell Trevor only." He locked his eyes on Trevor. "But Trevor, if you betray my secret, know that it is on pain of death."

Trevor's eyebrows shot up. "On pain of death? As in, you'd kill me?"

"Yes. But I will not kill you quickly. In this case, 'on pain of death' means a *painful* death."

Trevor gulped hard. "It does?"

"You know of our Spanish Inquisition? Think Spanish Inquisition."

Trevor turned slightly green as Claudio whispered into his ear. I tried to hear what he said, but he kept his voice intentionally low.

"That's your number?!" Trevor cried. "I wouldn't have guessed that, I—"

"—On pain of death!" Claudio shouted, cutting him off. Trevor hushed up, but a second later he turned to me with a knowing nod. A nod that he knew would drive me crazy. I hated it when the two of them did their "boys club" thing, and I resented them all the more for treating such a serious topic like a joke. Had they suddenly become thirteen-year-olds?

"Good, you two keep your little secret," I snapped. "I don't care anymore." I was sure I could find out Claudio's number later, when he was sober and acting like an adult, so I simply shook my head as if I had no interest whatsoever. I'm a good liar when I need to be—even when I'm mostly lying to myself.

"Do you guys want to know how many women I've slept with?" Trevor asked, lifting the thermos to his mouth.

"No!" Claudio and I shouted simultaneously, causing him to choke a little. That ended that.

Perhaps from disappointment, Trevor turned the spotlight back on me. "You told me you slept with 'a few' men in New York. 'A few' is almost a number."

"When did I say that?" I asked, surprised and now even more irritated. Why did Trevor insist on filing away factoids about me? And why was he so damn good at it?

"In Barcelona. You told me you slept with a few men in New York, but that your friends slept with more."

"So, I slept with a few men, who cares?" I shot. I relaxed my voice slightly. "But yes, fewer than my friends. I don't go in much for drunken one-night-stands."

Claudio was in mid-sip when he quickly pulled the thermos from his lips. "Now there is a question, Kauhlie. One that perhaps you will not find so intrusive."

"You have an awful lot of questions today." I rolled my eyes. What little gem did he have in store for me now?

"Who are your female friends in New York? You must have girl-friends, but you barely talk about these women at all."

"No one you know, so what difference could it make?" I replied, answering his question with a question and not bothering to hide my perturbation.

"I am only asking, Kauhlie." His eyes glimmered as if the alcohol had won the battle for his wits. "It is called making conversation."

I relented a bit, humoring him for the sake of getting the day back on course. "I had a few girlfriends, I guess. Cicely… though I haven't seen her in a long time—she probably thinks I'm still in the city. I hung out with Madison, but Maddy can only talk about the men in her life, it's pathetic. And Susan. We went to law school together, but she's less of a friend and more of a gossip."

"So, that's three… three non-friends," Trevor jumped in, holding up three fingers like a toddler. "Who else?"

"Bethany and I got along okay when she wasn't being a total bitch. And then—"

"—Kauhlie, who came to your going away party in New York?"

I paused. I hadn't thought of that night in months. "I didn't really have a party. I didn't have time for that kind of thing."

"Nobody threw you a party *at all*?" Trevor asked, drunken pity in his voice.

"A few of us got together for drinks. A fun night. Everyone bought rounds for me."

"Who came?" For someone with a midday buzz, Claudio was being awfully persistent.

"Well, there was Jake from my last job. José too. Tom stopped by. And my friend Bill showed up later on," I answered, counting each guest as if they were points in a debate. So far, I was up to four. Impressive, Callie, impressive.

Claudio chuckled as if he'd been told an impolite joke. "Ah, I see now. I did not think you were that kind of woman."

"'That kind of woman?' What does that mean?" I snapped. And why was this "pick on Callie" day?

"Kauhlie, I mean the kind of woman who only has male friends, who does not get along with other women."

His words punched me in the chest, knocking the wind out of me. In reply, I managed to utter something that sounded vaguely like an objection. Claudio sipped from the thermos coolly, oblivious to my shock. Ass.

I sucked as much air into my lungs as I could, then growled, "I get along just fine with other women."

"I do not think so." He chuckled again. "It sounds like you do not."

"Yeah, Callie, I don't think you've ever mentioned a best girlfriend." I could see Trevor flipping through his mental Rolodex of "Callie facts" as he spoke.

Claudio shrugged his shoulders and added, "I am only saying that

I do not see you keeping in touch with many people from your home. Men or women. Certainly no women."

"That sounds sort of truthy," Trevor agreed. I snarled at him.

"What does it matter to you, Claudio? I came here to get *away* from home, away from the people in my life. Women included."

"You know, women often do not trust women who cannot be friends with other women," he added, pissing me off even further.

"He has a point, Callie. You don't even keep up with Susan and Jane, and they were really nice to us."

Retorting, I shot daggers at Trevor even as I directed my words at Claudio. "I have women friends, just not right now. Because I'm spending all my time with you two gentlemen." I said the word *gentlemen* scathingly—meaning, of course, "assholes."

"It does explain a few things, Kauhlie," he continued smugly.

I whipped my finger through the air like I was slicing through his argument with a switchblade. "I don't know what it explains, since it's not even true."

"Obviously, it is true. Otherwise you would not be so defensive. You are too sensitive about this subject."

"Don't tell me I'm being too sensitive! "You're telling lies! About me!"

"It *is* true, Kauhlie. Women friends are not for you. You even favor Teddy over Toni."

"How can you like one better than the other?" Trevor pleaded, frowning. "All kittens need love." This earned him another blistering glare from me, which shut him up.

"Your cats, Claudio? You're basing your theory on your cats? What kind of bullshit is that?" I yelled. Yes, I favored Teddy over Toni, but only because Teddy had a habit of cuddling at my feet and tucking his tail under my toes, turning himself into a fuzzy slipper. But that wasn't the point. The point was that Claudio was the only person in the universe who could've known as much. What right did he have to drag our private time into this? With Trevor right here and everything?

"But, Kauhlie, I do not think—"

"—Stop! I've heard enough!" I whipped the thermos from his hand and took an angry swig, emptying it.

"Who are you to judge me?!" I shouted. "You and your flamenco-dancing, womanizing ass!" I shot up from the bench. "I'll sleep with whoever I want! I'll be friends with whoever I want!"

"I did not say who you should be with. I only meant that—"

"—And if Teddy prefers snuggling at my feet rather than by your big hairy ones, I'm damn well going to let him!"

Claudio raised his voice slightly. "There is no cause for that! I only said…"

"I heard what you said! Say it again, I dare you!" Waves of fire exploded through my head.

Even more sternly, he countered, "You are now very emotional. I do not care for this!"

"Why shouldn't I be emotional? When you're *assuming* things, attacking me? I'm an accomplished lawyer with an Ivy League degree, not some pathetic, friendless, loser!" I flung the thermos to the ground violently; the impact sent a red squirrel scurrying away. "You know what, Claudio? We're done. We're finished!"

"Done?" he asked, dumbfounded.

"That's right, we're done!" I turned on my heel and stomped up the bank. I got about ten steps away before I whipped myself around. "I have plenty of women friends. I don't need you! Go to hell!"

∽

I turned off my phone and stuffed it into a drawer. Between Claudio and Trevor, the damn thing wouldn't stop buzzing. Obviously neither was in my good graces right now, but I did answer one—and only one—of Trevor's texts, when he asked if the two of us were still meeting for dinner. In its entirety, my message read, "Not today. Not tomorrow, either." He was welcome to infer whatever he wanted from that—I wasn't going to clarify.

Once I'd stomped away from the riverbank, I'd kept on stomping. For a good two hours, pure rage kept my pace swift and my footsteps heavy. Not a single person dared cross me as I made my way through the city. Anyone who saw me coming had practically jumped out of the way, and those who hadn't at least had the good sense to remain quiet as I pushed past. Hell hath no fury like a woman scorned, and the *madrileños*, it seemed, had a collective respect for that.

When the aching in my feet had finally outweighed the anger in my blood, I'd flagged a taxi. The area had been getting more and more residential, and by that point I had no idea where I was, with no idea how to get back. I was lucky to snag one when I did—taxis had been getting increasingly scarce.

I was still too livid to eat when I'd arrived at my hotel, and so I'd opted for an angry shower—scalding hot water; scouring my skin until it was raw. It didn't help and, in a way, it made things worse: Claudio and I had showered together once, and my loofah became sandpaper as I scrubbed away at the memory.

I cursed our five weeks together. I cursed *el duende* and the night I met Claudio. I cursed Picasso and his Embrace in the Street. And I was pissed at myself, too. How stupid had I been? For all his charm, all his wit, Claudio was a viper in disguise—I should've seen that coming. He'd been judging me this whole time, taking pity on "friendless Callie." And who was he to demand my number like an entitled brat? Or to throw Toni and Teddy in my face and weaponize privileged information? Why the hell had I let him in in the first place? I'd fallen for his suave demeanor and his abs, never suspecting that I was breathing his poison. What was next? Billboards blaring my flaws? Skywriting screaming my secrets?

I rang room service and irately ordered a bottle of white. If my Spanish was barely serviceable on any given day, now it was a total disaster. "*Envíalo inmediatamente!*" I demanded, except "*envíalo*" (send it) came out more like "envelope-o," and "*inmediatamente*" (immediately) had far too many syllables for my enraged tongue. It probably would've been easier to run to the corner market, but I didn't want to risk bumping into Trevor. For all I knew, he could've been camped out in the lobby, waiting like a scolded puppy for me to throw him a bone.

Hoping it would calm me, I pulled out my copy of *The Sun Also Rises* and opened it to the first page. My sanctuary-in-writing had never failed me before, but now, all it inspired in me was loathing. Not for the book itself, but for Hemingway and his stupid calls. I'd been perfectly ignorant of my own misery until that evening on Seventh Avenue, but now I'd obviously failed at the enlightenment quest mister-literature-on-high had sent me on. I flung the well-worn paperback against the wall, where it hit the corner of a generic, floral print—an affront to art itself—that had been mocking me since the day I'd checked in. Both fell unceremoniously to the carpeted floor with a less-than-satisfying thud.

I waited impatiently as the waiter from room service uncorked my wine. He fumbled with the corkscrew nervously as I wrapped my fingers on the dresser. I gave him a nice tip to compensate for my rudeness, but even my "*Gracias, señor,*" came out angry.

I drank my first glass in great gulps. I drank the second glass more slowly, muttering to myself before every swallow. After that, I started to calm my rage—if not my thoughts. Maybe I was overreacting? Maybe Claudio hadn't been judging, maybe he was merely curious about my past love life. Who wouldn't be? And as for the no-women-friends thing, maybe he'd simply noticed something about me that I hadn't seen in myself. Maybe that's what it meant to be in a real relationship? That didn't excuse him from being an asshole about it, but I felt my shoulders relax at the thought.

I pulled the damp towel from my head and ran my hand through my snarled, wet hair. I grabbed a hairband from my nightstand: the memory shot through me. *Her* hairband, pinched between my two fingers, with Toni inspecting it alongside me. How many women had she watched Claudio parade through his apartment? What secrets had her royal highness refused to divulge? Cats are like that—treacherously silent.

My anger returned, flooding through me like a tsunami. I grabbed the wine, poured myself a third glass, and gulped it down. Of their own accord, my eyes began darting around the room, searching for something, anything, that would make some sense out of this fresh hell. What they found instead was my reflection in the mirror, a wounded, dejected woman I barely recognized.

No Claudio. No Trevor. No Hemingway. No Picasso. I didn't even have Teddy *or* Toni anymore. It was just me and my wine now. There was only one thing left to do, the one thing I hated doing but knew I needed. I whipped the window's curtains tightly shut, then secured the room's deadbolt before shoving the chain-lock into its slot as well. I even pulled the hotel's phone off its receiver, just in case.

With the room as secure as I could possibly make it, I gave in. I plunked myself onto the bed, grabbed a pillow to scream into, and let the hot, choking tears roll down my cheeks. Callie McGraw: international disaster, international disappointment.

CHAPTER 15

THE SAGE AND *UN NIÑO*

I spent the entire next day in my room alone. I hadn't used room service often during my stay, but that day it became my one and only connection to anything beyond the four walls surrounding me. Because I couldn't deal with anything beyond those four walls. I could hardly bring myself to get dressed; the room's complimentary bathrobe was clothing enough.

I'd managed to make up with *The Sun Also Rises*, but that was all the forgiveness I had in me. And even then, as I'd flipped through the pages, my broken heart wasn't in it. Instead, I'd spent most of the day streaming movies and binging on wine and ice cream. Stupid Claudio.

Self-pity wasn't my thing, so the next morning I forced myself out of bed well before Trevor could possibly be up, slunk out of the hotel, and headed out for a run. Only by now, after months of indulging in nothingness, I was fully out of shape. Running in the dawn light should've quieted my mind and reinvigorated my body, but instead it left me drained physically and frustrated by my weeks upon weeks of caloric overloading. My waistline had adjusted itself since I'd arrived in Spain, and not for the better. Claudio had probably been judging me for that, too. I bet all his other girlfriends had perfect, sculpted, taut waists that never expanded even the tiniest bit.

After a good hot shower and some general brooding, I decided spending the rest of the day in my room wasn't an option—I'd allowed myself to fall to pieces yesterday and it had done me little good. I knew of a small, family-owned café on a nearby back street that Trevor and Claudio hadn't been to—when Claudio wasn't with us, I would sometimes tell Trevor I needed a *siesta*, but instead sneak off for some "me" time. My secret café seemed like the only safe public option in all of Madrid, so that's where I headed.

Just me, my coffee, and my thoughts. None of my thoughts were very pleasant, though, so I started doodling to keep myself occupied. Napkin after napkin, many featuring Claudio with fangs, horns, or a forked tail. It was surprisingly therapeutic.

At some point an old woman came in, taking a seat at the café's only front-window table. She'd been here a few times before, and I'd been studying her. I'd always felt a little voyeuristic, so I'd told myself I was observing local life, like an anthropologist. In truth, though, I was just being nosy, and she intrigued me.

Her hands, gnarled with age but with strength still in them, wrapped around her cup as if trying to absorb every bit of warmth radiating from her coffee. Her silver hair, pulled back in its usual tight bun, gleamed in the sunlight. The creases in her once-supple face deepened each time she took a measured, deliberate sip from her cup. As always, she was dressed tastefully and conservatively, and as always, she had a single rose with a longish stem pinned to her blouse. The stem drew me in; anyone else would've clipped it close.

Usually, I observed the woman without her noticing. Today I must've been off my game—no small wonder, all things considered— because she glanced up and caught me before I could pretend I hadn't been looking. Her eyes smiled as they met mine. The rest of her face followed, transforming into a welcoming grin. I felt awkward, but I smiled back.

She motioned for me to join her. I hesitated. She waved again, nodding her head in encouragement. I couldn't decline now, so I grabbed my coffee and sat down at her small table for two.

"Hello," I said, unsure of where to begin.

She didn't reply, but she smiled again. This time, her smile said, "Nice to meet you."

"Do you speak English?" I asked. "*Hablas el inglés, señora?*" I translated, hoping I got the words right. I vaguely remembered a rule about addressing one's elders with a special verb form, but I didn't know what that form was, and I didn't want to offend her.

"A little." She held up her hand and extended her thumb and forefinger outward in a pinch, leaving only a little space between the two. Not much English could fit between them. I mirrored her movement, keeping the space between my fingers open only a smidgeon, indicating that my Spanish was worse than her English.

"Read *sí*; speak, not good," she began. "My husband, he made friends with the American author. Long ago. I learn then." Her eyes glistened, as if she were pleased by her accomplishment. I was pleased for her.

"My name is Callie."

"Callie. Good name. Pretty name. Pretty like you." I smiled politely as she continued. "I am called Francesca Maria Fernandez."

"Nice to meet you, Señora Fernandez."

She nodded in acknowledgment. "I see you."

"You see me?"

She nodded. "*Sí*. I see you here, before now—and I watch you."

"I've seen you here before, too," I replied, hoping there was a translation issue in the mix. Could she have been watching *me*, when I thought I'd been watching *her*?

"Not all the days," she continued. "Some days I see you."

"I only come here when I can be alone. This place is my hideaway." Her eyes told me she didn't understand the last part, so I clarified. "Hideaway—a secret place, a special place."

"*Sí*. A special place. For me, too. I take my coffee here, then I meet my husband. All the days, coffee first, then my husband. We talk about many things. He makes me not lonely."

"That's so sweet," I sighed. My shoulders slumped even as I forced a smile. I thought I had someone I could always talk to, too... until two days ago.

"But I watch you. Here. You always have the small sad, but today your sad is much."

"No, I'm not sad," I said gently. "Not exactly sad. I come here to think sometimes."

"Lonely, maybe? Yes. I think you are lonely?"

I didn't answer, opting to stare into my coffee instead. *Lonely* wasn't the right word for what I was. Not even close.

"A nice boy? But he is gone now?"

I looked up in shock. My mouth moved, but no words came out. How could she have known that? Was I really so transparent?

"Lonely. Tell me."

I didn't know what to say, so I said... everything. All the words I hadn't spoken to anyone in the last two days came pouring out. I started with the night I'd met Claudio, then I kept on going, barely taking a breath in between sentences.

"And then he said I was the type of woman who couldn't be friends with other women! I have a career! I'm driven! I'm starting my dream job in a brand-new city in a few months! I don't need a gaggle of girl-friends holding me back! He *insulted* me, insulted my intelligence!"

Señora Fernandez lifted her plate of *almendrado* cookies, offering me the last one. Her eyes were full of sympathy, but I could tell she'd barely understood a word I'd said. Which didn't deter me in the slight-est from continuing.

"I'm an independent woman! I make my own rules! I define what is-and-is-not right for me! And anyway, who is he to talk? He can sleep with every woman on Earth, but I'm the one with the problem? Who knows how many women he's had?"

"Many women?" Señora Fernandez asked, shaking her head. "Some men, they do this. From woman to woman. Sometimes many women at once. Very bad. Not like my husband, with me for many years." A hint of pride gleamed in her eyes. "Only me. Only him." She clasped her hands together firmly. "Strong!"

"Right!" I agreed. "And if I'm not enough for him—me and me alone—then good riddance! I am woman, hear me roar!" I growled ferociously to drive the point home. In hindsight, that was probably excessive.

She stared at me, bewildered but not shocked. Whether or not she grasped my words didn't matter—she understood. Decades of wisdom shone in her eyes.

"Grrrr!" I growled again, making a claw with my hand.

"Grrrr!" she repeated, clasping my "claw" with both hands. She looked at me intensely, an empathetic smile on her lips. The heat from her coffee-warmed hands transferred to mine.

"The man, he must add to your strong. A man who steals your strong, he is not a man. He is… is…*un niño*."

"A child?" I asked, not sure if I understood.

"A child, *sí*. Not a man. Like my husband is a man. I must go talk to him now." She rose slowly from her chair. "You have the strong. A *man* adds to your strong."

I sat there agog. I'd never thought of relationships that way before: just because I didn't need a man to *make* me strong didn't mean a man couldn't *enhance* my strength, complement it. That's the man I needed to be with. Not some suave Spanish playboy.

Señora Fernandez shuffled toward the exit and turned abruptly as she opened the door. "I see your strong. You must see it, too. To take away your sad. The small sad, the big sad. Let no one steal your strong."

⤜

With Señora Fernandez's words echoing in my mind, I'd sent a text to Trevor later that night saying he could meet me for second breakfast. I was now seated in my usual spot at our café, my hands wrapped around a steaming cup of salvation. As I swirled the black richness in my cup, I inhaled the aroma of my coffee's redemptive powers.

I hadn't slept much last night—and even less the night before. The first night, whenever I'd closed my eyes, I kept replaying the fight over and over in my mind, then extrapolating all manner of scenarios from there. Last night, Señora Fernandez had kept me up. How could her aged eyes have seen me so clearly, when I couldn't even see myself? Because she was right, I *was* lonely. In fact, I'd been lonely for years, even if I hadn't really known it. Maybe that's why I'd let Trevor latch onto me in his puppy-dog way. Maybe that's why *Embrace in the Street* had made me cry. Maybe, under this Spanish sun, that's why I'd been so quick to fall for Claudio. Maybe my entire world wasn't supposed to be me, myself, and I.

I'd been awake well into the wee hours, pondering what it took to sustain decades and decades of a happy marriage. I'd imagined Señora Fernandez and her husband together, day after day, year after year. I'd wondered if they still held hands in public, or if they were the type to bicker contently through their golden years. The pair must've been intimate in simple, everyday ways—ways reflecting a depth and mutual understanding I'd never fathomed before. She knew how best to quell her husband's upset stomach, he knew exactly how to massage away the tension in her neck, and they put each other first—nothing like my parents. Theirs was a bounty of a shared life, constructed from the small moments. Surely, that's how they respected each other's strong, built a new strength together.

The café door opened slowly. I'd already planned what I wanted to say to Trevor, but now I would apparently be saying something else, because Claudio had walked in. He'd probably muscled Trevor into going his own way for the morning. Fabulous. If my traveling companion wasn't such a pushover, he would've landed right back on my shit list.

Claudio walked to my table, an uncharacteristic slowness in his step—his smolder and his swagger had vanished. I trained my gaze on him, hoping every degree of the hellfire in my eyes was searing his insides.

Most men would've run for the hills, but not Claudio, who pulled out the chair across from me, sat down deliberately, and sighed. His eyes were pained and full of longing. He opened with an utterly unoriginal, "Kauhlie, I am sorry."

I crossed my arms and whipped my face toward the wall, shutting him out. Why did he presume I was ready to talk so soon—or that I'd be ready to talk at all? What part of, "We're done," hadn't he understood?

"I should not have said those things," he added after a long moment.

"Because they weren't true!" I exclaimed, commanding, with my very tone, that he agree.

"Because they were not true," he concurred. At least he was smart enough to admit that much.

"And because they were mean!" I shouted at the wall, still refusing to look at him.

"And because they were mean," he granted. "Although I did not inte—"

"—And because you were a giant asshole!" I demanded.

He hesitated. "Kauhlie. Please do not make me say such a thing."

"And you were a giant asshole!" I repeated, emphasizing both *ass* and *hole*. I would have my confession in full, or I'd write him off here and now—and he knew it.

"Yes, Kauhlie, I was an asshole," he acquiesced.

"Giant." I insisted.

"Yes, giant. A giant asshole. That was me."

I relaxed my shoulders slightly and turned to him. Now that we'd established the basics, I was almost willing to hear what he had to say.

"I must apologize. I was only teasing. I did not know I would hurt you. I had drunk too much for so early in the day, and I was trying to be funny."

"Funny? You have a terrible sense of humor, my friend." I took a gulp of my coffee and hid a wince: I'd burned the daylights out of my mouth. Claudio made me so angry that I forgot the necessity of sipping hot beverages.

"I know. It was not funny. I should not have assumed. You said you were not close to your girlfriends in New York, and I took it too far."

I crossed my arms again. "And you had no right to demand my number. Especially not with Trevor there."

"And I had no right to demand your number," he echoed penitently. "I should have *asked*—in private."

"You were disrespectful. My life is mine to live, not yours to judge! No matter how many men I've slept with. No matter who my friends are!" I kept my back stiff and my arms crossed, letting my words fill with anger.

"This is very true, Kauhlie. I do not know what I was thinking."

"You had no right to attack me like that! Margaritas are no excuse."

"No, they are no excuse. Alcohol is no excuse."

"I trusted you, you know. I told you about my parents. I told you about Hemingway and his calls. I don't open myself up to many people. Not like that. *Never* like that."

"You have told me many things, Kauhlie. Many private things." He reached across the table to brush my hair from my face. I shot out of his reach, batting his hand away with a slap.

"I break sometimes. Don't you know that?" I said. "And I showed you that—my broken places. That's how much I trusted you! Or *thought* I could trust you."

"You can trust me, Kauhlie, I assure you of this. I made a mistake." He forced a smile. "Giant asshole, as you say."

"Exactly. A giant asshole. Why should I trust a giant asshole?"

"I am remorseful, Kauhlie. I was very wrong."

"You made me feel small. You *enjoyed* making me feel small! That's why you are a giant asshole." I slammed both hands on the table. "That's the real problem here."

"Kauhlie, I have apologized. I am penitent. And I apologize again now, with sincerity. But Trevor is outside. He wants to see you, he feels bad too."

"Why does Trevor feel bad? He wasn't the giant asshole, you were." If anything, Trevor was a collateral asshole, but I left that point out for the moment.

"Yes, Kauhlie, but can the three of us now move forward? We are good friends, you, me, and Trevor."

I thought about it for a moment, taking my time with my still-steaming coffee. "Okay. Friends... that's okay."

Claudio almost reached for my hand, but he had the good sense to hold back. "And you and I, we can move forward together?" he said, pleading in his eyes. "Just you and me in our way?"

His words hung in the air. I gazed deep into my coffee as if reading tea leaves. But the answer wasn't in that cup, it was in the pit of my stomach, in the knot tightening there. Claudio had betrayed me, and he'd done it for his own amusement. I could maybe admit there was a seed of truth in what he'd said, but that didn't give him permission to steal my strong.

My mouth went dry. "*Un niño,*" I whispered into my cup. Of their own accord, my hands balled into fists as I steeled myself.

"*Un niño?*" Claudio repeated. "There are no children in here, Kauhlie, what does this mean?"

"It means no."

"No?"

"No, Claudio. The three of us can be friends, but that's all." I paused intentionally, then threw in a scathing, "You'll have no problem finding someone else, anyway."

A deep shadow crossed his face. A part of me was glad of it, even as the rest of me ripped apart. I fought back a moan of hurt and frustration as he said, "My dear one, I made a mistake. One drunken mistake. And I am sorry for it. Do you truly mean what you are saying?"

"Really. I demand better!"

"I will be better, Kauhlie," he implored. "I will be better for you. Please, Kauhlie."

"I thought you *were* better—that's the issue. I don't need someone who can maybe *become* better, I need someone who *is* better, who's strong *with* me. I can't be with you anymore, not like that. I *won't* be with you."

Claudio's entire face fell, his eyes becoming blank and hard—emotionless. He ran his fingers through his hair, gathering his thoughts. He did the same a second time. Then he nodded slowly as if he were accepting a truth he'd never before contemplated.

"We will go back to being friends, Kauhlie," he agreed, the words heavy in his mouth, his voice as flat and blank as his eyes. "If that is what you want."

"Friends."

"Friends."

The cruelest word in the English language.

CHAPTER 16

A FRENCHMAN AND A TARTIFLETTE

Claudio and I didn't see each other for a solid week, but after a few days of distance we agreed we wanted "friends" to mean "actual friends," not just, "exes who don't hate each other." We had Trevor to consider, too— without Claudio around, he was regressing into his stodgy, socially inept, self, and he'd begun clinging to me in weird ways again. We both felt Trevor deserved better than to get swept up in our wreckage, so we committed to hanging out twice a week. I felt a little like parents staying together for the sake of their kid, but that actually made me feel *better* about the whole situation. It was more than my parents ever did for me.

Fridays were a 'Trevor care" day, and this Friday we'd all gone to the Plaza Mayor at my request—a site we hadn't visited yet. The sweeping plaza, once the heart of Old Madrid, was jubilant with all manner of people dining, taking pictures, and enjoying the music of the various street performers. I was now an expert at discerning locals from tourists (easy); recognizing Spanish folks who weren't locals was harder, but I had a handle on that, too. Equipped with this skill, I felt more and more like I "belonged" in Madrid.

Streaks of orange colored the dusk sky, and lamplights illuminated the square in a welcoming glow. The evening's warmth invited us to linger as we weaved through the archways lining the plaza and peered into the stores beyond. This was window-shopping at its finest as far as I was concerned but it bored the hell out of the guys, and so they'd left me to my own devices for a while. Claudio had said he would "be right back," while Trevor had perched himself on one of the few benches and had commenced people-watching.

The wafting music drew me, carrying me toward it. The guitarist's tones had a distinct rhythm, and the man sang in a cadence I hadn't heard in Madrid before. The clinking of euros landing in his open guitar case contrasted with the music sharply, but I tuned those out. I focused in intensely, listening and swaying my hips gently.

"That is not a Spanish song, I must tell you," a voice came over my shoulder. An accented male voice, one I didn't recognize.

"Excuse me?" I turned and found myself facing a sandy-brown-haired man who was only slightly taller than me. He wasn't a typical tourist, although he definitely wasn't Spanish, either.

"*Oui*, it's true, this is a French song in translation. He is an imposter."

The man's light-blue eyes glowed under his raised eyebrows. He looked like he knew all the answers, if I only could figure out the right questions; at the same time, his air said he'd be perpetually disappointed at my never finding the right questions. I accepted the challenge.

"How do you know that?"

"I am French." As he spoke, he raised both eyebrows high before lowering them dramatically, as if he'd just revealed a spectacular plot twist. I giggled before I could help it.

"Well, Mr. French… *Je parle assez bien le français. J'ai visité France plusieurs fois*," I said, telling him my French was strong and explaining I'd been to his country many times.

"*Mais vous êtes américaine, oui?*" he replied, asking if I were American. Switching back to English, he continued, "That is why I spoke American to you." His eyebrows waggled up and down.

"Yes, I'm American. An American named Callie." I tried to keep from giggling at his eyebrows again, but a small laugh escaped with my reply.

"Hello, Culleee." He said my name with the emphasis on the last syllable, with the "ie" sound trailing into an "eee" string—in sharp contrast to Claudio's pronunciation. I liked it. "Culleee" made me sound chic and sophisticated. I could almost picture myself in an underground Paris café, a glass of Sauternes in one hand and my lit cigarette, in an opera-length holder, in the other. This, of course, utterly ignored my hating dessert wines and not being a smoker.

"It is my distinct pleasure to meet you, *mademoiselle,* "I am Jean-Francois."

"Jean-Francois, really?" I blurted out. I thought Frenchmen were only named Jean-Francois in movies. I collected myself before he could answer. "Of course ... it's nice to meet you." I smiled at him and he smiled back.

"I am from Paris," he explained with an air that only Parisians could pull off.

"No kidding," I replied, a touch of sarcasm in my voice. "I never would've guessed."

"There!" he cried, making me jump a little.

"What?!"

"What you just did, Callie." He pointed at my face excitedly.

Except for breathing, I hadn't done much of anything, as far as I knew. "What are you talking about?" Maybe this guy was a nutjob, who knew?

"With your eyes. You rolled your eyes!"

"I did? I didn't mean to. I'm sorry."

His face exploded with delight. "No need to apologize. Your eye roll, it was... so much like the women of my beautiful city. I *loved* it!"

This guy was laying it on a little thick. I'd been to Paris enough times to know the whole eye-rolling thing was a bit of a stereotype, yet something about him still intrigued me.

"An American in Madrid, yet a woman so reflective of my home." He looked deep into my eyes and took my hand, then began leading me… somewhere. I was about to break away from him when he said confidently, "Let me show you around the Plaza Mayor."

When Jean-Francois said he wanted to show me around, I think he meant, "walk around the square holding my hand." He didn't show me much of anything, except for the statue of King Philip III in the plaza's center. He claimed some distant relation to Phillip III's daughter, who—for reasons I didn't care to wrap my head around—was called Anne of Austria. Equally dizzying was that Anne of Austria had become queen of France at some point. I was nonplussed by Jean-Francois' "nobility" blood; Jean-Francois was nonplussed at my being nonplussed.

As the moon was starting to rise over the plaza's five-story buildings, I asked, "What brings you to Madrid this weekend?" I paused in thought. "I mean, you don't live here, do you?"

He scoffed slightly. "No, I do not live here," he replied, waving his hand drolly. "I live in Paris, of course. I have lived there all my life."

"So you're visiting friends this weekend?"

"No, not at all," he answered, as if I'd just asked the most painfully dull question in the world. "I own an import-export company, and I have many customers in Madrid. I am here so often that I keep a *pied-à-terre*. Having my own *appartement* is much more convenient than hotels."

"What's more convenient than hotels?" came Trevor's voice from behind, startling me. My back had been turned to his bench; I never saw him coming. "We stay in hotels, and it works out just fine, doesn't it, Callie?"

"Nothing, Trevor, never mind," I answered, a little annoyed that he'd chosen to pop back up at this moment. I wanted to hear more about Jean-Francois' company. When I was in law school, I had initially wanted to specialize in import-export law—it sounded so exotic. My interest didn't last long, though: I quickly realized that the *products* being represented traveled to exotic places, while import-export *attorneys* stayed at their desks. Yet Jean-Francois had found a loophole. He wasn't a lawyer, of course, but here he was, traveling between Paris and Madrid and doing the fun part.

As I made introductions, I realized I was still holding Jean-Francois' hand. "Oh, Callie, not another one," Trevor whispered to me. I ignored him. What did "another one" mean?

Jean-Francois let go of my palm to shake Trevor's hand—leaving Trevor no choice but to shake back. He almost managed to speak a full, socially acceptable, sentence to my new friend, but he didn't exactly succeed.

"We were enjoying a walk around the plaza, Trevor," said Jean-Francois cordially. "We should continue to do so. Together."

He took Trevor's right hand with his left and took my left hand with his right. Trevor clearly had no idea what to do; holding another man's hand totally threw him off. He was visibly relieved when, after a few yards, Jean-Francois naturally dropped his hand—although my new friend still held onto mine.

We strolled around for a while, with Trevor loosening up a bit and asking a bunch of dorky questions about this store or that one. I almost had to pry him away from a caricature artist who, much to the delight of the crowd, was drawing under a streetlamp. Trevor insisted that he and I needed a caricature together, but I vetoed the idea outright—I didn't want anyone, not even a cartoonist, making me look like a fool in front of Jean-Francois.

Claudio soon caught up to us, emerging from the sea of unfamiliar faces like a wraith. I'd almost forgotten he'd come with us today. I was glad of it; this last half-hour or so was the first time since we'd broken up that the man hadn't popped into my thoughts every ten minutes.

Trevor perked up. "Look, Claudio!" he cried, "Callie's made a new friend. Another one!" I ignored Trevor's "another one" for a second time. Why did he keep saying that?

"A new friend?" Claudio parroted, looking as if he'd missed something. He examined me, Jean-Francois, and our entwined palms (in that order) as his face lit up, then fell in recognition. I couldn't help it; I took a wicked pleasure in the falling part.

"Yeah. This one's French," Trevor chuckled.

"Kauhlie, you are becoming so… European." Claudio mustered a smile. He began speaking to Jean-Francois in French, extending his hand for a handshake. Jean-Francois had to drop my hand to shake his. I couldn't tell if Claudio was being his usual affable self, or if the handshake was a deliberate move to part Jean-Francois' hand from mine. I suspected a bit of both.

The two conversed for a few moments. I caught some of it but not all—their French was much too fast for me to keep up, plus Claudio's Spanish accent made his French hard for me to follow.

Once they'd stopped tittering between themselves, Claudio slapped Jean-Francois on the back before turning to me. "Indeed, you have found us a new friend, Kauhlie. "We will be your entourage!"

Never in my life had I wanted an entourage, but tantalization prickled through me. I didn't know what would happen between me and Jean-Francois, but I sure as hell like the idea of Claudio seeing me with another guy. To remind him of all he'd lost.

Jean-Francois and I had been out together twice—once with Trevor, once without—since the evening we'd first met. Tonight was the first meal with all four of us, and I was sure dinner with Jean-Francois in the group would be different. Good-different or bad-different, I wasn't sure. I largely didn't care, either, so long as "different" was on the menu.

What I did care about was the seating arrangement, which I carefully but clandestinely orchestrated as we were shown to our table. Me, Jean-Francois, Claudio, Trevor, in that order. I wanted to sit next to Jean-Francois for obvious reasons, but I also needed to sit *across* from

Claudio. As his ex, giving him a clear view of me with my date seemed the least I could do.

Before Jean-Francois came along, there was only one expert among us on food, wine, and all things European. Now there were two. I enjoyed the battle of the know-it-all titans as dinner became epically wrapped in Continental testosterone. Claudio suggested; Jean-Francois counter-suggested. Jean-Francois pontificated; Claudio counter-pontificated. Eye rolls. Sighs. Heavier sighs. Exasperated shoulder-shrugging, extra points for which went to Jean-Francois. To my mind, the French had perfected the shoulder-shrug, and Jean-Francois' shrug had an unexpected sexiness to it. The whole meal morphed into a new type of delicious.

"No, no, no, Claudio, my friend!" Jean-Francois objected. "We French have mastered potatoes in a way the Spanish never will."

"No, *my* friend," Claudio challenged. "Have you not heard of our *patatas bravas*?" He rolled his eyes.

Each of them now used the word *friend* in the same way folks in the American South sometimes said, "Bless your heart." Both meant, "Go to hell." I relished every minute of it.

"Callie… you're an expert," Jean-Francois began, turning to me. "Who prepares potatoes the best? We French, or the Spanish?"

"I'm not an authority on starches," I replied, which was nearly a lie. Sometimes I *craved* carbs—potatoes au gratin, steak fries, or heavily garlicked mashed potatoes. A date once ended very badly because I couldn't say no to the garlic mashed potatoes.

"But surely our *tartiflette* is more sumptuous than any other dish?" Jean-Francois asked. I knew the potato, onion, bacon, and cheese casserole well. Probably too well. Pretty much anytime I'd found myself in a French restaurant, a *tartiflette* had found its way onto my plate.

"I do like that," Trevor interjected. "I had that a bunch of times when I was trekking through France."

Jean-Francois nodded at Trevor before replying, "You can tell us about your adventures in France another time, *oui*?" His dismissive tone said, "Hush, the grown-ups are talking." I didn't care for that, but I let it slide. Trevor could inspire that kind of impatience in anyone.

Jean-Francois raised his index finger as he turned to me again. "Or… what about our *gratin dauphinois*? Surely this is heaven on a plate?"

Boom went the culinary dynamite. We had a winner.

"You can't beat *gratin dauphinois*, Claudio." I said with honesty. The tantalizing dish of thinly sliced potatoes baked in cream and garlic—sometimes with cheese—blew just about everything else, potato-based or otherwise, out of the water.

It went from there. Wine: I think that went to France. Sausage went to Spain. Seafood was a tie—Mediterranean seafood went to Spain, while Atlantic seafood went to France. Beef, chicken, and lamb were debated vigorously during an extra carafe of wine. Well, two extra carafes, actually. Jean-Francois only drank French wine and ordered a half-carafe for himself, while we shared a full carafe of an aged Tempranillo.

All the wine in the world couldn't tame the heated debate at our table. I lost count of the number of times one man shot daggers at the other, their eyes conveying, "You are wrong," I have bested you," or simply, "You must be crazy." Whenever I agreed with Jean-Francois, I made damn sure Claudio knew it, which turned the debate into a devilishly satisfying game for me.

After the check came, and over the avid objections of Claudio, Jean-Francois declared France, and himself, the overall winner. "Even you cannot disagree, my friend. French food is better food than Spanish. That much is clear." He shrugged his shoulders as if there could be no further argument.

"No, it is not clear," Claudio said curtly. "We could debate this for centuries, but still you would not win. This is how subjectivity works." Normally I would've agreed with him, but I wasn't switching camps now.

"The cuisine in France is… *la fantaisie*," he countered, before finishing the last sip of his French wine. He turned to Trevor. "That is French for 'the fantasy,'" he clarified.

Sometimes Jean-Francois could be a jerk. I'd already figured that out about him, but his urbanity generally made up for it. And I wasn't about to rebuke him with Claudio watching; there could be no hint of discontent, not tonight.

"Yes, I got that one," Trevor replied, clearly ready to leave. Uncharacteristically, he pushed back, "Sometimes French is just fancified English." I was glad he got the shot in, even if Jean-Francois ignored him.

As we left, Claudio excused himself, saying he had a call with his father in New York. He didn't have a call with his father, that much was obvious to me; he was merely sore from "losing" the debate. *Un niño.* I said an overly polite goodbye and let him sulk.

The night was warm and invigorating, and it wasn't too late—just before midnight—so Jean-Francois offered to walk us back to our hotels. The three of us made our way through the streets, slightly drunk and laughing along the way.

We'd just said goodnight to Trevor when I turned to cross the street to my hotel. Jean-Francois tenderly took my hand and anchored me to him. "*Reste avec moi un peu plus longtemps, ma belle,*" he urged.

"Stay with you a little longer?" I asked, translating to hide my intrigue—and the heat creeping through my body. It wasn't every day that someone addressed me as "my beauty."

"*Oui*, I have something I would like to share with you. In my apartment. A small surprise."

"I love surprises! How far away do you live?"

"It is only a little surprise, Callie, and my apartment is only a little way from here."

We walked for about ten minutes before Jean-Francois flagged a cab with elegant ease. I was caught off guard, and I hesitated as he opened the door for me.

"Wait, I thought you said your apartment was only a little way off?" I asked.

"It is. A little way by foot—and a little way by cab. It's not far." The taxi's door stood open, beckoning me to adventure.

I eyed him dubiously. "You should've mentioned that, don't you think?"

His eyebrows shot up. "*Excusez-moi*, I didn't think you would mind. But perhaps you've had too much wine tonight? Should I take you back to your hotel instead?"

"No! I've had just the right amount of wine, and I still want my surprise." Jean-Francois' eyebrows lowered, but his eyes lit up joyfully.

Five minutes later, we pulled up outside a six-story building with a small balcony attached to each unit. I couldn't tell exactly because it was dark, but I think the brick was painted in one of the bright hews so common to Madrid. We'd passed the magnificent arch of the Puerta de Alcalá a few blocks back, so I had a rough idea of where we were.

A long, narrow lobby led directly to a small but bright elevator, which creaked as it made its way to the fourth floor with an almost-painful slowness. Each floor had only two units, and as we exited, Jean-Francois led me to the right. A resounding *clunk* reverberated through the hallway when he unlocked the door with his key.

"*Voilà!*" He opened the door widely, ushering me inside. "My Paris in Madrid!"

The apartment was on the smaller side, but lushly decorated in a modern Parisian style—the muted color pattern contrasted with the rich fabrics, and gold-gilding adorned the accent pieces. Simple yet splendidly elegant.

Jean-Francois made a beeline for the kitchen area, quickly turned on the oven, and then looked over his shoulder, his blue eyes twinkling. "For your surprise!"

"Tell me!" I demanded.

"No, no. You must wait, Callie," he cautioned as he waggled his finger back and forth. He waggled his eyebrows, too, although I don't think it was intentional. I stifled a laugh. Those eyebrows were going to do me in, I just knew it.

"I don't like waiting!" I cried.

"*C'est vrai.* I have noticed this about you. Perhaps you have noble blood as well, for you are accustomed to having your way, no? He smiled in amusement. "But wait you must." He then pulled a pan from the refrigerator, purposely shielding it with his body. He popped the mystery dish into the oven with an almost comical alacrity, spun around, and sent a devilish glance my way.

Practically floating over to his wine rack, he asked, "Callie, will you join me in a glass of wine? I have several you would like."

"No, thank you," I said, surprising even myself as my old instinct fell out of my mouth. Back in the city, I had a rule about not drinking with a guy the first time I was alone with him in his apartment. Madrid wasn't New York, but good sense was good sense, and Callie McGraw looked out for herself. Always.

Jean-Francois seemed puzzled, but he recovered quickly. "Then I will pour you a mineral water," he replied, opening the refrigerator. He pulled out a liter of water and a container of plump raspberries. He poured, then dropped two raspberries into each glass after squeezing them firmly between his fingertips. A droplet of juice trickled down this thumb.

Touching only the base of the glass, he slid my water across the island to me. I received it with only my fingertips, my fingers brushing against his. I pretended a spark of electricity didn't run through me.

I swirled the raspberries around to even out the flavor. Jean-Francois did the same. We drank our first sip in unison. "You like, *oui*?" he asked, knowing the answer.

"Yes, thank you. This is wonderful." As simple as it was, it was perfect.

"I know," he said, almost bragging. "I only buy the freshest of berries, and I only drink the finest French mineral waters."

We smiled and flirted for a few minutes until I heard a beep. Jean-Francois' eyes darted over to the oven, then back to me. "Callie, your wait is over!"

"It's about time." I laughed. "That smells fantastic."

The small, square pan he set before me was half-filled with something that was a lovely deep yellow color and had browned cheese on top. "*La tartiflette!*" he exclaimed. "This is only the leftovers—I made it last night—but I thought it would be a perfect end to our evening."

I leaned over the pan and took in the heavenly aroma. "Jean-Francois, you're amazing!"

"Yes, I am." Clearly, he was not a modest man, but I didn't mind—not with a *tartiflette* literally on the table.

He handed me a fork as he walked to my side of the island. "We will indulge straight from the pan. It is more delicious this way, and I like to share in my home when eating. It is more… intimate." He sat on the stool next to me, scooting in an inch or two closer than was strictly necessary. "Now, Callie, please take the first bite."

Deliciousness exploded in my mouth. I might've moaned with pleasure, Jean-Francois might've enjoyed my moan. I couldn't believe this man had sexy, gourmet leftovers sitting in his refrigerator. Before this moment, I'd never thought of leftover food as being sexy—any unfinished takeout in my fridge in New York had usually been the most gross, unsexy food imaginable.

We ate in heavy forkfuls. At one point, a piece of potato escaped from my mouth and landed back in the pan. I didn't care. Neither did he. As we were finishing up the last bites, he leaned in closer to me. Very close. Even closer. Closer still.

My head was completely clear now. It all made sense. The spring night. The potatoes, the onions, the cheese. Paris in Madrid. A soft kiss as Jean-Francois' lips met mine. This was a man who wasn't trying to steal my strong, he just wanted to be with me. For tonight, for tomorrow, for next week—just me, just him.

We didn't speak as I led him to the bedroom.

CHAPTER 17

A THEATRICAL DETOUR

"Microtheater!"

"What's that?" I asked.

"It's what we're doing after our dinner," Jean-Francois replied dryly, as if the question itself bored him.

"Does it have micro-actors?" Trevor asked through a bite of lamb.

"Trevor, don't talk with your mouth full," I scolded. "How many times do I have to tell you that?"

"Sorry, Callie."

"You're in the presence of a lady."

"Who, you?"

"Yes me! Now quit it."

"I said I was sorry, Callie."

"What is this microtheater?" asked Claudio, slightly irritated. "You did not answer Kauhlie's question... or Trevor's, for that matter."

"I'm surprised you don't know of it, Claudio, being such a man of Madrid." Oddly enough, Claudio let the dig pass. Continuing, Jean-Francois explained, "It is an artistic movement that started in this city. It is now spreading across Latin America."

Trevor was going to ask a question, but his mouth was full again. He glanced at me before letting the thought remain private. Every once in a while, I had the sneaking suspicion he was learning something.

I rapped on the table impatiently, urging Jean-Francois on. Getting any useful information out of him could be like pulling teeth. He wasn't terribly generous with his knowledge; he liked knowing things others didn't. This might've bothered me, except I was a lawyer. I knew tons of stuff he never would, and he knew it.

"Of course, there are no micro-actors, Trevor, only micro-plays. Fifteen minutes each. Several of them in an evening, each in its own tiny theater." Jean-Francois sipped his French wine before raising his eyebrows. "And if this is not intriguing enough, there's a *pièce de résistance*. The theater itself,"—down went his eyebrows—"is a converted brothel! Each—"

"—You mean the theaters are… the rooms where women would—"

"—Conduct their business? Yes, *mon chéri*, presumably."

I shivered. World's oldest profession or not, that grossed me out.

"Not to worry, Kauhlie, I am sure they have cleaned since then," Claudio offered, chuckling slightly but also intending to comfort me. I smiled at him for that.

Jean-Francois pretended to ignore us both. "Each theater is fifteen square meters, and the audience is only fifteen people. And best of all, tonight is… the monthly English night! I bought us tickets because I know how much my Callie loves the arts."

"Jean-Francois, you're incredible!" I cried, kissing him on the cheek. He'd missed the mark with "the arts," but I attributed that to a translation issue, and it was a sweet gesture.

"I'm incredible? Yes, if you insist," he agreed, accepting my kiss. Reacting to two very different things, Trevor shook his head approvingly, while Claudio grimaced ever so slightly.

The theater wasn't far—a short walk. Claudio's testosterone took over as we entered the lobby; he sliced through the crowd to the bar where he ordered us our usuals. The three of us trailed after him.

"Kauhlie, I asked for extra gin. I know how you like your drinks," he said, handing me my cocktail.

"Well done." I toasted his glass and sipped. The extra gin warmed me.

Jean-Francois pulled out the program he'd grabbed on our way in. "We will start with 'The Trench,'" he announced. "It seems the most engaging of the plays."

Examining the program from over his shoulder, I said, "That looks serious. Military serious. Wartime stuff."

"Tonight is not a night for comedy," he countered. "Tonight is for true theater—in micro-form!"

"Yeah, let's go to 'The Trench,'" Trevor blurted out. "That sounds deep." One of these days, his puns were going to kill me. Even Claudio groaned.

We made our way downstairs, where all four theaters were housed. We found "The Trench," which fortunately had four audience-slots left. "You must crawl to go in," the ticket-taker instructed us in his best English, pointing to the long curtain covering most of the doorway. "To not get shot by the soldiers."

Apparently tonight was interactive theater. Great.

It was dark inside, a deep dark; an usher directed us to crawl to the right wall and seat ourselves on the floor with the other audience members. The house lights raised, artillery rumbling in the distance.

My eyes adjusted to the lighting, revealing our surroundings: A World War I trench. Not a trench on stage—we, the audience, were *in* the trench, with four soldiers leaning against the opposite wall. All four men, Americans, bore hangdog expressions, as if they'd been worn out long ago.

The perspective illuminated the insidiousness of trench warfare. The stage-effects immersed us fully; the theater smelled of grease and earth and gunpowder, and the "bombings" shook the floor, the stage lights flashing like thunderbolts. I didn't know if we were supposed to talk to the actors, but I peppered in my own comments and challenges. My engagement was rewarded when one soldier offered me (and me alone) a cigarette. I smoked my trophy proudly in front of everyone, suppressing my coughs. The thing tasted awful. A Pyrrhic victory, maybe, but I was still the winner.

The play ended with a direct-hit in the trench—the entire room shook—obliterating the four soldiers and, presumably, us as well.

Agog, we crawled out of the theater the same way we'd come in. None of us spoke—none of us were sure we were still alive.

"What the hell was that?" Trevor asked, once he was assured of his corporeal form.

"Something very powerful!" Claudio answered.

"I loved it!" exclaimed Jean-Francois. "So true to life! But perhaps we should have a glass of wine, to temper the intensity."

"No!" I shouted. I had been floored by "The Trench," and now I was eager for something lighter. "We need to keep going! "'Fiesta' is starting now—that sounds fun!" I grabbed Jean-Francois' hand and pulled him down the hallway.

An usher escorted us into the next theater. We hadn't needed to crawl to enter, but once inside, we were directed to sit in the first row of what looked suspiciously like a jury box.

A voice boomed through the darkness. "The prisoner stands accused of murdering our Nationalist civilians!" A spotlight illuminated a lone, devastatingly handsome man on a makeshift witness stand. A second spotlight shone on the speaker, a general in uniform. "He's a Republican traitor, a slaughterer of women and children!" he continued. As he spoke, the first spotlight widened to reveal two soldiers on either side of the accused.

As it turned out, we *were* in a jury box. We, the audience, were jurors in a kangaroo court. A far cry from the bordello this room once had been.

"Boo!" cried someone behind us. Shocked, I did a quick count of the audience: besides the four of us, six other people were in our row. Ten people sat in the row behind. That meant five "jurors" were part of the play. More interaction than I'd bargained for.

"He is guilty of high crimes against Spain!" the general shouted. "He must pay with his life!"

"Traitor!" cried another juror. Dissenting, someone else shouted, "Let him speak!"

The accused man, Diego, had been a prominent matador. As gorgeous as he was now; apparently he'd been even more beautiful before the war—too beautiful to be gored, they'd said, that's why he always triumphed in the ring. When he'd joined the Republicans, he was appointed a squad leader for that very reason: if *el toro* couldn't maim him, neither could bullets.

The accused didn't have a lawyer. Neither did the general, who fired off a litany of crimes. Now and then, a guard would butt Diego with his rifle, usually for no discernible reason. With each disruption, the judge gaveled madly and shouted fervidly, always in the army's favor.

My blood boiled, my teeth clenched. I'd spent my entire post grad-school life working in law, respecting the courts. What kind of justice was this? Why did they bother having a trial at all?

Diego admitted he'd fought for the Republicans, serving for a few months before shrapnel to the knee had brought an end to his soldier-ing—and to any remaining years in the bullring. As proof, he lifted his tattered pant leg, showing the scarring.

Members of the jury hissed. Others called him a true Spaniard. Someone threw a cabbage; it hit the witness stand with a *splat*.

The general whipped the jury into a divided frenzy. He insisted the prisoner had led an attack on civilians—an unarmed village in the north—decimating the town. The general claimed they had witnesses, although none testified. The judge ruled none were needed. A trial of hearsay, pure scapegoating.

Diego wept, begging desperately. He'd never been so far north, had never been to that village—and he could never kill children. He would swear loyalty, from this moment until his dying breath, to the Nationalists, to Franco, to Spain.

The jury erupted—first just the actors, I think, but then almost everyone joined in. "Liar!" one woman cried. "A traitor against Franco!" shouted another. "Guilty on all counts!" the man behind me cried. More and more agreed—definitely not just the actors. "Hang him!" they yelled. "Death to the traitor!"

Only one man remained on Diego's side. "This man's no murderer!" It wasn't nearly enough.

The two guards grabbed the condemned, manhandling him as they led him away. Diego pleaded for clemency, prayed to God for mercy. The frenzy grew—the jury disintegrating into a mob.

The room went completely dark, shocking the jury-mob into a collective silence. A calculated beat. A harsh spotlight. A noose dropped from the ceiling, swaying ominously.

I rushed out of the theater, pushing past the other patrons in a mad dash. That was no court, not law-in-action. That trial was the antithesis of all I knew as a lawyer and believed as an American.

"What the hell was that?!" I shouted when the others caught up to me.

"Kauhlie, you must understand, it was a commentary on our civil war," Claudio replied. "It was not long ago, many people still remember their grandfathers and great-uncles who fought. That is why the whole jury became upset, not just the actors."

"What happened in there wasn't justice. That's not how the law works!"

"It is not how the law works in America, Kauhlie, but it is how it works in some other countries, I am sorry to say."

"And am I *in* one of those countries *now*?"

"No, that did not happen here, I assure you. We had real courts to address these matters. The play was a reimagining. In the Spanish Civil War, everyone lost—all of us. That was the message of the playwright. I believe that is why she titled her work 'Fiesta.' For the irony."

"Your civil war was so very violent. Very messy," Jean-Francois huffed. "So many killed. *Vraiment terrible.*"

"And who are you to say?" I barked, concentrating my anger on his snobbery. "Your revolution was bloody as hell. People starved! Both your king and queen lost their heads. Literally. So, don't judge!"

"Ah, *mon cher*, this play has upset you too much," he snorted, affronted. "Perhaps Trevor will take you home."

I balked, as did Trevor. "Jean-Francois, don't you dar—"

"—Let us now see 'Still,'" Claudio jumped in, keeping me from exploding. "And then we will all have a drink. Together, as friends."

"That sounds good," answered Trevor, pulling on his beard. I'd never blown up at him directly, but he'd been in my orbit often enough to know the signs of impending disaster.

"No, I'm going for that drink *now*." Shooting a dirty look at my so-called boyfriend, I pointed to the concession stand. "Alone." Walking away, I called over my shoulder, "Come get me when you're done." My entourage gawked, but they wisely gave me my space.

Two plays, two wars. Fascism corrupting the court. Sickening. Maybe I wasn't a litigator, but, "Innocent until proven guilty" was high up on the reasons I'd entered law in the first place. Callie McGraw, American patriot?

⤲

"Kauhlie, we missed you," Claudio said, walking up to the concession stand. "But you did not miss much. That one was not so good."

"Yeah," agreed Trevor. "Mushy stuff." He cocked his head, making a snoring sound.

"No, that's not true," said Jean-Francois, disagreeing as usual. "It was a reflection on the one who got away. A piece about a man who built his life with another. Very authentic."

"At least that's better than corrupt courts and trench warfare," I said, mostly to Claudio and Trevor, half-ignoring my date.

"Our hero did not end up with the wrong person, but certainly he was not with the *right* person," Claudio offered. "There is a difference."

"That doesn't sound like my type of thing," I granted. Remembering a play my mother had dragged me to in Chicago—an overnight "girls" trip to spite my dad—I lowered my voice so only Claudio could hear. "Sounds like my parents. *They* chose wrong when they chose each other."

Claudio faked a chuckle, then rolled his merry ruse straight into his next question to protect my privacy. "The last play is, 'The Lovely One.' You will join us?"

"Yeah, Callie, come on," urged Trevor. "It's no fun without you."

"Yes, *mon cher*, I brought us here tonight for you." This wasn't exactly a plea for my company; Jean-Francois was reminding me who'd paid for the tickets. Ass.

I agreed for Trevor and Claudio's sakes and hopped down from my stool. Jean-Francois did not take my hand as we walked to the final theater. I didn't want him to, either.

The setup for this play was more traditional, although it didn't come with chairs; we were seated on the floor along the far wall. The house lights came up, revealing the bedroom of an upscale apartment.

A pretty, young-ish woman in a silk robe sat at a vanity brushing her hair. Her husband lounged in a recliner, reading a newspaper. He peered up and spoke first.

"Darling, shall we pop over to the Isle of Wight next weekend? It says here, once the season starts, it'll be rather impossible to get proper accommodation."

"If you'd like, dear. I have no feeling on it," she replied. Meeting her husband's gaze in the mirror, she added, "Now be a love and fetch my compact. It's on the chest, just there." She waved her hand vaguely.

The man, twenty years her senior, retrieved her makeup dutifully. Handing it to her, he asked another question—something equally commonplace. Again she vacillated in disinterest, powdering her face.

They chatted about trips, galas, and the charity event they were preparing for. She was palpably bored. The only thing she was interested in was her preening—that, and her wine. Every once in a while, her husband would top off her glass, literally and figuratively revolving around her. It came out that she used to have money, but he was the only one with money now. Tonight's charity was his cause, not hers. She didn't care if the orphans were starving or the whales needed saving, as long as her mascara was perfect.

Rising, she began, "Well, if we must go to this ghastly thing…" She untied her sash, letting her robe slip to the floor. The audience gasped; all she'd been wearing underneath was lingerie, stockings and garters included. "I suppose that gown shall do nicely. Dreadfully kind of you to buy it for me, dear." She waved her hand vaguely again.

Her husband removed the lace evening dress from the closet door, bringing it to her with a sweeping elegance. She stepped into it, purposefully keeping her back to the audience. She nodded, and he zipped her up obediently. That was as close as they ever came to touching.

She seated herself again, applying her lipstick. "Are you ready, my dear?" the husband asked once her mouth was painted. He enjoyed dressing her, ogling her, that much was clear. What else kept them together wasn't clear—other than his money. No passion, no connection, between them. They reminded me of my parents that way.

A spotlight zeroed in on her. "Now I am ready," she declared. She rose, turning to the audience as if she were royalty, stunningly vibrant and almost impossibly beautiful.

Until that moment, I'd thought the play was garbage. Yet the effect was complete; her false splendor, a wasted marriage, a wasted life. Two wasted lives, actually; his and hers. I sighed. This too, I realized, was much like my parents.

"That was so sad," I said, shuffling out of the theater. I was exhausted at this point. This was supposed to be a fun night, but it had turned into a personal emotional roller coaster for me.

"Indeed, Callie. Their life together was a lie," Jean-Francois agreed. "A lie held together by ennui."

"No, I don't think ennui kept them together, it kept them apart. They could've had a good life if they'd made an effort, but neither of them cared enough to make that effort."

"Good thing they didn't have children," Trevor remarked innocently enough. "That woman wouldn't have liked being a mom—unless she could've worn her kids as jewelry, huh Callie?"

Trevor couldn't have known it, but his words cut too close to the bone—that was how my mother regarded me. She'd been more concerned about her career than her lipstick, but the result was basically the same.

I swallowed hard before answering. "I guess so, Trevor," I uttered, shooting a pleading look at Claudio. With memories of my mom flanking both sides of this play, I needed him to divert the conversation before I publicly lost my shit.

Claudio didn't disappoint. "Very astute of you, Trevor," he began gently. "Now that our theatrical experience is complete, let us go have a drink."

Yeah, that's a good idea," Trevor replied with relief. "I think we all need one, Callie included."

With the gnawing in my gut, all I wanted was some space and a hot bath. "Gentlemen, go on without me. I'm tired," I announced. "I'm done for the night. I'll get myself a cab."

"But I thought you were... *passer la nuit avec moi*?" Jean-Francois objected.

"You'll just have to sleep alone tonight," I shot. Seriously, I was in no mood. And anyway, hadn't he practically called an end to our evening smack in the middle of our microtheater night?

"Callie, are you feeling okay?" Trevor asked, genuinely concerned.

"I'm okay, thanks. Just tired, alright?" As his frown deepened, I smiled slightly in reassurance. "Have fun with the guys, and I'll see you for first breakfast. Just you and me, I promise."

His face eased, his eyes lit up. "Okay, Callie, first breakfast tomorrow." Trevor really did love our alone-time breakfasts.

"I understand, Kauhlie," Claudio began with a sincere empathy. "Come, I will call you a taxi. We will all get together for drinks on another night."

CHAPTER 18

WHEN EVERYTHING
WAS DYING

The day was hot. Not just Madrid-hot, but hot-hot; the type of heat that envelops you like an unwelcome blanket, that sears the streets so intensely you can smell the asphalt. An insidious, unrelenting heat—a preview, perhaps, of the third circle of Hell. All of Madrid seemed either listlessly lazy or contemptuously cranky... or, for some, both at once. Trevor had said this probably would be the hottest day of the year, and for once I didn't disagree with him.

With the sun high overhead and the heat sticking to my skin, I called it quits after a light lunch—a salad accompanied by plain, old-fashioned ice water. It was too hot to eat anything but rabbit food, and too hot to eat was generally my cue to exit. At that point, I needed air conditioning, and fast. Trevor said he wouldn't mind a cool shower himself, so we'd treated ourselves to a cab back to our hotels before parting ways for the afternoon.

One thing about hotels in Madrid—and, I'm told, in Europe generally—is that air conditioning in rooms isn't a guarantee. I'd rented a small window unit once the spring's warmth started creeping toward summer-y hot, but it didn't provide what I'd call an arctic experience. That wouldn't do for a day like today: what I needed was real relief, so I'd made my way to the guest lounge just off the lobby. The hotel's entire first floor had modern, monster air conditioning. I bet that's how they sucked in unsuspecting summer tourists.

After stopping at the bar for a frosty cocktail, I found a comfy chair right under a vent. I'd never noticed before, but my hotel offered a surprising array of magazines, many of which were in English. I snatched up a copy of *The New Yorker*—backdated four months—and commenced my cooling off. I especially enjoyed the jet of icy air dancing over my sandaled toes.

Midway through my second article, my phone rang. Damn. I should've left it in my room. I pulled it out of my pocket reluctantly and glimpsed at the caller ID. This wasn't a call I could ignore, and it was from the last person I expected. I sighed and hit, "Accept."

"Dad?!" I forced some brightness into my voice, even though I had no idea why my father was calling me. Outside of the holidays, we usually only spoke when there was big news.

"Hello, Callie, how are you?"

"It's been a while, Dad. Is everything ok?"

"Of course, of course, everything is fine. I'm busy, as usual. Very, very, busy!" He launched into a soliloquy about the happenings at his firm—my dad could bore anyone to death with earnings-report summaries and financial-statement analyses. As a corporate lawyer, financial analysis was something I was damn good at—my math skills were one of the reasons I'd advanced so quickly—and I did enjoy working with numbers. A love of financial statements was among the few things my father and I had in common, yet he managed to suck all the fun out of it.

"That must be very exciting, Dad. I'm glad you're doing so well. Keep this up and maybe you'll finally make VP." The last part was a bit of a dirty shot on my part; my father had been trying to make vice-president for twenty years and we both knew it.

An awkward pause settled between us, and I knew he was trying (somewhat desperately) to think of a new topic. I wasn't about to help him—I mean, how hard was it to talk to your firstborn daughter?

"How are things in… wait… Spain? It's Spain, right?"

"Yeah. I've been here for a while now."

"My little girl's in Spain. All grown up, a world traveler!"

"I like it here. Different culture. Different way of life. If I didn't have my new position starting in August, I might not come home." I didn't know if all the words coming out of my mouth were true or not, but I couldn't bear another awkward silence between us. Thankfully, Dad didn't notice when I choked on the word *home*. Where was "home" for me these days?

He changed the subject. "Callie, I called to wish you a happy birthday! You're another year older today." From his tone, he was clearly expecting a father of the year award for remembering.

"Dad… my birthday was… *yesterday*."

"No, it wasn't. It's today."

"I think I know when my own birthday is, Dad…" I hadn't told anyone in our group about my birthday, and I thought I'd blissfully escaped any mention of it this year. I hadn't celebrated since I'd turned thirty. That night should've been a high moment in my life—goodbye twenties, hello womanhood—but my party had been a major disappointment. I'd rented out the back room at my favorite watering hole, but most of my friends had been too busy to make it, so my celebration was attended only by acquaintances looking for an excuse to drink. That was when I'd sworn off birthdays for good.

"No, your mother's birthday was yesterday. Your birthday is one day after hers."

"No," I muttered, trying to keep my voice from trembling, "it's the other way around. Mom's birthday is the day after mine."

"Wait now. Let me check." I heard him fumbling through the pages of his daily planner. Yes, my father the Luddite still used a pen-and-paper planner. More than one assistant had quit over this.

"Ah, here it is. Oh, yes... I'll be damned... Your birthday was yesterday."

"Right," I uttered through clenched teeth of frustration. My birthday had been on the same day for over thirty years now; he'd had better than three decades to catch on. "Dad, I know you meant... but... I... you..." I pulled myself together and stopped blithering like an idiot. "I mean, you used to forget when I was a kid—and sometimes Mom's too."

"Maybe that *is* right," he conceded, no hint of apology in his tone. "She used to get so mad when I'd forget your birthday... and then I'd rush out and get her a present for the next day. Can't say I care so much about her birthday anymore, though."

"No, not really, I guess." Hell, not even my mom cared about her birthday anymore. She'd opened a craft store a while back, and the riveting, dog-eat-dog competition between local arts and crafts vendors now consumed her every waking moment.

"Well, anyway, happy birthday!"

"Thanks for trying, Dad. You'll get it right next year."

"I will. Callie, I'll do my best. But right now, I have to go. Marian and I have the day planned."

"Right. Marian." Just the sound of my stepmother's name grated on me. I generally tried to be civil for the sake of... well, I guess, civility itself... but I'd never liked the woman. She didn't particularly care for me either, so that worked out nicely.

"We're driving up to visit Gretchen. She's staying on campus this summer." Gretchen was my half-sister, the older of the two daughters my father and Marian had together. "Gotta go, Callie."

"Dad?"

He paused before answering. A long pause.

"Yes?" he finally uttered. The word was hard. "What is it?"

"Nothing," I retreated. I didn't really know what I wanted to say, anyway.

"Happy birthday again."

"Yes, thanks."

"Let me know when you get back Stateside. Bye, Callie."

"Goodbye, Dad."

⁓

I was an intended pregnancy. I was not an accident, a surprise, or an afterthought—that much I knew for sure. I knew this not because my parents filled my childhood with joy and love, but because my mother and father planned everything. The concept of spontaneity was alien to them. Still is.

Or maybe I should clarify: my parents wanted their *idea* of a child. When it came to *having* a child—a living, breathing child with needs and wants and dreams—things got murkier. Enter Callie McGraw, an actual child, an in-living-color kid to nurture and raise. An actual human being, and far more real than what my parents envisioned.

When I was younger, I used to imagine my parents, pre-prenatal, sitting at our kitchen table, a yellow pad with a line drawn down the middle in front of them. A "Kids: Pros and Cons" sheet. I could see them carefully writing each objective advantage and disadvantage in the appropriate column. Occasionally something subjective would creep in. "It might be fun," or, "We should try it."—much like they were contemplating an exotic vacation. Every reason they listed was less about what they might gain and more about what they'd miss out on. Not one single reason was about *me*, the child they would have.

I was a precocious kid, partly because I was smart, but largely because I was a voracious reader whose parents didn't care about "age-appropriate material." Any time I wanted to know something I knew I could find the answer in the library. With all that reading, by the time I was approaching middle school, I'd figured something out—or thought I had. It occurred to me that my mom and dad might've had another "pro kids" motive: namely, having a baby to save their marriage. The togetherness, the teamwork, the "We're all in the same boat," mentality. The problem was, my parents' marriage was like a dinghy with a slow leak, and I was the anvil they threw on board.

The tension in our house was always present. Not knowing any differently, I'd thought this was normal. Much of the time, good ol' Mom and Dad fought about me: if I forgot my homework or got kept after school, whose fault was it? Who was going to shuttle me to this activity or that one? Who taught me to eat like this, or dress like that? Who was being the better parent?

Growing up in this tempest, I thought I was the cause of their problems. I truly believed that for a while, until I met a few of my friends' parents who got along—and didn't weaponize their children. I was nine or ten by the time I realized my parents fought long before I came on the scene. Of course, just because my nine-year-old brain worked out the truth didn't mean I believed it deep down, where it counted. Deep down, if I'm honest, a tiny part of me *still* believes it.

The divorce should've solved a bunch of problems, yet my parents continued fighting—went out of their way, I swear, to keep fighting. And when they weren't fighting, they were hoarding grenades. As a pubescent kid with a rebellious streak, I was both the main grenade and an easy target for their anger.

The night I gave up on them remains my most vivid childhood memory. I was in eighth grade. It was late fall—when everything is dying. My father hadn't moved out yet, but I'm pretty sure they'd filed preliminary divorce papers. For dinner that evening, my mom had made a pot roast—overdone and leathery. There was no love in that pot roast, no love at that table.

Like most nights, we ate in near silence. Any attempt at conversation only underscored how far apart we all were, and we'd learned it was better to keep communication to an absolute minimum. I don't know why we were still eating together at that point; each meal became yet another thwarted bonding experience, one that only separated us further.

After the awkward tedium of loading the dishwasher with my mom, I retreated to my room and picked up my copy of *The Sun Also Rises*. I was only on my second or third reading back then, the pages not yet dog-eared and worn. I'd just gotten to the part where Jake Barnes and Bill Gorton were fishing their cares away in Spain's serene Burguete region. I'd never been fishing myself, but in that moment, I would've given everything I owned to be in Basque country with a rod and reel. Anything to get away.

The door to my parents' bedroom slammed. From the sharpness of the impact, I could tell it was my father who'd done the slamming this time. Not that closing the damn thing mattered. The doors in our house were cheap and thin—more symbolic barriers than real ones.

The yelling followed, like usual. Tonight's fight started with not caring. He didn't care about her feelings. She didn't care about his needs. He never did care. She never cared, either. He'd never made anything of himself. She'd undermined him at every turn. Around and around they went, hurling accusations.

I put my headphones on to drown them out, only to find the batteries in my Walkman were dead; I couldn't wade back into the Spanish countryside's cool waters. Their battle seemed that much more explosive because we'd just turned on the heat for the season, and our air ducts were open. I heard everything, as if there were no secrets in our house. Yet there was one secret I hadn't known—at least not until that night.

"You never supported my career!" she accused.

"That's not true! I always said you could do whatever you wanted!"

"How could I? Your promise was hollow! What was I supposed to do?"

"My promises are never hollow! You never did anything with your career. You could've, but you didn't. That's not my fault!"

"It *is* your fault. You went off to work each day, but I was stuck in this house for six full years! Do you know what six years off does to a woman's career?"

A pause, a cavernous pause. That's how I knew what was coming would be worse than the shouting.

My mother's voice became low and cruel—her doomsday voice. "You know I never wanted children," she hissed, her tone dripping with regret. The way she said *children* was antiseptic, frigid. I was "the children." Me. I was the only one. The unwanted one.

My father objected viciously. "We discussed it! We made that decision together!"

"You *made* me do it!" she shouted. "You talked me into it... and then everything changed. Everything!" Another pause. I held my breath. Her voice became low again. "If it weren't for that—for having children—we probably could've worked things out. I think we would've been fine."

I waited for my dad's rebuttal. I waited for him to launch a verbal assault to top all verbal assaults. To remind her of the truth. To correct her. To accuse her of twisting reality. To defend me, his only daughter. I sat there in suspended animation, waiting for my dad to set her straight.

I'm still waiting. Because the words that came from my father's mouth that night were not the words any daughter should hear.

His defeated voice wafted through the vent. "I know." I could practically see him shrinking in concession. "I know."

A chill ran down my spine, my skin contracted. Goosebumps rose on my arms, the meaning of his two words sinking in. My father had surrendered the battlefield—it was done and agreed. They would've been "fine" if not for me. He didn't fight her, not even out of paternal instinct.

Tears rolled down my cheeks and splattered onto my precious novel. Ink from the type mixed with my heartbreak and began snaking in a salty river to the bottom of the page. I rolled over and covered my face with my book. *The Sun Also Rises*, my only protection, my only escape.

That was the night I'd decided: if they didn't want me, I didn't want them. I wasn't dumb enough to run away—I knew what could happen to those kids—but I would show them, anyhow. I'd never be like them, never have kids. Hell, I'd never even get married. I'd work my ass off in high school, get myself a college scholarship, and I'd never ask them for a damn thing. I would push myself until I achieved the career my mom never had, and I'd couple it with the success my father never attained. I'd become a living reminder of their failures—all of them. At thirteen, I vowed this to myself.

And I'd kept that vow. I'd had a setback here or there, sure, but I never failed myself. Because, whether my parents liked it or not, I was—and am—Callie McGraw.

Chapter 19

Claiming My Strong

Yes, Callie, as I've told you, I know that book well enough," Jean-Francois answered with his usual know-it-all swagger. "For an American writer, it is a nice novel. But what I have not told you is this: your beloved book is a lie."

I very nearly shot up from my seat, right in the middle of lunch. "A lie?" I hissed. I would have none of this. Cranky and especially difficult all afternoon, Jean-Francois had been skating on thin ice: now the first cracks rent through my patience. Gearing myself up for a full defense, I repeated, "My book is a lie?!"

"Oh, man; oh, brother," Trevor groaned anxiously. He was the one who'd brought *The Sun Also Rises* up—I'd only told Jean-Francois a little about my love for it—so whatever came next was arguably his doing. I launched a look at my traveling companion telling him as much.

"A lie, yes," Jean-Francois continued coolly. "The characters were not carefree as you say, but rather careless." His waggling eyebrows screamed, "Prove me wrong, if you can." I was sick to death of arguing with those damn eyebrows.

He continued after a bite of his black-truffle omelet. "They ate and drank and lusted themselves into blindness… so pathetically concerned with themselves, like so many Americans. So drunk they did not see what was coming, and they were fools for it." He leaned back in his chair, as if literally resting on his laurels. What laurels he thought he'd won, I wasn't sure.

"Fools?!" I snapped. "Are you talking about the novel? Or are all Americans pathetic fools to you, Jean-Francois?" This time I did jump up from my chair, catching the attention of several patrons and causing a ripple through the café. "Why are you trashing my country? Why are you trashing the *one* book that changed my life?"

Before he could answer—and well before I could jump down his throat for his answer—Claudio spoke up. "Perhaps what our friend means to say is that Europe was only a playground for the characters. Running from World War I… they never thought to look *forward*. Remember, the war here in Spain was only ten years away, with the Second World War coming on its heels."

Jean-Francois' finger shot into the air. "Yes—our friend here has explained it well. But it wasn't only the characters, it was the author as well. An American hiding from himself in Europe." He waved dismissively. "Hemingway and his 'artist' friends confused valiance with drowning their sorrows in wine."

I'd grown used to—and bored with—shooting down Jean-Francois' constant criticisms, but this was beyond the pale. "That's not true!" I cried. "Hemingway survived the horrors of the first world war! You might need wine, too, if you'd lived through that! Hell, you couldn't even sit through 'The Trench' without wanting a drink!"

I couldn't be sure, but I thought I saw a small smile flash across Claudio's face. He alone knew about my Hemingway calls, and his subversive delight bolstered me as I continued. "That war stole the future of a generation. A lost generation! That's what Hemingway lived, that's what he wrote!"

"Your Hemingway was a reporter, *chérie*. He should've known better.

The signs of more war on the horizon were clear to the trained eye—to a *sober* eye. You're smart enough, you should know this."

"I'm smart *enough*?" I could run intellectual circles around this man, and we both knew it—in fact, that was the source of the underlying tension in our relationship. I clutched my glass tightly, willing myself not to throw my wine in Jean-Francois' face.

Claudio reached for the last pork kabob and overturned his water in the process. The mess was no accident, I was sure of it—I'd never once seen him spill anything. Annoyance prickled through me, but the disruption did diffuse my impending tempest.

"It's not personal, Callie," Jean-Francois remarked casually as he finished mopping up his side of the table. "The book was a lie, and that's all there is to it, *mon cher*." He shrugged his shoulders, as if leveling the temple that was my book was no big deal.

"The novel is true and pure, a portrait of a moment! Hemingway couldn't see into the future any more than you can!" My voice was much too loud now, the patrons around us pretending not to listen. "The novel changed my life! Why can't you understand that?"

He crossed his arms defiantly. "Hemingway was a fraud. Above all else, his novel reflects his fraud. You should read our French writers, they are much more authentic."

Trevor's lips moved as if he were about to say something, but then his eyes took over. They shifted nervously between Jean-Francois and me—finally landing on me. Without a word, but with unmistakable dread on his face, he got up and scurried away. He didn't abandon me completely, though; he huddled by the pastry display-case, pretending to choose a dessert. In reality, he was preparing to duck for cover when I launched my grenade.

If Jean-Francois were truly a smart man, he would've followed Trevor. But he wasn't. "Hemingway deluded himself," he continued. "All his characters did—all he did—was run around Europe licking their wounds. Tell me one thing your beloved characters did, Callie. One *real* thing."

"They reconciled their pasts!" I countered. "World War I stole their futures. They had to face that… and eventually they did. They needed time to process their trauma!"

"'Processing trauma,' is so self-indulgent, so very shallow," he griped. "The rest of us merely—as you Americans say—suck it up and go on with our lives." He stared at me with cold eyes. "Hemingway wrote a shallow book for a shallow audience." He waved dismissively, as if he hadn't taken a direct stab at me.

An icy silence filled the table. I took a deep breath to steel myself. A waiter cowered in the corner, unsure if he should intervene. The breadstick in my hand crumbled under the force of my clenching fist.

"The book is not shallow! Hemingway was not shallow! I am *not* shallow! Stop trying to steal my strong!"

"Steal your strong?" Clearly offended but also confused, Jean-Francois turned to Claudio practically begging for help. Claudio, in a masterstroke of mimicry, merely wiggled his eyebrows and shrugged.

I erupted. "*The Sun Also Rises* is my strong! A big part of my strong! And just because you don't understand it doesn't mean you get to take it from me!"

"This is true," agreed Claudio, not hiding his irritation any longer yet maintaining his calm. "My friend, you are not giving due consideration to Kauhlie's interpretation, or to how deeply she has connected to this work. Disagreement and disrespect are not one and the same."

A sliver of me appreciated Claudio's sticking up for me and trying to keep the peace, but the rest of me was *done* with peace now. Done with a lot of things, in fact. I slammed my palms on the table, shouting at the top of my lungs. "You know what? Jean-Francois, you need to leave! *Stay* away from me! You're nothing but a faux…" My voice caught in my throat—I was so furious I couldn't think a fitting bon mot. "Faux… intellectual!" Not my most brilliant insult ever, but it got the job done.

"'Faux' does not describe me, Callie, I am being truthful. Unlike your Hemingway, who—"

Cutting him off, I sprung from my chair again and grabbed his carafe of French wine. "I'm sick of your criticisms!" I slammed the decanter down so hard burgundy droplets leaped onto the tablecloth. "I'm sick of your *arrogance*." I pronounced the word in French, infusing contempt into all three syllables. "I'm sick of your superiority." I stuck my nose in the air like the snootiest of snobs. "But most of all, I'm sick of *you*!

With that, I spun around and stormed toward the door. I was half-way across the café before I realized Jean-Francois was supposed to do the leaving, not me. Ah well, Callie, screw it. Who says I have to be perfect?

With the entire café now staring, I resolved to make this a truly dramatic exit. Jean-Francois shouted in a stream of French—including a few expletives—that I was too incensed to translate. I let him blither on like the fool he was as I flung the door open, whipping my napkin into the air. "Go back to Paris!" I cried, "No man on Earth steals my strong!"

That should have been that. Things should have ended on my awesome line, but they didn't. Jean-Francois needed to have the last word—like always. Jumping up from his chair, he cried, "Stealing your strong? Such women's nonsense! Bah!"

I could not let that man have the last word. I could not let that man have *that* last word. Women's nonsense? Just who did he think he was? I didn't have a comeback ready, though, so I bought myself a second to think.

"Jean-Francois?"

"*Oui?*"

I still had nothing. What I needed now was a screenwriter, someone to craft a scathing riposte. But screenwriters were in short supply in this café, so I spat out the only thing that came to mind.

"*Au revoir!*" My words dripped with scorn. I gave Jean-Francois a mock farewell salute, dismissing him before I thundered through the door.

I don't know why I said, "*Au revoir.*" I don't know why I mock-saluted him. I doubt either had the intended effect. As I stormed back to my hotel,

I thought of a dozen stronger comebacks and more-fitting gestures—a few of which would've even been suitable for polite company if executed well. That ate at me, but at least I'd foiled Jean-Francois' last word. That was a win for this woman and her "nonsense." A win for Callie McGraw.

⌘

I curled up on my bed, equal parts pissed at Jean-Francois and relieved that I'd severed myself from him. Asshole. On the other hand, I'd just broken up with a man because of a book. Who does that?

"No," I told myself, "you didn't break up with him because of a book. You broke up with him because he's an ass." I found my own voice reassuring, despite the undeniable fact that I was sitting alone in a hotel room talking to myself. "No one steals your strong, Callie."

The kicker was that I'd known Jean-Francois was a jerk, but I'd willfully ignored that fact, pretty much in its entirety. Under the guise of refinement and urbanity, he'd effaced me—or tried to. He didn't succeed, of course, but it took effort to be around him. Sure, I'd shot him down again and again, but why had I been with a guy who needed shooting down in the first place?

If I were being brutally honest with myself, I knew the answer to that question. After Claudio, I hadn't wanted to be alone. The emptiness in my chest and the sourness in my stomach had been entirely, unnervingly new, and I'd hated it. I'd never given a fig about being alone before, but I'd also never faced a void inside like that one. Claudio had made me happy, profoundly happy, and maybe that was the scariest thing of all. Yet at the same time, I didn't want him back, didn't trust in him—or in 'us'—deeply enough to want him back.

A too-easy remedy was finding someone else, or letting someone else find me. When we'd met, Jean-Francois had just been some guy in a plaza, no different than a thousand others who'd hit on me over the years. But with him, I'd let it happen. I'd *wanted* it to happen. I'd latched onto him as my life-raft—anything to keep me afloat. In those terms, I guess any guy, even one whose eyebrows waggled as much as his tongue, would've sated the pain I'd been hiding inside. Was still hiding inside.

Crap. Had I just had my first rebound relationship? Jesus, Callie, how juvenile.

My head was spinning—or maybe the room was spinning, and I was along for the ride. Either way, I wanted to tune out everything. Going back to basics seemed the only thing to do, so I pulled *The Sun Also Rises* out of my nightstand. Yet beginning at the beginning seemed *too* basic, so I closed my eyes and thumbed my way to a random page.

The copy I'd brought to Spain was my original, the one I'd bought in middle school. Ragged and worn and with a delicious old-book smell, its pages were well-browned, and the back cover was held on with several applications of lovingly placed book tape. I revered this copy, I'd almost never removed it from its shadow box in my old living room. I hadn't wanted to put it in storage, and it seemed only fitting to bring my holy-grail-of-copies with me on my Spanish quest.

At any given time, I also owned at least two other copies; one was a cheap paperback I could stand to lose—over the years, I'd peppered the coffee houses, parks, and subways of New York City with abandoned books. The remaining copy was of slightly better quality; I used that one for everyday reading. I generally shuttled it between home and office, because, honestly, I didn't have all that much of a life in New York.

I took my time letting my fingers pick their spot, trusting that my hands knew what my soul needed. My eyes fell on the page and straight into the festival of San Fermín. In the first moments of the revelry, when the streets still felt fresh and clean, when the throngs were still gathering. When anything felt possible.

My eyes caressed the lines. After Claudio, I'd wanted to feel as if I were at the beginning too—like anything was possible—but Jean-Francois had never made me feel that way. Not really, not in any way that counted. Severing myself from him was more of a beginning than he'd ever been capable of offering me.

I fell into the scene. Spanish streets in the summer sunlight. Dancers dancing, fifers fifing. Wild drumming as the procession began. Lady Brett Ashley in a wreath of garlic cloves. Jake Barnes on the hunt for wine-skins. I forgot about Claudio and Jean-Francois and my rebound relationship. I forgot about my travels and my future job. I forgot about everything and simply lost myself in reading. No one would take this book from me, not ever.

My phone rang. Jean-Francois had interrupted my reading several times, and I'd responded to each of his calls with a firm and satisfying press of the "Decline" button. But this time the caller ID didn't display his number—all that showed on the screen was "Madrid." Because Jean-Francois was too much of a snob to use a public phone, I figured Trevor was trying to reach me. He'd let his phone run out of charge more times than I could count.

"Trevor, I'm okay, real—" I began.

"—Thank you for defending my novel, Callie," came the now-familiar voice, "but it wasn't necessary. The test of time is my ally."

"You heard that?" I replied, taken aback. "You heard him tearing you down?"

"Of course I heard. I am very close to you."

"You're here in Madrid?" I asked, remembering the caller ID. "You told me to embrace you on the streets of Madrid. But where are you?"

"You must find me, Callie."

"I'm *trying*," I said a little defensively. "But I think I... I... got distracted." I kept the angst out of my voice as best I could.

"Perhaps your French lover was a necessary detour. A detour that is now complete."

"Yes, agreed." I fell silent. Was Ernest Hemingway really giving me relationship advice? And was this the best use of his from-beyond-the-grave counsel?

I steered the call back on track. "I've been in Madrid for eons, without a single sign of you."

"You found *el duende*, Callie. *El duende* is my love of the Spanish people."

"Okay, but that was when I first arrived in this city!"

"You found your strong, Callie. Very well done."

"That wasn't you, that was Señora Fernandez! I don't—" The memory of the old woman's voice stopped me in mid-sentence. "*My husband, he made friends with the American author.*"

Hemingway chuckled softly, as if he were amused by his own well-guarded secrets. "She was always so kind to me, Callie. You've done well in taking her advice to heart."

"You mean you sent—"

"—The Fernandezes loved me, as I loved them."

I reeled. "You're not playing fair! You can't disguise your clues!" Literary master or no, my life wasn't a plotline to be toyed with.

"I have left many clues for you, Callie, but you've been… *distracted,* as you said. I left one for you in *Guernica.*"

"In Guernica? You told me Madrid. I dropped everything and came to *Madrid.*"

"I left it with my friend Picasso."

I nearly dropped the phone. The bull. The hidden bull.

"And I left a clue for you at the fiesta."

The gears of my brain twisted, making the connection. "The matador? The one on trial in the play?"

"Of course. Nobody ever lives their life all the way up except bull-fighters, Callie."

"That's Jake's line! He said it in chapter two. Everyone knows that!"

"No, not everyone, Callie." He chuckled again, a kind laugh. "But Jake was right. Nobody ever lives their life all the way up except bull-fighters.

Trying to pull the pieces together, I remembered the flamenco club, named for the matador's deadly strike. "You want me to go back to Estocada? To where I found *el duende?*"

"No, Callie, don't look back. Never look back. But you must find me. You have less than three months left, and I'm still waiting for you."

CHAPTER 20

A CANADIAN IN MADRID

"Why a hotel bar?" asked Trevor. He eyed me up and down, something he didn't normally do. Hey, I looked good, and I knew it.

"Bars in big hotels have such an elegance."

Trevor shook his head incredulously. "Is that why you're so dressed up?"

"Yeah, because we need some of that elegance in our lives. Run back to your room and put on a nice shirt and jacket. Something with a little style."

"Do I have to?" he asked, sounding like an eight-year-old.

"Yes, you have to. Now be quick about it."

"But what's the difference?" Trevor persisted. "Isn't that the same thing we always do, just in a glitzy location? Why can't we go to one of our normal places?"

"Because we always go to those places!" I countered. "Because we need to do something different. Because I dressed up tonight. And most of all, Trevor, because I want to!"

He relented. "Okay, Callie, if it will make you happy." He began trudging away across the street, back to his hotel. I didn't think throwing on a jacket was a big deal, but apparently I'd underestimated Trevor's recalcitrant inner child.

"And Trevor, those sneakers are a catastrophe," I called after him, pointing to his more-than-well-worn Chucks. "I know you have a pair of decent shoes. You wore them to Susan and Jane's. Grab those."

He smiled goofily, relieved that I'd given him specific instructions. He could now let his general anxiety rest for a moment, knowing that all he had to do was follow directions.

I still didn't know what to make of Hemingway's last call, but I did know what Jake Barnes would do if he were in a celebratory post-breakup mode like me: dress himself to the nines and paint the town red. He'd find the lushest, poshest bar in town and dance and flirt and drink until the summer night swirled with redemption. So why couldn't I?

There were a couple of high-end hotels in Madrid, and I picked the one with the fanciest, most-sprawling lounge. Located in the Cortés Quarter, it was only a mile or so away—although we would need to take a cab so my makeup wouldn't melt as we walked. I texted Claudio with the address, grateful that I didn't need to give him dressing-up directions too. He was always dressed well.

Twenty minutes later, Trevor reappeared looking more handsome than I'd ever seen. He'd even brushed his beard, which only usually happened once a week (at best). Ten minutes after that, the two of us met Claudio outside the lounge.

"Kauhlie, you look wonderful tonight," Claudio said, greeting us with literal open arms. It wasn't just his usual politeness, either. Behind his eyes, I could see a glimmer of attraction, like the way he used to look at me when we were together. I didn't mind that one bit, but I wasn't going to seize on it either.

"And Trevor, I must say you do clean up nicely," Claudio continued. "But you must loosen up. This is much too many buttons—you cannot live your life if you cannot breathe!" He reached over and undid the button on Trevor's collar along with the two below it. He grumbled but didn't object otherwise, although he did refasten the lowermost button as soon as Claudio turned away. Trevor wasn't brave enough for a three-button peepshow.

We strode into the lounge and directly up to the bar. The grand, columned space—a story and a half high—was teeming with activity. The crystal chandelier cast rainbow-ribbons of light onto the dance-floor, and most everyone had dressed for the occasion. This wasn't just a lounge, it was practically a ballroom.

With our drinks secure and our tab open, we slid through the crowd and slipped into one of the last unoccupied leather-and-velvet booths. A placard on the stage announced that the house band would begin their set at midnight.

"You were right, Callie, this place is really something. We should've done this a long time ago."

"I will admit it is a nice change of pace," Claudio agreed.

"See, I told you. There's a certain splendor to a hotel bar. A lavishness." I raised my glass, and my two friends clinked in. Claudio smiled; I turned away from him. Without Jean-Francois as my shield, his smile was dangerous.

Trevor had just returned from the bar with a plate for the table when a voice cut through the hum around us and landed smack in our tapas. "Oh my God, is that English?!"

I scanned the room and found the owner of the voice, a tall blonde woman who was rapidly approaching us. She sliced through the groups of mingling patrons with a confident precision. "You're from the States, aren't you?" she asked, holding her oversized glass of wine forward. It reached us before the rest of her did.

"We are," Trevor muttered through a mouthful of olives. Gross. Was he ever going to stop talking with his mouth full?

"I thought so! I could see it across the room, and when I heard you talking, that cinched it."

"Great detective work, lady," I said baldly. I'd been enjoying having just the three of us together, and I resented her for busting in uninvited. Or maybe I resented her for her legs, which went on for miles.

"Oh, I'm sorry. I'm Stephanie. I could tell you were from the States because I'm Canadian!" For some reason, she waved her glass in a wide circle as she spoke.

"You're an awfully loud Canadian," I remarked. Every Canadian I'd ever met had been friendly, unassuming, and—most of all—quiet.

"Honey, we all have to break out of our mold sometime!" I couldn't disagree with that, even if it came through a loudspeaker. In a sense, wasn't I breaking out of my own mold by coming to Spain?

"It is my pleasure to meet you," Claudio said, friendly and polite as always. "I am Claudio, and this is Callie and Trevor. We are a trio of good friends." I balked. A "trio of good friends?" Did he just go out of his way to mention he was single?

"You're not from the States, though." Stephanie poked Claudio's chest with the index finger of her wine-free hand. "You're Spanish, aren't you?"

"Yes, I am one hundred percent Spanish once again," he responded proudly.

"Once again?" She smiled at Claudio, too widely for my liking.

"It is a long story," he replied. "I was born in Madrid, and I am now back in Madrid." Now Claudio was the one smiling too broadly for my liking.

"Claudio has lived all over Europe." I jumped in. I put my arm through his. "Trevor and I are Americans." I put my other arm through Trevor's arm. A united front.

"Americans? Honey, we're all Americans. We're all from North America—all of us from the US *and* Canada. Everyone in the US says, 'American this' and 'American that'—but we're Americans too. Your country is funny that way." Her wine-hand moved too abruptly, causing her beverage to slosh violently in her glass. My eyes widened in anticipation of the impending disaster, but her wine splashed safely back down into its home without a single drop spilled.

"What brings you to Madrid?" Claudio asked, still smiling too much. Geez, one leggy blonde and the man went to pieces. Damn playboy.

"I work in advertising, and my company sent me here."

"Advertising? That's cool," Trevor said, truly impressed.

For the first time, Stephanie fully acknowledged Trevor's existence. "It is… isn't it?" She turned back to me and Claudio. "I'm in the middle of an eight-month stint. A client is rolling out a product globally, and I'm focusing on Spain's market. I'm hoping they'll extend my stay— the falls in Chicago are so cold. Especially downtown by the lake, you know?" She motioned around the lounge as if a cold front were hiding somewhere in the room.

"I thought you were Canadian?" Trevor asked, his eyes following Stephanie's hand. She'd continued gesticulating even though her mouth had stopped talking.

"Born and bred!" she boomed. "But there's not what you'd call a ton of advertising opportunities in Winnipeg. And I'm the best at what I do, so when I hit that ceiling at home, I jumped into the major leagues."

"No use being a big fish in a small pond," I said. Between her volume and her gestures, it was hard to picture Stephanie in a small anything but, hey, I could respect her drive. When it came time to choose between going big and staying home, she went big. And from the looks of her manicure alone, she was doing damn well for herself.

We took turns telling Stephanie how we each landed in Madrid before the conversation began moving in its own direction. Stephanie drove that movement, because the woman could *talk*. Maybe she could've talked without dripping all over Claudio, but there was no denying she was super smart and *super* funny.

"Another round, and this one's on me!" Stephanie shouted as she waved for the waiter—it was late now, the band was warming up, and table service had started. The waiter sprung to her aid. She said something in Spanish, then moments later more cocktails showed up. Other than Claudio, I'd never seen anyone get served so fast. Stephanie was used to getting her way, that much was apparent.

"I switched to gin and tonics to keep up with you two," she began before turning to Trevor. "But honey, I am not sure what you're drinking, so I took a guess. I hope you like it."

Trevor took a long sip. "It's delicious! And it's blue!" Stephanie laughed loudly. I'm not sure why, but her laugh made Trevor smile. It was a blue smile from the blue drink.

From there, and despite our being in a classy lounge where everyone else knew how to behave, we began trading bar stories. Stephanie might've had the look of a model, but already I could tell she was a bar-stories type of woman.

Bar stories are different from regular stories. Bar stories—good bar stories—are devoid of deep meaning. Deep meaning is eschewed because it mixes with the alcohol and brings everyone down. Also, bar stories can't be too long or complicated. Besotted audiences often can't follow complexity, and they're prone to interrupting the storyteller—everyone involved needs to be able to pick the thread back up easily. Acoustics need consideration, too: in a packed bar, it's hard to hear every word, so folks need to be able to fill in some stuff on their own. More importantly, bar stories need a seed of truth, but not too much truth. Too much truth can also mix badly with the alcohol and kill a good buzz. Lastly, a good bar story comes with an uproarious punchline, one that invites every listener to throw their head back and laugh loud, drunken laughs. In sum, good bar stories must be compact and go down easily, just like a well-mixed cocktail, but still have a kick to them, too.

"...and that's what the monkey said!" I finished. Everyone roared. Stephanie's volume brought a new meaning to the word *roar*.

Claudio's story was even better. He spoke with more gusto than usual, intentionally racing toward the punchline. "...Wait, that's not a saxophone!" More laughter. That one *was* funny.

Not to be outdone, I saved my best for last, exaggerating a tale about my Canadian friend as wildly as I dared. "So I said, 'That sounds great.' And he replied…" I paused for comic effect. "'…Callie, you're so delicious… I want to douse you in maple syrup and spank you with a hockey stick!'"

My audience of three laughed until they hit the ceiling, and I laughed at their laughing. Mirthful tears started rolling from our eyes—from all eight of our eyes. Callie McGraw, entertainer extraordinaire.

Stephanie was drying her tears when Trevor, almost in mid laugh, abruptly frowned. "Wait, Callie. Really?" he asked. "That's sort of mean." He'd wiped the blue of Stephanie's mystery cocktail from his lips but, as the light caught his teeth, I could swear they had a bluish tint.

I couldn't help myself. I grabbed his face in both my hands, gave him a, "Were you born yesterday?" look, and kissed him square on the mouth. Stunned, Trevor turned a shade of pink previously unknown to humankind.

This, of course, started another round of laughter to the ceiling. Trevor stuttered and faltered and muttered, but not one single real word came out. The rest of us screaked again and again, holding back riotous tears. Soon even Trevor joined in: the goofiest, dorkiest smile took over his face as he tittered (yes, tittered) along with our laughter.

Stephanie actually doubled over in her chair. "Oh, my God, Callie. You're so hilarious!" she cried, finally coming up for air. When she slapped me on the back a little too hard, I took it as a badge of honor. I was the undefeated Bar Stories Queen for the night.

I leaned back in the booth and into the inevitable post-uproar lull. With the lounge still buzzing around us, a comfortable semi-silence spread across our table. Somewhere during the evening, Stephanie had won me over; I didn't just like her, I already thought of her as a friend. I didn't even mind her hanging all over Claudio. I mean, I couldn't really blame the woman for that—Claudio was easy on the eyes, no matter who was doing the looking.

"Okay, guys," I started once I'd had enough silence, "it's time for one more toast."

"Okay, Kauhlie, but what should we toast to this time?

I smirked. I knew exactly what to toast to… and I'd prove a point to Claudio in the process. Sometimes I loved my lawyer's brain. I loved it even more when a little alcohol was greasing its gears.

"To paraphrase a very good book…" I began.

"Oh, no," laughed Trevor, "we're doomed now."

"To paraphrase a very good book…" I repeated, raising my glass in Stephanie's direction, "Women make awfully swell friends!"

Claudio didn't miss it. I knew he wouldn't, although he barely let it show. His eyebrows knitted together for less than a second before his face relaxed into a wide, "Touché Callie," smile.

"What book is that from?" Stephanie asked, much more loudly than was needed. No surprise there.

"We will tell you another time," Claudio cut in, chuckling and keeping his tone warm. "Otherwise you will not get home until dawn— and perhaps not even then."

I could've lay into Claudio for that one, but I let his return-fire go unchallenged. The shot was gentle enough, and there was magic in this night. Magic that came from decadence and elegance intermingling with the vulgarity of bar stories.

"Well, Callie," said Stephanie, still laughing slightly. "I'm sure we're going to be best friends!"

&

And we did become best friends—best bar friends, that is, which some-times can be a good start to a real friendship. The four of us got on splendidly and, over the next two weeks, Stephanie became a member of our group. She had a job, so that slowed her down. Work occupied her weekdays, but her weekends and most evenings were magnificently free, and we spent them well. In the limited time she'd been in Madrid, she'd found all manner of interesting bars and cafés, some of which even

Claudio had never been to. I was impressed. We spent a lot of time in such places—three expatriates and an ex-expatriate.

Stephanie challenged me, but mostly in a good way. We complimented each other. In fact, she complimented each of us in one way or the other. I didn't even mind her volume anymore, not even when Claudio referred to it as her "natural exuberance."

I wondered, though, if Stephanie herself were a clue from Hemingway: despite her brains and looks, she was a bit of a bull in a china shop—forever dropping things and accidently whacking passers-by with her wild gesticulations. So far, Hemingway's bulls had been more literal than that, but I supposed a literary hero could take any type of license he wanted.

"It's not easy being an expatriate, you know," Stephanie said one night as our second round of drinks (not including our wine with dinner) arrived.

"I don't know," I replied. When you're an expat, you don't have family around, you don't have old friends and their hang-ups weighing on you. You have the luxury of squandering your time and hanging out in cafés. It's a great life."

"Sure, I like hanging around and drinking. It's a terrific way to relax," she replied.

"Blowing off steam anywhere is good." I pointed out. "You don't need to be in a foreign country for that."

"I disagree, honey. It *is* different when you're not in your own country, your own culture." She swirled the ice in her glass. "I have to admit I was a little lonely before I met you guys."

"I don't remember being lonely when I came to Spain," I said.

"You met me your first night here, remember?" Trevor quickly chimed in. "You weren't really on your own, unless you count the ride from the airport."

"Oh, that's right." I chuckled as I remembered the Trevor I'd met in Barcelona. Harmless enough. True then, still true now.

"I could hang out anywhere, foreign country or otherwise," Trevor continued. "I'm good at it."

"You're pretty good at hanging out, Trevor. I bet you're good at it when you're at home, too."

"You're getting pretty good at it yourself, Callie." He beamed at me with a wobbly smile. The mutual admiration society was hard at work tonight.

"No, it is different." Claudio piped up. He'd been unusually quiet, as if something were bothering him; his dissent startled me. There was a certain depth to his tone, a speaking-from-experience gravitas. "Stephanie is right. It is different when you are living in another country." His words hung in the air, his eyes looked more intently into his drink than usual. "Being an expatriate means you are somewhere else. You are an 'other' when you are somewhere else."

"Being different can be good," I countered. "Even being an 'other' can be good, if you challenge stereotypes and all that."

"In the United States, it can be good, because you thrive so greatly on individualism. It can be good here, too, but Europe is much more… tribal in a way. So many nations, so very many cultures and identities." He paused, scratching his jaw thoughtfully. "There is a certain dislocation that comes with living outside your own country."

"I feel liberated," I said, which was mostly true. I felt a little obligated, too, with my uncompleted quest hanging over me, but I wasn't about to get into that with Trevor and Stephanie around. "I don't feel dislocation."

"You don't?" Claudio was surprised. He lifted one eyebrow purposefully, alluding privately to Hemingway. "I know you have given much thought to your time in my beautiful country. But have you also thought of what comes next?"

"Of course. I'm going back to a fabulous job when this is done," I answered. "Back home."

"Home? You are returning to the States, this is true, but to a whole new city, a whole new coast. So let me ask you this: what is home, Kauhlie?"

"Right!" Stephanie interrupted in full megaphone mode. "What *is* home?"

Claudio nodded. "Think about Stephanie. She probably feels triple dislocation. She is from Canada, but she lives in the United States. And now she is here, all the way across the Atlantic. Which is her home? Winnipeg? Chicago? Madrid? All three, perhaps, or none of the above?" He shrugged his shoulders. "Where is home for Stephanie?"

"Oh, my God, you so totally get it!" Stephanie cried, her eyes gleaming with an appreciative relief. "That's exactly how I feel." She ran her hand down his arm lightly, cooing. "How did you know that, Claudio?"

"Because I lived it for much of my life, Stephanie."

"You know you're home when you *feel* home." I interjected. "Right now, I don't need home. I like being an expatriate." I spoke with conviction even as my stomach dropped. I'd given up my lease on my Village apartment, and New York was now well behind me. Ostensibly, I had an apartment in California, yet I'd never set foot in it. If I didn't even know where I *lived*, how could I know where home was? Aw, hell—this was going to keep me up nights.

"Being an expatriate is often like living in a bubble. It is not the real world, Kauhlie." I couldn't tell if Claudio was responding to me or merely continuing his own thoughts. "It is like time stands still… until you make a decision."

"A decision? I've already made my decisions."

"But have you really, Kauhlie? Or has circumstance decided for you? You have not had to make a decision about what comes after Madrid."

"Yes, a decision, Callie," Stephanie interjected, as if she *knew* what Claudio was talking about. "You don't have to make a decision as an expat, because you know where you're headed. But for the rest of us, we must decide what comes next."

"Yes, this is right." Claudio paused as if he had something deep to convey. "Most expatriates, we must make a decision. Is our new country temporary? If so, for how long? If so, how deeply do we invest ourselves in our temporary life? Which emotions can fly free, and which must be reined in, if only out of necessity?"

"Yes!" Stephanie nodded. "That's exactly it. Dislocation in three parts. Literal, philosophical, emotional."

"Emotional is the big one," Claudio agreed. "Because if it is not temporary, if it is the rest of your life, then you are facing something powerful. You must give up what you used to call home. You must make a new home. You must commit to something—or to someone—and you must embrace it in your heart, fully and completely."

"Geez, I didn't know that's what I was doing," Trevor said pensively, his eyes wide. "I was just taking some time off."

"It is your decision to make, Trevor, my friend." Claudio dipped a crust of his bread in what remained of the table's olive oil. "But make it you must."

I couldn't take this waxing philosophical anymore. "Whatever! Listen, I've had enough of this psycho-babble."

"Psycho-babble?" Claudio asked with a puzzled look. "These are reflections of experience."

This conversation was now much too heavy. "We were having such a nice evening together…" I saw that everyone was finished with their drinks. "Look, it's late, we're done. Let's call it a night."

"I am in no mood for sleep now, Kauhlie," he answered firmly but not crossly. "We have unearthed truths tonight that require meditation. I think I will have a final round."

"Yes, we've hit on some truths," Stephanie echoed. "I think I'll have one more, too." She spoke quietly for once (quiet for Stephanie, anyhow), as if she were mulling over the meaning of life itself.

"I'm ready if you are, Callie. I'll go with you—I do my best thinking in bed, anyhow." I had expected Trevor to follow me out, but I was also thankful for his offer. I still liked that about him: I could always count on Trevor.

"I will see you for breakfast tomorrow, my friends, yes?"

"Second breakfast" corrected Trevor. With Jean-Francois gone, he had more or less quietly reinstituted our first-breakfast coffee-and-a-bun start to the day. He protected our alone time just as quietly, even though one of us was usually cranky and hungover in the mornings. I didn't question it.

"And we'll see you for dinner tomorrow, Stephanie." I said, mostly so she wouldn't feel that Trevor and I were ignoring her.

"Yes, dinner and drinks. But for now, you go on *home*." She chuckled at her own joke, weak as it was.

I hid a bristle. I liked Stephanie—I really did—but like I said, she challenged me. And sometimes she didn't know when *not* to challenge me, if only for the sake of not making waves. See, the thing about Stephanie was that she had to win—even when the contest was only in her head. I figured advertising execs *had* to be that way, or else they'd never sell anything. I'd won Bar Stories Queen on the night we'd met, and some part of her resented me for it.

With the question of "home" weighing in my mind, I didn't want to get fired up. Plus, I was sleepy from our drinks and the heat, so I handled Stephanie like any overtired lawyer would: I instantly constructed a brilliant, foolproof, retort in my head, then delivered it as one hefty eye-roll before walking away. Goodnight, Stephanie.

CHAPTER 21

SEX NEVER CHANGES ANYTHING

(SITUATIONAL IRONY)

"Do you think they're right, Callie? Do you think I have to choose?"

I opened the door to our favorite second-breakfast café and motioned for Trevor to go in first. "Yes and no. The part about choosing your home was bullshit, but you do need to make a decision soon. You've been floating around Europe for... how long now?"

"Gee, I've lost track. And I haven't even gone to Germany yet. I still want to do that, my German is almost as good as my English."

"Then go to Germany," I replied, pulling out my chair. "Go visit a Bavarian prince or something." I was unusually sluggish for this time of day. I didn't know what had gone wrong with my first-breakfast coffee, but it was a bitter, gritty brew. When I'd complained, a second cup just as bad appeared in its place. I'd taken only one or two sips of each, and I'd been in a dangerously undercaffeinated state ever since. Even the morning air—the coolest it had been in weeks—hadn't invigorated me. I needed strong, black, good coffee, and I needed it immediately.

"I don't want to go alone, Callie. Besides, I like the way things are now."

"Then don't go to Germany. But do decide on *something*. Go back and finish your PhD. Get that damn dissertation over with."

Trevor sighed an undeniably brown-and-gray sigh. He picked up his menu and pretended to study it. He put on a good show, but neither of us needed a menu—we'd been here a thousand times. I shouldn't have mentioned grad school, at least not without a good buzz to ease him.

"Or try the Vatican," I suggested, smoothing over my flub. "There's lots of color in the Vatican. All those Renaissance artists."

I caught the eye of a familiar waitress as she rushed by. She knew what I needed. She shrugged her shoulders and explained, "Fresh pot soon, *señorita*."

"Where's Claudio?" Trevor asked evasively, pulling on his beard. "He's late."

"He'll be along in a moment," I replied, deferring and dropping the subject. Claudio was often late to second breakfast; he was only ever punctual after noon. We sometimes teased him about being on "Spanish time."

Ten minutes later, right after my coffee arrived, Claudio came through the door—followed by Stephanie. I was thrown by this variation: Stephanie never joined us for breakfast. She'd taken her American-workday hours with her, and she was in the office by nine each morning. Why was she here?

"Good morning, Kauhlie." Claudio's voice and manner signaled caution—like he thought I might bite. A fair enough assumption on the best of days, never mind on days that had started with a cup of mud.

"Hullo," I muttered before plunging back into the blackness of my coffee. I said the same to Stephanie with my eyes.

"Good morning, Claudio! Good morning, Stephanie! Great to see you both!" There was too much enthusiasm in Trevor's voice. He would do anything to avoid the PhD conversation, even if it meant being engaging.

The pair sat down at the same time. Stephanie gave Claudio a weird look, he returned it with a look just as weird. My decaffeinated mind went back to the same thought loop: Stephanie never joined us for breakfast; why was she here? I took a long, hot sip of caffeinated wisdom, and it came to me: they'd spent the night together. Damnit.

"Welcome to second breakfast, Stephanie," said Trevor brightly. "I hope you'll be joining us more often?"

"I don't know, honey. I… took this morning off for… a change of pace." She and Claudio chuckled conspiratorially. I wanted to hurl. There was no way I acted like this when I was first with Jean-Francois, right?

We stumbled through our meal. I picked at my scrambled eggs with asparagus. The conversation was forced, but I don't think Claudio or Stephanie noticed. I don't think Trevor noticed either—only me. Okay, maybe I wasn't being the greatest conversationalist.

Finally, Stephanie had to leave for work. Claudio excused himself to hail her a cab. She took his arm as they walked out. Sickening.

"Well, that was pleasant," Trevor remarked. He meant it.

An edge to my voice I hadn't been expecting came out. "They're sleeping together." Having stated the fact aloud, I realized I'd been seething the whole meal.

"You mean, like, *together*?"

"Trevor, please try to keep up." I shook my head in exasperation.

"Oh, well, that's… something new." His eyes sparkled, and he broke into a goofy grin that smacked of possibility.

Fortunately, I didn't have to think too much about Trevor's odd reaction, because just then Claudio sauntered back in, a cup of gelato in his hand.

"Trevor, my friend, I must speak to Kauhlie. I have bought you dessert from the cart outside." He handed over the treat. "Please leave us."

His tone was haunting. Claudio's "Please leave us," wasn't a suggestion, it was an order. An order that came with a frosty bribe. An interesting maneuver. I gave the man points for that one.

Trevor looked at me with his, "Do I have to?" face. I felt bad for him, but I knew I needed to hear whatever was coming. Assuring him I wouldn't be long, I suggested that he take his gelato to the bench outside. He cautiously sniffed Claudio's offering as if he suspected poison, but in the end he relented and let us be.

"Kauhlie, you are very smart," Claudio began, sliding into the chair opposite mine. It was a clever opening move, a good start. He'd really thought all the angles of this thing through—it was hard to argue with bribes and blatant flattery. "And I expect you know by now: I spent the night with Stephanie."

"Yeah, well, I did notice the new notch on your bedpost." My words were acid.

He frowned. "There are no notches on my bedpost. Never have been, never will be. I am a single man and free in this regard. The women I sleep with are free in this regard as well. Consenting adults."

I crossed my arms: he was right, of course, and technically I didn't have a say in any of this. Which counted, as far as I was concerned, for exactly nothing. "Go ahead, you just keep ratcheting up that number of yours."

He grimaced, and I knew I'd hit my mark perfectly: in a moment or two, Claudio could very well run out of patience. "Kauhlie, I am speaking to you as an adult. With respect. You once said that I am disrespectful. This is not something I want to be in your eyes."

I eased up a little—not much, but a little. Not with my words, but with my body language. It was the best I could do for the moment.

When he saw I was giving him a little rope, he continued. "I supported your taking a lover, Kauhlie. I am asking that you do the same for me." He scratched the scruff at his chin. "It is most important to me that there be no awkwardness between us. That nothing changes in our group."

Claudio's "taking a lover" jumped out at me. So sophisticated, so refined. Yet so completely untrue. What really happened was that Jean-Francois had served me a leftover potato casserole, and I'd started sleeping with him. I preferred Claudio's version of events.

Even still, I strung the moment out, swirling my spoon in my cup despite having long finished the coffee inside. I didn't want to deal with this new complication, not now: I'd thought I had a handle on our foursome, and I'd been looking forward to calm waters and focusing on finding Hemingway. Damnit.

I raised my defenses as I pulled every muscle of my face into a grin. "Of course not. We agreed to be friends, so we're friends. You and Stephanie do as you please." I let the forced smile fall from my face in a heap. "Sex never changes anything."

Claudio was so relieved that he missed my sarcasm. His eyes brightened, his shoulders relaxed. He smiled crookedly. Then he motioned stiffly as if he were tipping his hat, which was extra-strange because Claudio never wore hats. So much for things not being awkward.

⌁

Dinner was torture. From the moment Claudio and Stephanie strode in together, I'd been in hell.

Stephanie couldn't stop smiling and laughing much, much too loudly at Claudio's jokes. Claudio wasn't that funny—I was the funny one. She'd touched him every chance she got, pokes and taps and nudges, all of which made me cringe. Claudio's laugh wasn't right either, his pitch was way too high. Even Trevor was insufferable. Something had gotten into him, and he seemed excited, almost jubilant; nervous, cautious, pliable Trevor had been replaced by a doppelganger. And their manners—so much conviviality. Who were these people? I felt like I'd been watching our dinner on TV rather than living it; everyone at this table was a bad actor trying too hard. This particular episode was titled, "A portrait of inanity."

I'd grabbed my wine glass as soon as we'd been served, and I'd almost forgotten to toast everyone. Claudio had taken the lead; he'd raised his glass and blathered something about "friends, good times," and some other garbage. After listening to that, I held my wineglass with both hands like a precious goblet—a goblet of indifference—and drank in gulps.

I'd tuned out most of our meal. Instead, I'd immersed myself in my lamb chops, which the chef had coated in a black-olive and rosemary crumble. A delicious distraction: I lost interest in anything beyond my next bite of lamb… or beyond my chorizo-and-bacon mashed potatoes. The wine had helped, too, of course.

"That's so ironic!" Stephanie shouted as the waiter was clearing our plates. I wasn't sure what she was referring to exactly, and I didn't know why she needed to shout it even more loudly than usual—we were all right next to her. Nonetheless, irony was the only mildly interesting topic all night, so I threw my hat into the ring.

"I love irony."

"Callie! You're here after all," Stephanie replied with saccharine delight.

"We thought we'd lost you to the mashed potatoes," added Trevor. "I'm the one who usually zones out, not you."

"You ought to be ironical the minute you get out of bed." I quoted. That was one of Bill's lines from *The Sun Also Rises*, and it was high on my list of favorites.

"Oh, no!" Trevor and Claudio both groaned in unison. Claudio touched two fingers to his forehead as if he were suddenly fighting a headache.

"Okay… That's… something to consider, I guess?" Stephanie spoke slowly, trying to understand. Her brow furrowed. She hated being left out of the loop.

"Okay, Kauhlie, tell us what chapter that is from."

"Twelve. Bill and Jake are talking about—"

"—What book?" Stephanie interrupted, frustrated. "You guys are always talking about some book. *Which* book, exactly?"

Claudio caught her up on the specifics as succinctly as he possibly could. I waited as patiently as I possibly could.

"Oh, well why didn't you just say so, honey?" Stephanie finally burst out. "I'm with you now… I'm no idiot, you know. I just needed some context."

"Irony is integral to the novel," I explained. "In this scene, Bill is encouraging Jake to be more ironic to further his writing career."

"Really? That's so interesting." Her tone dripped with sarcasm, like she already knew everything there was to know on the topic. Stephanie had a look in her eye that I didn't like but could read clearly: we hadn't filled her in on things quickly enough, and she'd taken it as a slight.

She paused before firing her salvo. "Do you even know what irony is, Callie?" A broadside attack, intentionally insulting.

I shot daggers at her. "Irony is when the real meaning is different from the literal meaning—the incongruity often results in amusement."

"Not bad." She was clearly impressed, but her expression came with a heavy dose of mocking. "I bet you practiced that definition for a long time."

"No," I said firmly, lying. I'd actually practiced it many times. Being able to define irony at a moment's notice was on my bucket list. When I was feeling particularly obsessive, I'd even practiced it in front of a mirror.

"That would be pathetic," I continued, layering my lie like any good fabulist. "Who goes around practicing a definition?"

Stephanie's eyes gleamed even as they narrowed. She'd honed onto something, and that something was me. "But that's not the whole story, is it Callie?"

"What do you mean?"

"You defined what's called 'rhetorical irony,' but irony is more complicated than that. What about situational irony? Hmmm?"

"Irony is complex, and it's highly adaptable," academic-Trevor cut in. "That's why it's such a popular device. It shows up everywhere—novels, plays, essays, you name it."

"That's right, honey," Stephanie agreed before turning back to me. "Situational irony is when something is incongruous with the principles of the speaker, or out of synch with the character experiencing the event."

"Isn't that sort of the same thing? Like Trevor said, irony is adaptable."

"No, Callie. It's not the same thing. Not at all—you're missing my whole point."

I didn't expect, nor had I prepared for, an irony battle. Prep is a necessary component to winning any debate; if I'd seen this coming, I would've brushed up. I knew the subject well enough, but even five minutes of review would've bolstered me. Crap.

"Yes, there are many types of irony, Stephanie," Claudio spoke up. "Like many branches of the same tree. They all lead back to one fundamental principle, as Callie described."

Stephanie smiled too placidly at her new lover, putting on a show for him. My lamb chops came dangerously close to liberating themselves from my stomach.

"Well, if you're so interested in the nuances of irony, Stephanie," I began, using my best debate voice, "Go ahead and define dramatic irony... if you can."

"Oh, that's *easy!*" she cried shrilly, so loud that she disturbed the tables around us. "That's when you have developing situational irony that the audience sees but the character cannot."

Damnit, she was right. I really had nothing left to counter with, and my head was beginning to swirl from drinking too much goblet-wine. Why did my buzz have to kick in *now*?

Trevor jumped back in, giving me an opportunity to collect myself. "Stephanie, what about Socratic irony? You know—feigning ignorance to challenge the other person, so you can point out the faults in their position."

Stephanie held up her finger, acknowledging his point. "Very good, Trevor darling." Then she moved her finger forward, touching it to his lips and hushing him. "But now we're getting into the philosophy of rhetoric, and we don't want to overwhelm poor Callie."

Overwhelm poor Callie? Did this woman really think Callie McGraw, cum laude Yale Law graduate, didn't understand the principles of rhetoric—something I was literally trained in? What was her problem?

"I get it!" I shouted, slamming my fist on the table. "I get it all. I get all the irony!" Claudio glanced at Trevor, his dark brown eyes screaming, "Take cover!"

Stephanie mocked my choice of words. "All the irony? No one says it like that!"

I kept going. "Yes. All the irony. All the iterations of irony. Because irony shows up in law, too. All the time. Some cases are ironical by their very nature!"

"Oh, that's cute, Callie," she demeaned. "Falling back on law like that." She yawned at me in mocking, her mouth wide and gaping.

"What, am I boring you?"

"Your reasoning does, Callie, but not the irony at this table. I know all about irony and you clearly *don't*, no matter how much you try to hide it. You are situationally ironic; the incongruity is amusing to everyone here."

"—Stephanie!" Claudio's deep, firm voice dammed up whatever vitriol was about to spill from my mouth. "I do believe you have made your point." In response, she reached over and squeezed his hand affectionately, her eyes glowing with self-proclaimed victory.

"We can debate, Stephanie," I started, trying to hold back my anger. It didn't work, because the rest of my sentence betrayed me. "But there's no need to be a raging asshole." Feigning shock, she asked, "You call women assholes?" She let go of Claudio's hand in the process. At least I'd accomplished that much.

"Yes, when it fits," I responded.

"When what fits? When the asshole fits?" She laughed. "That's weird." Trevor began to chuckle, but wisely suppressed it.

Her face turned grave. Somber. And then, just when she could've backed down, when there was still a glimmer of hope for the evening, Stephanie uttered the one phrase that drove me berserk. She said it softly, more softly than I'd ever heard her speak. Her softness sliced directly into my flesh.

"I win."

I gasped, a guttural noise erupting from deep in my throat. I stood up, overturning half the table in the process. "I'm done! I can't stay here anymore—not with this... this..." My mind flooded with insults as I searched for the right barb. Overwhelmed with choices, I blundered out, "this... harpy!"

The amused expression spreading across Stephanie's face pissed me off even further as I turned to storm away. I was halfway across the room when I heard her ask, "Trevor, Callie can be kind of a bitch, can't she?"

Trevor raised his voice to meet her volume, making sure I heard his reply. "Only when you get to know her."

Good ol' Trevor.

CHAPTER 22

DIFFICULT TRUTHS

I strode down the street, my head buzzing with anger. Was this how things were going to be from now on? Did Stephanie see me as a threat, just because she and Claudio were sleeping together? I hadn't seen that coming, and I was pissed at myself for missing it.

I was halfway down the block when I heard, "Kauhlie!"

My temper and I kept trooping forward. Wide, deep, disciplined steps evidencing my fury.

"Kauhlie! Wait! Please!"

I whipped myself around. Claudio was fifteen paces behind, jogging forward. He waved his arm like he was hailing a cab. I put my hand on my hip and waited for him to reach me.

"Kauhlie, I do not know what happened back there. I am sorry."

"I'll tell you what happened," I shouted. I kicked a wad of trash on the sidewalk purely for the pleasure of kicking it. "It's simple. Your new girlfriend thinks keeping you for herself means degrading me."

Claudio hesitated. "I do not think that is what happened." He paused, considering what I'd said. "But Stephanie does have some rough edges, this is true."

"I've been friends with plenty of women," I spat back, knowing the full weight of my words. "Some women tear other women down as soon as a guy enters the picture. That's how insecure they are, deep down!"

Not that I was any saint in this regard. I'd torn down any number of women myself, but never over a man. No, when I threw someone under a bus—male or female—it was on fair turf, and usually only after they'd tried shoving *me* into traffic. Sometimes, corporate law could be that way; I'd done what I needed to do to stay competitive.

"Kauhlie, I think perhaps you are conflating two things that ought not to be conflated. Besides,"—and here he shot me a chiding grin— "you have some rough edges yourself."

My expression, which I felt contort indescribably in consternation, revealed my exact thoughts about his comment.

He spoke again before I could untangle my lips. "Let me clarify. I only mean that both of you have strong personalities."

My expression contorted again, but not quite as sharply this time. Claudio got a few points for rephrasing, but he was still in the red. In the red via Stephanie.

"So what is it? Why did you run out here?"

"Because I do not want us to fight again, Kauhlie, and I want you and Stephanie to remain friends. I know it is never good when you storm off like that."

"I don't storm out of places randomly," I said, annoyed. "It's not like it is a 'thing' of mine or something."

"Kauhlie, it is very much your thing." He softened his tone and added, "At least it is one of your things. You have a lot of things."

I didn't like the sound of this at all. "What things? How many things?"

"I do not know. I have not counted. A handful."

I crossed my arms. "List them," I demanded.

Claudio knew he wasn't getting out of this one, so he conceded. "Well, there is your *The Sun Also Rises* thing."

I raised my palms in the air. "That's not a thing, that's my salvation!"

"And then there is… your Hemingway-calls thing." He took on a sheepish tone, unsure if he should mention it.

"That's a secret thing, and don't you dare use it against me!" I jabbed his shoulder too hard with my index finger. Not enough to hurt him, but more than was strictly needed to make my point.

He threw his shoulders back, straightening his posture solemnly. "I will guard your secret well. I give you my word."

I nodded sharply and quickly, conveying, "I know," and, "Thank you," and "Sorry for jabbing you." All three in one nod.

A delivery truck roared by, giving me a moment to collect my thoughts. I shook my head to clear it. "Fine. So that's three things. That's not a lot of things."

"Those are the first three, Kauhlie. And there is your drinking thing. You drink a lot."

"So do you!"

"But it is different with you. I drink to celebrate, to enjoy, but you…. So often you seem… sorrowful."

This conversation wasn't improving. Weren't we supposed to be talking about Stephanie? It was too hard to stay mad at her while being psychoanalyzed, and also (as Claudio knew too well), I hated being psychoanalyzed.

I walked over to what looked like an old bank and plopped myself on its granite steps. Claudio followed and sat next to me, scooting in close but not *too* close. He smiled at me as if to say, "I must be the one to tell you the truth, and for this I am sorry."

"What's wrong with a little sorrow?" I burst out. "I've… been through stuff. You know that."

"Yes, your parents, I understand." He turned his gaze to the traffic. "I do not say this to be callous, but we have all… been through stuff. Yet we do not all… drink as you do."

"It's not like I drink to forget, or anything like that."

"No, Kauhlie. You do not drink to forget. You drink to ignore.

Perhaps it is because you do not have your work to distract you now, and so you drink to ignore." His eyes smiled but his lips did not.

"Drink to ignore? Ignore what, smart guy?"

"This, I do not know. I have not figured it out yet."

I frowned. "I'm not a riddle to be figured out!"

Claudio chuckled softly. "And this is a thing. This right here. Making an argument. You *like* making arguments."

He wasn't wrong, but I failed to see anything problematic here. Arguments made the world go around. Arguments, debates, challenges. "Of course, I do. Why wouldn't I?"

He gazed softly at me before replying, "You start arguments, yes, but another one of your things is that you *win* arguments."

"It would be pretty dumb to start arguments I couldn't win. What kind of masochist would that make me?

He chuckled again, more freely this time. "You win arguments, just like you have won this argument." He leaned over and put his hands tenderly on my cheeks, then gently kissed my forehead—his warm lips on my skin felt good, too good. Too comfortable.

I turned my eyes downward as he continued. "You are the winner of this argument, and you won the argument in the restaurant, too."

I looked up at him with pleading eyes. "Is it really important to you that I stay friends with Stephanie?"

"It is, Kauhlie. It is."

"Then I'll try. No guarantees, but I promise I'll try. For you."

He broke into a grin. "That is all I am asking. And I will have a word with her. The combativeness she exhibited tonight, whatever the root of it, is not... her most attractive quality." He stood and brushed the dust from his linen pants.

"I will see you tomorrow, okay Kauhlie? It is Saturday, it will be all four of us."

"No, I... I... think I'll take the day to myself. Go to a museum or something. But tell Stephanie no offense."

"You would go to a museum without me? Am I not still your favorite art ambassador?" His eyes twinkled, teasing me.

I balked. Of course, I wanted him along. But I couldn't say that, because with Claudio came Stephanie, and I'd had enough of the new-lovers sideshow for now. I needed to steel myself for the many Claudio-and-Stephanie days to come, and that meant clearing the slate with some "Callie time." I needed to put some serious hours into my quest, anyway. I'd been on high alert for clues after Hemingway's last call, but so far I'd found nothing definitive.

I couldn't say what I needed to say, so instead I focused on logistics. "Will you take Trevor to second breakfast tomorrow? Babysit him through the afternoon?"

Claudio threw his head back and laughed. "Yes, we will babysit Trevor. Do not worry." His "we" stung a little.

He kissed my hand before walking away. He was about five yards down the street when he turned and smiled over his shoulder at me. "Winner!" he called back exuberantly. Claudio followed this with a big thumbs-up as he continued toward the restaurant.

As he disappeared, I counted six things—and only one of them even remotely good. Six Callie McGraw things, plus one promise from my lips, and at least one proclaimed win from Claudio. But standing there alone on the sidewalk, I didn't feel as if I'd won anything.

∽

I felt weird going back. I hadn't been to my secret café since the day I'd spoken with Señora Fernandez, but I'd thought of her often, and I wanted to meet the husband she was so deeply, unfailingly committed to. Hemingway had approved of her sage advice: I wondered if I could learn more from her.

With the afternoon gloriously free, I planned to meet up with Señora Fernandez before heading to the Monet exhibit at the Museo Thyssen-Bornemisza. But now that the café was in sight, I couldn't will myself to go in. There was no way to recapture the day we'd met, no way the heat of her coffee-warmed hands could again comfort my own, at least not in the same way. So I resolved to do the only rational thing: spy on her.

Of course, I needed to be cleverer this time. Clearly Señora Fernandez was a sly one—I'd never once noticed her watching me during the entire time I'd been watching her. At the very least, I needed a disguise. Before choosing my stakeout point, I stopped at a gaudy tourist shop and bought a baseball cap that had "*Viva España!*" printed across the yellow and red of the Spanish flag. I also put on my sunglasses and pulled my hair into a high ponytail. The mirror in the shop told me it was a good disguise. Well, a good enough disguise, at least.

I got into position about fifteen minutes before I was expecting Señora Fernandez to show, my eyes peering between the café's entrance and the street from which I'd seen her approach. I was thankful that smartphones made surveilling easy—anyone, anytime, could be stopped in the middle of the street, as long as they were glued to a small, glowing screen. I positioned myself in an inconspicuous spot, but I also took full advantage of this new twenty-first century norm.

As expected, Señora Fernandez shuffled down the sidewalk, right on time. Her conservative dress hadn't been altered much for the summer's heat, and she'd knotted her hair into its usual bun. As always, she'd pinned a rose with a longer stem to her blouse. She walked into the café without breaking stride, which I took to mean she didn't see me. So far, so good.

I knew she usually spent about twenty minutes inside, and—since I needed some caffeine too—I used the time to nip around the corner and grab a cup of reconnaissance-fuel. Returning to my spot, I sipped my coffee slowly, waiting for my mark to make her move.

And move she did. She shuffled for the first block, but then Señora Fernandez picked up speed—maybe it was the caffeine kicking in, or maybe she was just cagier than I'd anticipated. I'd been maintaining a safe distance as I followed, but her change in horsepower threw me off: when she rounded a corner, I rushed up behind her too quickly and had to duck behind a street vendor to stay out of sight. Too close a call, even for an amateur. The woman had a lot of stamina for her age. I was impressed.

After some fifteen espionage-filled minutes, Señora Fernandez turned onto a block lined on her side with a long, wrought-iron fence; the shrubbery and trees beyond made it look like a garden of some sort. I hung back on the corner, watching as she opened the only gate and walked resolutely through. I jumped into action and had closed the gap between us by about half when I heard the *clang* of the gate as she shut it securely.

The cemetery wasn't large, at least not as large as it looked from the outside. Señora Fernandez made her way to the back of the grounds—her head and her spirits high. She came to a stop in front of a grave, looking down at it longingly. She sighed visibly before reaching for the rose on her blouse. Unfastening it took some effort, her time-ravaged fingers struggling with the pin. With the rose still in her right hand, she knelt down—a surprisingly fluid and practiced motion—and she made the sign of the cross, beginning her prayers.

She placed the rose against the gravestone gently. Then she leaned back on her heels and, with an even more surprising pliability, eased herself into a sitting position. Her words began to flow, not just from her mouth but from her entire body. She gesticulated animatedly in a conversation so lively that I had trouble believing one half of the participants were departed from this world.

"*Coffee first, then my husband. We talk about many things. He makes me not lonely.*" Her words flashed through my mind. She could've been talking to her husband about anything, from the Spanish senate to her breakfast that morning. This ritual, this daily rite in this cemetery, kept loneliness from Señora Fernandez's life. It all seemed so natural, she looked so rejuvenated, and it was as if her husband *wanted* her to tell him these things—I could almost see his headstone leaning ever-so-slightly forward, hungry for her words.

I got lost in the sweetness, the sincerity, the intimacy. Then all of a sudden, that same intimacy became cloying, its weight pressing down on me: what I was doing wasn't appropriate. This was their time together as husband and wife; I had no right to intrude. "Till death do us part," didn't apply to the Fernandezes.

I was turning to leave when something caught my eye. A lone tombstone sat on the other side of the cemetery, set apart from the other graves by a low fence—almost like it was lonely. With its loneliness calling to me, I made my way to it. Once, this grave had lovingly been tended to, but the weeds and the elements had now ravaged this poor, isolated, plot. No one had been here for ages.

The gravestone was in Spanish, of course, and faded by the decades. The name, a long male name in the Spanish tradition, was almost illegible, although the date, 1899–1961, was clearer. I probably wouldn't have attempted to translate the epitaph save for one intriguing word: *matador*. My mind conjured up images of a vibrant bullfighter on the razor's edge of life as he eluded—at the last possible instant—*el toro* once again. And again. And again. Reaching sixty-two, this matador survived the many battles of youth yet never knew the trials of old age.

I stared at the epitaph for a long time, tracing my fingers over the faded markings and working through the Spanish as best I could, sounding out the syllables in whispers. The inscription calling to me, challenging me. I pulled out my phone and translated a couple of key words, but otherwise I was determined to do this myself. Again and again, I read the three simple lines, beseeching them to reveal their meaning. My tongue twisted around the words, the grooves of the etching rough under my fingertips. Slowly, insight breached my ignorance, a translation emerging in my mind: "Born of Woman, Given Life by the Bull, Passed in God's Grace."

My breathing shallowed as I absorbed the words. Who was this man? Did he have regrets? Did he have enough time? Was he truly given life by the bull? And what secrets had he taken with him to this forlorn grave? The questions flashed through my mind as I gasped for air. The sky above me swirled, the ground beneath me swelled. A lifeless matador in a lifeless place. Had he lived his life all the way up? If so, what was I supposed to learn from him? Why had Hemingway brought me to this desolate place? And how could this forgotten matador help me find him?

CHAPTER 23

THE ULTIMATUM

I kept a cool-ish distance from Stephanie over the next week. Not that I avoided her, exactly, I just leaned on a degree of separation whenever I could. I even excused myself from dinner one night, saying I had a conference call with Matt and his human resources director. With San Francisco being nine hours behind Madrid, my ruse worked perfectly; I got a whole night—and a whole bottle of wine—to myself. I spent much of it studying up on irony, just in case the topic came up again.

Claudio, though, *didn't* stay away from Stephanie. Or rather, Stephanie didn't stay away from him. If she'd been handsy before, now she was downright clingy—a clinginess that exceeded even her volume. She draped herself over Claudio so obviously and so often that even Trevor commented on it. Claudio didn't seem to mind having a leggy blonde attached to his hip, although I did catch him bristling when she offered to walk him to the restroom. Seriously Stephanie, let the man pee in peace.

Saturday arrived and I very seriously thought about playing sick. But I knew skipping out would only add tension to my tenuous truce with Stephanie, and it would probably upset Claudio as well, so I headed to the train station. We'd planned the overnight trip to Toledo during those few glorious weeks when there were no couples among us. It had seemed like a good idea at the time.

The ride was swift—only thirty minutes—and I found myself intrigued by the city's history, which Claudio filled us in on, by the time we'd pulled into the station. The entire city was a World Heritage Site: Roman, Visigoth, Arab, Jewish, and Christian influences all intermingled in this crossroads. A walking tour would take us past the city's monasteries, bridges, and castle, and we'd end the day at a spa where our poor feet would be treated to massages.

I should've been able to enjoy the day, but a sinking, discomforting feeling shadowed me. I wanted this trip to be over with, wanted to go back to Madrid where I could escape to my familiar hotel room if I needed to. I pasted on smiles and oozed out pleasantries all day, and I didn't take the bait the few times Stephanie tried to rile me, but the truth was I felt trapped. Trapped by this medieval city and its splendors. Trapped by the promise I'd made to Claudio. Trapped by my own damn stupidity; I should've faced up to my feelings the morning Claudio had apologized, instead of pushing him away at the first bump in the road.

On our ride from Madrid, Trevor and I had planned a detour to the Catedral Primada Santa María de Toledo, which housed a de Goya I wanted to see. It wouldn't be a long detour—the cathedral's collection was small—but when the time came for us to wander away from the walking tour, a palpable relief seeped into every crevice of my body. An hour or two when I wouldn't need to watch my tongue or duck Stephanie's barbs. Even the thought of seeing an original de Goya paled in comparison to watching Stephanie walk away. Walking away with Claudio, of course, but I guess I couldn't win them all.

Claudio had made reservations for us at a restaurant across the street from the spa, to save our re-tenderized feet from any unnecessary walking. Initially, Trevor was going to skip the foot rub, claiming his toes were too ticklish, but I convinced him otherwise: not wanting to be alone with the happy couple, I needed him for backup. The massages did the trick for our aching feet, but by the time we were seated at the restaurant, we were all a little cranky—it had been a long day by any measure.

We were also all ravenous. We guttled our appetizers as if they were the last plates of food on Earth. My chicken with leeks and crème had just arrived when the conversation turned to literature. I resolved to remain quiet: if anyone at this table still had doubts about my favorite book, they hadn't been paying attention. I dived into my plate and stayed there—or at least I tried to.

"*Don Quixote* is set in this region," Stephanie announced as if she alone had read the book. "Not in the city, obviously, but nearby." I rolled my eyes as I jammed my fork into my dish. "*Don Quixote* is *my* favorite book," she continued, shooting me a glance.

As she said this, and just as I was opening my mouth, I felt a string of leek fall from my fork and hung there. It slapped against my chin and stuck. I tried to inconspicuously peel the leek away with my fork. I missed it. Then I missed it again. Its juice began running down my chin. So much for being inconspicuous.

"Here, Kauhlie, let me help you," Claudio said kindly, reaching out with his napkin. Before I could stop him, he wiped my chin—leek and juice—for me.

"Aw, Claudio's such a good *friend* to you, Callie," Stephanie said. By "friend," she meant, "Friend and only a friend, and don't you forget that," but I let it pass.

"Quite," I muttered.

"Callie, sometimes I feel like we've gone down the wrong path together. Do you not like me because I'm Canadian?"

"Not at all. I'm not maple-phobic. I'm maple-friendly." That's what my mouth said, but my thoughts screamed something else – *I don't care where you're from. I don't like you because you're a bigger and louder know-it-all than I am, and crassly insecure.*

"Well then, I think we could still be great friends." Stephanie shouted the last part, as if loudness could make it true.

"Sure," my mouth lied. We could be amicable and civil, but only because I'd promised Claudio as much. Obviously, Stephanie and I were long past bosom buddies now.

"We could be a team," she continued without taking a breath. "Just like in *Don Quixote*."

I shrugged my shoulders, deferring, and reached for more wine. Whatever she was setting me up for, I didn't want any part of it.

"I'd be Don Quixote because I'm a natural leader—"

– You're not a natural leader, you're a natural blowhard. –

"—and you could be my Sancho Panza."

– Harpy! No one wants to be Sancho Panza. Hell, his name means 'big belly.' Wait, is she calling me fat? Some of us have curves, Stephanie, we're not all walking skeletons like you. –

"—You could carry my shield—"

– I'm not your servant! –

"—and my lance too, Sancho."

– I'll tell you where you can stick your lance! –

Once Stephanie stopped blathering, I forced a smile and molded my tone into something passably lighthearted. "Thanks, but I think I'll pass on that one."

"Oh, Callie!" she shouted, pointing at my mouth and laughing. Obnoxious as usual.

"Callie, you have leek-tooth," Trevor helped, motioning to his own teeth. I ran my tongue along my mouth; a big piece of leek was indeed blanketing my front tooth.

"I cannot help you with that one," Claudio said, shaking his head and chuckling.

I swiped at my tooth with my finger before I smiled at Trevor, asking for an inspection.

"Nope. Still there."

I dug at it harder this time, then smiled again.

"Still… there." Trevor grimaced slightly.

Damn this leek.

Stephanie reached out a manicured finger now that she'd managed to stop laughing. "Here, honey. You need my help."

I instinctively recoiled. The last thing I wanted was her finger in my mouth. It would be a finger of pity, and there was always the chance I'd bite the damn thing off. I wiped violently at my teeth with my napkin.

"Yup. Got it!" Trevor reported. He said it like he was proud of me, which was weird even for him.

"Sancho Panza is so cute when she gets food in her teeth," Stephanie teased.

— *I'll kill myself, or you, before I let you start calling me that.* —

"That would be a hilarious nickname for you, Callie. Sancho Panza," Trevor joined in.

"Shut up, Bilbo," I spat. "Or no second breakfast for you tomorrow." I was ready to claw Trevor's eyeballs out, but he retreated into himself with that scolded-puppy-dog look of his. I couldn't go ripping at his eye sockets when his tail was between his legs.

"I bet I can get that nickname to stick, Callie!" cried Stephanie. "Just like that leek on your tooth." She burst out laughing again. Trevor did his best to hold back, but he tittered. Claudio said nothing; he did not look pleased.

"Stop calling me that!" I steamed. "Dial it back, Stephanie." I left it there: Callie McGraw, the very epitome of restraint.

"Don't be mad, Callie. It's better than a nickname from your little book," she shot, her voice again saccharine.

Really? That's where she was taking this? Stephanie was now treading on sacred ground and she knew it. She'd laid a challenge I *couldn't* leave unanswered. "What's wrong with my book?" I snapped, my volume meeting her own.

"Oh, nothing. It's a cute little read."

I took a deep breath. I didn't remind her that *The Sun Also Rises* had been analyzed countless times, in every possible way, and still remained in print after almost a century. I didn't remind her that everyone from eminent literary scholars to hungover and barely-coherent college kids had examined its allegories and layers of meaning, yet no one had ever declared it, "a cute little read."

What I did say is this: "It's not 'cute.' It's a modernist masterpiece."

"Masterpiece is a stretch, Callie. It's a decent read, but *Don Quixote* is *literature*." The way Stephanie pronounced *literature* reeked of affectation. Like she'd spent a lifetime critiquing novels in some ivory tower. Like she alone judged what constituted literature and what did not. Like the very idea that someone might hold a differing opinion was offensive.

Claudio spoke up, his tone grave. "There is room enough for more than one masterpiece in the vast canon of English literature. We all know this well." His tone clearly said, "Change the subject, Stephanie."

I would've been more than willing to do just that, but Stephanie merely grabbed Claudio's arm and continued. "*Don Quixote* is a masterpiece of comedy and tragedy all rolled into one. Cervantes was a masterful writer."

I sighed. "Cervantes was a pretty good writer, I'll grant you that, Stephanie." Claudio's eyes bugged out a little when those words came out of my mouth. With my eyes I explained, "I'm *trying*, Claudio, I really am."

"Cervantes is one of the greatest writers of all time, Callie," academic-Trevor piped up. "Some consider him the best ever—the father of the modern novel." I knew this was Trevor's area, but I hurled a look at him anyway: this was no time to go rogue on me.

"There are many great writers. Pitting one against the other is fruitless," Claudio interjected, actively trying to steer the conversation somewhere—anywhere—else. "Perhaps we should begin planning our next trip together. There are many wonders in Spain."

For once, Stephanie completely ignored her new lover. "What Trevor said is true, Callie. Cervantes is the vastly superior writer. I'm right and you know it, honey."

My anger exploded behind my eyes and landed squarely on Trevor. He shrunk in his chair and asserted quietly, "I'm getting a PhD in Comp Lit, Callie, I *do* know what I'm talking about."

"You don't have your doctorate yet, Trevor, and with the way you're wasting time, you never will! I actually got my JD."

He scowled hard and slumped his shoulders—I knew that one had hurt, and badly. I thought Trevor would probably make an excuse to leave, but instead he did something I barely thought he was capable of: He fought back.

"Yeah, sure," he began defiantly. He paused, winding up for something good. "But your degree came only *after* you'd spent six months working for an intern! *That* was a waste of time."

By itself, I could have lived with the insult. I could've cut Trevor some slack, especially considering I'd fired the first volley. But then he started filling Stephanie in on the full story, ignoring my protests. That put him high on my shit list, but what happened next was truly the straw that broke the camel's back. I was the camel. Hell, by this point, I *felt* like a camel, with reserves of frustration stored in my hump.

"Callie, that is remarkable!" Stephanie cried once the story was over. "You are so… sad." She raised her voice and repeated, "You are *so* sad."

That was the breaking-straw. Stephanie did not say, "That was sad." She did not say, "You were so sad." No, she said, "You *are* so sad," and she'd gone out of her way to *repeat* it. A direct hit across the bow. Intentional. Calculated. Precise.

I bolted from my chair, blood rushing to my head and my rage transforming into the Four Horsemen of the Apocalypse. Destruction incarnate. I grabbed my wine, intending to throw it in Stephanie's face.

My stomach cramped, I doubled over: my promise to Claudio. The glass fell from my grip and shattered. The entire restaurant turned and stared.

"Claudio! Outside!" I screamed.

"Kauhlie?" His eyes said, "Wait, what did I do?"

"Now!"

He got up slowly, unsure of what was happening. I grabbed his forearm and heaved him toward the door, leaving a stunned Trevor and a steaming Stephanie behind.

Outside, I whirled around, looking Claudio dead in the eyes. "I want her gone!" I demanded.

"What?!"

"You heard me. Gone!"

"But, Kauhlie, she and I are..."

"I don't care what you and she are! She *enjoys* making a fool out of me, and I won't stand for it! Get rid of her!" I stomped my foot against the slate sidewalk, pretending I was crushing Stephanie's head.

"Perhaps she only wanted to share her love of *Don Quixote* with you?" He countered tenuously.

"Stop making excuses. That's bullshit and you know it! You warned her. Twice!"

He hung his head and shook it. "I did try to change the subject," he ceded, "but she did not want to listen."

"I've *tried* with her, Claudio, I've tried. All damn week. But instead of backing off, she went in for the kill!"

"Yes, Kauhlie, I have seen you trying, I will grant you that. You have been on your best behavior. While Stephanie... has not."

"And now I'm *done* trying! Nobody makes a fool out of Callie McGraw, do you hear me?!"

"What do you expect me to do?"

I crossed my arms tightly. "I'm going back to the hotel, and you're going back inside. I don't care how you do it, but I want her gone. For good! I never want to see her again! She's banished, do you understand?"

"Kauhlie, I cannot simply... I mean... she is my—"

"—I don't care what she is to you. If you care about what *I* am to you, you'll end it now. Tonight. I barely have two months left in Spain, and I'm *not* spending it as the butt of that woman's joke... not even for your sake!"

Claudio paused, sizing up the situation. His eyes went blank, his face expressionless. "I do not care for ultimatums, Kauhlie. And have you considered: what if I do not want her to go?"

"Buddy, you have a choice to make, and I hope for your sake you make the right one. Because otherwise, don't bother coming back yourself."

His face betrayed not one single emotion. I couldn't tell what was going on behind those eyes, not even one hint. Had I pushed him too far?

I softened the slightest bit. "I don't like ultimatums, either. But I think you know this isn't working. It's time to let her go."

Claudio scratched his scruff of a beard and grunted almost defiantly. "That is a decision for me—and me alone—to make." He said it firmly, but I couldn't read any emotion beyond that.

I stiffened again—if he wasn't giving me an inch, I wasn't giving him one either. "You have a choice, and you'd better make the right one!" I threw my hands in the air, then turned on my heel, leaving Claudio alone in the dusky evening light.

∽

The next morning, I had the sneaking suspicion that I'd truly overplayed my hand this time. "Me or her" was a brazen move. All or none. Us versus them. No gray area, no wiggle room. A calculated risk. But, like many calculated risks, a decent night's sleep skewed things differently. Last night, I thought I'd been holding all the cards, but now, in the light of day, I wasn't so sure which cards, if any, I had in my hand.

I obsessed as I showered and packed up my overnight bag. Would both Claudio and Stephanie fail to show up at breakfast? She would be gone… but he'd be gone too. Bittersweet. No, not bittersweet. Bittersweet implied more sweet than bitter; losing Claudio would always outweigh being free of Stephanie. Bitter with a side of relief, maybe. I wondered if there was a word for that.

As I dressed, a new thought occurred to me: what if *both* of them showed up at breakfast? What if Claudio called my bet? What would I do then? Had I been bluffing all along? But no, that wasn't his style. I was pretty sure it would be all or nothing—either he would come to breakfast alone, or he wouldn't show up at all. He wasn't prone to conflict, and bringing Stephanie to breakfast was guaranteed conflict—he wouldn't want his scrambled eggs with a side of war. Right? I wasn't sure. I might've really screwed up.

I did one final sweep of the room, checking to see if I'd left anything behind—not that I'd brought all that much stuff with me in the first place. I swept up a stray bobby pin from the vanity, another thought hitting me: Would *Trevor* be at breakfast this morning? What if Claudio had made him choose? What if he'd weaponized Trevor the way my parents had weaponized me? Which side would Trevor be on? He'd never pushed back at me like that before; would I lose him too? Shit. I'd placed my bet without gauging the odds, and now I stood to lose so much more than I'd wagered.

I sat myself on the bed and purposefully waited, going as far as setting my timer on my phone for ten minutes. I would not be the first (only?) one to arrive at breakfast this morning. I watched the clock count down. Patience not being one of my strengths, this took every ounce of self-control I had. I was also desperately craving a cup of coffee, just as I did every morning. I focused on that—that one small discomfort among this storm—as the clock ticked down; the rest was too much to fathom.

Some three years later, the timer went off. It had been long enough—surely even Claudio would be at breakfast by now, if he were coming at all. I grabbed my stuff and trudged to the elevator. More waiting. After a solid minute of torture, I opted for the stairs—four flights down. Something to burn off this nervous energy, something to keep this uncertainty at bay. Had I sabotaged the rest of my time in Spain? Would it be just me from here on out?

In the hotel's restaurant, I saw Trevor sitting alone at a table for four, hunched over a steaming cup of coffee. Relief swept through me even as I felt a chill slither down my back. No Claudio. My mouth went dry.

Trevor slowly raised his eyes from his coffee as I approached. He didn't say anything, nor did he wave. Not even on our worst-hangover mornings did Trevor fail to wave. A brown-and-gray pall hung over him, one so heavy it was almost visible.

"Good morning!" I tried to be bright, but I couldn't pull it off. Usually, my volcanic explosions missed Trevor almost entirely, but this time I'd launched molten lava and burned him—a third-degree burn that had scorched far more than flesh.

"Callie," he whispered. The bare minimum of a greeting, but at least he was speaking to me. That was something. I could work with that. I *had* to work with that. I owed Trevor at least that much.

I panned the room one more time for any sign of Claudio. Nothing. I ached at that fact, but as I beheld my faithful travel companion, I knew I had to make things right between us, and I needed to do it now, before his wounds festered. Maybe I could go to Claudio's apartment in Madrid and apologize later—if he'd even hear an apology—but right now I need to focus on Trevor.

"Listen, I need to say," I began, my voice soft, gentle. Trevor's worn-out eyes were heavy, but they urged me to continue. "I owe you an apology. I'm sorry for what I said last night about your degree. I was angry at Stephanie, not you. It was wrong of me to take it out on you, and I'm sorry. Can you forgive me?"

Signs of life awoke in his eyes. "Really? You mean it, Callie?"

"Yes, I mean it. I really am sorry. I'll do better. Be better." I reached for his hands, which were still wrapped around his coffee. I held my hand there gently. The brown and gray around him lightened. He smiled.

"I'm sorry too. I didn't mean to make things worse. It's just that I don't want to go back to school, not ever. But then you… and then I… I mean… she attacked… and Claudio didn't… you were…."

I squeezed his knuckles reassuringly. With Trevor descending into non-language, I knew this was really tough for him—he probably felt even worse than I did. "It's okay, Trevor. I know. I get it."

His eyes brightened even more, as if the first green shoots of spring were peeking through the thaw behind them. Maybe things would be fine with just me and Trevor again. We made a great team, in our own way.

"Apologies traded, apologies accepted," I offered, adding cheer to my tone. It wasn't exactly fake cheer either; I felt better, too.

"Apologies traded, apologies accepted," Trevor echoed. "And I'm glad of it, Callie."

Just then, a cup of coffee came out of nowhere and landed in front of me. The waiter's hand moved so quickly that I almost didn't see it retracting.

"I didn't order this, *señor*," I said. "*No ordenélo*," I repeated.

"*Sí, señorita*. No, you." The waiter cocked his chin, indicating beyond my shoulder. "He order." At this, Claudio slipped into the seat next to me. The waiter deftly set down another cup of coffee before walking away.

"Good morning, Kauhlie," Claudio said with a grin.

"Claudio!" My heart lifted instantly, although I tried to rein in the smile on my face before it betrayed too much. Keep it cool, Callie, keep it cool.

"I thought you would want your coffee right away. It is black, just as you like it."

"That was nice of you, thank you." I didn't know what to say next, so I went for something banal and nonchalant. "Did you sleep well?"

Claudio's eyes sparked just a little. "I have had better nights, but I am okay."

"Oh, I know!" Trevor burst out. "The mattress in my room is terrible. My back is killing me!"

"Yes, the mattresses here are not very good," Claudio agreed. He took his first sip of coffee. "You must come for a dip in my hot tub when we get back to Madrid. That will help your back."

"Gee, do you mean it? That *would* help." Trevor replied, stretching in his chair.

"Of course I mean it. You are welcome anytime. As are you, Kauhlie. We are a trio of good friends."

CHAPTER 24

A MATADOR EMERGES

It was amazing how effortlessly we returned to our just-the-three-of-us rhythm. In many ways it was like those early weeks after Trevor and I had met Claudio. With so much extraneous drama gone, our trio went back to simply having fun. Claudio made jokes. I made jokes. Trevor laughed at all of them. My jokes were funnier than Claudio's.

We made a bucket list of sites to see, and during the days we visited them all—the Royal Palace, Cybele's Fountain, the Temple of Debod, and of course the Museo Sorolla, which was dedicated to impressionist artist Joaquín Sorolla, and which the guys had to practically drag me out of. Claudio happily played tour guide on our excursions, and Trevor behaved himself for the most part. Through it all, I kept my eyes well-peeled for Hemingway clues, questioning everything yet finding little.

We were all a little burned out on restaurants, so we started cooking more in the evenings at Claudio's apartment. I still couldn't cook to save my life, but Claudio was very patient, even on our first "returning-to-home-cooking evening," when I managed to murder several tomatoes that I was dicing for our tomato-and-tuna tapas. Our main course that night was braised rabbit in *salmorejo* sauce, a dish from the Canary

Islands, with *sofrito* rice. Shortly after the rice went in and we'd all cried "*Veinte minutos!*" I grabbed a wooden spoon to stir the grains. Claudio had gently caught my wrist an instant before I dug into the yellow rice.

"Just like when we cook paella, it is not good to stir the rice. A big no-no, Kauhlie."

He'd said it gently, almost comfortingly. His words were not nearly as panicked as when we'd cooked together the very first time, when I'd almost made the same mistake. Claudio's "no-no" was even cuter than Teddy, who'd immediately resumed his habit of curling around my feet.

It was also my job that evening to cut up the rabbit. That wasn't pretty, but Claudio good-naturedly showed me how to chop Bugs Bunny's unfortunate cousin into sixths. It was soothing having Claudio that close to me and guiding my hands, even though I was wielding a potentially deadly weapon.

Our cooking together brought other changes as well. Claudio started sneaking me glances. Smiles too, warm ones. And the touches. Most were safe-zone touches—lower arm, congratulatory pats on the shoulder, mock handshakes. But every once in a while, he'd lightly slide his thumb over my wrist, or press his palm into the small of my back. Not that I minded even one little bit. And hell, anytime I could orchestrate a "legitimate touch" moment in the kitchen, I did the same to him.

There was never any true hand-holding. No hugs, and there was definitely never any kissing. But sometimes at dinner we pushed our chairs an inch or two closer. Claudio's eyes were brighter. Our passing glances morphed into almost-lingering looks. Sometimes, if Teddy and Toni were scampering under the table, we'd go as far as letting our knees touch. Really hot stuff.

After a particular triumph of home-cooking one night, the three of us sat back from the table, stuffed and approaching tipsy.

"Guys, I know a great game we could play," I said, the idea coming to me.

"I love your games, Kauhlie."

"I do too," Trevor added.

"That's because my games are awesome." Explaining my idea, I poured more wine for each of us. The game was simple: we each had to describe the type of book we would write if we were to become authors. The guys initially groaned, but once I added a, "no Hemingway stuff" rule, they were in. Of course, with that rule, I now needed time to think about my answer, so I suggested Claudio go first.

He took a moment, clinking his butter knife against his glass as he thought. Then he focused his gaze on me. "I would write a cookbook, Kauhlie."

"What?!" I almost couldn't have been more shocked. Here was this world traveler, a polyglot of high business and finance, saying he wanted to write a cookbook. Not a thriller with international espionage, not a mystery full of murders and plot twists. A cookbook.

"Why does this surprise you? As I have told you, preparing food for another is to give them life. But it is also sharing yourself. Food can be a way to share love… and a wonderful way of sharing a story."

The gears of my brain felt clogged with molasses. "You're going to have to spell that one out for me, big guy." What in the world was he getting at?

"It is a simple idea, and it is a complex idea. I would pick my recipes very carefully… and, as a whole, they would tell a story."

"A story?" Trevor asked, his academic tone creeping in. "Food can be a supporting element in a story, but not the narrative itself."

"Ah-ha!" Claudio cried, as if a lightbulb had turned on over his head. "This is where you are not using your full imagination, my friend. This is not high literature, this is a book of passion! I will take my readers on a culinary journey, one that reflects my life through the recipes I choose. My readers will come to know me in this way."

"Huh, I never thought about it that way," replied Trevor slowly. "That's kind of sneaky."

Claudio threw his napkin on the table and laughed heartily. "I suppose it is, if you are not prepared for it." He sipped his wine. "Trevor, do you know they say you can see into someone's soul through the food they cook?"

"Who says that?"

"Hush, Trevor," I hissed. I was busy watching Claudio and the light in his eyes. I turned back to him. "Go on." A lock of his hair had sprung free, dangling at his forehead and holding there just so. I almost didn't care what he said next, as long as I could look at his gorgeous black waves.

"Kauhlie, food can be passion, too—a *pasión* for life, but also a *pasión* for the people you cook for." He held my gaze for an extra heartbeat, his soft brown eyes enveloping me.

I had to get control of myself before I melted into a pile of Callie-goo. However awkwardly, I leaped from my chair and announced, "My turn!"

"Okay, Callie, you can go next, but remember the rule," Trevor responded. I couldn't blame him for that; I reached down and grabbed Toni as he continued. "What kind of book would you write?"

Toni squirmed in my arms, slinking and twisting. I shifted her in my lap as I sat back down, hoping she would stay put. She did, but I could feel her resentment emanating from her sleek and restless tail.

"Personal growth and development," I answered. "That's what I'd write."

"Oh, no, Kauhlie. Not one of those 'Fifteen steps to living your dream' books?" Claudio smiled slightly, but I also knew he wasn't exactly kidding. "Please tell me that is not what you mean."

"Ugh, give me some credit. My book would be a novel where the protagonist happens to be a woman. She would go on a journey—an emotional and literal journey—where she learns about herself."

"A chick book," Trevor interrupted.

"Chick book? What is a chick book?" Claudio asked, puzzled.

"Chick-lit," clarified Trevor. He recited dutifully: "Novels with frothy plots aimed specifically at female audiences.

"Frothy plots?" Claudio turned to me. "Now that could be something." He winked.

I ignored Claudio as a defense against turning to goo. (Oh, God, that wink.) "No, Trevor, not chick-lit. A novel about a woman who discovers herself! What's wrong with that?"

"That sounds boring, Callie." Trevor sighed. Toni sprung from my arms as if also objecting. Traitor.

"Oh, yeah, then do better if you can!" I challenged.

At this, Trevor's face plunged into itself. He picked up his wine glass, then put it back down without taking a sip. Muttering to himself, he rearranged his cutlery, then scooped up Teddy before releasing him almost immediately. He tugged at his beard as if trying to pull open his own mouth. It was quite a show.

"Perhaps you need a touch of liquid courage." Claudio chuckled gently, reaching for the bottle of anisette and pouring a shot. Trevor grabbed the glass like a lifeline and swallowed the liqueur in one gulp.

"Okay, well… here's the thing. I would… I'd write…"

I clapped Trevor on the back, encouraging him. "Come on, spit it out. I know you can."

"… a book about my alter ego!" The words rushed out of him in one great swoop, then a sheepishness shadowed his face.

"I was not aware you had an alter ego, my friend. This is new information."

"Yeah," I added, teasing. "Who's your alter ego? A salesman maybe?" That wasn't bland enough, so I expanded. "A salesman in outer Mongolia?"

"No, Callie! Listen, I'm trying to tell you guys something."

"Kauhlie, play nice. Our friend is bearing his soul, I believe." He turned to Trevor. "Go ahead, tell us. We are listening."

Repeating the angst show, Trevor toyed with the various items on the table. He pulled at his beard again, this time hard enough that it had to hurt. "In my alternate life, I'm… a matador!"

If Claudio had shocked me, Trevor had fully pulled the rug out from under me. Mild-mannered, brown-and-gray, over-academic, awkward-dork-weird, Trevor. I was so astonished I couldn't cobble together a response.

Claudio saved me from having to speak. Very graciously, he said, "Well, I must say, you hide this alter ego well."

Trevor's face went defiant yet bashful at the same time. "What do you guys think I'm thinking about all day? I have a rich inner life!"

He had a point. Trevor rarely seemed fully tethered to reality, that was true. "So you've had a "Walter Mitty" thing going on this whole time?" I asked, now that my brain and my lips were reconnecting.

"Gee, I knew you'd understand, Callie." He smiled at me with relief and goofiness.

"Now that is a story I have not read in years," Claudio interjected. "'The Secret Life of Walter Mitty' is very Don Quixote-esque in a way." I shot him a look of warning. Outside of a heart-to-heart we'd had after arriving back in Madrid, we hadn't mentioned Stephanie at all—even Trevor sensed she was an unwelcome topic. I wanted to keep it that way.

"But why a matador, Trevor?" Claudio continued, recovering from his fumble. "This does not seem like you." Teddy jumped onto his lap like a living exclamation mark.

"That's exactly it!" Trevor cried, throwing his arms up. "Because a matador is everything I'm *not*. And since I've been in Spain, my alter ego has been a matador." He grabbed his spoon and began rubbing it with the tablecloth, as if he were polishing antique silver. Almost as a confession, he whispered, "It changes with where I am, my alter ego. *That's* why I decided to travel."

"Okay Trevor, tell us the story of your matador. We're behind you." I squeezed his hand quickly. After all that had happened since my Seventh Avenue call, who was I to judge anyone else's version of sanity?"

"I would fight in the ring, of course. I'd be gored now and again, but I'd always recover, and the people would love me for it. They'd come from across the country to see me. But I would be fighting *for* something, too, and that would be the crux of the story. I'd fight to balance old-world traditions with twenty-first-century ways."

"That is noble, Trevor, and wise. If we are to preserve our traditions, we must also embrace a certain flexibility," Claudio pronounced, Spanish pride in his voice. "The world is changing now, and so rapidly."

"And I'd wear the *traje de luces*, but a modern one. With real lights sewn in. LEDs maybe, but not tacky ones."

"That would count as the color you've been searching for, Trevor," I replied thoughtfully, not questioning the idea of a non-tacky LED *traje de luces*. Yet, now that he was explaining it, this alter-ego thing was making more and more sense. "And you'd have that bright red *muleta* to wave in the ring!"

"Plus, the *capote de brega*, Callie. That cape is pink on the front, but I'd get to choose the color on the back." Toni meowed from Trevor's feet in approval.

"But, my friend, you realize you would have to fight *el toro*? Face-to-face, man-to-beast. Only the bravest of us can do this—and do it time and time again."

Trevor's face turned grave, his gravity spreading across the table like a spill. "That would be better than comp lit for the rest of my life. I'm just not into it anymore—the teaching part especially. For me, that would be another kind of death, a slower one."

Because I'd taken one too many cheap shots at Trevor's lack of direction, I tried to make up for it now. "Yeah, Claudio! Every time he stepped into that ring, he'd be living his life all the way up!"

Claudio bristled slightly. "Kauhlie, we said no Hemingway tonight. That was one of his lines. You have told me this many times."

"No, it's okay," Trevor jumped in. "Just because it's Hemingway doesn't make it less true. In my novel, I'd live my life all the way up!"

A revelation shot into my mind and directly into my legs, catapulting me from my chair. "Then let's live it for real!" The idea was so obvious, so fitting, so *perfect* I couldn't believe I hadn't thought of it before—San Fermín's famed festival was a big part of *The Sun Also*

Rises. "Let's go to the running of the bulls!" I bounced on the balls of my feet with delight. "Claudio, when do the bulls run in Pamplona? That has to be coming up soon, right?"

Wonder smoldered in Claudio's eyes. He pulled out his phone, looking up the dates for San Fermín's eight-day festival. The seconds slowed as I waited for his reply. How many times had bulls invaded my dreams over the years? How often had they haunted me in the depths of the night? Trevor's matador needed to face them, sure, and in my gut, I knew I did too. I hoped against hope there was still time. Time enough before I went back to the States, time enough to live *my* life all the way up.

"It is in three days, Kauhlie."

"Three days! We *have* to go!" I squealed the words like a schoolgirl.

"Wait, no, Callie. We never talked about this. We can't just…"

"We're talking about it *now*. Come on, Trevor, after what you just told us, don't you want to let your alter ego fly?"

"But Callie, that's one of the most famous festivals in the world. Where would we stay? You think we're going to find three hotel rooms now?"

I shirked. He had a point. Necessities of life and all that. Damnit.

"This may not be a problem," Claudio began. "My cousin keeps an apartment in Pamplona, but she is not in the country and will miss the festival this year. I will call her." He trained his eyes on Trevor. "If you are both willing to go. The *encierro*, the running of the bulls, is not for the faint of heart!"

I caught Trevor's eye and held his gaze, my own eyes begging. Pleading. Yearning. I needed this. So many of Hemingway's clues spoke of bulls and matadors—maybe this is what he wanted of me all along.

"Look, Trevor, I'm going. Even if you don't. Even if I have to sleep on the street. But I want you to come. This is something I think we both need to do."

Trevor tried to free himself from my gaze, but he just couldn't manage it. I started feeling like a bully, so I broke out of the stare and sat back down. Toni and Teddy zipped from the room in unison, off on their own adventure.

With a little breathing room, Trevor relaxed a measure as he thought. Yet when he replied, his tone was shyly serious. "Only if you swear not to make fun of me."

I was confused. "We always make fun of each other, that's what we do. Why stop now?"

"No, I mean my alter ego. That's off-limits."

"This is fine by me," Claudio pronounced. "We all have secrets, and"—here he trained his eyes too-knowingly on me—"friends do not exploit each other's secrets."

Claudio was right. If Trevor needed this thing to remain our unspoken secret, then that's what I'd do. I thrust out my palm for a handshake. "Off-limits, Trevor, I promise."

Trevor didn't take my hand as I expected—he left me hanging there, arm outstretched like an idiot. Avoiding my eyes, he gazed into his tablecloth-polished spoon as if it were a crystal ball. "Thank you, Callie, but there's one more thing," he began, almost afraid to add a second condition. "I don't want to go to the *encierro* on the first day. Or maybe not on the second day, for that matter."

"They run the bulls every morning," Claudio replied reassuringly. "There will be many chances to experience the run. We need not rush."

The question jumped out of my mouth of its own accord. "But why wait? Why not go as soon as we can?"

The anxiety show repeated for the third time—at this point, there wasn't an item within arm's reach that Trevor and his nerves hadn't fiddled with, adjusted, or relocated. "Because, Callie, I need... to...." He cut himself off, pouring a second shot of anisette.

"Kauhlie, I believe Trevor needs time to grow used to the idea. Even for spectators, the running of the bulls invigorates the blood!"

Trevor gasped audibly with relief. "Yes, that's it exactly." He finished the last drop of his anisette, then whispered, "I'm not as brave as my alter ego, Callie."

Waiting an extra forty-eight hours wasn't a deal-breaker, especially since the festival lasted over a week. Plus, after all this time together, Trevor was finally able to state his own needs. That counted for a lot, too.

"Deal." I held out my palm again, fairly confident that our negotiation was now successful.

This time, almost eagerly, Trevor grabbed my hand and shook it. "Thank you, Callie."

I didn't waste a single second. "Good, now let's go! We've got to move! Claudio, call your cousin. I'll book our tickets. In three days, we live our lives all the way up!"

PAMPLONA

CHAPTER 25

VIVA SAN FERMÍN!

Our trip to Pamplona started in the most unexpected way—with a shopping trip in Madrid. Claudio had advised us to pack only our incidentals, not clothing, although he'd been vague on the reasons why. I'd pressed him on it, but I didn't get anywhere—a consequence of an excess of wine that had induced more sleepiness than intoxication.

Trevor and I had foregone first breakfast together so we could meet Claudio for the ten o'clock train. I'd ordered room service, and I hoped Trevor had done the same; without coffee to start his day, there was no predicting how his weirdness could leak out. I wanted a no-distractions morning, because I was focused on one thing: getting to our platform on time.

I slung my very-light travel bag over my shoulder as I stepped off the elevator, which hadn't landed quite flush with the floor. This happened often enough, and I'd learned to avoid this booby trap for the most part, but this morning my mind was on the streets of Pamplona, on the *encierro*, on the nightmare creatures that had plagued my dreams for years. I stumbled hard, stumbled again trying to rebalance, and before I knew it, I'd stumbled my way right into Claudio's chest.

"And good morning to you, too!" He laughed as he caught me, hugging me with his strong arms. "That was quite a hello, Kauhlie. I hope you will greet me this way more often." He smelled fresh, like soap and sandalwood, with the slightest tinge of bleach wafting off his white-linen shirt and pants. I inhaled an extra breath before I pulled away, just so I could smell him for a second longer.

"What are you doing here?" I asked, forcing my head on straight and my body fully upright. "You're supposed to meet us at the station, and not for another thirty minutes yet." Another thought occurred to me as I spoke—Claudio was early. He was never punctual in the mornings, never mind early. What was he doing here?

"Ah, Kauhlie, I must admit I am guilty of a white lie." He reached into his leather duffle and pulled out a long red sash, which he began wrapping around his taut waist. "We are not on the ten o'clock train. Our train is not until noon." With his sash now around him like a belt, he fumbled in his bag again and pulled out a matching red handkerchief.

"Why are you white-lying, and what are you doing with those red... accessories?" I wasn't sure how these two pieces fit together yet, but he surely was up to something.

He finished tying his handkerchief around his neck, then stepped back and threw out his arms, showing off his raiment. "I am telling white lies for white attire, and with the reds, I am making myself ready for the celebrations!"

I grunted something. Maybe I hadn't had enough coffee after all.

"Do not be cross, Kauhlie. I changed our tickets because you and Trevor must be properly attired for the festival, and so I am taking you shopping!"

"Couldn't we shop in Pamplona?" I moaned. I really wasn't loving this unilateral game-change of his.

"We cannot. I thought of this. At this late date, the shops in Pamplona will be stripped bare of traditional dress. Whatever is left over will be gaudy and touristy. This will not do. You must have an authentic Spanish experience!"

I nodded. He did have a point. We didn't exactly plan this trip to the letter, and if we needed traditional dress, it was better to bring it to Pamplona with us, even if that meant Claudio had to change our tickets.

"And even better news. The noon train is direct, no transfers. Now we do not have to stop in Zaragoza for second breakfast."

"That is more convenient," I agreed, "and we won't have to worry about Trevor wandering off in the station. Where is he, by the way?"

"He is probably outside by now. I texted him earlier." Claudio's eyes lit up with charm. "But I wanted to surprise you, Kauhlie." His pupils became even brighter. "It has been some time since I have surprised you, a negligence I hope you will forgive me for."

I swooned. I had little control over my thoughts at this early hour, and my mind flashed back to Buen Retiro Park, to our first kiss. To my first *complete* kiss amid the Dr. Seuss trees. I pushed the memory away, but several seconds had passed, our banter interrupted. Anything I said now would sound stilted.

Claudio sensed this. He offered me his elbow. "Come, we must go."

We picked up Trevor, and then Claudio swept us into a taxi. I thought he would take us to a chain store of some type, but instead we pulled up in front of a boutique, one that—even from curbside—was bursting with extravagance.

"I have made an appointment for us, to ensure timely service," Claudio explained as we piled out of the cab. "You will need several changes of clothing, and you should expect to ruin them all during our week. But I do not want either of you to hold back on this account. Today, I will take care of the bill!"

We weren't two steps inside when two attendants appeared—a woman for me and a man for Trevor—who both over-affably offered us *café con leche*. Not being one to pass up free coffee, I accepted. The woman then whisked me off to the selection of whites she had prepared—several pairs of pants and a half-dozen tops. There were fewer options for the requisite red belt and scarf, but she'd managed to pull together two choices for each. With service like this, I was seriously afraid I might never set foot inside a department store again.

"This red is fantastic, Callie," Trevor remarked as Claudio paid. "Like the *muleta*, but without the threat of a bull. The best of both worlds."

I bit the inside of my cheek. A hundred clever comebacks had raced through my mind, but I stopped even one of them from coming out of my mouth. "Trevor, if your alter ego is off-limits, you can't set me up like that, okay? Behave."

"Okay, Callie. You're right. I'll be good."

Claudio insisted that we wear one of our outfits out. Trevor's selection fit him well, but the cut of his pants was relaxed, while Claudio's pants were fitted perfectly through his thighs, showing off his flamenco-toned muscles. He'd bought himself several more pairs as well; my week was definitely looking up.

Because we'd dawdled too long, we had to dash for the station. No time for second breakfast, which Trevor groaned sorely about since we'd now be going direct. Bribing him to hurry, I promised to buy him a snack from a newsstand. With only minutes to go before our train left, I loaded up on prepackaged goodies. Truth was, I hadn't been looking forward to a three-hour train ride without a bite to eat, either. Maybe I'd been spoiled by abundance. Or maybe I'd embraced abundance for the first time in my life, I didn't know which. I didn't have time for a meditation session on the topic, though, and I tossed the assortment of very-unhealthy food into my bag as I ran to catch up with the guys.

Boarding was well underway when we reached the platform. Revelers abounded, most dressed in whites. I scanned the crowd and noted there were almost no tourists; it seemed all of Madrid was on its way to Pamplona. We couldn't get a triple seat together, but we did manage to find a pair of empties with a third open directly in front of them. It took some scrambling to snag all three seats; Claudio and I took the pair, with Trevor settling into the third.

Claudio leaned over the seat and clasped Trevor's shoulder. "My friend," he began as he reached for the scarf at his own throat. "I am sorry to say, but it is time to remove these." His eyeballs shot over to me, prompting me to undo my scarf as well. "We are premature, you see."

"Do I have to? I really do like it," replied Trevor, twisting around awkwardly. "It feels fancy."

"I am afraid so. Tradition dictates that the scarf not be worn until the festival opens tomorrow at noon. See how none of the other travelers are wearing theirs?" He swooshed his hand through the air. "I wore mine for demonstration, but now we must be authentically Spanish!"

The attendant at the boutique had tied my scarf too tight; my clunky hands couldn't loosen the knot. Without a word, Claudio reached over and began undoing it for me.

"Aw!" whined Trevor, "Does that go for the belt, too?"

Claudio laughed, calling the attention of the man in the third seat in our row. He explained Trevor's fashion dilemma in Spanish. The man laughed too, before offering a suggestion in a stream of Spanish.

"*Señor* is correct!" Claudio chuckled. "He says the scarf is a no-no, but if it means so much to you, Trevor, you must wear the belt to Pamplona. He says you must harbor a great love for the *encierro*!"

Trevor's face lit up. "That's a fair compromise. I can do that." Claudio translated, then the man held out his hand—across Claudio and over the seat—for Trevor to shake. Much to my amazement, Trevor reached out and grabbed the man's hand appreciatively.

The train lurched forward. A man in the back shouted, "*Vamonos!*" which set off a chain reaction—with similar celebratory cries, passengers across the car confirmed that our trip was now underway. Someone toward the front had brought a guitar and began strumming boisterously. Bottles of wine appeared as if by magic. The aisles filled as people began singing and even dancing. A woman pulled out a *chiflo* and started playing the sharp flute brightly. Someone else had castanets and a flair for using them. Communicable chaos. Chanting. Singing. Beer. More wine. Laughter.

Ninety minutes later, when we were deep into the Spanish countryside, the party started to slow. The dusty hills were whooshing by outside, baking under the summer sun like clay pots. The calm outside penetrated our car, lulling us collectively. The singing and chanting gave way to a murmur, then the murmur faded away, too. Soon, all that was left of the party was the gentle guitar melody coming from the guy in row four.

I could feel sleep creeping in as I watched the hills roll by. Claudio had been nodding for a good ten minutes, and now, half-asleep, he reached over and put his hand on mine. His touch radiated warmth, a warmth I absorbed, cherishing it. The guitarist strummed, I slipped away.

I awoke later with my head nestled on Claudio's shoulder. His hand was still on my hand, and his head had fallen on my head. Not wanting to wake him, I stayed perfectly motionless. He still smelled fresh, sandalwood again filling my nostrils. I tried not to move as I glanced down at my watch, which was barely in my field of vision. I'd only been asleep for a half-hour, but it felt like a lifetime.

We still had another hour before reaching Pamplona, so I shut my eyes again. Not to sleep, but to take the moment in. The rhythm of the train was fast and steady now, the car around us quiet now. The world around us perfect now.

∽

I slipped out of our borrowed apartment while the guys were still asleep, my jailbreak made easier because Claudio and Trevor were now roommates—they were sharing the back bedroom with its two double beds. I, very unapologetically, had the master bedroom, and fortunately for me, it was closest to the front door.

I didn't want to subject Claudio and Trevor to a *The Sun Also Rises* moment, but in the dawn light I'd bolted upright in bed: the opening of San Fermín's festival was only a few short hours away. I'd read that chapter hundreds of times, but I'd never once lived it. To forego the ceremonial opening for sleep was pathetic. The rockets, the intrigue, the revelry. The excitement, yes, but the risks too—wild roisterers, a plaza packed with intoxication, the scorching July sun above the unrestrained masses. That part was daunting, but to hide from the good because of the bad seemed cowardly. This was no time for cowardice: a once-in-a-lifetime adventure awaited me.

I hesitated as I closed the hallway door. Sneaking off by myself was slightly mad, I couldn't deny that. I didn't know Pamplona at all, I barely spoke the language, and for all I knew, even in my whites, I screamed "helpless tourist." A headline flashed in my mind. "American Expat Trampled in Pamplona—but Not by Bulls." A hell of a way to go out.

I reflected on this possible fate, staring blankly at the hallway's ornate clock. Just as the minute hand jolted forward to twelve past nine, I snapped myself out of it, grousing at my own absurdity. So what if I made the evening news? At least I would go out *trying* to live—I'd have accomplished that much.

"Am I here to live my life all the way up or not?" I asked aloud. The only reply I received was the ding of the elevator arriving.

I knifed my way onto the crowded street. Already, throngs of people were milling around, and luckily the morning wasn't too hot. I reached into my pocket to make sure my scarf was still there; feeling its bulk somehow made me more confident. All that stood between me and the Plaza Consistorial's opening ceremony was a little more than two hours and a little less than two miles. Both seemed manageable, even though I had no idea how to get from here to there. I didn't want to pull out my phone and follow a map, so I scanned the street for clues.

A group of young men stumbled by, singing and passing a large bottle of wine between them. Rowdily buzzed, obviously, but they also looked like they knew where they were going. I followed, keeping a few paces behind, taking in the splendor of the morning and watching the modern world transform into the brightly colored balconies and cobblestoned streets of Old Town. I was sure I was going the right way—the crowd thickened by the block, the frenzy growing ever more palpable. A sea of white surrounded me, I was a droplet in that sea.

When at last the plaza's magnificent Baroque town hall was in sight, I ducked into a café decked out in the green, red, and white of the Basque flag. The place was packed. I managed to slither to the counter where I slammed down an espresso like a pro, then grabbed an order of knotted churros. I slipped back into the streaming crowd, enjoying my fried breakfast and practically dancing my way the last few blocks. Fiesta was in the air, and the air was infectious.

Just as I was cramming myself into the plaza (along with thousands of others), my phone started blowing up—a text every sixty seconds. It was nearly ten-thirty now, my flight had been discovered. As soon as I claimed an inch of space within the chaos, I pulled my phone from my pocket and scanned through the messages. So many texts. All were from what remained of my entourage, begging to know where I was. All save for the first one.

The first text was earlier, I'd missed it somehow. "Yes, Callie. You must live your life all the way up to find me. I am in Pamplona." My heart jumped. I checked the timestamp: twelve minutes past nine. When I'd asked the question aloud to no one.

I mistook the *pop* of a champagne bottle for the bursting of my insides. Hemingway was texting me now? Texting? How did he learn to do that? More to the point, why was this the *one* question he'd chosen to answer? One question out of dozens, one question after months and months of asking. And what was I supposed to say in reply?

The dervish around me faded as my world became no bigger than my phone's screen. I focused intensely, weighing my options for a reply. I tapped out a few words, then deleted them. I tried again. Again. And again. I was stuck: I had nothing to say—or maybe I had too much to say. A message from Trevor popped up, breaking my concentration. I deleted it immediately in a fit of frustration.

I shoved my phone back into my pocket and refocused on the raucous spirit in the plaza. A woman, her hair wild and her midriff exposed, offered me a swig of champagne. Her boyfriend encouraged me: "*Bebe todo!*" The bubbles cooled my throat, the sticky-sweet liquid dribbling down my chin and onto my whites. The woman twirled me around, shaking her supple hips to the music streaming from her phone. This wasn't just *el duende*, this was something more, something even more transformative.

I tried to lose myself in the elation, but the text kept haunting me: "I am in Pamplona." I'd been following Hemingway's trail of breadcrumbs for five months, and now that I thought of it, he had never once declared his location so specifically. Was I closer than ever to finding him? Yes, surely. Or probably. Maybe. A definite maybe. Yes, I was definitely maybe much closer. Either that or I'd botched the whole thing up. Both seemed equal possibilities. Anxiety slithered through me, the quicksilver in my veins contrasting with the morning's frenzy. Damnit, what did this man want from me? And why couldn't he just send GPS coordinates?

The sun was creeping toward high noon now. I panned the plaza, turning around as best I could in what little space I had. Latecomers swarmed into the square, packing the rest of us that much more densely. Not a single person among the thousands seemed in the midst of an existential crisis—so why should I be? Why this quest, why this burden, why this angst? All these whys, all this woe, when centuries of tradition and celebration were before me. A freedom as pure and essential as fresh air, all now before me.

The crowd roared as the festival's officials filed onto the platform. Any moment now, the mayor would make his proclamation before launching the *chupinazo* rocket into the air. The crowd became one as they waved their reds, the swatches of crimson undulating like a great patchwork blanket across the square. From all around came the chant, "*Viva San Fermín! Viva San Fermín!*"

The anticipation became my clarity. I could reply to Hemingway now. I *had* to reply to Hemingway now, because this was *my* moment, not his. I was here, I was in Pamplona, and I would live every instant of this fiesta fully. I pulled out my phone again. I responded in his own terse style, needing only seven words and knowing that he would understand all I was packing into them. My thumbs flew over the keys: "It is fiesta, and fiesta is good."

CHAPTER 26

UNTIL WE SHARED ONE SKIN

The ash of the old man's cigarette was almost an inch long. It hung there, refusing to break free, clinging to the smoldering cigarette between his two wrinkled fingers. Fiesta was defying the laws of physics. The man was one of hundreds on this narrow street, being jostled and shuffled by the mob, yet the ash hung on, unyielding.

The madness was freedom. Every twist and turn of Old Town's streets brought adventure, titillation, intoxication. Two voluptuous young women walked hand-in-hand, their abandon turning the heads of a group of singing young men—they collectively lost the thread of their song as they gawked. A couple who we'd seen several times debated heatedly, pointing and stomping their feet as they walked; this went on until the woman hopped up on her tiptoes and kissed her boyfriend passionately. Flags from the balconies waved at the slightest breeze - none of those flags were Spanish. Culturally, Pamplona was Basque country, and green saltires greeted us everywhere we turned.

The saltires were much more welcoming than the homecoming I'd received after yesterday's jailbreak. The guys had been really upset when I finally made it back to the apartment, but thankfully, during fiesta, the rising Spanish sun absolved us all with each morning. That absolution had saved me, and we'd started the day on a bright note.

"Claudio, where are we going?" Trevor asked. His words were drowned out, never reaching Claudio's ears. Trevor turned to me like I knew the answer—as if I wasn't completely lost. I was trusting that Claudio knew where he was going, although even he looked a touch overwhelmed. He was trying to hide it, and it was cute as hell.

After a few minutes the street opened up, rows of open-air cafés on either side. Claudio guided us toward the third on the block. Even from the street, the scent of cured ham made my stomach growl and mouth salivate.

"Ah, yes, I knew it was around here somewhere!" Claudio cried triumphantly. He opened the door for us. With a flourish, he announced, "This is the best charcutier in the entire country, and so this is where we begin our food-journey."

I hadn't been aware that we were on a food-journey, but I didn't knock it either. It was well past time for second breakfast for one thing, but more importantly, the dozens of cured hams dangling from the ceiling were enticing my taste buds. One of them had been taken down and was being spun slowly on a vertical rotisserie. A butcher—one of six frantically trying to serve the crowd—deftly shaved off paper-thin sheets of the delicacy with his sharp, curved knife.

The shop was as crowded as anywhere else in Old Town. Everyone was standing—either at the end of a long counter or at small, round tables. We claimed a space for ourselves at the far end of the counter, where we ordered a charcuterie board—various samplings of ham and sausage balanced by marvelous cheeses. The house ale, brewed on-site especially for fiesta, complemented it all beautifully. Claudio was right; these had to be the best butchers in all of Spain.

I would've gone in for seconds, but Claudio encouraged us to keep moving. He asserted that there were too many delicious things to eat in Pamplona and too little time to eat them. From my experience, this was true of all of Spain, but the excitement flickering in his brown eyes made me want to move on as well. It seemed possible that we'd be having third, fourth, and maybe even fifth breakfast today. Who was I to argue with that?

Our next stop was also in Old Town, and Claudio was clearly looking for a specific spot as we sliced through the thrall. The cobblestones were damn hard to walk on—uneven and deep-rutted. Who designed these things?

"*Pinchos!*" Claudio exclaimed as a tray of toothpick-skewered appetizers reached our table. (Wait, we'd only been here for two minutes, when had he ordered?) He gazed softly into my eyes. "Kauhlie, I have very much wanted to share these with you."

"Then I'm very much looking forward to eating them!" Not my most original reply, but as long as I kept my mouth moving, I was that much less likely to blush. Blushing at guys had never been a problem before; I don't know how Claudio did that to me.

"*Pinchos?*" Trevor asked. "Aren't these tapas?"

"They are… and they are not, my friend. They are Basque tapas, you might say, and they are native to this region. Literally translated from Spanish, a *pincho* is a spike or skewer, and *pinchar* means 'to pierce.'"

"So that's why they have toothpicks? Little piercing skewers?"

"Exactly, Kauhlie. In the Basque tongue, they are called *pintxos*. But in any language, they are delicious!" He held out a shrimp-on-toasted-bread creation for me. It was just a little too big to comfortably eat in one bite, but nonetheless a smile crept across my face as I chewed. I enjoyed being fed via toothpick. Via toothpick by Claudio.

"I like this *pinchos* concept," Trevor declared, grabbing a toothpicked treat. "But I think we need a pitcher of beer, too." This was an excellent suggestion, and before we knew it, a couple of besotted hours had slipped by.

Our last stop was a real restaurant, not a café or bar, that served only "the most authentic Basque cuisine," as Claudio put it. It was early for dinner—early for Spain in general, but early for fiesta in particular—and a break from the crowds only added to our epicurean enjoyment. We started with scallops in their shell, soaking in a sherry-ginger vinaigrette. Then the three of us split an open-faced quail-egg sandwich, before gluttonously moving on to trout stuffed with ham. We washed all of this down with even more beer. By the time we were finishing up, I didn't know if I was more drunk than full, or more full than drunk. None of that mattered. It was fiesta.

⌇

It was time to do some serious nightclubbing—Pamplona style. We'd taken a late but much-needed siesta after our food-journey. I'd awoken completely sober but utterly energized, and now I wanted to dance.

Claudio led us across the Plaza del Castillo and down a crowded side street lined on both sides with clubs. Each club was small and narrow, like a shopfront, and it was easy to see that most ran deep into their buildings. Flashes of red, then blue, then red again, spilled out onto the sidewalks. Every club had a distinct type of music coming from within, the sounds leaking onto the narrow street and mixing with the roisterous multitudes. An untamed street where even the air smelled like fun.

"How about this one?" Trevor asked as Claudio peered in from the sidewalk.

"No, this one will not do," he replied, pushing forward into the crowd while reaching back and grabbing my hand so we wouldn't be separated. With my free hand, I did the same to Trevor: if we lost him amid the crush, who knew when we'd ever find him again. The three of us slithered through the thrall together, chain-link style, until we reached the far end of the block. Claudio stopped short. "This one," he declared.

The bar jutted out into the narrow room, creating a bottleneck. Squeezing past the bar's stacked-up patrons was no small feat, but we managed to make it to the crowded dancefloor. Claudio indicated that he would get our drinks. And Trevor, after barely surviving the fight to the back of the club, followed him, presumably to help carry the cocktails. This left me on my lonesome on the outskirts of the dancefloor.

Normally this wouldn't have been a problem, but as soon as the guys disappeared, I felt like I was being watched. I panned the room: I *was* being watched: three men were huddled together, conspiring and eying me. One man smiled at me, but it was a lewd, ravenous, objectifying smile—I was a piece of meat to him, little different from the hams at the charcutier. For the first time in Spain, I felt unsafe.

I wasn't about to let this asshole get away with intimidating me; I fixed my eyes on him and held his gaze, warning him to keep his distance. Within a few seconds, he became visibly uncomfortable. He motioned to his friends, and the three of them began pushing their way out of the club. I claimed my victory silently: Callie McGraw, pervert thwarter.

The guys returned a few minutes later bearing the sweet relief of alcohol. Gin and tonics for me and Claudio, but Trevor's drink was brightly colored and sweet-looking. A touch of something sugary sounded soothing, even with my gin and tonic in-hand.

"Can I try a sip of that?" I shouted over the cacophony. He handed the glass over. "That's fantastic! What is it?"

"I don't know. I found it!" Trevor's eyes lit up as he spoke, an extra-goofy smile sweeping across his face.

"You what?!" I screamed, horrified. "Are you trying to get us all roofied?"

"Oh my God, Callie, I'm kidding." He laughed. Claudio laughed too—so hard he almost spit out his drink.

"Don't do that to me!"

"Sometimes you're so intense, Callie." He mock-punched my bicep. "Chill a little."

Trevor was right. I was too wound up, being too literal; while "pervert alerts" had been common back in New York, I wasn't quite so used to them anymore. The alcohol would help, I was sure, but really the only cure was to dance—and dance hard.

The three of us had been out dancing many times, and we always ran into the same challenge: mathematics. When the guy-to-gal ratio isn't even, dancing dynamics are tough to calculate. Some guys can dance with any number of people, as long as there's at least one woman on the dancefloor; others insist on dancing one-on-one with a woman. Most guys, like Claudio, fell into a hybrid of the first two. For him to join in with his tantalizing dance moves, one of the women in the group had to be partnered *primarily* with him—other guys were free to take part, providing they didn't challenge his alpha-male status. Trevor, by contrast, fell into the first category. As long as there was a woman in the mix, he was good. No alpha-male thing happening, but no real dance moves either.

I grabbed Claudio's arm and pulled him onto the dancefloor, squeezing in as best we could. I loved his dance style: Claudio employed a minimum, deliberate, amount of movement. For him, less was more. Every move had rhythm and was filled with a restrained passion. The conservation created a reservoir of energy: when he did let loose, it was in a spectacular, flamenco-inspired fervor. And when he finally did break free—when the dancefloor parted and all eyes turned to him—I adored being the woman he was dancing with.

Trevor was the opposite. His elbows and knees flew everywhere, and he moved like his entire body was double-jointed. He used all the energy he had in his tank all the time. He danced like nobody was watching, even though the eyes on any dancefloor regarded him as a car accident in progress. That didn't matter, though; as I danced with my two favorite men, it was clear Trevor was having a blast, Trevor-style. Fiesta was feeding his soul, he seemed freer and braver than ever. I nodded at him in time with the music to encourage him—like he really was doing everything right. Like his flinging elbows weren't a concussion waiting to happen.

Our dancing could only continue for so long, because Claudio was dancing *with* me and Trevor was really only dancing *near* me; after a while, this always got clunky. But I wasn't danced out, so—

after another round of cocktails—we decided to move to a different club. Claudio shout-whispered something into Trevor's ear, and then we were off.

The night air wasn't exactly cool, but it was refreshing. I breathed it in deeply as I looked down to the next block. The atmosphere there seemed even more hedonistic, beckoning to me.

"Guys, I'm going to find a club over this way," Trevor announced, pointing down the street. "Maybe back to the one Claudio didn't want to go to earlier."

"Naw, we're going this way." I pointed in the opposite direction. "Come on!" Claudio gently placed two fingers on the small of my back. I knew the touch well. A familiar touch from when we were together. He was asking for some alone time with me, asking that we let Trevor wander off on his own for a while. That's probably what Claudio had been whispering about before we'd stepped outside. I locked my knees into place before they could betray me; no way was I going to start swooning.

"Okay, well, I'm going this way... to find me some *señoritas!*" Trevor exclaimed, waving his arms. The alcohol was clearly having its usual effect, but this was bold for him. Fiesta bold.

"You do that, big guy," I said, giving him a thumbs up and a wink. I guess the alcohol was having its usual effect on me, too.

Claudio guided me down the street as the prime-clubbing-hour crowd squeezed in tighter around us. He clearly was trying to protect me from being jostled and shoved, and he was doing a good job. With his forearm, he blocked several revelers from colliding with me, and he even put his shoulder into one particularly rowdy guy.

"Let's try this one!" I shouted, pointing to a truly wild-looking club. Claudio eyed it carefully before nodding in approval. He cleared a path to the entrance, then kept on clearing a path to the bar, leading but holding my hand as he pushed through the people. He got us another round of gin and tonics. The gin tasted cheap, but I was getting to the part of the evening when I didn't care.

The dancefloor here was even more packed than the first club's. White and red blurs gyrated with abandon. Claudio claimed a space for us, and I nestled into the opening. He placed his hands on my hips as we moved as one to the rhythm.

The low ceiling pressed down on us, dancers on all sides pressed in on us, and Claudio and I pressed together unabashedly. Sweat and heat and movement and energy. Intense heat, sultry and sticky, clung to my skin, shrinking my world. I inhaled Claudio's scent—earthy and comforting and tantalizing. I lost myself in the haze of this Spanish Fiesta. This Spanish fiesta with Claudio.

Lights flashing in a dizzying swirl, the dancers moving as one organism. One life thriving beneath the pulse and the heat. From the speakers, the music boomed louder, its rhythm moving through my body as if I were made of air. I closed my eyes even as I continued moving. When I opened them, Claudio swooped me in even closer. My heart skipped a beat.

We pressed against each other until we shared one skin. The mass swayed and popped around us, but we were no longer a part of the crowd. We were an island, a universe, unto ourselves. Claudio leaned down, becoming blurry in his nearness. I reached up and wrapped my arms around his neck, gazing into the brightness of his eyes. He pressed his lips to mine. The world melted.

CHAPTER 27

CALLIE'S PERFECT DAY

Claudio and I stayed out all night having a blast, reacquainting our lips in the process. We never went to sleep, we just kept going. It wasn't until sunrise that we headed back to the apartment for a brief recharge. That's where we found Trevor sprawled on the sofa, his red belt around his forehead, snoring loudly. The man had obviously drunk himself silly. I was glad of it; what else was fiesta for?

After a cool shower and a fresh set of whites, I almost felt like a million dollars. I was still wired, but a hangover was starting to creep in. I figured the best thing to do was seek caffeine and carbs before we headed to the *encierro*; I peeked into the bathroom where Claudio was showering and told him I would be right back. I slipped out the door without waking Trevor.

The sun, shining brilliantly in the sky, had been up for maybe an hour. Its beams reflected off the colorful, unfurling awnings above the shops and cafés, their owners preparing for another profitable fiesta day. I suspected that under normal circumstances, no merchant in all of Basque country would be open this early, but today the neighborhood had no shortage of stragglers drifting back from the clubs. Stragglers who needed sweet-bread *ensaimadas* to soak up the alcohol in their stomachs.

The city was rebounding from a night of revelry, just like I was. Entering a small plaza, I paused in the street, breathing in the freshness of the day and taking in the morning light. I indulged for a long moment, trying to burn the scene into my memory. Today I would face the creatures of my nightmares; today I would live my life all the way up. With the sun shining warmly on my face, the streets were full of promise. And, after my night with Claudio, I felt in my soul that this was the opening of a Perfect Day.

That precise moment is when my day took a turn for the worse.

I lost track of my steps, catching my toe on a bit of uneven pavement and stumbling hard. I shot my other foot forward to compensate, but I still twisted my ankle. I teetered hard, foolishly trying to save myself. Both legs buckled. My arms flailed outward trying—and failing—to grab ahold of anything that would keep me upright. I went down, my body slapping against the pavement like a side of beef hitting a butcher's table.

I screamed something—something indecent, I'm sure—as the sting of asphalt-against-flesh surged through me. "Shit!"

I lay there for a moment, not moving, shocked and mortified. I attempted to get my bearings from my new ground-level perspective. I had an excellent view of the gutter.

As I began hoisting myself up, an older man appeared out of nowhere and grabbed my arm. "Shit," I muttered, my sandal threatening to slip again.

"*Mierda*," the old man said as he heaved me up. I reclaimed my balance. "*Mierda!*" he said again, a helpful look on his face.

"*Mierda*; shit" I repeated, as if I were paying for this language course. The man nodded back with a kind smile. Seeing I was alright, he walked off, as if happening upon a woman literally in the gutter was nothing unusual.

I'd been fresh and clean only moments ago, but now streaks of asphalt-black—along with some unidentifiable gray stuff—stained my whites. The side of my sandal had a large scuff mark across it, which seemed permanent. Aside from those patches where the shopkeepers had hosed off their sidewalks, I hadn't thought the street was wet, but somehow my outfit was now damp in places. During my graceless swoon, my sunglasses had rolled underneath me; I picked up the crushed and mangled frames with two fingers, pinching the end of the optical carnage. I flung them toward an overflowing trash can, where they bounced off the top and landed with a hard *clunk*.

I wanted to retreat before anyone else saw me in this sorry state, but now I needed coffee more than ever before. I walked across the plaza, limping on my swelling ankle and headed for the café where we'd had first breakfast yesterday. The host observed my wish to seat myself on the front patio, but not before taking a silent inventory of the grime sprawled across my outfit. Callie McGraw, walking disaster area.

The host wasn't without mercy, though. My limp must've been more pronounced than I thought, because almost as soon as I sat down, he reappeared with good wishes and a zip-top bag full of ice. "*Ese va ayudarte mucho, señorita.*" He grinned gently, his eyes telling me he'd seen more than one fiesta casualty over the years. I loved him for that. And I loved his coffee, which he'd brought without my having to ask. Right then, it was the best coffee I'd ever tasted.

Soon, I saw Trevor and Claudio making their way through the plaza. With their contrasting strides and matching whites, they made an odd pair—Claudio confident and smooth, Trevor ambling yet somehow jerky. They made even stranger roommates, now that I thought of it. Of course, the roommate situation might not last too long. I didn't know if I was ready to welcome Claudio into my bed again, but the possibility was far from out of the question.

"Kauhlie, you must not make a habit of running off," Claudio began once he was within earshot, "but thank you for your texts."

I rose halfway out of my chair as he bent down to give me a kiss-on-the-cheek hello, but Trevor was first to notice the state I was in. Which was saying something—did I really look that pathetic?

"Callie, what happened?! Did the bulls already run? Did they run *over you?*"

"I took a tumble. Nothing serious."

"Are you alright?" Claudio asked, genuinely, pointing to my ice pack.

"I'm fine. The ice fixed me up, it's not even swelling anymore. An extra-hearty first breakfast, and I'll be good to go, go, *go!*"

Eggs!" Trevor cried. "We need eggs!"

"Right! Maybe *huevos rotos*, or an omelet. Good hangover food."

"We have time to eat, my friends, but then we make our way to the course. The bulls run at eight o'clock, and we must secure our spots early!"

Trevor didn't speak, but whatever boldness fiesta had bestowed upon him last night dissipated before my eyes. He sank into himself, becoming smaller in his chair. He tugged at his beard, then began pulling at the handkerchief at his neck as if it had become too tight.

"Come on Trevor, this is what we came for," I encouraged. "You know it's time. You owe it to yourself—and to your alter ego!"

"Yes, Kauhlie is right, you must do this. You need only be brave for a brief time. The *encierro* is intense, but it is over within a few minutes."

At this, Trevor's ultra-tensed face relaxed into his more-usual tensed face. He flagged a waiter and ordered a screwdriver to bolster himself. I couldn't fault him for that, and a little hair of the dog might help the hangover he was harboring.

The cocktail arrived swiftly, and he drank it in two large gulps. "I think I can do this." He slammed his glass down on the table to convince himself.

"Yes, you can do this! Your inner matador can do this. You, me, and Claudio, we can *all* do this, and we'll do it together."

Apparently, this was exactly what Trevor needed to hear because, without a single word, he rose from the table slowly and strode boldly into the street, his head held high and his chest puffed out. With deep, sweeping strides, he began circling the small plaza, waving as if greeting a cheering arena. Claudio and I stared in astonishment, our respective jaws on the ground. For the moment—in this moment—Trevor was a matador, and this matador was leading our way.

"I want to be up front, right against the fence," matador-Trevor declared as we approached the course. "Claudio, find us a good spot."

Claudio grinned like a proud father. Taking orders wasn't his thing, especially not from other guys, but this morning he was happy to make an exception. "This is the very best spot on the Plaza Consistorial, I have chosen it carefully. Now all we must do is make our way to the front."

The streets of Old Town were transformed. With centuries of practice behind them, each festival morning the good people of Pamplona erected the run, putting up fences and gates and creating a corridor leading to the city's arena, the run's terminus. Once the bulls had been corralled post-run, the fences would be pulled down… only to be erected again tomorrow. The half-mile course wasn't a straight shot—it was filled with turns and hills—and in addition to the crowds on the streets, thousands hung from windows and balconies above. And everywhere, in every heart of every person, anticipation loomed.

The crowds grew thicker, everyone vying for a good view. Claudio managed to claim a space for us against the fence. I pushed back the memories of my nightmares, now flashing in a great swirl in my mind, and stepped up on one of the fence's wooden slats. Leaning forward, I marveled at the waiting runners.

Dozens of runners, mostly men, milled about, smiling and joking. At least most of them were. Some were visibly (and understandably) nervous. One man who thought nobody was looking scrambled over the fence to safety—I could see his disappointment in himself even in his gait. I pitied him: I thought he was damn brave for making it as far as he did, but I knew he would face taunting and ridicule for his last-minute, yet very-sensible, decision.

Everyone on the course was dressed in white and red as tradition prescribed. Everyone except for one guy who was sporting nothing but tennis shoes and a British-flag-adorned Speedo bikini-brief. He pranced and strutted his stuff for all to see, as if anyone cared. He didn't even have all that much stuff to strut, and the Union Jack across his ass looked awfully flat.

Claudio read my mind. "Worry not. The bulls will seek him out, for sure," he winked, curling his lips into a sly smile. His one rebellious lock of hair broke free, as it so often did. I didn't reach up to smooth it back into place, but the restraint took effort; I longed to feel his hair slipping through my fingertips.

"Time for reconnaissance," Trevor declared. "How long until the bulls run?"

"Reconnaissance?" I asked. "What reconnaissance? We're already here, we have a great spot."

"No, I need to surveil the run. A matador faces the ring alone. This is my ring." He held his chin high, evidencing his conviction. Matador-Trevor was still leading the way.

"There remains time enough to explore briefly," Claudio said, "but do not delay."

"I won't. Save my place for me."

"Whatever you and your alter ego do, you must not cross onto the course. Not even before the opening rocket," warned Claudio. "If you do, you are very likely to be arrested. If that happens, you will not face *el toro* today. Nor tomorrow. Maybe not even the next day." His eyes narrowed, becoming even more grave. "And we both know you must experience the running of the bulls *today*. This morning. Now."

"This morning," Trevor agreed. "*This* is the morning."

He took off, pushing through the people behind us. With that, Claudio and I were alone—except for the crush of festival-goers surrounding us. Claudio leaned down and whispered in my ear, "I had a fine time last night, Kauhlie. Fiesta agrees with you." He caressed my upper arm, just brushing my skin.

Goosebumps rose on my neck, my senses growing keener. I could smell him again, his post-shower freshness. I wanted to burrow myself in his chest, as I had done so many times last night, but I forced myself to turn and fix my gaze far over the fence. Now wasn't the time for this, not with the fever in the air and my nightmares lurking at the edges of my mind.

I concentrated on the crowd's buzz as I counted to twenty silently, purposefully. Steering the conversation back to the run, I said, "So explain how this all works. Why are the runners here and not at the start of the course?"

Claudio cleared his throat—a throat-clearing that seemed to swallow the intimacy that had passed between us. "Groups of runners line the route, jumping in when the bulls approach. In a moment, the police will allow these brave souls to spread out on the course and pick their spot for the run."

"Pick their spot?"

"The spot where the bulls will catch them."

Part of my mind froze. "They don't really catch them, though, do they?"

"Not if things go right. Normally, the bulls run swiftly past." I turned around, looking at him quizzically. He grinned, raising his left eyebrow. "Ideally, things go right."

The crowd shifted en masse, pushing us much closer together, Claudio squeezing against me. I didn't mind that at all. He reached out, turning my wrist so he could glance at my watch. "The *encierro* is strictly coordinated. In a few minutes, the first rocket will signal the release of the bulls. Six bulls and a few steers."

The joke launched out of my mouth before I knew I'd spoken. "Steers? I thought you needed balls to run this course!"

A grimace flashed over Claudio's face—he must've heard that one before. "The steers are castrated and more docile, but they are helpful.

Most bulls like to run in a herd. The steers help create that herd, they all want to get to the end."

"What happens when they reach the end?"

"Many things. But for these bulls, not much. At least, not until this evening. Then they will star in the bullfight!"

"That all sounds pretty straightforward," I replied, a little disappointed, a little relieved. His description didn't at all match the restlessness and anticipation of the thousands around us.

"Perhaps it sounds that way. But I promise you, in less than nine-hundred meters, there is more peril than I expect you are imagining." He looked deep into my eyes, pulling me into the foreboding within. "So very many dangers for the runners." His stance changed, reflecting an ominousness. "This is fact." Totally over the top. I giggled despite myself.

"Kauhlie, I am serious. There is grave danger."

"Grave danger?" I bit my lip to suppress another giggle.

"Yes. This course in particular. The Curva de Mercaderes, for example." He pointed down the run, to the furthest spot we could see. The turn there was sharp, maybe a full ninety degrees, and at the bottom of a slope. "Velocity, plus speed, plus—"

"—I know that equation!" A bubble of a giggle slipped out; my lack of sleep and general uneasiness were bringing out a giddiness I'd never experienced. A defense mechanism perhaps. I straightened my face and my tone. "That has to be a tough corner to round."

"It is. Many bulls cannot turn in time, they slam into the wall… and whatever is between them and the wall. This is why it is called, 'Hamburger Corner.'"

I bit my lip even harder. His earnestness was too much. Hamburger Corner was too much. Just… too much. I burst. Not a pleasant, jokey laugh; a full-on unrestrained laugh, poorly timed and even more poorly received. Even the four women behind us seemed slightly offended.

His eyes went blank, he squared his jaw. "Kauhlie!" he chastised,

"This is real! Such injuries are not funny." I couldn't tell if he was hurt or angry.

I put on my best "I'm sorry" face. I was indeed sorry. This was serious stuff, and since I'd never told Claudio of my nightmares, I couldn't explain my odd behavior. "I'll be good," I promised. "Tell me more? What other dangers?"

He relaxed a measure. "The runners themselves can cause problems. The course is narrow in many places, and there are many, many runners." He bent down and half-whispered the next part. "Do you recall the... scar on the back of my thigh?"

I nodded to hide the rush shivering through me. Of course I remembered. A raised, whitened crook just below his firm buttock. My eyes had followed its curve countless times, studied the contrast between the once-injured skin and the rest of his muscled flesh. I'd never asked about it, partly because I didn't think Claudio would explain, but mostly because we were usually busy doing... other things.

He threw his shoulders back. "I earned that scar, right here in Pamplona. San Fermín blessed me!" At this, he turned to the crush of people behind us, raised his arms in the air, and repeated his words in Spanish. Cheers of support and encouragement and awe answered him.

"You've run with the bulls?" I asked in a rush of breath. It didn't seem possible. Even now, here, with the opening moments away, I didn't think running with the bulls was something regular people—sane people—did. Why in the world would anyone risk their life like that?

"For several years, yes. And in this particular year, I did not escape *el toro*. Up ahead, at the end of the run... the tunnel into the arena is perilously thin. A bottleneck forms there. Always. I knew this, but I was not careful enough. I fell at the moment the herd rushed by... and I tell you Kauhlie, bulls do not stop for traffic!"

I gasped. "You mean to tell me that scar... is a hoofprint?"

Something behind his eyes sparked. "More or less, yes. I was lucky, *el toro* only nicked me. Only his front leg, and he did not step on the bone—or else surely I would have been crippled."

"You never told me that?" I muttered through my shock.

He shrugged. "There are many things I have not told you, Kauhlie. I am a private man."

"Did you ever run again?"

Claudio's eyes twinkled as he laughed. "Of course, I did. It was not *el toro's* fault, I was in his way." He shrugged with the ease of a man who *didn't* have a hoofprint embedded in this thigh.

My hand moved of its own accord. I ran my fingers lightly—so lightly—over his leg, where I remembered the scar. A timid touch, a bold touch—both in one. "Does it ever... still... hurt?"

His eyes became deep velvet pools as he met my gaze. "No, Kauhlie. This is one wound that time has healed. Much like you and I are healed."

He slipped his arm around me, pressing me against his broad chest and resting his chin gently on the crown of my head. I closed my eyes, my eyelids heavy, my nostrils inhaling his scent. The world became small again, the madness around us disappearing. The sun on my hair, his arm around me, his chest firm and strong, yet welcoming. Safe, cherished, sheltered. No nightmares here, not ever. I could stay in this embrace... just here... just forever.

"I love you."

The words startled me. Did he say that? No. They were my words, from my mouth. My voice. I fought the urge to recoil, but a tension had already seeped in between us; Claudio's body growing taut, mine stiffening. My words—words I'd never said to any guy, not ever, not once. Too soon, too soon! We weren't ready for this, were we? Wait, was *I* ready for this? What the fuck, Callie?!

I pushed myself away. Not by much, an inch or two, just enough to depressurize. But wait. The milliseconds were flying by—Claudio hadn't reciprocated. In fact, he hadn't said a word. He *had* to say it back, get everything out in the open; he *had* to, right?

More milliseconds. I went to code yellow. He looked down at me, his eyes blank and unreadable. He caressed my hair, a plastic smile on his face. Not a word. I'd opened the door for him, all he needed to do was step through. That's all… one little step, three little words. Silence. Code red! He turned and fixed his gaze far over the fence, just as I'd done moments earlier.

The last vestiges of my Perfect Day evaporated, my heart sinking, my humiliation complete. Three words—mine spoken in hope, Claudio's left unsaid—had left me exposed and cruelly vulnerable. Damn Claudio. Damn him.

CHAPTER 28

NIGHTMARES & NEW YORK

We heard the bulls before we saw them—a low rumble growing steadily louder as the beasts turned onto the long straightaway. The crowd turned as one, all craning their necks for a better view. Some chanted in anticipation, others prayed anxiously. The runners directly in front of us tensed: some stood dead still, testing the air, while others hopped in place, warming up and getting ready to jump forward into the rush of bulls. The guy in the British-flag Speedo began waving his thin, pale chicken arms as if he were conducting an orchestra. I was sure he was high or crazy or both; a good goring would set him straight.

"Oh, man! This is intense!" Trevor began rocking on his heels, and I was surprised to find I was doing the same. I steeled myself for the arrival of my nightmares. Goosebumps covered my arms. Any moment now, the bulls would thunder by, and I wasn't about to miss a second of it.

Claudio put his hand on my shoulder intending to pull me from the fence-rail. I shrugged him off hard. I'd managed to stay civil until Trevor had returned, but that's all I'd managed—the last thing I wanted right now was his touch. When he self-consciously retracted his hand, I was glad of it.

The herd was close now, maybe two blocks away, barreling down the street. A breakneck pace, faster than I thought possible. Runners ahead jumped into the bulls' path, swarming into the herd for a fleeting moment. At the last second, before a bull could catch them, they would swerve to one side—all hoping *el toro* did not swerve with them.

Incredible, magnificent beasts, so much larger than I'd anticipated. Rampaging nightmares—every fear I'd ever had made real, here in front of me. The beasts' heads bobbed up and down, every stride propelling them forward like giant battering rams. Such majestic, unbridled strength—the muscles in their bodies visibly pumping. Their velocity, their power. Suffocating on an insidious dread, I trembled in sheer, fearful awe as the Hell-beasts drew closer. I tried to remind myself that I was on the safe side of the fence, that the bulls couldn't catch me here. It was little comfort. The fence was flimsy, thin, almost symbolic—even more symbolic, perhaps, than the doors in my parents' home.

The rush blew my hair back. Trevor shouted something enthusiastic but unintelligible amid the chaos. The runners directly in front of us had jumped in a second earlier—a leap of faith like no other. The crowd exploded as a bull swung its head, his broad skull knocking a man clean off his feet. I recoiled involuntarily from my perch, my whole body shaking.

Agog, I had no words. Trevor fought back welling tears of wonder and awe. Claudio was speaking earnestly to a man on the other side of him, although how either could form coherent thoughts right now was beyond me. The herd thundered on as if we were thin air, insignificant and inconsequential.

I scrambled back onto the fence-rail, watching the bulls' powerful hind legs propelling them, muscles throbbing, tails flailing. So many glorious creatures, all moving with a single shared purpose. A stampeding torrent of nightmares.

"It is not over," Claudio suddenly cautioned, his face grave.

"There's more?" asked Trevor. He rephrased. "I hope there's more!"

"There is one bull left, I counted. Five bulls only, plus the steers. My friend here"—he gestured to the man he'd been speaking to—"agrees. One bull remains unaccounted for."

"How can a bull disappear?" Trevor asked. I was glad he posed the question; I really didn't want to speak to Claudio right now.

"He has separated from the herd. This can happen when *el toro* becomes distracted." Claudio's eyes burned. "This is very dangerous."

We heard a solitary set of hooves striking the cobblestones, followed by shouts from the runners up the course. They parted with a terrified synchronicity, all trying to melt into the fences. *El toro* was alone… and pissed off. The animal's rage surpassed even my anger at Claudio.

Pastore shepherds, armed with nothing but thin and fragile herding sticks, appeared out of nowhere, shouting to each other over the chaos. *El toro* didn't slow. Most of the runners had managed to dive out of the way, but a few remained, the guy in the British Speedo included—the Union Jack on his ass transformed into a *muleta*. Slowing to almost a trot, the bull zeroed in on him, waiting for the right moment to catch Speedo guy and his love of Queen and Country. I gasped in fear—I'd only been kidding about his needing a good goring.

Man and bull were close now, no more than twenty feet away. I thought for sure the poor sop was done for, but just as the beast attacked with his massive horn, Speedo guy dived to one side, landing ass-up against the far fence. Lucky bastard.

"Callie! The horn missed that British guy by an inch! Maybe less! His ribs almost—blammo!" Trevor cried, equal parts thrilled and terrified, just as a matador should be.

Yet all was not well. Halfway between us and *el toro*, one of the runners—a tourist—began panicking. Knowing he couldn't outrun the beast, he'd had the good sense to throw himself flat on the ground. Now his good sense had abandoned him. It was in his eyes: the dread, the irrationality, the loss of control. Terror propelling him, he sprung up—the worst thing he could've done. The sudden motion caught *el toro's* attention, and he acquired a new target.

"*Bájate, bájate*!! Get down, you idiot!!" Claudio screamed with every bit of air in his lungs. I couldn't tell if he'd gone bilingual out of sheer horror or intentional practicality, and there was no way the kid heard him over the uproar. This poor kid from who-knows-where, a college kid probably, who'd thought running with the bulls would be fun and games.

"Callie, no!" Trevor buried his head in the crook of my neck, unable to watch the spectacle. "The *pastores* can't control it! He's doomed!" My eyes grew wide as the same realization hit me: there was no escape for this boy. The only question that remained was whether he would live or die.

The bull lowered his massive head, surging forward. He hooked the boy's leg in his horn, the two coasting forward as one. Shrieks and wails from all sides. Then *el toro* swung his neck violently, flinging the boy free. The impact of his body shook the fence—this fence that now seemed more symbolic than ever. I recoiled in self-preservation, the boy landing at my feet. Twisted like a rag doll, he gazed backward through the slats, terror and desperation in his moist eyes.

As the beast backed away, I almost exhaled with relief. Almost. *El toro* was not done. He raked his hoof, establishing his dominance. With a running start, he plowed into his victim, thrusting his dagger-like horn clean through the boy's leg. He screamed in utter agony. Blood erupted—more blood than seemed possible from one human limb. Fighting to free himself from his victim, *el toro* bellowed and snarled, but the horn was too deeply embedded in the boy's flesh. Enraging the animal further, he screamed again, more desperately this time. The mighty beast jerked his head upward and shook it forcefully. Then again. A third time. Finally, his horn freed itself from the boy's leg. A trail of blood spurted through the air, spattering across my hair and face and shirt.

El toro, still not satisfied, backed up again, pawing and raking the ground, preparing to charge again at the shattered boy. Whacks from the *pastore's* poles did nothing to deter the beast; their shouts did even less. Screams enveloped me; screams rose from me.

To my right, a white flash streaked over the fence. Claudio. Landing on the course with surprising alacrity, he ran behind *el toro*. Just before the bull began charging the crumpled pile of a boy, Claudio grabbed his tail and pulled with all his strength.

El toro did not like this at all.

The bull snorted fiercely, folding himself around nearly in half, struggling to hook the tormentor at his tail. But the more *el toro* went after Claudio, the more leverage Claudio gained—he forced the beast into a spin. The crowd went mad with terror-tinged cheering, Trevor included. Man and beast spun around three times until—at the precise moment when the bull was pointed toward the open course—Claudio let go. The centrifugal force sent *el toro* surging forward. The stunned animal forgot about the tormentor at his tail and the bleeding-and-moaning boy, and he began racing down the course.

"Claudio saved his life!" Trevor shouted. "He's like Superman!"

I forced a shrug. "It was okay." Saving that boy was undeniably amazing, but I wasn't feeling at all charitable toward Claudio right now. And the cacophony spinning in my head—the carnage, the anguish, the horror—was crowding my few remaining rational thoughts. More gore than in my worst nightmare.

"No, wait," Trevor continued. "He's Spain Man, remember? I guess Spain Man really is a superhero after all!"

"Yeah, sure Trevor, a superhero, whatever." Claudio, the man who'd bested a bull with his bare hands; Claudio, the man too cowardly to say, "I love you."

The next thirty minutes were just as surreal. The crowd indeed treated Claudio like a superhero. With the medical team frantically tending to the mutilated boy, Claudio became a micro-superstar—every man, woman, and child within fifty feet rushed to take his picture, shake his hand, clap him on the back, or pray over him in thanksgiving to San Fermín. A local reporter covering today's *encierro* snapped his picture. The story would run in the "Best Gorings of the Day" section.

We somehow broke free of the madness and began making our way to the Plaza del Castillo. Not one of us spoke. We were processing—the bull, the boy, the blood, the crowd lauding Claudio. Plus, the "I love you" debacle. I couldn't be mad at Claudio now, not with his being a hero, but my anger, embarrassment, and frustration were simmering in the background too. I'm sure my humiliating expression of love was somewhere in his thoughts as well, even though he showed no hint of it.

We wandered into a café, and Claudio made drinks magically appear. Not our usuals—a Spanish liquor I'd never seen before arrived in small glasses.

"Here. Drink this. It will help," he offered. I tossed it back. It burned as it slid down my throat. I coughed hard.

Always the philosopher, Trevor whispered, "That was ferocious."

"Yes." I didn't have more words. I stared into my empty glass, suddenly realizing that something was stuck to my forehead. I reached up: my hair was damp-ish, sticky, and matted against my skin. Blood. The boy's blood. I shuddered, trying not to wretch.

Claudio pulled out his phone. "You should see yourself, Kauhlie. Let me take a picture of you, so you will always remember San Fermín's mercy!"

"No! What's wrong with you?!" I blocked the lens with my hand—my fingers were now bloody, too. "I'm good." A stranger's blood coating my hair, a stranger's blood coating my shirt—why in all hell would I want a picture of myself now? Grizzly, sickening. This was a moment to forget.

Claudio sensed my revulsion. "Then I will get you a second round. That, too, will help." I perked up. Another round was exactly what I needed.

Trevor raised his hand like a kid asking for a cookie. "Yes. A second round." Whatever matador lived within him had obviously been steamrolled by this morning's reality. We wouldn't be seeing matador-Trevor again for a good while, I was sure of that.

Claudio kept trying to flag a waiter, except there was no waiter to call. He panned the café twice, but help was nowhere in sight. It was the height of the breakfast rush now, I imagined the waitstaff was busy flying from table to table on the front and back patios.

As if his mouth had just reconnected with his brain, Trevor interrupted Claudio's silent search. "You totally saved that kid! He was done. Stick-a-fork-in-him done!"

Claudio turned to Trevor. He shrugged his shoulders as if facing off with a bull and saving a life were part of a typical day at the office.

"He was a goner, Claudio," Trevor repeated, revving up for a long babble. With his neurons now firing, I knew he had a queue of painfully obvious thoughts threatening to fly out of his mouth. I couldn't let that happen now.

"Trevor, stop! You're distracting him. Claudio has a purpose—getting our drinks—and you're keeping him from that purpose."

"Right, Callie. Sorry."

Claudio, his adrenaline rush fully faded, gawked at me as if to say, "There is no one to serve our drinks. All is lost."

"Look at me!" I cried. "I'm covered in blood. I need that second round!"

Trevor leaned forward, examining me. "Yeah, you have some blood right there." He extended his index finger and thumb. "Right here. It's drying and making your hair curl." He snapped the blood-crusted curl. "It's sticking out like you used the world's worst hairspray."

Lasers shot from my eyes. Trevor withdrew his hand as if he'd burned himself. It took everything I had not to punch him, and he knew it—we'd been through too much today, and now alcohol was on the line. "It… it's really not so bad," he uttered, trying to mollify me. I shot lasers at him again.

"Do not worry, Kauhlie. I will find us another round." Claudio rose abruptly, leaving his phone on the table. "Trevor will help me," he added, grabbing his arm and hoisting him up. "Between the two of us, no waiter shall escape!"

I leaned back and closed my eyes. The depth of an exhaustion I didn't realize I was harboring seeped into my eyelids. A second round, a hot bath, sleep, food. Then I could deal with anything else. But first, I needed those four things. Starting with that drink.

Claudio's phone rang. I looked around to see if he was nearby, glancing at the screen. A call from the States—a 212 area code. A Manhattan caller. I snatched up the phone, gawking in disbelief at the screen. Who the hell was calling him from New York? What was he up to now? What was he keeping from me? My stomach jumped: my Perfect Day just kept getting better and better.

❧

"Why won't you tell me?!" I cried. "Who's calling you from New York, and at…" I counted the hours between time zones, "three-thirty in the morning?" Three-thirty in the morning? Someone stumbling in drunk, I thought, someone with cheap mascara running down her face and her miniskirt hiked up to her navel.

"I know many people in many places," Claudio answered. I hated him for his evasiveness.

"If you had nothing to hide, you'd tell me." He opened his mouth, but I cut him off, plowing through. "Who do you know there, and why is she calling you?"

He winced just slightly. "It is not important right now, right here."

"You're telling me some girlfriend of yours in New York is calling you, and it's not important?"

"I did not say any such thing." Claudio's eyes turned hard and blank. "I said it is not important right now. Right now, we are in the throes of fiesta. Let it be, Kauhlie."

"So, you admit there's a girlfriend in New York? And you admit this on the same day I told you I love you?"

Trevor's mouth fell open. "You told him you loved him?" His eyes grew wide and maybe a little sad. "Is this a lovers' quarrel?"

"No!" We shouted back in unison.

"Maybe," I countered.

"Maybe?!" Claudio asked, surprised and wary.

"Yes, maybe!"

"O… kay," Trevor nodded, pulling on his beard nervously and clearly trying to come up with an out. He pushed his chair back. "I think I'm going to the bathroom."

"No, you're not! Stay right there! Pee yourself if you need to. Claudio has some explaining to do, and I need a witness!"

"There is no girlfriend, Kauhlie. Do not put words in my mouth." He began undoing the red handkerchief at his neck—like he was literally hot under the collar. "This morning has been very taxing, physically and emotionally, for all of us. And you did not sleep last night—I think perhaps you are not at your sharpest."

"I'm always at my sharpest!" I shouted. A real shout. Patrons turned, their eyes bugging out at the sight of my bloody hair and stained whites. Callie McGraw, the very epitome of sharpness.

"This is not true! Otherwise, you would remember that my father is in New York. That is who called." He crossed his arms firmly, becoming a stone sentinel.

Damnit, he was right—I'd forgotten. Not that I was giving in. "At three in the morning? I'm not that gullible!"

"Yes, at three in the morning. My father does not sleep well. Never has. And right now, he wants me to move to New York, to fill a position at the company he just founded." He lowered his voice to a growl. "So, there you have my so-called girlfriend, Kauhlie."

"Oh." My worst comeback ever by far. I felt like a fool, defeated.

"And in the future, Kauhlie, I advise that some trust will go a long way. My father is pressuring me to move back to New York, but I do not want to think about it now, during fiesta. I should not have to answer for such things—to you or anyone else!"

Something in my head clicked. "Wait, you said 'back' to New York."

"Yeah, you said 'back,'" Trevor piped up. "When did you live in New York?"

"Exactly!" I shouted. "All these months, and you just happened to gloss over that?"

Claudio's eyes grew harder and colder. "I have lived in many cities. New York was a minor point—it was over half a decade ago, and I was there for no more than a year."

Anger surged through me, shooting into my very fingertips. An absolute betrayal. He hadn't merely visited New York City as he'd implied so many times before, he'd *lived* there. We could've been trading life-in-the city stories all this time, sharing quips and anecdotes that only New Yorkers find interesting. Something that could've brought us closer together, but he'd held it back. Intentionally.

"You lived there when I did?! What next, you're going to tell me we were neighbors?"

A sly smile on Claudio's lips. He fought it, but in the end the left side of his mouth gave him away. I didn't know what could possibly be so amusing. Damn him.

"Almost neighbors, yes. I was in Chelsea. On Seventh Avenue." He acted as if he were completely justified in keeping this from me.

"One neighborhood away?" The table shook under the force of my fist. "Barely a mile away?!"

"One mile is a world in New York City. You know this well, Kauh-lie. And do not forget," he held up one unrepentant finger, "I did not know you back then. You cannot fault me for the linear nature of time."

"Scoundrel!" The insult flew from my mouth before the word registered in my head. "I *can* fault you for time—I've known you for over four months. That was a material omission. A prosecutable crime when under oath!"

"I am not under oath," he snapped, his words ice. Claudio's patience was growing as thin as that ice, which was fine by me.

"Not telling me something important *is* a lie. No different. When you asked for my trust only five minutes ago! You kept this from me on purpose!"

"It is not a time I remember well, nor do I want to remember it now. Working with my father… he is not an easy man. If I omitted it, it was for this reason only."

"Not *if* you omitted it. You *did* omit it. And now you can go omit yourself!"

Claudio's thin ice cracked violently. "This is not an appropriate way to address me!"

"Good—then leave. Omit yourself. Get out of my sight!" I picked up my third round—the round our waiter had hastily dropped off in the middle of all this. I threw it back in one gulp. It burned my throat and almost made me cough again, but I held firm, slamming my glass down.

"Yes, perhaps that is for the best!" Claudio rose in tempered anger before throwing a wad of euros on the table.

"Don't go!" Trevor cried. "You two can work this out. Come on, it's fiesta!"

"Trevor, my friend, I will see you back at the apartment. Do not worry on that account. "*You*," Claudio shot fiery daggers at me, "and I are good friends."

CHAPTER 29

A SPECIAL CIRCLE OF HELL

The table was wet. Wet with my tears. Wet with my snot, my sweat. Because the moment Claudio had made it out the door, I'd buried my too-heavy head in my arms and wept—an aching, open, uncontrollable, exhausted weeping for all of Old Town to see. I didn't have it in me anymore, I really didn't. My face-plant in the street, the lack of sleep, the unreturned "I love you," the nightmare of bulls, the crippled boy, the gore and blood (Oh God, the blood), the rescue, Claudio's secrets, the fight. How much could one woman take in a single morning? I didn't even care about being in public—tears flowed through my entire body, unrestrained.

"Callie, you know you two are like this, two roller coasters colliding in the night," Trevor soothed, the poor man bewildered and trying like hell not to run for cover. For a good long while, he'd silently sat next to me with all the patience and bravery he had, cupping my blood-stained hand and letting me fall apart. He'd even fended off the manager, who I think had asked us to leave. Bloodied, filthy patrons having emotional crises apparently weren't good for business.

"It'll be okay," he cooed. "He should've told you about New York, but it'll be okay."

His words barely registered—Trevor seemed far away, blurry, a mirage. The café was barely registering. I needed to faint. I needed to scream. I wanted the Spanish voices buzzing all around to quiet and just let me be. I wanted to... to Not. To void. To become a vacuum where there was no Claudio, no Spain, no mad Hemingway quests, no goring bulls. An existence of Not. Work, gym, sleep, repeat. Like I used to be, on autopilot without knowing it. That had been a perfectly valid life, a safe life—just me and my demons. Anything else could be buried under corporate-ladder-climbing and a pile of legal documents. And whenever that failed, strong alcohol liberally applied took care of the rest.

"It's... not... ohh... kay!" I pulled the sentence together between wrenching sobs. "That man... turned me... into... a... frog!"

"Callie?" Trevor gently lifted my face from the table. His touch felt odd, his hands shaky. I didn't want to move, but I didn't have it in me to fight him. "Callie, do you need me to... get some help?" he asked. "Is there someone I should... call for you? Someone back home, maybe?" His eyes were wide with alarm, greener than I'd ever seen them, and brimming with concern.

Some rational scintilla flickered deep in my mind: I sounded like a lunatic. Not like an overwhelmed woman having a tough moment, but like someone breaking-with-reality and in need of psychiatric care. Callie McGraw and her snapping point.

I gulped down deep swallows of air, each breath tempered, until I forced a calm. "No, Trevor, not like a fairy-tale frog. Like the frog in the pot. Don't you know that old story?"

His eyes relaxed. "The one where you turn up the heat, little by little, until the frog's been boiled without realizing it?"

"Yeah, that frog. Claudio waited until I felt safe and warm, then he turned up the gas. I'm the frog in his pot!" I buried my head in my arms again.

"You're not a frog," Trevor offered gently, displaying his talent for overstating the obvious. Not that I didn't appreciate the effort—he really was doing his best. Better than his best, even if he was being too literal. "Besides, Callie, Claudio doesn't even like frog's legs."

I couldn't laugh at his unwitting joke. "And it's not just that. What have I done here, all this time in Spain? Nothing! All these months and not one damn thing to show for it, unless you count a mountain of hangovers."

"That's not true. You're much nicer now—nicer than when we first met. Less... jaded. Like, all your good parts are freer now, you're letting them show."

I peeked up from between my arms. The blood in my hair had transferred in clumpy streaks to the backs of my palms. "You really think so?"

"I know so. You haven't even made fun of my alter ego once."

"I promised I wouldn't," I sniffed.

"Yeah, but would Barcelona-Callie have done that? Given her word, *and* kept it? On an easy target? I don't think so."

I thought about it as best I could—now wasn't the best moment for unbiased retrospective analysis. I shrugged slightly in agreement.

"Spain has been good for you. The art, the sites, the expat thing, all of it."

I blew my nose in my now-filthy napkin. "But what good did it do? Where did it lead me? I... found someone I thought I really connected with... but I wound up... a frog!" The image of a belly-up amphibian jerking around in boiling water flashed in my head. That was me, the frog. Too humiliating.

Trevor managed to talk me down over the next hour. He wasn't a bad listener, actually, when he put his mind to it. At some point, he even managed to steer me out of the café and onto a reasonably secluded bench outside. I'd never seen a manager look so relieved in my life. The air outside felt cooler, too, from the breeze. That helped.

"Listen, Callie, I think Claudio was right about one thing," Trevor began, breaking a lull in our conversation. "This morning was hard. That was scary—all of it."

I exhaled exhaustion and defeat. "Yeah, it was. Even before the boy. When I saw those bulls, all sorts of things went through my mind."

"What things? You can tell me."

"Terrible things. All the things in my head—all the stuff I don't talk about." I ran my hand through my snarled hair. "All my nightmares, all the stuff on the edges of my consciousness—they were all right there, rampaging down the street."

"That's what it was like for you? It didn't show—not really."

"Of course, it didn't show. I... don't show things like that." I focused my gaze across the plaza. "But yeah, that's what it was like for me."

Trevor scooted closer and put his head on my shoulder. "I get it, the world is like that for me sometimes, too. I never see it coming until *boom*! I'm in the nightmare. Grad school was that way."

I leaned my head on top of Trevor's head, his head still on my shoulder, and hooked my arm through his. We sat quietly, the plaza buzzing around us, compatriots to the last. He understood. Or at least he understood enough, and that was okay.

"I have to tell you something, Callie," he said, his tone shaky and feeble. I didn't reply, but I lifted my head from his to give him some space and signal that I was listening.

"My... my alter ego is gone. Vanished."

"Gone?" I had no idea about the comings and goings of alter egos, but sudden vanishings didn't seem like the norm. If there was a norm.

"The bulls took him. My matador... I think he's with the bulls now."

This, of course, made no sense to anyone but Trevor, but I buoyed him up anyway. "That's okay, you're still here, that's what counts." I smiled as best I could before asking, "Have your alter egos disappeared before?"

"They have, but never so quick. Never like this. They usually... fade out of their own accord."

I considered this, grasping for a reply. A woman across the way threw a crumpled coffee cup toward a trash can. She would've missed the shot, but a gust corrected the trajectory. "Well, do you think your matador is happy? With the bulls?"

Trevor clenched and unclenched his fists a few times as he thought. "I think he is, yeah. But I also think… it'll be time for me to leave Spain soon. I get lonely without an alter ego, and the world gets too scary again."

"Do you think it's almost time to go home? I'm here for two more weeks. We can fly together most of the way, I bet."

"No, I don't want to go home. Not even if I'm going with you, Callie. What I want to do is *decide*." He slumped, sighing. "By the time we get back to Madrid, I have to decide what's next. That's all there is to it."

"I think you got what you needed from your matador," I mused. "Maybe he disappeared so you can move on to something new. And a deadline is always good for decision-making, right?"

"I'm not good at deciding, Callie."

"You *decided* to leave school. You *decided* to come to Europe. You did that. So you can decide what's next. But then you have to *act* on your decision."

"Yeah, that's the tough part."

"No doubt. But it's the hard things that count the most."

We leaned our heads against each other again, falling quiet. We stayed like that, watching the plaza, solidarity connecting us, until a new thought burst into my mind.

"Damn Hemingway!" I cried, pulling away from Trevor and soliciting a dirty look from a passing man. "Damn him! This is all his fault!"

"Callie, you're losing me again," he said cautiously. "What's Hemingway got to do with any of this?"

I hesitated, planning my words carefully. Even with all I'd confided in him today, even with all he'd confided in me, I wasn't ready to confess my Hemingway calls to Trevor. I'd already abutted that invisible, delicate sanity-line once, and I didn't want him worrying about me—not when he already had so much on his mind.

"He made me *believe*, Trevor! He made me think, if I came to Spain, that I could have my own private *The Sun Also Rises* experience." That wasn't the whole truth of it, of course, but my material omission was far less damaging than Claudio's. "That I could be like his characters!"

"Why would you want to be like them? They're losers. Every single one."

My hackles raised reflexively, but I had just enough energy to push them back down. "They're not losers. They represent things."

"No, they really are losers." His voice turned cautious. "Listen, I'm not saying this to be mean but... the characters just drift around Europe, full of nothing but entitlement. Nothing holds importance, nothing has any meaning. The book isn't a blueprint for how to live your life."

"But they live in suspended animation, almost. That's so easy!"

"That's not easy, that's bleak. You just said so yourself... it's the hard things that count."

"I guess I did say that, huh?" Me and my big mouth.

"A life devoid of meaning? That sounds like Hell. A special circle of Hell, one for cowards too cowardly to know they're cowards." He met my eye, his own eyes full of conviction. "You are *not* a coward."

My stomach lurched from the certainty in Trevor's gaze. I broke free from his eyes and concentrated on the scuff mark on my sandal. "Sometimes I *am* a coward," I admitted, tears welling up again. "But I didn't know that until I came to Spain."

"Then you learned something about yourself. That's good, right?"

Was it good? I honestly didn't know. Ignorance is bliss—people say that for a reason. I'd never understood it until now.

"I think I have it, Callie!" Trevor beamed like a leprechaun who'd just thwarted some dolt trying to steal his gold.

"Have what?" I wasn't sure where he was going with this. But hell, where were any of us going with anything, ever?

"I only know one quote by Hemingway." The leprechaun-smile on his face grew. "It's apocryphal, but it fits."

"Well, don't keep me in suspense."

"He said, 'To hell with them. Nothing hurts if you don't let it.'"

"Yeah, that sounds about right," I admitted. I'd spent the whole of my adult life ignoring the things that hurt.

"But you know what, Callie?" Trevor forced back a titter. "That's really shitty advice." He tittered again as he punched my shoulder, then his titter grew into a full-on laugh.

I didn't want to, but I laughed back. Just a giggle at first, then harder. Then even harder, my sides beginning to seize. Harder still, until I was crying again, this time in mirth. Good ol' Trevor—the counsel and catharsis I needed.

⁂

"Come on, it is time to wake up," came the familiar voice. "You have been asleep for many hours."

So groggy. Who was bothering me? Who was this shapeless some-one sitting on the edge of my bed?

I rolled over in a sleep-defending huff, pulling the sheet far over me. "Urugh!" I argued.

A gentle nudge—followed by a stronger one. "You must eat some-thing, at least."

"Urugh!" I cried again. A compelling counterargument if I ever heard one. Were I a litigator, I could win in court with an argument like that. And who was bothering me?

"I have made you a tray, Kauhlie."

My eyes shot open under the sheets. What was Claudio doing here? And where, exactly, was I? This wasn't my bed, was it?

The memories flooded back, whirring together in my mind like a headache. Claudio, something about Claudio. What was it?... Ah—I wasn't speaking to him. Why wasn't I speaking to him?... Oh, yeah, that's why.

"Damnit, what do you want?" I hissed, still under the covers.

"To start, I would like you to eat something. You've—"

"—You said that already. Try again." Another thought panicked its way into my mind: was I dressed, or was I lying here ass-naked with nothing between us save for this sheet? I did a quick check-in with my hands. Fabric... okay. A tank top... good. Sleep-shorts... definitely good. I could now defend my position with the full surety of someone wearing underpants.

"You have been asleep for nearly twenty hours. Almost an entire day. This is not so good."

"It's called being tired! I'm tired—of you, especially. And what the hell are you doing on my bed? Haven't you heard of personal space!" The possibility of returning to sleep was growing further and further away, but this mattress could still be my redoubt.

He hesitated, and even from under the covers I knew he was scratching the scruff at his jawline. I felt Claudio's weight lift from the bed as he stood. "Pardon me. I have taken a liberty that is no longer mine to take."

"You got that right, buddy." Damnit, I was fully awake now. And I had to pee. Double damnit. Why didn't this redoubt come with plumbing?

Through the sheet, I saw his shape move away and reposition itself on the hope chest at the foot of the bed. "While you are considering my ills, Kauhlie, I admit I have come to you under a false pretense. You must eat, yes, but... in truth I have come... to confess."

That got my attention. In one great swoop, I shot up from the covers and locked onto his eyes defiantly. "Oh, *now* you want to play nice? Why should I trust anything you say?"

His pupils turned into quizzical, earnest tunnels. "Because... I have brought you coffee?"

"Not good enough." A bit of a lie. Caffeine cured many an ill—and now that he'd mentioned it, the fresh-brewed aroma was heavenly. I reached over to the cup of exquisite darkness, cradling it to my chest before taking my first sip.

"I am sorry about New York." He said it plain and simple. "I should have told you about my time there with my father."

"Well, it's a little late for that, don't you think?" Caffeine and outrage for breakfast; they complimented each other surprisingly well.

"I do not think so, Kauhlie, not if you are willing to listen. And I should not have been so defensive yesterday, either. *El toro* got into my blood, I am sure of this. The morning was… demanding. For everyone."

"Fine, okay," I said, far more interested in my buttered roll than in a nightmare of bulls. Now that my stomach had turned on, I was ravenous, like I hadn't eaten since I'd landed in Spain. Which was contrary to all evidence, but still.

"Kauhlie, there is a reason I did not tell you. My father is an exacting man, this is true, but it is not the work that troubles me."

I leaned forward slightly as I chewed. I guess I could listen. I could do that. As long as food came with his white flag. Claudio really was a masterful negotiator.

"This is not so easy." He grinned nervously. "Growing up, I did not know my father as well as you might think. My mother either, for that matter."

"Boarding school. Switzerland. Right. You've told me."

"It was what they wanted," he continued. "It was what was *expected*." He glanced into the mirror on the dresser, then turned back to me. "My parents are overly concerned with… status. Boarding school for their only child was necessary for that status, but it was not what I wanted. I wanted to… be with my parents. To be a family. Not just for the summers—every day."

"That's not unreasonable for a kid." I could understand that much, although I wasn't sure why Claudio was giving me this history lesson now. Didn't I have my own demons—bulls included—to deal with?

"But the trouble was… the year before I went to college, my parents no longer wanted to be… with each other. That shattered me, Kauhlie."

He covered his face with his hands. "Shattered me." A vulnerability emerged that I'd never seen in him before.

I softened a little, empathy betraying me. I knew that shattering too well. "I thought your parents were together?"

Claudio shook his head. "They are... and they are not. They are happy in their marriage, but only because it is not a marriage. It is more of an 'arrangement' than anything else."

"I see. That is hard," I said—I knew. "Status again?"

"Status... and assets... and taxes." He sighed in dejection. "This is what my parents now base their union upon. And the day when my mother told me, she said it matter-of-factly—as if they had been living apart for some time, and it was not so emotional for her anymore."

He ran his hands through his black waves three full times. I was listening, but I took the opportunity to polish off my bun in two huge bites. I was still chewing when he continued. "I did not see them together much after that. The few times when I did, they talked very little—a wall between them. That was even worse. When the three of us were together, but not together. When I understood we were no longer a family."

I let his words hang there. I wasn't without sympathy, but I had no idea what any of this had to do with a job offer in New York. He'd softened me up some, but I wasn't about to let all my defenses down yet. I crossed my arms.

"Some years later, my father had a position for me. By that time he had moved to New York semi-permanently. I thought working for him might bring us closer, that I could get to know my own father."

"Did it?" I wanted to know, despite myself. "Did it bring you any closer?"

"A little, maybe. He is a hard person to get to know. He likes to keep a measure of distance. You remind me of him in that way, Kauhlie."

I uncrossed my arms for the sole purpose of re-crossing them. "Oh, like you're a warm and fuzzy open-book?"

Claudio forced a chuckle. "Perhaps I am like him in this way as well. Perhaps you can count it among my ills. The ills I am offering to you, in honesty and for peace."

I leaned back on my pillows, the realization hitting me. That was our problem. He needed space, I needed space: that space—that need—stood staunchly between us. I covered my face with my hands. I couldn't deal with that last thought while my bladder was screaming—and it looked as if relief was still a while off.

"And what does any of this have to do with moving to New York now?" I finally asked, keeping the attention on Claudio.

"Because my father took a mistress, Kauhlie, when I was living there. It is not right that they should live this way, as husband and wife. My father has a wife, and that wife is my mother!"

I held back my surprise. "That's not... very European of you. What happened to living in the moment, to *el duende*?"

"Marriage is not living in the moment, Kauhlie. Marriage is *every* moment—it is a life and a vow of living! My father with his false wife... this I could not bear! This is why I left." His eyes shone with tears that he wouldn't let fall. Not crocodile tears, either, the man was hurting. "But now my father says I should go back. He says this time will be different. He has left her, but I do not place my faith in this. They have parted several times before."

"So then don't go? There's nothing that says you have to go." I mean, it wasn't like *I* was in New York anymore. It wasn't like we could transplant our relationship—such as it was—across the Atlantic.

"But it is a great opportunity, Kauhlie. A big step up. I will not find a position at this level, not now. Maybe not for some years. I would be a fool to pass it up. And I would move back now, if not for the mistress. To betray my mother in this way...."

"Well, what does your mother think of this?"

"She has long been upset, and she would *prefer* I not go. She believes my father should be more discreet. As she is discreet in her affairs."

Claudio's antilogic was fighting against my caffeine—and pressing against my bladder. "Your mother's affairs are okay, but your dad's aren't? How does that work?"

"My mother has taken lovers, this I know. Her current one is in Greece, where she winters. But they do not pretend to be husband and wife. They... are more quiet. This is not ideal to my mind, but it is not... so crass, not so vulgar."

"Claudio, that's a lot to hide. You could've told me—some of it at least."

He ran his hands through his hair again, freeing his one forever-untamable lock. "I do not speak of these things unless I must. But this is not an excuse. I should have told you, and I should not have lost my temper. I am... trying to figure this out—it is an unexpected complication."

I wiggled down the bed and reached for his hand. "*Some* people think nothing hurts if you don't let it. I guess I used to think that, sort of. But keeping stuff this big to yourself, that's not good for you—or for us."

Claudio's face lit up for the first time since he'd awakened me. "So then, there is, as you say, an 'us?'"

I jumped back, pulling my hand away. "Don't get carried away there, buddy! How many other secrets are you harboring?"

His eyes sparked devilishly, his lips curling. "Dozens," he replied. "And, as best as I am able, I hope to share them with you. In due time."

My heart leaped before sinking to my stomach. In due time. How much time was that? Two weeks left, Callie, two weeks. Could I love this man for only two more weeks? And what about that love—the whole "I love you" debacle? If I let him back in, we wouldn't be on square terms. I was deep into this novel while he was still dancing in the margins.

"So, you love me then?" I asked straight out. This was too important of a question to skirt, plus I still needed the bathroom. Soon.

Claudio didn't answer. He turned his head, fixing his eyes on some far point outside the window. I knew that trick—the same one he'd pulled on the Plaza Consistorial yesterday. I wasn't letting him get away with it, not this time.

"Out with it," I demanded. "Yes or no—it's not that hard."

He pulled his gaze from the window and pretended to be looking at me, but really he was looking beyond me, at some utterly fascinating spot just behind my shoulder. "It is hard, Kauhlie. I am not a man to discuss these things. I have done all in my power today to evidence the depth of my affection." His eyes shifted from the spot on the wall and landed directly on mine, although they had turned blank, unreadable. "Let that be enough—for right now."

My two thoughts crashed into each other. "Damn you and your space, Claudio," smashed into "Don't push him, Callie. Maybe that's enough, for now." Where was the middle ground?

"Then I take it back," I declared. "I'm taking my 'I love you' back."

His face turned into a question mark. "I do not believe you can do that, Kauhlie. This is not a possible thing to do?"

"It is, and I am," I retorted. "You've been downgraded. From now on, I will merely have"—and here I imitated his voice—"'a depth of affection' for you."

Claudio laughed, as the rest of him leaned toward me, his body scooting back onto the bed in the process. He enveloped me in the crook of his arm. "Very well, Kauhlie, that is very fair."

I relaxed into him, trying to make sense of my every waking moment today. I sighed contentedly. Claudio touched his fingers to my chin, guiding my lips upward for a kiss.

"Claudio?"

"Yes, dear one?"

"I have to pee."

CHAPTER 30

MR. HEMINGWAY, I PRESUME

Second breakfast came at three in the afternoon, after I'd taken a shower. I was still ravenous, so I decided to raid the fridge rather than heading out to a café. Even though I was just making eggs and bacon, when Claudio saw I was preparing to cook, he took over immediately. Which, in all honesty, was for the best.

Trevor dutifully reported that he'd drawn me a bath when we'd come back to the apartment yesterday. I had no recollection of it; not even one soothing, soapy bubble remained in my memory. Not that I doubted Trevor in the slightest, plus supporting evidence abounded— chiefly that I hadn't been covered in blood when I'd been pried from my exhaustion-coma.

"Kauhlie, if you are up for it, I have a surprise for you," Claudio said as I loaded our plates into the dishwasher. "Something you will very much want to see."

"You know I love surprises! What is it? Let's go now!" With my stomach full and a second cup of coffee in me, I felt fantastic.

Trevor chuckled for no discernible reason. "Callie, don't you think you should… adjust your wardrobe first?"

Damnit, he was right. I was still wearing the light, waffled bathrobe I'd found in the closet. "Hey, at least I'm still in white," I countered. "All I need is a red scarf and I'll be ready to go."

"I vote for pants, Callie. I'll wager this is a pants-wearing surprise."

Claudio nearly spit out his tea in laughter. "Our friend is right. Pants are indeed required. But that is the only clue I will offer."

"So, it's a surprise *and* a mystery?" I clapped my hands in delight.

"It is a very special surprise, Kauhlie, and you must agree to not ask questions. It is only a short ride away, but I will brook no inquiries."

"Geez, what is it?" asked Trevor in a special display of obliviousness.

"Didn't you just hear the man?!" I turned to Claudio and smiled. "He said no questions."

"Not even tiny ones," he replied impishly. "I will not even answer your non-questions."

"My non-questions?"

"The questions you ask that seemingly do not relate to the matter at hand. The ones you ask when you are putting things together, when you are hiding your puzzle-piecing."

With a *clunk*, Trevor placed a fistful of silverware into the dishwasher. "I don't think Callie does that—do you, Callie?"

"She does," Claudio answered quickly. "It is her lawyer's mind."

"Right. And don't you forget it, buddy. Brains before beauty!"

His deep laugh echoed through the apartment. "I do not believe you will let me forget it!" He slipped his finger into the belt of my bathrobe, pulling me toward him and pecking me on the cheek.

"Yuck." Trevor scrunched up his nose. "We're back to this again."

Claudio laughed again, this time not so loudly. "Yes, we are back to 'this again,' my friend." He stood from his stool at the island. "And I am back to surprising my Kauhlie. If"—he turned to me, his eyes impish again—"she agrees with the terms. No questions."

"Fine, fine, no questions," I agreed. "Not even non-questions."

"And Trevor, the same goes for you. Do not try to do Kauhlie's work for her. Whether you know it or not, you are very good at that."

"I am?"

"You are."

"Yeah, Trevor, you're an awesome sidekick like that. The best Bilbo ever."

The lines of his forehead wrinkled. "I want my alter ego back," he groaned. "I would've zoned out of this conversation a while ago."

"We still have a few days in Pamplona," I countered. "After that, we'll figure out your alter ego. But right now, you're standing in the way of my surprise."

"What is wrong with your alter ego?" Claudio asked. "I was not aware of a problem."

"Claudio, my surprise!"

"My matador… I'll fill you in later. But right now, for Callie's sake, I promise. Okay?"

"It is settled then. Kauhlie, go put on your whites. I want to arrive before the crowds settle too thickly."

The cab ride was indeed short, but by now I knew the city just enough to discern that we were heading back to Old Town—to the Plaza del Castillo, in fact. On the ride, to keep both of us from asking questions, I resorted to playing the alphabet game with Trevor.

The taxi left us off, per Claudio's instructions, where the Calle San Nicolás intersected the plaza. Here, we could approach our destination from the south, on foot, so as not to "ruin the effect" as Claudio put it.

As we approached, I realized I knew the café well, if only in my mind's eye. A *The Sun Also Rises* surprise from Claudio to me—the very place where so many of the novel's scenes were set. Broad white awnings emblazoned with "Café Iruña" protected patrons from the afternoon sun. The polished-wood and frosted-glass doorway was choked with tables, with customers milling over their coffees in all the ease of Spain in July.

"I didn't think this place still existed!" I twirled around in enthusiasm. "So exciting!" I might've squealed like a schoolgirl as I hopped onto Claudio without warning for a piggyback ride. He laughed and grunted simultaneously, humoring me.

I shot my fist in the air. "Iruña, ho!" People everywhere turned. With all eyes on us, Claudio quickened into a half-gallop. Trevor scurried behind, utterly bewildered.

"Another café..." Trevor began as we reached the crowd of tables. "What's so special about this one?"

"That was a question!" Claudio cried. I jumped down and rushed the last few feet to the door while he was still speaking. "But you will soon discover the answer for yourself."

I gasped in delight at the sprawling, opulent space. The Iruña was far more beautiful than I'd ever envisioned, and it seemed transplanted from another time. All the magnificence of a bygone era: soaring ceilings, marble tables, globe lights glowing gently. A gleaming floor of black and white checkers, also marble, beckoned us further inside.

"This is incredible! If it wasn't for fiesta, I'd feel underdressed," I said, more to myself than anyone else.

"You are incorrect, Kauhlie. That is part of the magic here. The clashing of the casual and the luxurious. He would have it no other way."

"He who?" I asked.

"Another question!" Claudio said, raising his finger with a flourish. "Use caution. What is it you say in America? Three strikes and you're out."

"Three strikes *each*." I said. "That's how it goes in baseball. Three strikes each—play fair!"

"Very well, Kauhlie. I will play by this rule. But we are very close now... you may not have time enough to strike out."

"But I thought all this *was* my surprise." I kept my voice intentionally flat. If my tone didn't go up at the end, I wasn't making an inquiry, right?

Claudio called my bullshit. "Another question!"

"It was not! That was a statement of fact. Factually, I thought the Iruña was my surprise."

Trevor laughed. "She's got you on a technicality. Leading, sure, but still within fair play."

"I will never understand your American baseball."

"Yeah, and I thought this *was* my surprise," I repeated. "Jake and Bill and Mike did their fair share of drinking here!"

"I do not know so much about that, Kauhlie, but this café does hold a treat for you. Come. I have called ahead, as is required." He took my hand and led me through the light crowd, toward a side room.

"What lies in here is very special," he announced, approaching the curtained entryway. He leaned down and whispered in my ear, so Trevor couldn't hear. "Inside is what you have been looking for, I believe."

A thousand questions exploded in my mind, but not a single one came out of my mouth. "Let's go, let's go, let's go!" I urged, mostly to keep from bursting.

He walked into the no-less-opulent side-room first, holding the curtain open for me and Trevor. I had a view of the beautiful, fully stocked bar, but Claudio had positioned himself in such a way that he was clearly hiding something behind him. The spark in his eye betrayed him.

"Kauhlie, I have someone you would like to meet. May I please introduce you to," he stepped broadly to the side, "Mr. Ernest Hemingway!"

I was dumbstruck. There stood a slightly-larger-than-life-sized bronze Ernest Hemingway, leaning easily against the bar, his face brooding and his eyes staring at me.

"Boop! I found him!" I exclaimed, lunging toward the bronze effigy. The next thing I knew, I'd slipped my hand around the statue's arm as if we were lifelong friends. Which I guess we were, in a way.

"You say, 'Boop!' when you find something?" Of all the reactions Claudio had anticipated, "Boop!" was certainly not it.

"Sure. Boop, there it is! Boop, there it is!"

"I do not think people say that." Claudio shook his head, confounded. "You are misremembering, perhaps."

"Callie, I think Claudio is ri—"

"—This is no time for semantics, Trevor. I found Hemingway!"

"Found him? I didn't know you were looking for him. I would've helped!"

I sucked in my breath. I'd already said too much; I needed to tread carefully now. Poor Trevor's head might implode if he learned of my quest… if he found out I'd been keeping a secret this big from him.

"Hemingway loved Pamplona, and the Iruña was one of his favorite haunts, Kauhlie. He drank many a whiskey and soda in this very room."

On my tiptoes, I gazed deeply into Hemingway's metallic eyes. "Hello, Mr. Hemingway! Hellooo!" I paused, but the cold bronze eyes only looked straight ahead. "Don't you have something to say to me?" Nothing.

Three small glasses appeared, each full of sherry—one of Hemingway's favorite drinks. Claudio had ordered them with no more than a glance at the bartender. Even after all these months, I still wondered how he commanded such amazing service.

"Now I can have a drink with my three favorite men!" I cried. We toasted Hemingway, who did not return the gesture, and began sipping our sherries. It didn't take long for our drinks to disappear, only to be immediately replaced. Every now and again I'd challenge Hemingway to speak to me, but always he remained silent.

"Kauhlie, perhaps you should tell Mr. Hemingway about your personal-development novel. Maybe he will inspire you to write it, with Spain as your backdrop."

"I could do that," I mused. "My own semi-autobiography, full of metaphors and allusions. After all, have I not grown in Spain? Haven't I developed in Spain?" My questions went out to my audience of two (three?). The two drinking audience members nodded in affirmation, but Hemingway was silent—and somehow critical in his silence. Not about my unwritten novel, exactly, more about my life-choices. I wasn't about to let that stand, not when I'd been all over Spain looking for him.

"Gentlemen, give me a moment with Mr. Hemingway. He and I need to have a little chat."

Claudio called to the bartender in Spanish—telling him to keep the tab open, I think. Then he turned to Trevor and his sherry-reddened face. "Let us go to the front room and treat ourselves to some *pinchos*." He clasped my shoulder warmly. "We will not save any for Kauhlie, since she no longer wants our company." He winked at me, smiling.

"Get!" I ordered, laughing. "My bronze buddy and I need to parley!"

I waited until the guys disappeared behind the curtain. "Look here," I began, not caring that I was talking to an inanimate object in a public place. "I'm no author—and I don't want to be. But you"—I poked the figure's hard bronze chest—"have sent me on this wild goose chase, and now I want some answers! I found you fair and square!"

Nothing. I don't know what I'd been expecting, but I sure didn't get it.

"Seriously, Mr. Hemingway. *This* is where you've been all this time? In the back room of a bar?… But then, if I were going to find you anywhere, I guess it would be in *this* bar… So here I am! Impart to me your wisdom, Oh Grand Terse Poohbah!" I bowed in mock worship.

Still nothing.

I ordered myself a third sherry, and I drained every last drop of it. I made Hemingway watch—he didn't have any sherry.

"Come on, out with it!" I demanded. "Five and a half months of this, but *now* you have nothing to say? Haven't I done everything you asked of me? Haven't you tortured me enough?"

Trevor poked his head through the curtain. "Callie, are you alright in there? It's been, like, fifteen minutes."

"I'm just telling Mr. Hemingway a thing or two… about a thing or two," I retorted, my speech starting to slur, the room going rosy.

"And this is a confidential conversation, Trevor—I asked you for some privacy!"

"So long as you're okay. The food just came. I'll save you a *pincho* or two."

He disappeared again. I ran to the curtain and stabbed it with my finger to make sure he was really gone. I turned to the statue, eyeing it from ten feet away, at a loss for what to do next.

Hemingway winked at me.

Or did he wink at me? Statues don't wink, not usually. It had to be a flash of light reflecting off the bronze, right? It had to be the sherry, drunk liberally and too quickly. Or the July heat—that was more plausible. Anything was more plausible. Except... I *swear* that statue winked at me.

Doubt both gripped and emboldened me. Here I was; here he was. I tried one more time. "I found you, so what do you have to say for yourself?!"

My phone rang. I answered on the first ring, knowing full well who it was.

"You're so close, Callie," came his voice—and for once it didn't sound tinny or staticky, a crystal-clear connection. "I'm so close to you."

I trained my eyes on the metallic, pupil-less eyes of Hemingway and spoke directly to them. "Of course, you're close, I'm looking right at you." I poked his bronze shoulder, the one furthest from the bar, to make my point.

"Surely the people of Pamplona honor me too well, Callie, but you have not found me yet."

I pulled the phone from my ear, my gaze ping-ponging between the screen and the statue, feeling like I was on an otherworldly video-call and half-hoping the effigy would show some sign of life.

"I've been searching for you for months! And just when I think I've found you, you start talking in riddles again."

He chuckled warily. "You are so close now, Callie. You need only to live your life all the way up."

"I *am* living my life all the way up! I'm doing everything you asked. Personal growth, self-development, relationships! What more do you want me to do?"

"I have already told you." He set his voice more firmly. "Nobody ever lives their life all the way up except bull-fighters."

"That's why we came here. For the running of the bulls—the most nightmarish thing I've ever seen!"

"We all have nightmares, Callie. You must face yours."

Face my nightmares: a nightmare of bulls. The sherry in my stomach revolted, the taste souring my mouth. I swallowed hard, barely keeping it down.

"You mean… you want me to—"

"—I am here, in Pamplona. At the heart of your nightmare."

"But I can't just—"

"—You can. And you must, lest you never find me."

Every inch of my soul rebelled. "Isn't there another way?" I clasped the statue's face with my free hand. "There must be another way!"

"Live your life all the way up, Callie. Find me. I am here, but I am unable to wait forever. Now is the time."

CHAPTER 31

A FEVER OF THE BLOOD

Dinner that night was quiet, for the most part—for my part. I didn't feel like talking much, not after my face-to-metallic-face chat with Hemingway. In fact, except to tell the guys I was done with the Iruña, I hadn't said much of anything since I'd fled from the side room. I couldn't make conversation now: something in my throat had turned to stone.

With his eyes, Claudio kept asking if I was alright. Trevor did the same. I answered with my eyes, but I didn't know what they conveyed. I sipped my wine whenever I couldn't muster an eye-answer. What was this roiling feeling—this terrifying and twisted, excited and hopeful feeling? This sense that I might have power over my nightmares, if only I could muster enough courage to face them. But since when did personal growth and development require a threat to life and limb?

"Flan. I need flan," I burst out, interrupting Claudio and not caring about my rudeness. "Claudio, make that happen, will you?"

"Ah. My Kauhlie has a sweet tooth this evening. Very well, flan for us all!" He caught the waiter's attention and gesticulated in a specific pattern. Apparently, Pamplona had a universal sign for flan.

With that done, he placed his hand on my knee. A reassuring touch, not at all sexual. "Are you perhaps ready to tell us about your conversation with your idol? You have been quiet this evening."

"He's not my idol," I muttered, aggravated that his small and gentle question still felt like a push.

"No, Claudio's sort of right, Callie," academic-Trevor said. "An idol is a likeness. You were chatting with that statue, that idol, for a long time—like you had a personal connection with it. So it's *your* idol." He smiled goofily, pleased with himself.

"Not now, Trevor. Please. No nerdy stuff now."

"Sorry, Callie. Sometimes I can't help it."

Our desserts arrived, the decadent, semi-solid sweetness melting on my tongue and infusing me with comfort. Two bites later, the sugar rush had renewed my vigor. I was ready to make my announcement.

"Gentlemen, I've come to a decision." I paused until they turned their attention from their flan. "I'm running with the bulls tomorrow."

"You're what?!" Trevor cried, his face a frown of fear.

"You heard me."

"Kauhlie, are you sure about this?"

"That's insane, Callie. Don't you remember yesterday morning?"

"It's not something I want to do, Trevor, it's something I *need* to do."

"But why? Why would you do something so mad?" He held his hands up, palms out, as if saying, "Stop."

"Kauhlie, I do not understand. You have shown no interest in this before. Running with the bulls is not a decision to make lightly."

"I know that, but I have to. Hemingway told me to. At the Iruña."

"We leave you alone with a statue and some sherry, and *this* is what you come up with?" Trevor's voice was much too loud. "I won't let you do it, I won't!"

Claudio snickered slightly. "My friend, I hope you are not under the delusion that we 'let' Kauhlie do anything. She is of her own mind and will."

Hey, Claudio was learning. That fact didn't escape me, even amid the flan-rush and inner turmoil.

"But it's too dangerous! She could die!"

"Perhaps, but more likely not. No one in yesterday's *encierro* departed from this world, even though I have never seen *el toro* so fierce." He held his spoon up. "We will hear what she has to say. I am sure she has her reasons."

"Yes, *she* does," I snapped, annoyed that they were hijacking my announcement and talking about me like I wasn't at the table. "And she's doing it tomorrow morning."

"No, you're not. You're not!"

"Yes, Trevor, I am. I'm not asking you to run with me, but I've been *called* to do it." I flicked my eyes to Claudio as I said the word *called*. His eyes told me he understood my full meaning. His eyes also told me he understood how important this was, despite the fear burning in my chest.

"If this is something you must do, Kauhlie, then I too will run! It has been some years, but I remember the route well."

"No," I said. It wasn't an objection; it was an order—although I didn't mean it that way. I softened the tension around my lips. "Claudio, this is something I have to do on my own. Just me and the bulls."

"In your old life, did you normally take advice from statues?" Trevor cut in. His voice had the edge of a challenge to it; he really *was* scared.

"That's the point. This isn't my old life. I'm not that woman anymore!"

"Nothing hurts if you don't let it," Trevor recited. "Remember that?"

"And you yourself said that was shitty advice!" I wiped my mouth with my napkin, then threw it on the table. "You guys weren't a part of my old life—that's why I have to do this alone. It's time to live my life, *this* life, all the way up!"

Claudio jumped in before I could really get going. "Allow me a suggestion, Kauhlie. Do not run tomorrow, but the next day. Tomorrow, you and I will go through the course—every meter of it—so you will not be ill-prepared. Trevor's concern is warranted. I will not run with you, if that is your wish, but allow me a single day for coaching and training."

Thinking, I cut what remained of my flan into tiny pieces. Fiesta would continue for three more mornings and three more runs. I didn't want to run on the last day, when the crowds would again swell. But running on the penultimate day, that seemed okay. Some training seemed okay, too. A little tutorial might very well keep me from harm.

"I'll take you up on that offer," I replied. "That's fair enough."

"Good. Tomorrow, I will take you on a crash-course of the course!" He chuckled at his own pun; I didn't have the heart to tell him it was a terrible pun.

"I like training. I'm a fast learner. Did I tell you guys about the time I crammed an entire semester's worth of American history into one night before my final?"

"Twice," Trevor replied. "We all know you're smart, Callie. Which is why I can't understand your need to do this."

"If your matador came back, would you do it? If he *told* you to do it?"

Trevor pulled on his beard. "I guess I'd have to," he ceded. "But I wouldn't really *want* to."

"Well, that's what it's like for me. This is something I *need* to do, whether I want to or not."

"It has been my experience," Claudio began, "that once *el toro* beckons, there is no cure but rising to meet him. It is like a fever of the blood—a fever with but one remedy."

Claudio was dramatic, but he wasn't wrong. My veins felt itchy, as if the very vessels of my blood were standing on end and being pulled toward the run. That more than a full half of me objected out of fear and good sense didn't matter at all.

Trevor's shoulders relented, and I knew the prospect of tomorrow's cramming session had eased his nerves some. "I don't get it, Callie. Aren't you scared?"

"Terrified. But it's the hard things that count."

I was in good hands with Claudio. He knew practically every inch of the run, and he pointed out pitfalls both large and small as he coached me. Trevor shadowed us the whole way, keeping his fears and objections to himself. Mostly.

We started at the holding pens, then moved through the course to Pamplona's city hall. From there, it was only a few dozen meters to the spot where the boy had been gored. My pulse quickened at the memory, although no trace of violence remained—the blood fully washed away. Yet the memory haunted me; I could almost see the boy still there, crumpled and fragile.

Claudio grasped my shoulders and gently turned me to him. "Do not fret, Kauhlie. You do not need to start here. It is better if you begin further down, so you will make it into the arena before the doors close. Not everyone who runs makes it to the end in time."

Even with his words of coaching and comfort, I still couldn't push the image of the broken and bleeding boy from my mind. That could be me tomorrow, shattered on the cobblestones. Was I truly going to do this?

"Think of it this way, Kauhlie. This spot is not a point of sorrow. The boy was saved."

"Only because you saved him."

He shrugged. "If not me, another would have. The run is wider here than in many places. Room enough for rescues."

We spent extra time at Hamburger Corner—the ninety-degree turn that caused many a bull to slam into the wall, often taking a runner or two down as well. Claudio recommended I start my run a few meters beyond the potentially deadly corner, which was the most sensible thing I'd heard all day.

The Calle Estafeta's long hill was intimidating, a climb so steep I wondered how the herd could manage it. I didn't have long to think about it, though, because Claudio reminded me that the early morning street was often damp and slick, creating yet another peril. Wasn't running with my nightmares perilous enough?

"Here on the Calle Estafeta, the bulls often begin to tire. The hill is taxing, and this is where the greatest danger for *sueltos* exists."

"*Sueltos?*" My stomach lurched at the ominous word.

"*Suelto*, a straggler. A bull who pulls apart from the herd. Such as you witnessed the other day."

The boy's blood on my shirt, the smell of it, came back to me. My stomach lurched again, my nightmares flashing at the edges of my vision. Did I have it in me to do this? Maybe Trevor was right, maybe basing my life-choices on statue-advice wasn't the best idea.

The Calle Estafeta held yet another challenge. It was flanked on both sides by adjoining four- and five-story buildings, creating a corridor. Other parts of the run had exit points, as well as fences that runners could scramble over in an emergency. Here, the only emergency-option was seeking shelter in one of the shallow doorways… and maybe praying.

The hill declined a bit after it crested, and the course opened up into an intersection. When the fences were back up, things would become really tight here, with not much room for more than a bull and a couple of people to run side-by-side. And if for any reason *el toro* bolted to one side… whammo.

I imagined the herd careening single file down the cobblestones as we walked through the last stretch. With the end now in sight, Claudio pointed toward the arena's entrance, and I followed the movement of his fingertip until my eyes collided with a monument of granite and bronze.

"Hemingway?! What's he doing here?" I sprinted across the street, startling a driver. She honked angrily.

"This is Pamplona's official monument to your favorite author!" Claudio said as he came up alongside me. "I thought you knew of it." He pointed again, this time to a footpath adjacent to the arena. "And this is the Ruta Hemingway."

I sized up the sculpture. The torso and arms were granite, but the head was bronze and contained the same hard metallic eyes I'd seen yesterday.

"This doesn't make sense," Trevor cried, catching up to us. "Is this guy *everywhere?*"

"Apparently, yes. I guess there's no escape," I said, forcing a chuckle. Hemingway was indeed everywhere, including here, at the heart of my nightmares.

"He looks... like a Soviet fisherman," Trevor continued, examining the monument. "They say he had a soft spot for communists, you know."

I considered this, staring at the broad, oversized granite shoulders that seemed intentionally too wide for the metallic head. A stone, roll-neck collar, the type on a fisherman's sweater, enveloped Hemingway's neck.

"I do not think the artist intended a communist bent," Claudio said. "Exaggeration perhaps, but I believe this is Hemingway watching his beloved bullfights."

"No, communist... that's good," I declared, strangely comforted. "An omen!"

"Callie?"

"When I used to go running in Central Park, my workout music was Soviet marches. I must have told you that?"

"Oh yeah, you did... at Susan and Jane's. That was really funny."

Even after all this time, I was still amazed at Trevor's "Fun facts about Callie" memory. I still had to remind him to tie his shoes every other morning, yet he filed away every tidbit I'd ever shared about myself.

"What is this?" Claudio asked. "Soviet marches?"

Trevor burst into a truly expansive account, replete with details even I had forgotten. He truly was amazing, in his own way.

"Ah, yes, this is indeed an omen!" Claudio exclaimed. "The perfect complement to your run!" I nodded in agreement, and even Trevor now looked more at ease with my running. Omens could do that, I guess.

We continued the last few yards to the entrance. A locked, wrought iron gate told us, in no uncertain terms, that the bullring was closed to the public at the moment, but the red wooden doors remained open, revealing the passageway beyond. Utterly claustrophobic. Narrower than the narrowest part of the Calle Estafeta.

"I don't like this Callie. I'm going to hang out with Hemingway... you're not the only one who can chat with him. Come get me when you're done." Trevor scurried away, leaving me cowering in the shadow of the passageway.

"This is by far the most dangerous part of the run, Kauhlie. Not because of the bulls so much, but because of the bottlenecking."

"Is this where you...?"

"Where I fell, yes. Where I was blessed by San Fermín. Right in that spot there, halfway through. It took a long time for the medical team to push through the crowd and reach me, if I recall correctly."

I shivered, picturing a stampeding bull clipping his thigh. That could well be me tomorrow, too.

"You must remember that this passageway is perilous. The crowding is so severe that often runners cannot move forward for some time."

"But...?"

Claudio read my mind. "Yes, the bulls keep moving forward. That is what bulls do!"

I continued staring into the passageway, feeling like I was going to be sick. I swallowed, pushing back the sourness.

"Look closely at the bottom of the walls, at the sanctuary niches. If you are fast enough, you can roll into one for protection. Unless—"

"—Unless it's already full, right?"

Claudio smirked. "You truly are a quick study, Kauhlie. You will be magnificent tomorrow!"

Truth be told, I didn't feel I would be magnificent in the slightest. I felt somewhat more grounded and prepared, but "magnificent" was pushing it. A nightmare of bulls, all fighting to get through this one small space. Could I do this? Did I really *need* to do this?

"It is normal to have doubts, Kauhlie," Claudio offered, reading my mind again. "No matter our reason for taking part in the *encierro*, we all have doubts. Trepidation is part of the experience!"

"But what if... I see those bulls coming and I flip out? Like the boy."

He put his arm around me confidently. "You will not do that. You have a practiced mind. Practiced minds are not easily given to panic."

He held me close, swaying me back and forth. I wasn't so sure about his assessment of my "practiced mind." I didn't practice much of anything these days—and certainly not law. I guess, if anything, I practiced drinking. The art of intoxication. Did that count?

A contented sigh rose from inside his chest. "You need not worry, Kauhlie. I promise I will be waiting for you, here at the end."

I inhaled a few mindful breaths, his soothing arms still around me. "Here at the end?" I asked into his chest. "Can you get into the bullring if you're not running?"

"It can be arranged," he said. "I will arrange it." He stroked the top of my head. "We will only be parted for a few hundred meters, for I will be here at the end when you triumph! On this, I give you my word."

Something in my spine relaxed. Claudio's faith in me expelled my self-doubt. He would be waiting for me. He would be there after I faced my nightmares.

"Kauhlie, are you still glad Hemingway told you to run?"

I turned back to the narrow passageway. "Maybe," I replied shakily. "But I think I'll start searching for a new favorite book. Something safe, like *Walden* by Thoreau."

CHAPTER 32

LIVING ALL THE WAY UP

I couldn't sleep that night. I knew my nightmares would be waiting for me in the morning, and some part of my brain calculated that if I never went to sleep, morning would never come. That same part of my brain kept me tossing and turning until I decided to get up and do something more productive than sweating into my sheets.

It wasn't that late, really, only one-thirty in the morning. I'd gone to bed early figuring I would need the rest. Trevor and Claudio were still out partying—the clubs would just be hitting full swing right now. During fiesta, Pamplona never slept. The city and I had that in common at the moment.

I crept down the dark hallway in my bare feet, in search of a mid-night snack. I was nervous, sure, but not nervous enough to forego snacking. If anything, I was stressed enough to eat for no particular reason. I certainly wasn't hungry—we'd feasted only a few hours ago in celebration of my impending run.

I flicked on the kitchen light. My heart nearly stopped. "Claudio!"

He smiled sheepishly. "Kauhlie, I did not hear you coming."

"What are you doing here? In the dark?"

His sheepish expression continued, becoming his reply.

"Don't you know that's how people get stabbed?"

"Stabbed? You would stab me, Kauhlie? I do not think you would do this?"

"I sure would, big guy—you could've been a perv! I'd be perfectly within my rights to stab a midnight perv!"

Claudio, sitting at the kitchen island, pursed his lips in thought. "Ah. I do see your point. Perhaps I should leave a light on next time."

I reached for the bottle of bourbon I'd set on the counter when we'd first arrived. Oddly enough, I hadn't touched it since. Grabbing some ice from the freezer, I dropped cubes into two glasses before pouring a stream of the brown liquid in after them—almost before the ice cubes stopped "ka-chinking" in their glasses. Warmth from a healthy sip soothed me; I was ready to deal with Claudio.

"Are you going to tell me what's on your mind?" I asked, putting the ice away. "What's keeping you from partying in Pamplona tonight?"

"I was just thinking I would tell you after your run, so I would not distract you from your purpose."

The hairs on the back of my neck jumped up like guards on alert. What didn't he want to tell me now? "Well, now I *am* distracted. Out with it." I plopped myself on the stool furthest from him.

He hesitated slightly but forced the words from his mouth. "My father called this evening. He is pressuring me." He wrapped his hand firmly around the drink I'd poured for him.

I tried not to let my relief show—this wasn't something "new." An ongoing crisis seemed easier to deal with right now than a new one. "Well, it's not like you have to go," I said gently. "I mean, it's not like you *need* to work, right?"

"I do not need to work for a living, I am blessed in this way. But, yes, I do need to work. I believe in working. I have had much time off now, almost a year. Perhaps too much."

"Yeah, I'm feeling some of that myself," I admitted. "Going back to work, I mean. Having a direction every morning, something to grab onto."

"Yes—direction, purpose, accomplishment. It is important to have these things, to strive for these things. To be useful."

"But there's nothing that says you *have* to work for your father." The ice clinked in my glass as I lowered it from my lips. "You're not beholden to his wishes."

"I am not. But in truth, I have grown fond of the idea of returning to America. Americans are so very... vibrant. So very individual. It is embedded in your spirit."

"Then go to New York and find your own job. Your dad isn't the only employer in the city."

He smiled weakly, and I realized I'd just stated the obvious. Either I needed some sleep, or I was turning into Trevor. I hoped it was the former.

Claudio dipped his finger into his glass, playing with his ice. "I thought of this, but no, it is not a solution. My father is... easily affronted, in his own way. Doing this would cause more problems than it solves."

I swallowed the last of my bourbon, the mash colliding with my thoughts. "Maybe you should try the American Embassy!"

"What is this, Kauhlie?"

"The American Embassy in Madrid! Go work there. Win-win. Lots of Americans, but you get to stay in Madrid. The Embassy must need someone who..." It occurred to me that I didn't know exactly what Claudio did for work, not exactly. "...who specializes in... whatever it is you do."

He exploded in roaring laughter. "Yes, Kauhlie, this is exactly what I will do," he managed between breaths. "Work at the Embassy!" He slapped the island hard, not even trying to contain himself. Callie McGraw, problem-solver extraordinaire.

Watching Claudio laugh was a magical beauty—at least it was until one of us fell off our stool from the mirth. I won't say who nearly landed ass-down on the floor, but it wasn't me.

It took a couple of tries, but we regained our composure. "It is good to hear you laugh, Kauhlie. You have been solemn. It is the anticipation of the *encierro*. This I can see clearly."

"It's kind of a big thing, you know. For me anyway."

"You do not need to worry. I have told you everything you need to know to run smart."

I wrinkled my nose. "I don't know if that's a real guarantee—Claudio's Bull Running School."

"You want a guarantee?" He chuckled. *El toro* offers no guarantees!"

I frowned. "That's not funny, Claudio. I face my nightmares tomorrow."

He straightened up, squaring his shoulders. "I know, you have told me. I understand this is not easy for you. Especially you, who wants things buttoned-up, controlled and in control."

"What's wrong with that?" I didn't see how "controlled" was unreasonable. And hey, if I was the one doing the controlling, so much the better.

"Because life is not like this—it is eventful and unpredictable. You cannot prepare for everything, nor should you try."

"I like knowing where I'm going. I like having a plan." Again, I failed to see how this was unreasonable.

"Which is prudent, to a degree. But I must tell you something. An important thing." Claudio paused, trying to hide his hesitance by draining his glass. "You will not like it, and you must promise not to yell."

I crossed my arms abruptly. "I make no such promises. You'll just have to risk it, if you think it's so important."

"It *is* important. Do you remember what I once said of your drinking? That you drink to ignore?"

"I remember," I answered, bristling.

"I know now what you ignore in your drink. You do not drink, as so many others do, to run from your demons. You drink to ignore what you cannot control—for when you are not in control, your nightmares come unbidden. You claim your demons, this is true, but they are welcome by invitation only."

"You're so full of it!" I glared at him so forcefully my eyeballs throbbed. He leaned back in his seat, just in case I blew.

But I didn't blow. Not that I didn't want to—what right did he have to tell me about my own demons? Yet a deeper part of me knew he was right. Undeniably right. I didn't have a leg to stand on, and when I opened my mouth to retort, all that came out was a ridiculous, under-formed syllable, unflattering and unsexy. "Uhhhaa…"

He nodded in agreement with himself. "It is true—I believe this is true. And I also believe—and again you will not like this—you are drawn so greatly to *The Sun Also Rises* for a similar reason. The characters do not, as you claim, come to terms. They *ignore* their issues until terms come to them."

"That's not fair! You know that's not fair!" I cried. Yet as soon as he said it, I knew he was undeniably right once again. For the second time in twenty seconds. Damnit.

"I do not mean to be hard on you. But I see this in your drinking."

"Hard on me? Buddy, I'm hard as nails." Bullshit, of course, but Claudio didn't interrupt. "Hard as titanium nails!" Flexing my bicep, I reached for the bottle again.

"Wait, Kauhlie." He intercepted my arm in mid-reach, curling his fingers softly around my wrist—a somber touch that got my full attention. "Do not drink for the rest of tonight."

"What?!" I put—well, slammed—the bottle down. "Who are you to tell me what I can and cannot do?"

Claudio breathed out a growl, controlling his temper. He had more to say. I didn't particularly want to hear it, but I didn't stop him, either.

"Tomorrow you meet *el toro*. Tomorrow you face your nightmares. Run sober, Kauhlie. You do not need the bottle for courage."

"I don't *need* it," I snapped. "But it does help. Why are you denying me a little help?"

"I *am* helping you, dear one." He nodded almost without pausing. "You do not need liquid courage," he reached out with his index finger and ran it lightly along the center of my forehead. "You have everything you need inside here," he moved his finger down until he reached my heart. "And you have it here, too." His eyes became deep wells, the softest pools. Over the top as usual, but his sincerity knew no depths. For one pure instant, I believed him without question.

I would face my nightmares sober.

∾

I bid farewell to Claudio's calming brown eyes. He'd escorted me to the start of the *encierro*, near the corral at the Calle Santo Domingo, but now he could go no further. The course was for runners only—the brave, the determined, the crazy. I wasn't sure which group I belonged to.

I floated in a sea of swirling whites and reds as the runners began churning with excitement—any moment now, we'd be allowed to fan out on the course, each of us picking the spot where we would catch the bulls. I paid no attention to my knocking knees.

The gray sky above loomed over the damp, slick street. Slim streaks of sunshine peeked through the clouds, but the rays weren't yet strong enough to dissipate the morning's humidity. The air felt too close, a blanketing I didn't want or need. My body began tingling—fear and anticipation in equal parts. I wanted to be still, to focus, to crawl into myself, but again and again, the crowd swelled up against me before receding, undulating without a set rhythm. A disorienting dissonance: I was one with the great crowd yet alone amid this mass of humanity. My body no longer felt like my own as I was tossed to and fro.

The cheering of the crowd grew. I let go of any moorings and gave myself over to the moment. The first prayers to San Fermín started, signaling the last five minutes before the *encierro* began. I chanted in a language I barely spoke and sang words I didn't understand. I prayed along with the faithful, secretly hoping God—any god, actually—was listening.

The police opened the barriers, turning on a great human faucet. Bodies raced forward in a dense deluge. I became a drop in the great torrent as we surged forward. Cheers from the balconies above lifted our spirits and bolstered our bravery. A young woman on a lower balcony poured from her wine-skin, aiming the red wine into the eager mouth of a man a decade older. She missed, staining his face and shirt. They laughed freely, unconcerned about the impending danger.

I flowed on, pooling with the crowd at Hamburger Corner, then pushing myself forward—I knew not to stop here. The morning's pulse quickened as each moment drew us nearer to our fate. Nearer to my nightmares.

The Calle Estafeta loomed, the hill seeming so much longer now. I shifted my gait to increase my purchase on the slick cobblestones. About halfway up, the river of runners became a trickle, many having chosen their spots.

I found the place Claudio and I had picked out yesterday. This was a good spot. If I ran hard, I'd have a solid chance of making it inside the arena before the doors closed. I needed to be among those who made it into the bullring: I wouldn't be living my life all the way up if I didn't.

A collective exhale washed over the course. We were all in place, the only thing left to do was wait. My frenzied thoughts sent my head spinning: Was I doing this right? Was I really doing this at all?

I lunged forward involuntarily. Two full steps of fleeing. I glued down my feet, reminding myself why I was here. Running away was futile, anyhow—this was the part of the course without fences to scale or gaps to snake through. No escape. The street suddenly seemed much narrower, as if someone had squeezed the opposite sides together just for the *encierro*. All the parts of me that were shouting to turn back were now trapped. Those same parts were also crying for a drink, yet I didn't rue my decision to run sober.

A flash of light caught my eye. Above, in a second-story window, an oversized TV was showing the run. I squinted hard, sharping the image, and I cursed the guy whose head was smack in the middle of the screen. I needed to see the bulls the moment they were set loose, needed to witness the moment I began living my life all the way up.

The opening rocket fired, the crowd erupting like a volcano. I broke into a sweat. I couldn't pull my eyes from the screen, watching as the bulls thundered out of their corral. The beasts were still far enough away, but now their inevitability became palpably real. Every muscle in my body tensed—even my knees stopped knocking. I calculated in my head: in about ninety seconds, the bulls would be upon me.

I waited, gulping slow breaths to quell my nerves, the seconds ticking by. At the hill's bottom, a great surge of runners poured around the corner, their heads popping up like kernels of exploding corn. They propelled themselves forward in great leaps—running frantically while peeking over their shoulders, waiting for the herd to appear.

The wave of popping moved closer and closer. A strange, inexorable urge gripped me, compelling me to start running. I fought it back frantically. I plastered myself against the wall, clutching the building's cool stone façade. Running smart meant not running until my nightmares were in sight.

I knew why I was here, and the bulls were approaching. Even still, the herd surged around the corner seemingly without warning, running fast and hard. Electricity everywhere. My muscles tensed even harder in fight or flight.

Nothing could've prepared me for the force and energy of the majestic animals, for the crushing clamor and violence they brought. My vision blurred, terror transforming the great beasts. Before me was now every cruel and lonely night of my life, every wall I'd ever built, every empty achievement I'd claimed, every fear I'd ever had. I sprung forward, running before I knew my feet were moving, running *ahead* of my nightmares.

Other runners whipped past me in a chaotic stream, and the herd gained ground even more quickly. The first of the bulls roared past, his horn inches from my shoulder. I screamed as the animals overtook me, but I had no voice. Nothing came out, not a single word or sound—my breath taken away. I stumbled into another runner and almost fell, but I defied gravity and kept myself upright.

The last of the herd thundered by, creating a tornado-gust against my sweat-drenched body. *El toro's* flailing tail smacked me squarely in the chest, my heart skipping a beat at the impact, my skin horripilating. A touch of unbridled freedom, a brush of transcending perfection.

Callie McGraw, baptized by a nightmare of bulls.

The world swirled around me, crazy and vibrant, the universe unmoored. I ran on, knowing I would never catch the bulls again, knowing they had already bestowed upon all they could. Still, my future-self depended on making into the arena, into the heart of my nightmares. On living my life all the way up, here and now, and freeing myself from the prison of my own making.

The crowd exploded in cries of alarm and fear as the hill crested. The runners around me scattered like cockroaches, pressing themselves against the wooden fences that again lined the course. I didn't need to speak Spanish to decipher their dread. A *suelto*—a too-real reality rampaging loose.

Unprepared, I scanned the street. *El toro* saw me, and I saw him at the moment he surged. He lowered his head and swung his piercing horn, swiping dangerously close to my flesh. I sprang backward; had I been two inches closer, I surely would've borne the blessing of San Fermín for life.

The *pastores* flanked the beast with their feckless herding poles. They were lucky; *el toro* quickly tired of their taunting and ran on. Rejoicing runners leaped from the fences into the middle of the course, pushing forward once again.

I tucked in my chin and sprinted toward the arena. Rounding the last turn, the bronze-and-granite Hemingway came into view, his eyes peeking out atop the human mass. Without slowing, I shot daggers at the statue and screamed at the top of my lungs—a violent eulogy to every crazy, shitty, torturous, enlightening bit of hell Hemingway had put me through.

He was behind me now.

The great doors were starting to close just as I reached the arena. Along with at least a dozen others, I frantically clawed into the wood, forcing the hinges back open. I fought my way into the impossibly narrow passageway beyond. Claustrophobia descended. More and more runners squeezed through the closing doors, the passageway becoming so packed we couldn't move forward. If *el toro* were among us, surely we would not all make it out alive.

Even with the crowding, our shared relief was palpable. Every single one of us had made it into the arena, and the bullring was now only one archway away. A woman toward the back began jubilantly chanting San Fermín's prayer. In twos and threes, other elated voices joined her, singing together as one until the bottleneck burst.

I entered the ring victorious, my arms in the air. Thousands of people in the stands greeted me—or at least it felt that way, although most were probably cheering for the bulls. I danced with the other runners in triumph, arms and bodies waving wildly. Glorious pandemonium. I'd lived my life all the way up, and I would live to tell about it.

I saw him from across the ring, his feet firmly planted on the dusty ground—standing utterly motionless. Time slowed. Claudio became the sun, and everything in the ring—everything in the universe—revolved around him. Through the throngs of revelers separating us, the fire-spark in his eyes beckoned. I walked to him through the planets and the moons as they continued their revolutions.

"See, Kauhlie. I told you I would be here for you at the end."

I held him and he held me. Two stars intertwining as one.

MADRID
(MÁS)

CHAPTER 33
TEN MORNINGS FROM NOW

We left Pamplona that same day. I didn't want to stay a moment longer than necessary—I needed to leave the city on a high, victorious. A new Callie McGraw.

We found an empty four-person seater on the train. Trevor slipped into the seat facing us, and I nestled myself against Claudio's shoulder, half asleep the moment I plopped down. As my eyelids slid closed, the Spanish sun flickered across Trevor's face as he watched the world pass.

I faded in and out during the trip—each time I awoke, Claudio gave my hand a gentle squeeze. He was always there, just as he'd been there at the end of my run. It felt natural for him to be there. I loved that he was always there.

Some three hours later, I woke up fully as we reached the outskirts of Madrid. Claudio, still holding my hand, had fallen into a deep sleep, and Trevor was still gazing out the window. It seemed as if his head hadn't moved the whole ride.

He held his finger to his lips. "Shh."

I smiled slyly and mirrored him. "Shh yourself."

"Listen, I want you to know something," he whispered. He glanced warily at Claudio—whatever it was, Trevor wanted this to remain between us. "I want you to know I saw you, Callie. I was watching."

"You were watching me sleep?" I asked. "That's… umm… weird." And creepy. Maybe more creepy than weird. I hoped Trevor wasn't revealing some icky new personality quirk—anything was possible with him.

"No, Callie, don't be gross." He scrunched up his nose. "I was watching you this morning. I saw you run. I know I said I wasn't going to, but I did. On the Calle Estafeta, almost at the very top of the hill."

"You didn't have to do that," I said, grateful. "That must've been frightening for you without your matador."

"I had to, just… in case." His volume increased. "You were so brave!" Claudio stirred but didn't wake.

I shrugged. "It's something I *had* to do—I didn't have much say in it. I had to live my life all the way up!"

"No, Callie, you *were* brave. You barely flinched when the last bull showed up—that was the worst part. But watching you helped me decide. Now I know what I'm going to do next."

"Really?" I asked, surprised. It didn't seem possible Trevor was in the crowd, or that my run could've affected anyone but me. Yet I had to admit I'd been extra Callie-centric these last few days—something could've slipped through the cracks.

"I'm going to Berlin, Callie." He nodded in conviction. "That's what I'm doing next. I've decided."

"Good for you!" I replied, feeling my eyes light up. I really was proud of him: Trevor had met his own "deciding" deadline, and—for the first time since we'd met—he had a direction. "And Germany has wonderful national colors—black, red, and gold. Those are colors that match you, Trevor, colors that won't let you down."

"Yeah, I thought about that, too, Callie. Maybe there'll be color for me in Germany. Because I'm not going just to visit. I'm going to get a job, an apartment. A kitten, too. A whole life. No more floating around." He pulled on his beard as if encouraging himself. "I don't know if that counts as living my life all the way up, but it's *something*, at least."

I smiled warmly. "That's a fine start, Trevor. An excellent start."

"When's your flight, Callie? Your flight home?"

A lump formed in my throat. I hadn't thought of going home in ages—and in truth, I'd almost begun thinking of Spain as my home. Yet, in reality, I would be leaving soon. I began counting my remaining mornings on my fingertips.

"Ten days," I replied. "Ten days from tomorrow."

"Okay." He paused as if he wanted to say something more but couldn't. "I'll start making my plans in the morning."

I glanced at Claudio. His chest was moving up and down softly, but deeply, as he slept, which is how I knew it was safe to ask Trevor a few quick questions—Claudio wouldn't wake up until the train stopped its rhythmic lullaby.

"But why keep it a secret? Why don't you want to tell Claudio?"

Trevor pulled back as if a small bomb had detonated. "It's not like... I mean—Callie, I guess... I just wanted to tell you first." He fumbled with the red handkerchief still around his neck. "I wanted to talk to you alone... in the event that... because... in case—"

"Spill it out," I demanded. Not mean, but forceful. If Trevor was spiraling into non-language again, he needed a push. Plus, we were well inside the city limits now; we'd be pulling into the station any moment. "Come on, you're not being black and red and gold if you clam up now," I added more gently.

"In case you wanted to come with me!" His words rushed out in one long exhale, as if he were expelling them with all the breath he had.

"Come with you?" The thought fell from my mouth in a heap. "Trevor, I have a job waiting for me in San Francisco. People counting on me, responsibilities. I'd love to stay in Europe, but I can't."

Trevor wasn't surprised, although he couldn't hide the disappointment on his face. "But what if you didn't want that job anymore, Callie?

What if you *wanted* to come? What if you wanted to stay with me? What kind of a friend would I be if I didn't ask?"

I reached across the seat and clapped his shoulder. "Aw, Trevor, it's not like I *want* to leave you. That's going to be the hardest part—leaving my two favorite guys." I frowned. "It hardly seems fair, huh?"

He crossed his arms and pouted. "It doesn't seem fair at all."

"Look, we can always visit. Reunions in Spain. And you can come to the west coast whenever you want."

"That's what people *say*, Callie. That's what they always say, but it never happens. Or if it does happen, it's never the same." His pout became more crestfallen. "It's not fair!"

As the train entered the terminal, I pouted right along with him. No, it wasn't fair. Not fair at all.

The three of us didn't talk much as we made our way through the station, although we were all glad to be back in Madrid. As I unpacked in my hotel room, I thought about all Trevor had said. He was right—maybe the three of us would get together from time to time, although it would never be the same. It would never be this moment in Spain, the Spain we'd experienced together. This moment was growing short: only ten days remained. Long enough that it wasn't tomorrow; short enough that there weren't too many tomorrows left.

Yet at the same time, it didn't feel like the end. It still felt like the middle. I'd "found" Hemingway in Pamplona, in bronze and granite, but in my gut I knew my quest wasn't over. I'd lived my life all the way up, yet uncertainty still loomed. What did the rest of my time in Spain hold?

One piece that was still missing was Claudio. Was he thinking about what would come next? What did he want? What did I want? What did we want together, as a couple? Was "together" even part of the equation? Would we part ways ten mornings from now, virtual strangers thereafter? In ten days, I would be gone—maybe out of Claudio's life forever. Is that what he wanted?

Every inch of me itched; I longed to rush over to Claudio's apartment and ask him for his thoughts point-blank—not that I'd had great success with similar approaches before. With that in mind, and with an enormous amount of restraint, I resolved to wait three days before broaching the subject. This was something Claudio clearly didn't want to talk about—as messed up and wrong-headed as that was—so I could hold out. I'd just faced a nightmare of bulls; I could wait seventy-two hours.

Or maybe I'd wait just two days, that would be enough. Would that be enough? No, three days. Three was fair, three days left a full week to figure things out, and I didn't want to risk spoiling our remaining time. Hey, maybe these weren't our last days together at all? Maybe Claudio had some surprise-solution he was waiting to spring on me? Maybe, but in my heart, I knew that wasn't likely.

A pit in my stomach accompanied my every waking moment the next day. I tried to enjoy my waning time, but uncertainty gnawed at me. I told myself Claudio was just some guy, that Spain Man wasn't The Be All And End All of men. There were other fish in the sea, right? And very soon I'd be flying over that sea—and across a whole continent—to California. Thoughts of my new life in my amazing-yet-untested role as general counsel were creeping into my consciousness. The opportunity was still exciting, but starting a new job was daunting. That alone was unnerving enough, without having this idiot Claudio to think about. This idiot who probably loved me but was too dumb to say it.

Trevor was thinking about the future too. He babbled in excited streams about the art, literature, and culture of Germany. That evening, he delivered an enthusiastic diatribe on wursts: bockwurst, bregenwurst, currywurst, gelbwurst, knackwurst, leberwurst. From the way he was talking, it seemed no one in the whole of Germany had ever laid eyes on a vegetable.

Even more perplexing, Trevor started blurting out random responses in German, a language totally alien to me. Claudio spoke a few words of it—just enough to get by—but even he was confounded by the sudden bilingual gymnastics. Clearly, Trevor had a knack for German though; the complex syllables rolled off his tongue smoothly.

"But Callie, I have to practice," Trevor argued. "I haven't spoken German since grad school. "*Ich habe seit meiner Studienzeit kein Deutsch mehr gesprochen*," he repeated.

Trevor's resolve heartened me. For the first time, he was excited about his future. Not just excited about *not* returning to grad school, but excited about Berlin. By the next day, he had a plan all laid out; he'd stay at a hostel in the heart of the city while he job-and-apartment hunted. He knew which neighborhoods he wanted to live in and, apparently, he had a couple of second cousins in the city that he hadn't seen since he was a kid. His enthusiasm was even more unbounded than his general weirdness—maybe the kidnapping of his matador had been the best thing for him.

In contrast, Claudio seemed completely unaware of the changes to come. In many ways, he remained the same—timeless, no different than he was months ago. He smiled the same, ate and drank the same, told jokes the same. I couldn't read the man for the life of me. Was he really not thinking about what was coming? And if he wasn't thinking about it, what did that say about him—and us? Damnit, why couldn't he give me the slightest clue? I knew his father was on his mind, sure, but did that one issue consume his *whole* brain? Was there no room in his thoughts and heart for me?

Apparently not. Because on my second day of "not talking about it," Claudio truly flabbergasted me with a living-in-the-moment outburst. We were having cocktails at his apartment when he lit up suddenly, as if a brilliant thought had come to him.

"I have an idea for our next adventure!" he cried. "At the end of next month, we must go to Buñol, near Valencia, for the Tomatina Festival. It is great fun… there is nothing like hurling tomatoes at complete strangers to fortify the spirit!"

I bit my tongue for a second—wishing I could throw a tomato at Claudio and his lunkheadedness. I swallowed my frustration. "Claudio, I won't be around for that. I'll be back in the States." Geez, could he really be that obtuse?

"Yeah. And I'll be in Germany," Trevor added. He translated his response for no particular reason. "*Ich werde in Deutschland sein.*"

Claudio's face betrayed not a single emotion. "Ah, yes. I see now why that will not work."

"No, it won't," I replied flatly. "And for all you know, you could be in New York by then, remember?" Across the apartment, on the kitchen island, a basket of ripe tomatoes sat in full view. Would it really be so bad if I threw one at his head? Just one?

"Oh well," Claudio shrugged his shoulders, pretending to be engrossed in his gin and tonic.

Blood rushed to my face. I turned away so he wouldn't see my cheeks reddening. Claudio hadn't offered alternative plans, like doing something together in the US instead. Nothing but, "Oh well," and a shrug of the shoulders? Damnit. It's not like anything important was at stake here—just our relationship maybe ending. Oh well.

CHAPTER 34

THE GREATEST PLAN EVER

It's a funny thing. When asked to choose a superpower they want, lots of folks will say, "I want the power to fly." And I guess that's well and good, but I think it assumes too much. Among other things, it assumes that, once in flight, they'll be able to come back down. To return to terra firma safely. No one ever stipulates, "I want the power to land, too." Everyone focuses on flying without reading the fine print, as if safe reunions with solid ground are an implied part of the package. That's not how it works, though. Gravity and velocity are extortionists: the power to land costs extra.

I'm a lawyer and I traffic in fine print, but even I neglected to dig into the eight-point type in this case. After running with the bulls, I was flying in many ways, but with the Claudio question still not nailed down, I suspected I was circling a landing strip that didn't exist. That there was no way of getting out of this without crashing and burning.

It was now day three. I'd managed my "two days of not talking about it," and in that time, I'd formulated a whole new plan for me and Claudio. A feasible plan. A good plan. An *inspired* plan. I'd been on alert all afternoon for the right moment to bring it up.

"Kauhlie, I need to talk to you," he said seriously. "Let us go for ice cream. There is a shop one block down that sells the American kind."

I forced a sly smile. "Uh-oh. Whenever a guy says, 'I need to talk to you,' it's rarely good news." I was mostly joking and trying to keep things light, yet from his expression, I could tell Claudio and I were worlds apart on this one. Damnit.

"No, it is not like that," Claudio said. "Come—before Trevor liberates himself from my hot tub." After second breakfast, Trevor had rushed in to help a woman carry her grocery cart up a flight of stone steps. In the process, he'd wrenched his shoulder, which is how we'd wound up at Claudio's apartment during prime "floating around the city" hours.

We took our seats and ordered our sugary encouragement— mocha-coffee swirl for me, mint chocolate-chip for Claudio. He had an agenda, and so did I. Whether those two agendas would align remained to be seen.

"It is like this, Kauhlie. I have been thinking," he began, pulling napkins for us from the tabletop holder.

"Thinking about us?" I asked, oh-so-graciously segueing into *my* agenda before he even got started with his. I wasn't trying to cut him off, I was just really excited about my plan.

"No, not about us."

"You haven't been thinking about us? Not even a little?" Come on, Spain Man, throw me a bone, huh?

He slumped. "I did not mean it that way. I meant I have been thinking about my father." He paused, like he was lost in his own musings and was making a decision at that very moment.

I knew thoughts of his father were never far away. It was almost as if the less Claudio talked about him, the more prominent the man became in his son's mind. I was angry at my father and Claudio was angry at his father too, but they were different angers. Me, I'd given up on that front completely. For Claudio, something optimistic was mixed into his anger, as paradoxical as that seemed. Claudio still hoped:

Maybe this time? Maybe it can work with my father this time? It was like the man was playing emotional three-card monte with his son—my Claudio—and no matter which card Claudio chose, it would never be the right one in his father's eyes. Yet Claudio kept playing, lured by the promise of paternal love and admiration. A promise that the man would never, maybe could never, fulfill.

"I am going to take that job in New York. I will call my father this evening."

My heart soared and fell at the same time. New York subtracted thirty-five hundred miles between us (if there was an "us"), but it also left a twenty-five-hundred-mile deficit between The Big Apple and The Golden Gate City. Granted, I was still new to the serious-relationship concept, but who knew the damn thing would involve so much math?

But then, maybe this wasn't about me—wasn't about "us"—at all. I refocused on Claudio's well-being, and I did the only thing I knew how to do in these situations: play devil's advocate.

"Are you sure that's what you want?" I asked, keeping my tone neutral. "It didn't... go so well the last time—you said so yourself."

"It is, yes. I think this time will be different."

"Why? Why would it be different? Where's your evidence?" Keep that tone supportive Callie, easy and even.

Claudio sized me up as if he'd expected nothing less than my putting him through the wringer. "His false wife is out of the picture. She is moving elsewhere—to one of your other American states." He scooped up a spoonful of ice cream but didn't bring it to his mouth. "That means something. I *believe* that means something." He played with his mint chocolate-chip some more. "And I have changed, too. In many ways."

This sounded like wishful mumbo-jumbo to me. As far as I knew, Claudio didn't change—not really. I mean, look at where we were right now: I was leaving in a week, yet he acted as if our time under the Spanish sun was infinite, as if our worlds weren't on the cusp of reordering themselves. If he was going to move across a whole ocean on the premise of change, he had to be sure he was capable of it.

I tried not to be confrontational as I continued with my questions. "What's changed about you? Name one thing. One meaningful thing."

"Kauhlie, six years is a long time. I was in… a different phase of life then. I have changed. Maybe this would be a good opportunity to… to…." He lowered his eyes and gave up trying to finish the sentence.

"Time doesn't always mean change," I said. "Sometimes time *feels* like change, but it isn't. Have you thought about that?"

He nodded. "I have considered it. But what it comes down to, Kauhlie, is that this *feels* more right than wrong."

Claudio's "more right than wrong," wasn't at all compelling. I leaned back in my seat, now more confident that my plan was a good one—it would even give him a valid "out" with his father. My impending proposition became that much more compelling, if only in my own mind.

"Claudio, I've been thinking, too. What if there's another option. What if *I* offered you another option? A completely new one?"

He raised one eyebrow, intrigued. A good look. A hopeful look.

I took his free hand firmly in mine. Partly because I longed for his touch, and partly to anchor him in case he tried to run for the hills. "Come with me to San Francisco!" I burst out. Wasn't that the greatest plan ever? Wasn't it a shiningly brilliant idea, utterly spectacular?

His eyes bugged out a little as he hesitated. "What is this, Kauhlie?" Not a bad sign, per se, but definitely not the best one either. I'd have to sell the hell out of this thing.

"Listen, it's a good plan. Tell your father you want to open a California branch! San Francisco is full of companies looking for capital… or hoping to be bought out. You could make a killing!"

"I don't know." His brows knitted together. "My father probably would not want to invest in those kinds of companies?"

"Not interested in companies that make money? Not if he's the businessman you've told me about," I countered. "And you could be the one to figure all that out—it could be your 'gift' to him." Equal parts of attempted-helpfulness and tempered-hopefulness flitted in my stomach like butterflies. I had tons more to say, too. "San Francisco is a financial center in its own right; what firm wouldn't want offices coast-to-coast?"

More hesitation. "California? What would I do with myself in California?"

Claudio was asking all the wrong questions. "Not just California. *You* and *me* in California. You see?"

"Kauhlie, California is so different?"

Another wrong question. The man had lived in a bunch of European countries, plus the US. "Different" was what he was worried about? I couldn't tell if he was making excuses or honestly processing the curveball I'd just thrown him.

"It's not so different. San Francisco is very laid back—not like New York—it's a little like Spain that way. Lots of people speak Spanish, too." I nodded encouragingly. "And California was once a Spanish colony. You'll feel very at home." I was embellishing to a degree. I actually didn't know much about California in that sense. San Francisco was a cool, cosmopolitan city, though, and I could honestly see Claudio thriving there.

Thriving there with me. Us thriving together.

His eyes went blank—I hated that blank stare, but at least he was still in his seat. His words came out slowly. "I will consider this. Perhaps it will make good financial sense."

Good financial sense?! I just invited this man to move across the Western world with me—share his life with me—and he'd latched onto good financial sense. He sure knew how to slather on the romance and make a gal feel special.

I fought back a grimace and pulled myself together. "Honestly, I think it would be a win-win for everyone!" My voice betrayed too much enthusiasm, too much ardor. The kind of thing that always made Claudio uncomfortable.

He ran his hand through his dark waves and smiled cautiously. I worried.

We didn't say much after that. Our ice creams suddenly became super-interesting, and we finished our afternoon treat in relative silence. A heavy silence, like a weighted curtain, had unfurled between us. Neither of us knew exactly what was on the other side of that curtain, and we were both afraid of finding out.

"Claudio, did you decide yet?" I asked as the waiter cleared our table.

"No. I will consider it."

I fished a few euros out of my pocket for the tip. "How about now?"

"No."

We stepped into the afternoon sun. "Now?"

"No, Kauhlie, not yet."

Damnit.

⁓

We returned to Claudio's apartment to find Trevor looking like a puppy dog whose owner had abandoned him for Time and All Eternity—otherwise known as one full hour. I did feel bad, though, neither of us had remembered to text or leave a note, and we hadn't even brought him an ice cream. I decided not to mention the last part, for Trevor's sake.

To make it up to him, we let Trevor select our venue for the evening. Surprisingly enough, he wanted to go back to Limón y Lima. "Because that's where the three of us met, Callie," he pleaded. Which sounded fair enough, so after a light dinner, off we went.

We arrived early and managed to snag the same table we'd had on our first visit. Limón y Lima looked exactly as it had five months ago, five months that seemed like a very long time ago now. The gin and tonics tasted the same, too—a delicious blend of gin and tonic and lime. Also just like last time, Claudio seemed to know everyone at the bar. He had a glow about him as he greeted patron after patron.

"This is where it all started," Trevor began as we waited for Claudio to finish his hellos. "We're returning to the scene of the crime!"

"Crime? I don't think of our time together as criminal," I teased.

"Callie, you're a felony waiting to happen," he deadpanned.

I laughed harder than I intended to. It was true, in a sense; with all the times I'd blown up or stormed out, it was a wonder I hadn't been hauled off to some Spanish prison.

I was glad the club wasn't as packed as before. Not that the energy surrounding us was any less electric, it's just that there were fewer conduits for that electricity. It worked well, as far as I was concerned. After the crowds in Pamplona, I was burned out on screaming just to be heard.

"We only have a week left before we go our separate ways. Is there anything you still want to do before you go home?" asked Trevor. "Anything left on your bucket list?"

I was at a loss. I couldn't think of anything. I wasn't sure if I was going "home" either, not in the way Trevor meant. I had an apartment I'd never seen in a city I'd been to only once—a conference-visit lasting exactly forty-seven hours—and in no way did that constitute a home. It was enough to start my head spinning. I gazed at Claudio, still at the bar. That one untamable lock of his sprung free again, brushing against his forehead.

"Callie? Hello?"

"Sorry. I spaced out for a minute."

"I asked if there's anything else you want to do in Spain?"

"I think we've pretty much done it all now, haven't we, old chum?"

He smiled. "Yes, I think so." We clinked glasses and drank. The *clink* sounded just a touch bittersweet.

Trevor declared it was time to hit the dancefloor. He asked me to come with him, but I wanted to wait for Claudio, and I really wasn't up for dodging Trevor's knees and elbows at the moment, although I promised to join him in a little while. He waggled his hips all the way to the dancefloor, shaking his imaginary maracas as he shimmied.

Soon enough, Claudio returned, three gin and tonics in tow. "I apologize for staying away so long. I have brought an offering to make amends," he exclaimed proudly. His eyes moved to the dancefloor and Trevor's jerking hips. "Our friend will be glad of refreshment when he is finished... doing whatever it is he is doing."

I laughed. I was going to miss Trevor's unique dance moves. Claudio reached out, took my hand, and kissed it. "Kauhlie, I remember the first time I saw you. You were right over there." He jutted his chin toward the hallway leading to the restrooms. "And I was over there," he pointed across the room with his thumb.

"Yeah, I saw you seeing me," I answered. "Then I lost you in the crowd and figured that was the end of it." I distinctly remembered deeming him Spain Man and wondering if he was from a telenovela; I didn't see any need to mention that part.

"As if a mere crowd could keep me away!" he cried, exuberant. "Never! I thought to myself, 'I *must* meet this woman.'"

"And you came up with the very clever plan of buying me a drink. An original strategy!"

I might've been imagining it, but I think Claudio blushed slightly as he laughed. "Kauhlie, sometimes it is best to stick with the classics. For a woman of class!"

His last words were such a steaming pile of horseshit that I spat out my drink in shocked delight. A full spray that spewed across the table and onto Claudio.

His eyes sparked with amusement for an instant, then his expression turned sheepish. He reached for a napkin to mop himself up. "I thought one shower today had sufficed, but perhaps not. Very kind of you to rectify that for me, my dear Kauhlie."

I laughed heartily and easily. "Sure thing, buddy. What else could you expect from a woman of class?"

"I owe you a fresh drink. I do not believe the last one... reached its intended destination." He stood and offered me his hand. "Come.

There are many specials at the bar tonight, a full page of them. Perhaps we shall try something new."

Limón y Lima did indeed have a list of specials; apparently, it was their usual Tuesday-night promotion. I knew luring in mid-week clientele was tough for all sorts of businesses, but I guess this even applied to the hottest club in Madrid: partying and Tuesdays just didn't mix.

I picked a cocktail that could only be described as a gin and tonic pumped up on lime steroids and garnished with a small salad. It felt good to be back here. There was a certain comfort in reminiscing with Claudio in the place we'd first met. A certain tantalization in flirting openly and shamelessly with him.

At some point during my second salad, one of Claudio's friends approached us on his way out. He started the conversation in Spanish, then switched to English once Claudio began replying in a language I could readily understand.

"You and your girlfriend must join us Friday night, Claudio. I am throwing a party for my wife. She has launched her own company!"

"Thank you, my friend, but I am afraid my girlfriend and I have other plans. But you will give your Sonia my full regards and congratulations, *sí*?"

I latched onto Claudio's eyes the moment the man left us. "Girlfriend?" I asked.

He shrugged helplessly in response. I grinned at his helplessness. Maybe I had him right where I wanted him. Maybe this was the opportunity I needed—I'd neglected to mention something at the ice cream shop, something too important to let go.

"Claudio... I... have a confession."

"A confession?! Have you once again been up to no good, dear one?"

"Yes, I—wait, no! Up to no good? Honestly? Stay with me, this is serious."

"Then I, too, shall be serious. Very serious." He shot me his "genuine" smile. A dazzling smile full of even more horseshit.

I grumbled. Claudio obviously had a buzz—maybe now wasn't the time. But if not now, when? We only had six mornings left, and I was in too deep now to turn back.

"Look, I… just want you to know… I thought about it."

"Thought about what, Kauhlie? Are we thinking tonight? *Must* we think tonight?"

"I'm always thinking," I countered. "Now listen… just so you know, I thought about staying in Spain. Before you decided on New York, I thought about staying here with you." I searched his eyes for any trace of emotion. They went hard and blank as expected, but I could also tell I'd killed his buzz. That right there was a small victory.

A long pause settled before he spoke. "I never asked you to do that, Kauhlie. You have a life of your own in the US." He took a deep swallow from his glass. "I would never ask that of you."

"Good," I replied firmly. "Because I'm not doing it. I've worked too damn hard to get where I am. And honestly, this thing with Matt is my dream job." I bit off an inch of the sugared rhubarb stalk in my drink; it made a satisfying *snap* that emphasized my point. "I didn't know it was my dream job until I was offered it, but I'm damn sure I'll make a kick-ass general counsel. In San Francisco."

His eyes remained hard, but his tone was supportive. "That you will. There is no one I would rather have general counseling me." I was taken aback by that one; I'd expected a smart-ass remark, a much more pointed evasion.

I kept the momentum going while I still had it. "But then you decided on your own to leave Spain—I would never have asked you to do that. But since you're leaving, you should join me in California, like I said." I bit off another piece of rhubarb—this time it didn't make the dramatic *crunch* I was hoping for—before I went all in. "Because I love you, and we should be together."

Claudio's eyes betrayed a glimmer through their blankness, something I'd never seen before. He opened his mouth, but only a squeak came out—as if he'd picked out his words but someone had stolen them.

He kept opening and closing his mouth, no words coming out. I put my arm around his shoulder. "Do you love me?" I pressed, thinking a prompt would make things easier for him. He cocked his head as if preparing to recite pros and cons. (What cons?!) I jumped to yellow alert but succeeded in keeping my mouth shut until he spoke.

His voice came out deeper than usual, his words slow and measured. "I was of the understanding that... you had downgraded me." He rolled his neck in a half-circle, stretching awkwardly. "I thought our deep affection was enough."

Half the oxygen drained from the room, my face flushing with heat. "Oh, my God, you still can't say it?" Another thought stormed into my mind—an awful thought, its very existence as terrifying as a nightmare of bulls. "Do you feel it?" My burning blood turned to cold steel. "Jesus, you don't even feel it! You... stinking... piece... of... Spanish—"

"—Kauhlie, please. I am not like that."

"Not like what? Not warm and caring? Are you too cold inside to have real emotions?!"

"I did not mean... It is only to say... It does not work that way for me."

"How does it work, then? We have six more days, Claudio. Six. One hundred forty-four hours."

"I am fully aware, Kauhlie."

"Well, why haven't you said anything? Isn't this something we should talk about?"

"I don't know, I—"

"—Callie, it's been forever. You said you'd come dance!" Trevor cried as he wriggled up to the bar, shaking one invisible maraca. His flailing elbows and knees weren't especially well-received by the other patrons; he almost knocked a woman over.

"Not now, Trevor, we have a situation here!"

"A situation? What did I miss?" he asked after apologizing to the woman.

"Quite a few things!" I pointed accusingly at Claudio. "He can't say he loves me!"

Trevor's eyes narrowed into slits of green. "Dude, you can't say you love her? You suck!" Claudio shot him a look that I think was supposed to be stern but came out defeated.

"That's right, he can't say it! Even after I told him I loved him!"

"Kauhlie, is this necessary? Must we do this in public?"

"I said it twice, Trevor. I said I loved him *twice*! And you know what?"

"*Qué?*" blurted out the woman who'd been the unfortunate recipient of Trevor's dancing. She couldn't help herself. She needed to know "what."

"I'll tell you 'what,'" I said, turning to her. "This man can wrestle a bull with his bare hands, but he can't tell me he loves me!" She looked confused, so I attempted a translation. "*Ese hombre, muy duro como un toro! Pero... no puede decir, te amo!*" I had no idea how close I got to proper Spanish, but I got the gist across. The woman groaned as if to say "typical," as did her three girlfriends. One of them embraced me from behind, cooing sweet-sounding but undecipherable words in my ear. Her arms felt good around me. I needed that hug.

"Really dude? That's so cliché!" Trevor burst out. He was really riled up, like Claudio had slighted him instead of me. "Tell her right now!" he demanded. "You're lucky to have her, so tell her you love her! You know you do, so say it!"

Good ol' Trevor.

Claudio shrank like a guilty teenager on his stool. He called to the bartender, demanding a shot of vodka. He didn't so much as look at me, didn't have the decency to reply to Trevor. He seized on his drink the second it arrived. Mixing hard liquor like that was a sure-fire recipe for a hangover, and I sneered in satisfaction.

The four women around us were in an absolute fury. Over and over again I heard the Spanish words for *balls* (*cojones*) and *coward* (*cobarde*). We might've had a language barrier between us but, in that moment, we were a sisterhood. I was emboldened, as if I had a small army around me. A sisterhood plus Trevor, chock full of validation.

"*Señorita, baila!*" One woman exclaimed. "Dance! Dance!" She started pulling me toward the dancefloor, recruiting her friends in the process. "*No necesitas un hombre!*"

I understood that much clearly. "Right, I don't need a man!" I agreed. "And I don't need *that* man!" I grabbed Trevor's arm and began pulling him along too. "Trevor, come on, you heard her, let's dance. You, me, and these lovely ladies."

If Claudio didn't want me, screw him. I'd opened up; I'd put myself out there… and I'd been resoundingly rejected. So what? I'd faced my nightmares; this man couldn't keep me down. That a smoldering hell-fire burned in my heart was meaningless. There would be other guys, and—with or without Claudio—I could still dance.

CHAPTER 35

ALMOST LIKE A TRUCE

I'd neglected to pull the curtains fully closed before bed—precision and an excess of alcohol don't mix. A streak of hazy sunshine streamed into my eyes, blinding me as I tried to identify the buzzing half-ring now mimicking the pounding in my head.

I slammed my hand on my alarm clock. The obnoxious buzzing continued.

I rolled over and squinted until my eyes focused. On the night-stand, an orange light flashed in unison with the sound. The hotel's phone. The phone that never rang this early, not in all my time here.

I fumbled with the receiver. "What?!" I accused. That was my standard opening line whenever someone had the audacity to call me ten minutes before my alarm was set to go off. Sleep was precious. Especially with this hangover.

"Congratulations, Callie," came the voice.

"Congratulations on what?" I grumbled, before my mouth and my brain fully connected. Who was calling me at this uncivilized hour?

"On living your life all the way up. Truly well done."

Hemingway. I hadn't expected to hear from him again. And certainly not before breakfast.

"You found me, Callie. You found me in *el toro*, at the heart of your nightmare. I have been within you all along, I am the strength you hid from even yourself."

"What kind of crap is that?" I countered, not at all pleased. "I hauled myself across a whole ocean, did everything you said, and now you're saying you're not even here in Spain?"

He chortled with delight, as if I were missing something obvious. "I'm in Spain, but I'm also *not* in Spain."

I jolted upright, hitting my head on the headboard, adding a sharp pain to the throbbing one. None of this made sense—not that it ever did—and I was beginning to think I was still drunk. Why didn't this call come with an aspirin? Couldn't I get an aspirin in this damn hotel?

"I don't understand," I managed to squeak, despite my recent head injury.

"Callie, not everything in life needs to be understood fully. Sometimes you must enjoy things as they are… for what they are *and* are not."

"Hmmph!" I rebelled. "I *like* understanding. I *like* knowing." I paused to let my thoughts catch up with my mouth. A degree of cognition set in, and I admitted, "Maybe you're right."

"I *am* right. And you did marvelously at the *encierro*. A baptism by bulls. A feat you never suspected you were capable of only six months ago."

Just then the entire room tipped violently to one side; I shook my head hard to clear it, which was definitely the wrong move, and I almost dropped the phone. "Sure, okay… the bulls and I became bosom buddies, whatever. But you know what? With all this carrot-and-stick stuff, you're a shitty mentor."

"I don't think you mean that, Callie," he said gently. "I have helped you where I could."

I paused, rubbing my throbbing temple. These last six months had been the adventure of a lifetime, all prompted by Hemingway's Seventh

Avenue call. Where would I be without his guidance? I wouldn't have been able to sit still in New York, and I would probably now be working myself to death in a temporary legal gig, still living vicariously through *The Sun Also Rises*.

"No, I didn't mean that," I agreed, muttering. "I didn't." My mouth tasted liked sandpaper and damp dog hair. Did we really have to do this now?

"You chose this journey, Callie. Every decision was yours alone. Perhaps I left you a clue here or there, but nothing more."

"Yeah," I grumbled. "Yeah, okay." I took a deep breath, running my hand through my snarled hair. "Thanks for that. Really, I mean it. Thank you."

He paused, and I could almost see his eyes glowing with the pride of a mentor. "You have one more thing you must do before you leave Spain, Callie, and it is no small thing."

I groaned. Now what? Follow the magic flute? Find the pot at the end of the rainbow? Weave straw into gold?

"You must find peace with your Spanish lover."

"Claudio? What does he have to do with any of this?" After last night, I wasn't even sure my "Spanish lover" was still speaking to me. Hell, *I* wasn't even sure I was still speaking to *him.*

"Let me ask you this, Callie: when you were in Pamplona, did you run with the bulls?"

"What?!" What kind of question was that? And why was he changing subjects? "You know I did. Didn't you see me?"

A touch of frustration entered his tone. "I was watching, yes. But I ask again, did you run *with* the bulls... or did you try to bend them to your will?"

I thought back to the *suelto's* sharp horn. "I would've been gored if I did that. Shredded to pieces! I ran *with* the bulls. *Because* of the bulls."

"It is the same with your Spanish lover. Run with him, demand no more. Even if rejection is your true and greatest nightmare."

My stomach flipped. Now Claudio, the one man I'd truly opened myself to, was my bull? How much surrealism could I take before coffee? And my God, where was that aspirin?

"That's letting him off the hook," I replied weakly, my nausea growing. I rallied my strength. "I deserve better. I deserve more."

"You do indeed, Callie. You'll receive no argument from me there. But perhaps your Spanish lover is incapable of more. He has not faced his nightmares, as you have."

"I'm nobody's nightmare," I shot. I walked it back a little. "At least not anymore." A question occurred to me. "Claudio changed a bull's direction. He did that, why can't I?"

Hemingway's voice betrayed a bittersweetness. "His journey is different from yours. Intersecting roads do not always merge."

"Right," I agreed, although the word came out defiant. Tapping my fingernail against the receiver, I thought for a long moment. "I get that." I hesitated again, pushing past my headache to the raw understanding beneath. "Let him find his own Hemingway!"

The man laughed freely, a kind and full-bodied sound. "I will not speak with you again, Callie, but you've done so well. Now you must find your peace."

Some part of me panicked. The room swerved again; I clung to the phone like a lifeline. "But what if I need you? How will I reach you?"

"I am with you Callie, as always. And I will be with you when you leave Spain. A new life awaits you. I will be watching."

"Unacceptable!" I cried. "How come you get to—"

"—Find your peace, Callie. That's all that's left to do. Find your peace, just as you found me."

The line went dead abruptly, as it always did. I wanted to be still and think, but at that moment my stomach turned traitorous. I ran to the bathroom and parted ways with months of questions and uncertainties, along with any remnants of last night. Hemingway had asked one more thing of me—a big thing, sure, but he'd given me *specifics* for once. He'd said his farewells—I was on my own again—and completing my quest was now truly up to me.

I texted Trevor, telling him to have first breakfast without me, before stumbling back to the bathroom for a bicarbonate. I downed a double dose of fizzy relief as fast as I could, then I crawled under the covers, hiding and wishing it would all go away. No good. My mind whirled with thoughts, much as the walls were whirling around me. With my Spanish sisterhood backing me last night, I'd overdone it to an unconscionable degree. Geez, how many of those salads did I drink?

Great streams of shampoo bubbles swirled down the drain, the lavender aroma soothing me. I breathed in the steam, feeling my pores and my mind open. Hemingway was right. I couldn't impose my will on a bull any more than I could squeeze blood from a stone. I didn't know if Claudio was a bull, a stone, or *el duende* incarnate, but it didn't matter. The man was closed off, barricaded for his own reasons—reasons that had little to do with me. That wasn't going to change between today and the airport, now only five mornings away. Not when he'd had five months—my entire time in Madrid—to figure things out.

The revelation freed me. Claudio and I were good for each other, no doubt, but perhaps we were only good for each other outside of our "real" lives. A cocoon of bliss—mostly bliss—where we came together in kismet. Soon there was going to be a change, a big change, not a merging but a branching—two different directions. A reality we'd been pretty good at ignoring for months.

Claudio and I had intersected for a moment, but now that moment was drawing to a close. Maybe that had to be okay, maybe fighting it was the source of my pain. Maybe, if we were adults about it, we could salvage these last few Spanish days, no rules—no expectations—required. My new life in California would be just that: new. New, unencumbered, and free. Tears of mourning and liberation joined the bubbles swirling down the drain.

I ordered myself coffee and a croissant—I wasn't going to face this day without basic fuel. They took forever to come up from room service, but they did do wonders for my physical state. I was still hurting, of course, but conceding to reality—owning it—had lessened that pain. I resolved to make the effort and go to Claudio. To find that peace.

My intentions were cut short by a knock at the door. I finished doing up my jeans, then opened the door a crack, the safety latch still on. I found myself nose-to-nose with Claudio. He had a penitent look on his face, a look that was clearly accompanied by the remains of his own hangover.

"Kauhlie, I am sorry," he said, peering through the narrow opening.

"I'm sorry too," I replied, trying to meet him somewhere in the middle. "But you understand why I was angry, right?"

"Yes, I understand," I wasn't sure he truly got it, but I didn't want to quiz him either, and I certainly didn't want to do this with him in the hallway. I held fast to my revelation as I unchained the lock, re-opened the door, and ushered him in.

He came to an abrupt halt a few steps into the room. His eyes smoldered, vulnerability peeking through. "You must know, those types of things are not easy for me to say." His gaze never left me as I looked down at my feet and then off to the side. I forced myself to meet his eyes. "You know? Love. All of that," he continued.

I directed him to sit in the room's only chair before seating myself on the edge of the bed. A mere three feet of space between us, a sliver of a neutral zone.

"Yes. All of that. It's hard for me, too," I answered, staring into my hands.

"I am not so good with feelings, Kauhlie. Emotions are not my strength."

I took a steadying breath and looked up from my hands. "Listen, I wasn't looking for anything from you. Not at first. Not for a long time."

"I know. And I am sorry for running from you in Pamplona. For facing *el toro* instead of facing you."

I smiled slightly. This morning's revelation aside, at least I got an apology. A type of validation I'd never felt before flowed through me.

I looked straight into his eyes, bracing myself for the next part.

The important part. "But I have to tell you, Claudio, I'm not looking for anything from you now, either." I kept my voice flat but not dispassionate. "Not now."

"What does this mean?" His eyes almost went hard again, but somehow he forced them back to softness. The man really was trying.

"We only have a few days left. Let's not waste them. Let's be smarter than that."

"Yes, we are intelligent people." It was a question more than a statement. He couldn't tell where I was going with this, and his hangover was slowing him down. Which was okay—I wanted this to sink in gradually.

"Claudio, I have a plane to catch. You'll take me to the airport… and that'll be it."

"I am taking you to the airport?"

"You are. Don't argue."

"But what about California, Kauhlie? Yesterday you said I should come to California with you."

"Do you *want* to come with me?" I asked, my resolve cracking the tiniest bit. A hairline fracture threatening my reconciliation with reality.

"I do want to join you, but New York is where I must go. I cannot explain it fully. My heart tells me one thing, but my head tells me another. In this case, because of my father, I must listen to my head and not my heart."

Damnit, it never failed. Men always thought with the wrong body part.

I swung my legs freely, my kicks buying me a few seconds to regroup. "New York is a big city. California is a big state. There's a big country in between."

I let my words hang there. A long pause, painfully long.

Claudio, frowning, took in my full meaning before breaking the uncomfortable silence. "Ah. I see. We are like *Casablanca*, then?"

I smiled sadly. "We'll always have Madrid."

Simultaneously, we turned away from each other, hiding our faces.

"I am sorry, Kauhlie," Claudio repeated, still turned away from me.

"You keep saying that."

"I do, Kauhlie, and I am." He turned, then leaned forward as far as he could, extending his hand for mine. I did the same. Our palms met in the middle of the divide. We held them there, clasped together, almost like a handshake. Almost like a truce.

"All I know, dear one, is we have five mornings left. All I know is I care for you deeply. That is my world right now." He stood up, pulling me gently to my feet and wrapping his arm around me.

I smiled at him. My smile was swallowed up in his calm eyes, and he smiled back.

"Let us go to the lounge. Trevor is waiting. He declined to come up, just in case you decided to kill me."

I chuckled. "A smart move. I would've done the same."

Claudio winked—a maddening wink that almost made me want to take it all back and bury myself in his chest forever. "Although I have no doubt he would help you hide the body, if it came to that."

"Of course, he would. I honestly don't give him enough credit."

"He says he has news, Kauhlie, but he would not make his announcement without you."

"Loyal through and through." I pulled Claudio toward the door, grabbing my bag with my free hand. "Come on, we'd better go down."

The corridor was empty, which I was glad of—I hated the awkward semi-encounters of hotel hallways, and I wanted to be alone with Claudio for a few more minutes.

Once the elevator reached the ground floor, I released Claudio's hand. We stepped forward into the lobby together.

CHAPTER 36

A COLORFUL GOODBYE

"*Ich werde morgen nach Deutschland gehen.*"

"English, Trevor."

"I believe he said he is going to Germany," Claudio translated.

"Yes, we know that, Trevor," I said, once I understood. "You've told us that a bunch of times."

We'd met Trevor in the lounge, then decided some fresh air would do us all some good. The day wasn't too hot, and so we'd walked just a couple of blocks to a plaza. We'd settled ourselves on a shady granite staircase after grabbing coffees to go. A gentle breeze completed the effect.

"No, Callie, you're not listening. I said, '*morgen.*'"

"Again, Trevor, English." I knew he was hesitating on purpose. He knew that I knew. Yet this wasn't his usual hesitation, it was something else. He was leading up to something big, although I couldn't imagine what.

He fidgeted on the step, pulling on his beard. "Callie, '*morgen*' means 'tomorrow.' My train is tomorrow, after lunch."

"You're leaving tomorrow?" I asked, taken aback. "I thought you were staying until next week?"

"Yeah, yeah, yeah; no, no, no." Six syllables meaning, literally, nothing. We were back to non-language again.

"Three positives and three negatives. That equals zero." I put my hand on Trevor's shoulder in encouragement. "Take a deep breath and help us out."

"Leaving us so soon, we will miss you," Claudio added. He clapped him on the back gently. Sometimes getting Trevor's thoughts out of his mouth was like burping a baby.

"Well… I was going to leave next week, but you guys need a few days to…" he gesticulated in a sweeping circle, "figure this whole mess out."

Claudio laughed. "That is very thoughtful, but Kauhlie and I have figured many things out, you do not need to worry on that account. And we love having you with us."

"Love is a strong word," I shot under my breath, immediately regretting it. I should've been better than that. No more bitterness, no more expectations. I guess narcissism died hard?

"What did you say, Kauhlie?"

"Nothing, just talking to myself." I batted my eyelashes at him. It was better for everyone if we moved on, and quickly. And anyway, this was about Trevor, not me.

"Plus, I want to get started on my residence permit," Trevor continued.

"But surely a few days will make little difference? Certainly not enough to depart so suddenly?"

"It's a lot of paperwork, Claudio! I want to apply right away—it'll make getting a job easier. And once I get a job, I can probably get a Blue Card!"

"A Blue Card?" I gasped. "You're really going all-in on this, huh?"

"*Ja*. I'm not going back to the States. Not to live. No more brown and gray." He looked up at the beautifully clear sky. "Blacks and reds and golds. That's what I need."

"What about your degree? Will you finish it?" I asked it as gingerly as I could, since grad school was a sore spot. Yet I still wanted to know if Trevor had a plan on that front.

"I don't think so. I already have a master's, and I can apply to my school to get an advanced-study certificate for my doctoral work." He tore his gaze from the sky and sipped his coffee. "That's what they give to dissertation drop-outs."

"That may be to your advantage," I replied, thinking it through. "You won't be locked into teaching or research, like most PhDs in your field."

"Yes," Claudio began, throwing his hand up with a flourish. "The world will be your oyster!"

"Shakespeare coined that phrase. Let's leave him out of this." Trevor sighed heavily. "All this will be hard, but I'm going to do it."

"It's the hard things that count, Trevor," I offered, recalling our conversation in Pamplona. "Nothing hurts if you don't let it, right?"

A bemused and devilish smile spread across his face. "Leave Hemingway out of this, too. Geez, Callie."

Claudio's laugh echoed across the plaza, easing the mood momentarily. I think we all needed that.

I swirled my coffee in its paper cup, trying not to seem too eager about my next question. "But you'll come visit me, right? In San Francisco?" I really did want Trevor to come to the west coast once I got settled.

"Sure, Callie. They have that nice red bridge there."

I put my head on his shoulder, a sorrow creeping in. "Seriously, you *have* to come, okay? I'll have a guest room and everything in my new place. You and your next alter ego can stay whenever you'd like."

Seriousness crept across Trevor's face. "I'm not going to have an alter ego anymore, Callie. I'm going to be me, just me. All the way up. In living color."

"A man reborn! We must celebrate!" Claudio jumped to his feet, shirking the melancholy again. "What shall we do on your last day in my beautiful country?"

"Yes, old pal, let's celebrate! Today will be the stuff myths are made of!"

"No, guys, I think I want a quiet day. An a-lot-of-nothing day. But *a lot* of nothing. Cover half the city, if we can."

"You mean like a greatest-hits thing?" I finished the last of my coffee and crumpled my cup. It hadn't been very good; I wasn't sorry to see it go.

"Yeah, like that—only not like that. Appreciate the day for what it is." He turned to Claudio. "But I do want to see Toni and Teddy, the fuzz balls. Can we stop by your apartment?"

"Of course, my friend. In fact, let us start there, and then we will do a lot of nothing. We are quite good at that, no?"

I stretched my arms wide, taking Claudio's hand while wrapping my free arm around Trevor. "Yes, we're quite good at that, it's our one true talent. Let's make today count for nothing!"

We gave Trevor the day he wanted, letting him pick the sites and restaurants—some we'd visited before, some we hadn't. For nightcaps, we again went back to Limón y Lima because, as Trevor put it, "You guys managed to screw last night up pretty bad." He wasn't wrong, but it did feel weird going back after making such a big scene. The three of us had fun though, dancing until after midnight. Trevor even came dangerously close to achieving rhythm.

The next day, we met early, much earlier than we normally would. The weather had turned, it was hot again—Spanish-summer hot. We met for a first- and second-breakfast combo at a corner café we'd been to a million times before. None of us wanted to talk about Trevor leaving. We pushed it to the margins of our minds, and, with effort, we managed to avoid the subject completely.

"We're going for a walk, guys," I announced once we were outside. "As a team. A proper constitutional." I wedged myself in between them and hooked one elbow with each. We walked arm-in-arm, laughing and reminiscing. At one point, Trevor got the idea of naming all the museums I'd dragged him to. We lost track quickly.

"Well then, at least I taught you something," I chided. "An introduction to art. A thorough primer."

Trevor didn't miss a beat. "Yeah, there's a life-skill I can use."

"You don't use art, you *experience* art. It *enriches* you. You're fully enriched because of me." For effect, I agreed with myself imperiously. "Fully enriched, because of me."

I expected a snarky comeback, but Trevor grew somber, almost sullen. "That's true," he replied after a few paces. "I'm fuller now than I was before."

"Yes, we did have a magnificent breakfast, did we not?" Claudio teased, trying to lift the heaviness settling over Trevor. "I too am quite full!"

"No, I mean it. I'm fuller now because of you, Callie. You too, Claudio."

"I think you're going to have to explain that one," I said. "What does 'fuller' mean?"

He turned to me without breaking stride. "It's an adjective, Callie, meaning 'more full,'" he replied, as if I were a five-year-old kid asking silly questions.

"I know what it means! What does it mean to *you*?

Trevor shrugged. My linked elbow shrugged with him. "I don't know, I can't explain it. Just fuller. It's like I was kind of empty, only pretending I was full and getting in my own way."

"Self-sabotage is a sneaky one, my friend. And our Kauhlie is very good at challenging us!" My eyeballs shot over to Claudio before I could stop them. "In the best possible way," he added hastily. Nice save there, buddy.

We wandered around, doing a lot of nothing, until we came to a smaller park on the outskirts of downtown that I'd never much noticed before. "This is the Plaza del Campillo del Mundo Nuevo," Claudio told us. "Let us go sit for a while." We'd walked a couple of miles by then, a break was welcome. We found a broad bench a little way inside the park and made ourselves comfortable.

"*Mundo Nuevo*? That means 'New World,' right?" Trevor asked once we were situated. He was on my left, Claudio on my right. I felt secure and content between them. Just the three of us, with one more lunch to look forward to.

"It does indeed, my friend. Perhaps you have picked up more Spanish than you suspect."

"I don't think so. But I remember our tour guide said that a bunch of times. Callie, do you remember her? The one in Barcelona?"

"We went on a lot of those walking tours, Trevor. Which one?"

He snickered. "The one you made minced meat out of."

"Kauhlie made minced meat out of a tour guide?" Claudio put his arm around me. "Why does this not surprise me?"

I shrugged. "Her understanding of history was… skewed. I adjusted it for her." I kicked some gravel at a pigeon that had come too close for comfort.

"That was pretty kick-ass, Callie. That's when I knew."

"Knew what?"

Trevor hesitated, calculating his words carefully. He picked up a twig, snapped it in half, then pulled on his beard twice. "That I… I… wanted to stick around. That I… should follow your lead."

"That was on our second or third day together. You got all that from one speech on colonialism in the Americas?"

Trevor's cheeks flushed as he nodded. "You could fight. Like my matador."

I leaned back and crossed my legs with a dramatic swoop. "I'll take that as a compliment." I slipped my arm through his, locking elbows again. It was our pose for the day.

"Is there anywhere in particular you would like to go for your last lunch in Spain?" Claudio jumped in, pulling out his phone. "Tell me, and I will make it happen! Reservations—and the bill—are on me!

Trevor's whole body slumped. "Yeah, well… about that… um, there's something I need to tell you guys." He pulled up a weed, rolling it between his fingertips.

"What is it?" I asked, taking the stalk from him gently. "Come on, surely you know you can tell us anything." Claudio nodded in agreement.

"I'm going to leave early," Trevor announced.

I was confused; hadn't we had this conversation yesterday? "We know. We talked about that already, silly." I punched his shoulder lightly with my free hand. "You're leaving today."

"No, early—like now." Trevor's words came out in a rush, like there were no spaces in between them.

"Early? You mean no lunch?" I looked at Trevor and then at Claudio. "Can you do that in Spain, Claudio?"

"You cannot. It is against the rules," he replied. "I believe it is in our constitution."

"There you have it, Trevor. Skipping lunch is not possible in Spain. You've been here long enough to know the rules."

He laughed a little and I pulled him closer with our locked arms to make him laugh harder. "But, Callie, I'm packed, and I've checked out of my room. My bags are waiting for me in the lobby. I'm all ready to go."

"No!" I cried, the reality sinking in. "You said after lunch!"

"Yes, you did say after lunch," Claudio helped.

"I know, I know. I just don't like long goodbyes." He picked another weed and started pulling its leaves off the stem.

"Well, you can't go right now. Not this minute," I argued, feeling like the rug had been pulled out from under me. "I have something for you. A small something."

"Aw, Callie. That's why I wanted to do this quick. None of this goodbye stuff."

"It's not goodbye stuff." I started rifling through my bag—awkwardly because my arm was still linked with Trevor's. "It's a good *future* present." I pulled out the gift, expertly wrapped in yesterday's edition of *El País*, and held it out. "Now sit still and unwrap it," I instructed, mostly so he couldn't try one of those sneaky, "I'll open it on the train," moves.

"Kauhlie, that was very thoughtful of you. But why did you not tell me? I would have liked to contribute." As Claudio spoke, Trevor took the packet from my hand.

"Because it's not that kind of gift, Claudio." I turned to Trevor, who was examining the wrapped box with cautious curiosity. He held it up to his ear and rattled it, then sniffed it. God, he was weird.

"Okay, Callie, I'm all-in," he pronounced. He ripped off the newspaper, tearing right through the face of the Spanish prime minister. "Crayons?" Trevor smiled widely, but his smile was also a question mark.

"Yes, crayons! For living your life in color!" I cried. "Twenty-two colors. I told you I'd buy you some!"

Trevor's eyes sparkled, the green flecks glimmering. "Gee, Callie, you're such a good friend. I can't believe you remembered!"

"Twenty-two colors, Kauhlie?" asked Claudio, peering at the gift. "I think you have mistranslated. The box says twenty-four crayons."

I looked Trevor square in the eyes as I answered Claudio. "No, I didn't. I took the brown and gray ones out."

Trevor's still-glimmering eyes suddenly glistened with moistness. "Oh, Callie. No, no… You did that and…? Callie, I mean, oh…"

Claudio was fully puzzled by Trevor's reaction, but he helped him along anyhow, clapping him on the back firmly. "I believe the words you need are, 'Thank you,' yes?"

Trevor opened the box and slipped his pinky into the two-crayon void. "Yes, that's it exactly," he said, pulling himself together. "Thank you, Callie. I'll treasure these." He drew the gold one out and held the cylinder of wax and pigment up to the sun, as if peering into a kaleidoscope. "This is amazing," he whispered. I smushed my cheek against his and looked hard, but all I saw was a crayon—I couldn't see what Trevor was seeing.

"Now, my friend, what time is this train of yours?" Claudio interjected, mostly to steer us from the quicksand of melancholy. I didn't know a box of crayons could cause quicksand, but anything was possible with Trevor.

"In an hour and a half," he replied, glancing at the clock on Claudio's phone.

"That is plenty of time if we take a cab. Come, we will pick up your bags, then take you to the station!"

"Actually... I'm going to break it off here," Trevor responded with all the conviction he had. "I should break it off here."

"But we're the Three Musketeers! We should stay together until the last minute."

"Yes, together until The End!" added Claudio.

Trevor looked at me and then at Claudio, bravery in his eyes. "No, it's time. Really. It has to be now."

I was struggling with this more than I'd anticipated. "But we've been together for six months—all the way back to Barcelona," I objected. "I don't think I've ever had a relationship that's lasted this long. Even Claudio hasn't made six months! It's a very exclusive club."

"Callie, I..."

"Come on, you can put up with us for another hour or so, right?"

"Callie, please. You guys should have... some alone time. I have a new life to build in Berlin, and I need to start now."

I hooked his arm even more tightly. "I just thought... we had more time." Leaving now. I almost couldn't wrap my head around it.

"I know. We had such an amazing six months, Callie, a true adventure!"

I didn't say anything back. I couldn't. We should've had one more meal together, one more bottle of wine, but now we didn't even have one more hour. I kicked at the pigeon again as it wandered toward us. Couldn't that damn bird see we were having a moment?

Claudio broke the silence. "I am happy for the good times we had, but also sad to see you go. I am a little happy and a little sad—it is bittersweet." He stood up and extended his hand to our departing companion. "My friend Trevor, it has been an honor."

Trevor stood up and took his palm. "For me as well, Claudio." They shook and then did the guy-hug thing, complete with mutual claps on the back.

Almost by instinct, Claudio drifted back a couple of yards so I could talk with Trevor alone. "I'm totally going to miss you," I said, untangling myself from my bag as I rose.

"Callie, this is why I hate goodbyes. I'll miss you too." He rubbed his toe in the gravel.

"If we hadn't met, we wouldn't be saying goodbye now. Would that be better?"

He pushed his lips into a half-smile. "No, I wouldn't have wanted to miss knowing you."

I bounded forward and hugged him. He hugged me back hard. At first, it didn't feel natural—Trevor's hug had corners. But after a second or two, the hard angles rounded themselves out. An excellent hug from an old friend.

He smiled and began backing away.

"Take care of yourself, Bilbo."

"Not that name again!" he cried, rolling his eyes, still easing backward.

I forced a laugh. "You're the best Bilbo ever. Never let anyone tell you otherwise!"

"Good luck in San Francisco, Callie." He continued backing away. "*Auf Wiedersehen.*"

After another ten feet, Trevor faced forward and started walking away. He looked over his shoulder several times, and I waved each time. After the fifth or sixth wave, he stopped turning around and kept right on walking.

The ground went spongy, like it was suddenly too soft. I felt like I'd said goodbye to a part of myself, and I suddenly regretted never telling Trevor about my Hemingway calls. He would've gotten a kick out of that, but more importantly, Trevor would've understood.

I backed up a few steps—right into Claudio. He wrapped his arms around me.

"Do you think he was really packed and ready to go?" I asked, frustrated by the moistness in my eyes.

"No, he was not packed, not ready," he answered. "Of course not."

"But why would he leave early?"

"There is something you do not know, Kauhlie. Trevor was very much in love with you."

"What?!" This was no time for jokes. I turned around in his arms and searched his eyes.

"This is true. I sensed it the night we first met, and he told me so himself, when we were roommates in Pamplona."

"What? Don't you think you should've mentioned that?"

"No, Kauhlie. Because Trevor knew his love was not right for you. His love is quiet and unassuming, when you need a bold love—full of passion and life!"

I pushed out of his arms. "Oh, is that what I need?" I asked, not succeeding in hiding my annoyance. What the hell did Claudio know about love? And—on another note entirely—what kind of irony was this? Situational? Dramatic? Ugh, hadn't I just brushed up on this stuff?

"And I do believe," Claudio continued, "that it was important for his love to remain unrequited. Something to do with his robust inner life, perhaps."

I thought about it. That made sense—sense for Trevor, anyhow—although I didn't like it. "I still think you should've mentioned it. That's a big thing."

"I did what I thought was best for everyone, Trevor included, and I could not break his confidence," he replied gently. "Please, let us not fight now."

I turned and watched Trevor exiting the park. I waited until he was out of sight, then snuggled myself back into Claudio's arms.

"No, let's not fight now." More tears formed in my eyes. Claudio held me tighter.

CHAPTER 37

NO NEED FOR LEFTOVERS

My remaining days with Claudio were a whirlwind in slow motion. On the one hand, they flew by, but on the other, every minute seemed laden with a hidden weight anchoring me to my *Casablanca* moment. I tried not to think about that part, but no matter how hard I attempted to put it out of my heart and mind, parts of me kept falling to the floor—I'd have to sweep them up with my new resolve and press forward. I believe it was the same for Claudio, but the man was too damn hard to read to be sure.

We spent our days revisiting our favorite museums, lounging in my favorite cafés, hanging out in historic parts of the city, and checking out galleries Trevor would've driven us crazy in. Claudio even offered to take me to a bullfight because, as he put it, "You must experience the thrill of *una corrida de toros* for yourself!" I declined, though. I'd already conquered my bulls in Pamplona, I didn't need to relive it in any way. No animal, no nightmare, had a hold over me. Not anymore.

Part of me had been afraid our dynamic would become tinged by awkwardness without Trevor, but it didn't. I missed him, sure, and I looked forward to his texts, but now that we were no longer a trio,

Claudio and I had a new type of freedom—one we embraced despite its limited longevity. We laughed and lived and loved in a way that hadn't been possible before. We became truly a couple, focused solely on each other—on *enjoying* each other. We capped off each night dancing, and I loved being the pair everyone was watching. On the dancefloor time hardly existed, and the spectators surrounding us didn't know Claudio and I had an expiration date.

On my penultimate day, I told Claudio I needed a few hours to myself and went my own way for the afternoon. I wanted some "taking it all in time" before I left, but just as importantly, I had a late-afternoon phone call with Matt and his management team. We'd been trying to schedule it for a week, but San Francisco's workday didn't line up with Spanish time. I suspected Matt, in order to get his people to come in early, had bribed them with a swanky breakfast—I heard a fair amount of chewing on the line. That was gross, but by the time the call was finished I had my start date: August 15th. It would be a soft, pre-Labor-Day entry back into the professional world, yet it was a hard date. A real date to circle on my calendar. A date I could look forward to. Callie McGraw, hand-picked general counsel for San Francisco's hottest tech company.

The moment I'd hung up the phone, I called Claudio. I was really excited, almost giddy, but I didn't get very far with my news, because his mind was on something else entirely: food.

"Kauhlie, I would like us to make paella together tonight."

Softness slithered through me. Paella had been the very first dish we'd cooked together, exactly five months ago tonight. Was that intentional? Had Claudio remembered? Was this part of some grand gesture he'd been keeping secret? Oh, for heaven's sake, Callie, don't go down that road now.

I straightened myself up, literally and emotionally, and announced my big news proudly. After receiving my due congratulations, Claudio said he would run to the market. He wanted snails so fresh they'd practically still be moving, none of that canned stuff. I was more than happy to let him go gastropod hunting on his own, and I decided to make a start on my packing. That was something I needed to do alone—when company gets involved in packing, a trip down memory lane becomes inevitable. I wasn't falling into that sappy trap, not when I had so much ahead of me.

When I arrived at Claudio's apartment later, the lights were dimmed, and traditional Spanish guitar music was playing softly. On top of that, the aroma of baking bread wafted through the air. I'd found my peace with "my Spanish lover," and I accepted where we were headed, but why couldn't it work out with the guy who baked fresh bread?

Teddy greeted me even before Claudio. He wasn't exactly a kitten anymore, but he was still as affectionate as ever. The second I'd made it past the threshold, he slid between my feet, swirling around my ankles. Toni, as usual, eyed me from a privileged distance. Lest I forget, I was in her domain.

Claudio greeted me with a double kiss. "Kauhlie, I have taken the liberty of pouring for us that white wine you love," he said, handing me a glass. It was cool in my hand. The wine tasted liked crisp apples.

He returned to the kitchen. I seated myself in the living room, sinking into his plush couch. I took a mental picture of the penthouse and hoped my San Francisco digs would be half as nice—I'd seen realtor-pictures of my apartment-to-be, but they were clearly the rose-colored kind. Now that I had my start date, my apartment seemed much more real; I felt oddly eager to step foot in it for the first time. Hell, I might even hire someone to help me decorate.

Barely a moment passed before Claudio brought over a tray of tapas. "I also took the liberty of preparing the sun-dried tomato tarts you love." He set the tray on the coffee table as if presenting a masterpiece. To reach the tarts, I had to struggle to extricate myself from the depths of the couch. The effort was worth it.

He was pleased at my being pleased. Excitedly, he ran into the kitchen and brought over another tray. "Kauhlie, I have prepared an herbed chorizo for you as well. I fried it, you have always loved it this way." It didn't escape my notice that Claudio had used the word *love* three times inside of fifteen minutes, but a few bites of chorizo quickly distracted me—another tart didn't hurt either. By that time, I thought we were done with our pre-meal meal, but Claudio surprised me with gin-and-tonic sorbets as a finish to our appetizers. How he'd pulled all this together in two hours remained a mystery.

We chatted easily, as we always did, and flirted scandalously just for the fun of it. Teddy's extra-cuddly mood kept us well entertained; even Toni joined in for a while before deciding she was bored with us humans. The lighting added a touch of romance, while the soft-but-lively guitar music kept things light. Our conversation flowed freely except for one topic: my departure tomorrow. We avoided that like a quarantine-zone—we knew death was out there, and we ignored it as best we could.

"Isn't it time to start the paella?" I asked after a while. I wasn't hungry following our abundance of tapas, but cooking with Claudio was always fun, and I was looking forward to that part of the evening. Me, looking forward to cooking. Imagine that.

"You are right, I almost forgot. I do not know where my mind went!" He leaped from the couch, extending his hand and offering to help me up. I couldn't get up quite as quickly; Teddy had taken up residence in my lap. I gave him the boot, he gave me a yowl. All three of us moved to the kitchen. Toni yowled too, announcing she would follow when she was good and ready, not one minute sooner.

Once we'd laid out the primary ingredients on the kitchen island, Claudio asked, "Would you like to chop the meats or the vegetables?" He always pronounced every syllable of the word *vegetables*. I was going to miss that.

"You know I prefer the 'veg-e-ta-bles.'" He grinned at my imitation. "Hacking up meat feels so violent." I grabbed my favorite knife from the block.

"If I recall correctly," he began, placing his hand on the small of my back, "the first time we cooked paella together, *violent* does not begin to describe what you did to those tomatoes."

I laughed, touched that he remembered—maybe this evening didn't come with a grand-gesture surprise, but Claudio's remembering was enough. More than enough, considering our expiration date.

"Hey, learning to cook is a process, buddy," I chided. "And I told you about my relationship with the kitchen. You can't say I didn't warn you!"

"No, this is not exactly true." His eyes sparked with mischief. "No man could have been prepared for that slaughter. My beautiful tomatoes!"

"Just one tomato," I corrected. "You took over from there." I put my free hand on my hip. "But who starts a newbie out on a dish like paella? So much prep!"

"It does require some work, but this dish is the heart of Spain! It is well worth it!" he stepped away and opened the refrigerator. He lowered his voice and said the next part into the fridge. "Much like you are well worth it, my Kauhlie." Butterflies jumped in my stomach, but I pretended I hadn't heard. Keep those worms in their can, Callie.

We chopped and we diced, refilling our wine as needed along the way. Toni pawed at Claudio's legs, begging for fat scraps, which Teddy would then fight her for. Sibling rivalry at shin level. Their antics kept me on an even keel. The moment desolation tinged me, I could scoop one of them up for a cuddle. Claudio seemed to be going in for extra cuddles, too; tonight, we were both engaging in unspoken kitten-therapy.

We were in rare form as we prepared our meal, with our movements complementing each other like we were sharing a rhythm on the dancefloor. We were in absolute sync until, the moment Claudio was ready to begin browning the meats, I reached up to the pot rack and grabbed the large pan we'd used so many times before.

"Kauhlie, we do not need the big pan. It is only the two of us, and there is no need for leftovers." There was little emotion in his voice; he was simply stating a fact. As if his words weren't wounds on my soul.

I sighed, regrouping as best I could. "I guess you're right. No need for leftovers." I carefully rehung the larger pan, swapping it for a smaller one. By this time tomorrow, I would be thirty-thousand feet over North America, and transcontinental airlines generally frowned on bringing your own lunch.

He looked as if he were going to reply, but he turned back to the island and ran his blade through the chicken again. I let it pass and prepped the pan with oil. It began sizzling as Claudio threw in the chicken and rabbit. In went the beans, and after they softened, I added my expertly chopped (or at least not slaughtered) vegetables. I tossed in the snails, bidding them farewell: "In you go fellas." I hoped San Francisco's specialty markets carried fresh snails so I could try making paella on my own.

I knew it was now very important to guard the pan, so nothing dried out or burned. I kept one eye on the mixture as I began wiping up the island—we'd made a beautiful mess. I stirred the pan gently from time to time, taking in the aroma. Claudio, leaning against the counter, watched with interest.

"What?" I asked.

"Nothing. It is only that you have become an expert in the kitchen, I believe."

I wasn't buying that for a second, and for once tonight I wasn't letting him off that easy. "No really, what?"

"Kauhlie, it is nothing. Nothing at all. Do not stop."

"You're so odd." I turned back to the stovetop and adjusted the heat.

"*Claro que sí*," he agreed.

I gasped—a hiss of a sharp breath—and froze. Claudio never spoke Spanish to me. Had we entered an alternate universe? A new paella dimension, perhaps?

I shifted my attention back to the pan, which was drying out. I reached for the broth. Claudio instinctively reached for it at the same time, and his hand landed on mine. I raised my eyebrow. "Too slow," I admonished before moistening the mix. Since when was Claudio ever a step behind? The elephant in the room was killing me.

I pushed through, determined to make this our best paella ever. After a quick interlude of kitten-therapy, I reached for the canister of rice. "Prepare to call out!" I cried, packing an extra helping of enthusiasm into my five syllables.

"Kauhlie, I do not feel like yelling tonight."

"Come on, we always call out when we add the rice. It's our thing."

"We have a lot of things."

"What's so wrong with that, huh? One might say having a lot of things is one of our things." I tilted my head haughtily. "Mightn't one?"

He chuckled, brightening. "Yes, one mightn't."

I shrieked with laughter. "See, spending all this time together was not only your great delight, but I also managed to mess up your English."

"Yes, you have brought me many new experiences," he said with a touch of languor. He adjusted his tone and threw up his hands in mock surrender. "Okay, I give! We will call out."

I bumped my hip against his in victory before I started sprinkling in the rice slowly and evenly, just as he'd taught me. "*Veinte minutos!*" we both yelled in perfect unison. Startled, Toni and Teddy scuttled from the room.

As I was still adding the rice, Claudio slipped behind me. His chin on my shoulder, he gazed deep into the pan and whispered, "*Veinte minutos.*" He wrapped his arms around me and nuzzled my hair. "*Veinte minutos más, mi Kauhlie.*"

Claudio had been right—we shouldn't have called out. Because, with him embracing me and whispering into my ear, my mind turned back to time's waning. To the hours before my flight. *Veinte horas.* No, not twenty hours, more like thirteen hours. *Trece horas* left in Spain. *Trece horas* left with Claudio. *Trece horas* until my new life.

CHAPTER 38
THREE TYPES OF RED LIGHTS

I couldn't bring myself to spend the night with Claudio; I'd been sure I wouldn't sleep if I were next to him. I would lie awake for hours, watching the rise and fall of his chest and taking in his smell. At some point, I would roll over into my favorite position, and in his half-sleep, he'd drape his arm across me just so. Our perfect bliss. A trap—all my resolve would drain away, tearing asunder the peace I'd found. We did make love that evening, but I couldn't bring myself to stay. Claudio had objected to my going, but not too strongly. I'd stolen away into the night, leaving him alone in his bed.

In the morning, I packed much faster than expected; with yesterday's head start, I only needed to throw together my toiletries and a few sundries. When finished, I examined my bags, which I'd piled neatly on my bed. I hadn't accumulated much in all these months: I only had one more suitcase than when I'd arrived. Was this all I had after one-half of an entire year? I felt there should be more—how could so many months fit into so few bags? And, if I was taking so little with me, how could my time here possibly affect the life I would soon lead thousands of miles away?

I thought about the things I'd put into storage before leaving New York. All that stuff had been transferred last week to my yet-unseen San Francisco apartment, but there wouldn't be all that much waiting for me when I arrived—I'd only had two and a half rooms in the Village, and they weren't exactly crammed with material goods. Surely, New York had long forgotten me, would Spain forget me too?

Maybe, but I wouldn't forget Spain. I hadn't collected a lot of stuff, but I *had* collected experiences. Stuff could decay and disappear, but nothing could take away all I'd encountered here and the people I'd grown to love. I'd always have *Embrace in the Street*. I'd always have *Guernica*. I'd always have Trevor's exasperating weirdness and longing for color, Claudio's *el duende* and *pasión*. Maybe most of all, I'd always have Hemingway's otherworldly counsel. I would be taking all that with me as I flew away—each a brick in the foundation of my new life.

A horn beeped. Claudio had pulled up to the curb in his own car—a surprise since he so rarely drove. He stuck his head out the window and scanned the hotel until he found my room; his morning smile brightened his face when he saw me. I waved before collecting my things and taking one last look at my room. At the front desk, I left tips in individual envelopes for all the staff who'd put up with me for so long.

The bellhop wheeled my bags outside. Without the heft of my stuff, it felt weird walking out of the hotel for this last time—there was no finality to it. At this hour, I could've been on my way to first breakfast with Trevor, just like any other day. I hoped he would text while I was in the air; his cousin had put him in touch with a potential roommate, and he was meeting her this afternoon. With any luck, she would be someone who could appreciate Trevor's special blend of loyal, weird, dorky, and sweet.

"You're right on time," I said as Claudio greeted me. "You're never on time before noon." Wow, how often had Trevor and I teased him about that?

"I'm afraid *mañana* does not apply to transatlantic flights." He grinned slyly. "But I know myself well, so I built in extra time for my lateness. I planned to be here half an hour ago!"

He began helping the bellhop with my bags, loading them into the trunk. "Kauhlie, is this really everything?"

"That's all of it, yes. Hard to believe, I know."

"If you find you've forgotten something, I am sure my friend here…" he tipped the bellhop generously and explained his request in Spanish, "…will help me send it to you." The young man was effusive over his tip; if I'd left so much as a hairband behind, I was sure he would personally deliver it to Claudio.

"Thanks, but I'm not leaving anything here in Spain." I held back a sigh and a frown. Leaving nothing except Claudio.

Even though I was usually on foot, experience had taught me to expect heavy traffic at this time of the day, the last of the morning rush hour. I was looking forward to it in a way—it would force more alone time between Claudio and me. Hey, maybe I'd even miss my flight? That would mean one more lunch together, maybe dinner, too. I was getting on a plane today regardless, but who was I to argue if things got pushed back by a few hours? Couldn't I have my peace and a bonus lunch too?

But no. The city was remarkably empty. I'd never seen anything like it. Fate, it seemed, wanted me to leave Spain right away. We zoomed along as if Claudio owned the streets and had ordered them cleared. Even the traffic signals seemed to speed me on my way; green lights turned yellow as we approached, but almost none were red. Although, if asked in a court of law, I would have to testify that Claudio did run through one red light.

"Didn't you see that one?!" I cried, clutching my seatbelt as we whizzed into the intersection.

"Kauhlie, fret not. There are three types of red lights in Spain. Have I not told you this?"

"Three types of red lights?" Spanish traffic lights looked little different from American ones to me, and red was red.

"Of course, there are," he replied nonchalantly. "One type of red light is truly red. For these we stop, undisputed!"

"Okay…" I wasn't sure where he was going with this as the city zipped by.

"The second type is *mostly* red."

"That one looked pretty red, Claudio."

He ignored my comment and continued. "And the third is merely a suggestion."

"And that light you just blew? Which type was that?"

"That one was merely a suggestion. Not even mostly red." He laughed. "And like many suggestions, it was a poor one!"

We reached the airport in record time, without any more suggested red lights along the way. We pulled into my terminal's lot and found a parking space by the entrance—even the parking lot was championing my departure. Claudio popped out of the car and pulled out my bags right away, moving at a speed I'd only seen equaled the morning he'd rescued the boy. A life-or-death pace, all over some luggage.

Watching him on fast-forward, I couldn't take it. "Why are you in such a hurry to see me leave?" I demanded.

"What are you talking about, Kauhlie? You said I was to take you to the airport, and so this is what I have done." He flashed his "genuine" smile, the very picture of blind obedience.

"You set a record getting here. You had my bags out before I got my seatbelt off! I don't understand—what's the big rush?"

"But you have to go, Kauhlie, and I am very good at being late in the mornings. You cannot miss your flight!"

"That's not the point, and you know it. My flight isn't going anywhere."

He balked, puzzled. "This is not true. Your flight will leave with or without you. You know this, Kauhlie?"

"This is no time for technicalities! And you're still missing the point."

"What is the point?"

I took a deep breath. "Never mind. It doesn't matter." It didn't matter, really, not in the long run. Because there was no more long run.

I hopped up on my tiptoes and kissed him on the cheek. Let Claudio have his obliviousness, it would make this easier for him.

The walk across the terminal seemed much longer than it actually was. The airport was as empty as the streets, and with so few people around, the space felt cavernous. I checked in and sent my luggage on its way. We hardly spoke as we walked, but as we crept closer to my security checkpoint, I could sense Claudio's mood changing.

"Kauhlie, let us have a coffee before we reach your gate. We have time."

His matter-of-fact tone surprised me. After tearing at a breakneck speed to get here, now we had time?

I was already well-caffeinated from breakfast, and for the first time in my adult life I wondered if more caffeine was a good idea—I'd be in a flying tin can for the foreseeable future. Even still, I couldn't miss having one last coffee in Spain with the man I was leaving behind. Maybe I couldn't get a bonus lunch, but a bonus coffee would do.

We chose the gourmet place—when it came to airport coffee, it had been my experience that "gourmet" was the only way to get a decent brew—and situated ourselves at a small table. Claudio pulled out my chair for me, something he only ever did in nicer restaurants. I thanked him, but it came out too stiff, overly polite, and distant. An ocean-and-a-continent distant, like a part of me had already left.

"So, this is truly it, yes?" he asked, breaking the silence that had settled between us. He sounded as if he'd never been to an airport in his life, as if he'd only just realized I was going back to the States for good.

"That's how this works, big guy. When my flight leaves, I go away on it."

"Hmmm."

"Hmmm, what?" I asked. "Hmmm" wasn't even a word. With all the languages in his head, *that* the best he could do?"

"Nothing, Kauhlie."

I didn't press, and instead I steered the conversation to his own move. "You'll have to do this too, soon. Leave Spain. Fly away to New

York and not come back." His brows knitted together as he processed this, but I pretended not to notice. "Do you have a start date yet?"

He mulled for a moment more. "I do not, no. My father has not decided when my position will begin. It will be soon, I guess. I have not thought much about it."

I wanted to bang my head against a wall. I seriously didn't know how the man functioned. He'd tortured himself over this decision, he'd committed to relocating across the Atlantic, and yet he wasn't thinking about it? How could all that *not* be on his mind? And if all that wasn't on his mind, what was?

"But you are right. I will have to fly away from my beloved Madrid. I will miss being one-hundred percent Spanish, but it has always been my destiny to leave my beautiful city." He sighed heavily. "This past year has been good for me—in so many ways."

I softened a bit. If I loved this city as much as Claudio did, I might focus on living in the moment too. Leaving Madrid was inevitable for both of us, but it was hard for him in a way it wasn't for me. I was headed *toward* the rest of my life, while he was leaving his home. I squeezed his hand from across the table. He squeezed back.

A pang shot through me. We both had to leave, sure, but what if we changed the plan? What if we tried a cross-continental thing? I'd do one weekend a month in New York, he'd do one per month in San Francisco. A bi-coastal couple. I could probably do that. Not ideal, but Claudio clearly needed me, and maybe I needed him too.

His one unruly lock popped out of place, distracting me from my thoughts. I was about to float my coast-to-coast proposal when he grinned and asked, "Would you like a cookie?"

My mouth gaped; I had to consciously close my jaw. Here I was, considering a whole new plan for us, a potential future together, while Claudio was thinking about... cookies? It never ceased to amaze me how he could latch onto anything—anything at all—if it meant not talking about his feelings. So damn typical; *that* was the reason I'd made my peace.

I felt like a sap. I scratched the idea, relieved I hadn't spoken up after all. It would've been a recipe for disaster, anyhow: if we weren't together-together, a clean break was a mercy in disguise. At least we'd both be free to find happiness.

My tone turned saccharine. "No, thanks. I don't want a cookie."

"Okay, but they are really good here at the airport. If you change your mind, I will gladly buy you one!"

We lingered as we finished our coffees, but Claudio was distracted, pensive. Granted I'd never turned down a cookie before, but that wasn't it. Something was brewing inside him. When I looked closely, I saw he was sweating a little. What...? Claudio never sweat.

He took my hand as we left the café. His hand was clammy. That grossed me out, mostly from surprise, and I nearly let go. The man was nervous. Nervous about what, I had no idea, but definitely on edge—almost panicky. He stumbled over a table as we headed toward the exit, utterly graceless. Who was this man?

Even from outside the café, I could see there was barely a line at my checkpoint; even security wanted me to leave Spain this morning, it seemed. I couldn't fathom it; how could this airport be so empty? Sure, ten o'clock on a Wednesday wasn't a peak time for overseas departures, but this was ridiculous.

"You never got a cookie," I blurted out once we'd left the café, barely aware of my own words.

"What was that, Kauhlie?"

"You were so in love with airport cookies in there, but you didn't buy one."

He hung his head. "Neither of us truly wants a cookie today, I believe." The singularly saddest thing I'd ever heard him utter.

❧

An eeriness hanging over us, we'd made our way across the concourse toward security—another threshold Claudio couldn't, wouldn't, cross. With only a few yards left to go, Claudio stopped short decisively in mid-stride but didn't release my hand. I had to stop, too, and I wiggled free of my purse and carry-on. He took my hand again—my hand in his still-clammy hand—and raised it to his lips, kissing it tenderly.

Time slowed around us. Burying my head in his chest, I couldn't speak. Because this was it. This was goodbye. All of it was over, here and now. No matter what came next for me, Claudio and I were finished.

Without a word, Claudio lifted my chin, so gently goosebumps rose on my arms. Slowly, he ran his index finger down the center of my forehead. Then—just as he had before I'd run with the bulls—he moved his finger down and lightly touched my heart, letting his fingertip linger on my chest. I forced my knees not to buckle as he embraced me.

"Kauhlie, I love you."

Shock gripped me, my eyes shooting open. I didn't hear him correctly—I *couldn't* have heard him correctly. I met his eye. "You what?!"

"I love you, my Kauhlie."

I pushed him away and stepped back. "Are you kidding me?! We've been joined at the hip for almost a week! And now, minutes before my flight, you think *this* is the time to confess your love?"

"Yes. This is the time." He nodded sharply, agreeing with himself. "I must say it now. I love you."

"Well, you're a little late, buddy!"

He started bringing his finger to my forehead again. I grabbed it firmly. "Enough of that!" I snapped, not about to let my knees go weak again. "My future is on the other side of there." I pointed at the metal detectors.

He closed the few inches separating us, sweeping me against him and pressing his body to mine. "Perhaps not. Perhaps your future is with me?" He trembled ever so slightly as he spoke, as if he were afraid of the conviction behind his words.

"My future is in California, Claudio. You know that. We've already decided what we're doing here." I squirmed but didn't push him away. Yet I couldn't help but shout in frustration. "We've found our peace! You're not sticking to the plan!"

His brown eyes, now velvet, begged. "I cannot help my feelings." He brushed my cheek with the back of his hand, as if this one motion solved everything.

"What am I supposed to do with this, huh? What do you want me to do with this *now?*"

"New York," he replied, struggling to get the words out. An inchoate thought, not even a sentence. An utterance remarkably like Trevor's non-language.

"No, you're confused. I just *left* New York."

"New York with me," he said quickly. This time it sounded less like Trevor and more like a cartoon caveman. Was this really Claudio?

I wriggled out of his arms. "No, I'm not going back to the city, that part of my life is over. And anyway, you might hate New York—I'm not throwing everything away on the chance things *might* work out with your father!"

He clapped his hands together, palm-against-palm, in a steeple, begging. "Then stay with me in Madrid, my Kauhlie." His words were surer now, but not by much.

"Oh, even better! I'll give up my dream job and live the rest of my life in a country where I barely speak the language. Just for you."

"But we will live together in love." His voice evinced complete surety and sincerity.

"Now there's a plan that can't go wrong!" I did my best impression of him. "Kauhl-ie… let us live together in loooove."

"That is what I am asking. Madrid is my home. My father will understand if I back out."

"Oh, yeah? Well, you said it yourself—your fate is to leave Madrid. I asked you to come to San Francisco with me! That was the only true possibility for us, but there was no living in loooove back then!" I jabbed his chest with every sentence. "Remember that?"

"I remember," he replied, catching my finger before he succumbed to death by a thousand pokes. "I was not ready then. I am asking you now. Stay in Madrid with me… now." He turned my hand over in his and moved to kiss it.

I pulled back. "No more mushy stuff!" *Embrace in the Street* flashed in my mind, Hemingway's first clue to me. I pictured the two lovers in relief against the night, their whole universe each other. I trembled, remembering my tears as I took them in. The pair embraced *all* of each other. Not a half-embrace, not an embrace of sacrifice, but a complete embrace, every part of each other comprising one whole.

I knew my answer.

"Love isn't enough, Claudio, Madrid isn't enough. I worked my ass off to get where I am! It's not fair to ask me to give all that up! Not when I offered us a real way forward."

He didn't reply immediately, although the frown spreading across his face confirmed what I already knew. "San Francisco is something I cannot do. I am sorry."

"Well, so am I! And I don't care if you love me. I don't care!' I stomped my foot—actually stomped it—in sheer exasperation. Shocked, Claudio's eyes went blank and hard for an instant, then velvety and pleading again, then settled somewhere in the middle.

"Claudio, I have to go. Now."

"Go if you must, Kauhlie," he replied, focused on his feet. He raised his head and held my gaze. "But know you can come back. You can go through security, but you can still come back—right up until the point you board the plane."

"Goodbye, Claudio."

"If you change your mind—"

"—You're impossible!" I was about to elaborate on that point—on his being impossible, but he swooped up my face in his hands and kissed me. An *el duende* kiss, but somehow deeper, like our first kiss. This, our last kiss.

I melted into him, every inch of me dissolving. Every muscle relaxed, the airport disappearing. I wanted to stay in that kiss, yet I broke away, extricating myself slowly but deliberately. A gentle break, but a break nonetheless. A finality.

"Listen, you," I said tenderly. "I finally found myself. Spain did that… Hemingway did that. You were… are… a part of that, always will be. But you can't swan in at the last minute, say you love me, and expect me to walk away from my future. No. It's too late. Now is too late."

He smiled as if he understood, but his smile was sorrowful.

I smiled sorrowfully back. "That was a very nice kiss, though." Claudio's face lit up, and I instantly regretted my words. Hope burned in his eyes, even though no hope remained. "But it's still too late," I added.

His face fell again. "If you change your mind, Kauhlie, I will be waiting here for you."

"Goodbye, Claudio." Ignoring the moistness in my eyes, I kissed him on the cheek and slung my bags over my shoulder in one fluid movement. I didn't allow myself to hesitate as I walked away.

With almost no line, I was cleared to go through security in minutes. I faced forward the whole time, refusing to turn around, although I desperately wanted to. I knew Claudio was still there, and I knew how badly he wanted me to look back. I could feel his eyes on me, his hope on me.

His hope followed me into the waiting area. It stayed on me as I stared listlessly at the overhead TV. Still, I didn't look back—time and time again I didn't look back. After a few minutes, a last-call announcement crackled over the intercom. Until the call was repeated in English, I thought it was for my gate, but it was for the next gate over—for the flight to Kilimanjaro International Airport. I envisioned the famed mountain with its ice-capped peak. A strange and mysterious place, a wilderness of hyena's cries. I could hop on that flight, I thought, and disappear completely. No Madrid, no San Francisco, no New York. A whole new continent—no one would ever find me amid the snows of Kilimanjaro. A fantasy, of course, but in one way it would be no different from my future in California: both were lives without Claudio.

I'd been staring at the last man in the gate's line without realizing it.

He stepped forward and handed over his boarding pass, removing his Oysterman hat. He spun it around impishly on one finger as the attendant checked his pass, as if he were impatient for his next adventure to begin. Without warning, he turned abruptly, his eyes connecting with mine despite the distance between us.

I knew those eyes.

I knew that face, that beard, that wide and heavy brow. Hemingway. He winked at me, replacing his Oysterman. He tugged at the brim, cocking his head in approval. His smile widened, his eyes gleamed. Stunned, I instinctively spun around, checking to see who else he could've been looking at. No one was behind me except Claudio, still standing motionless by security, now gazing at the ceiling as if praying. I whipped my head forward, looking for Hemingway, but all I saw was the tan blur of a bush jacket disappearing through the doorway.

Before I could make any sense of it, my gate opened for boarding. Suddenly, all I wanted to do was start my new life, with all the possibilities it held. What did California have in store for me? What challenges, what rewards? I made a beeline for the attendant and his plastic smile.

Only two women made it into line ahead of me, but even that small delay was torture: I wanted to get on that plane. Yet my gaze turned again to Claudio—I couldn't help taking him in one last time. He perked up and waved, eager and expectant. I broke our eye contact, shaking my head. He understood my meaning—too late, much, much too late.

Eagerly, I faced forward, fighting to keep myself from pushing past the remaining woman ahead. The seconds felt like lead, my thoughts racing. Claudio's eyes burned into me, luring me back. But no. Screw Spain Man and his eleventh-hour, "I love you." I'd conquered my nightmares, I'd opened myself to love, and I'd found my peace. Another coast awaited me. I could welcome love—and willingly—on that coast, but only if the embrace came on a two-way street. Because that was the woman I'd been all along: I'd found my Hemingway, and he was me.

SAN FRANCISCO

California Company

I relaxed into my lounge chair and exhaled. I'd just refilled my wine, and now that I was comfortable again, I took a long sip. I loved my balcony—it ran the entire length of my apartment, kitchen to living room. I could see for miles, and to my west, the Golden Gate Bridge floated in the distance. Along with a nice glass of wine, that bridge made good company in the evenings.

My new job was fantastic—just as Matt had promised, only better. Being at the heart of a growing and dynamic team energized me, and I felt more professionally appreciated than I ever had in New York. The management team didn't make a single move without consulting me; I general-counseled to my heart's content.

My days were packed. New money continued pouring in from investors, and right now we were pulling together the final details before going to market. Our product was still tightly under wraps, but thanks to a clever marketing campaign, the entire industry was buzzing about us. No one knew exactly what game changer we were about to release, and the speculation, rumors, and anticipation fueled our brand. Without having sold a single thing, our company was already at the top of the heap. By this time next year, I had no doubt we would be a household name.

I was the one who'd vetted the marketers, and Matt had hired them on my recommendation. Because of their success, he gave me extra stock options as a bonus. A bonus, three months in! With so much happening so quickly, and with so much legal work to do, I'd hired myself a staff. Not a huge staff, but talented people who helped keep my work-life balance healthy. Me, the head of the legal department! Some days, I almost couldn't believe I'd had this in me all along.

The Golden Gate Bridge, with its stunning red contrasting against the blueness of the bay, often made me think of Trevor. I don't think I would've fully appreciated my view of the art deco masterpiece if it hadn't been for him. He was well on his way to finding his own color now; he'd found a job translating classic works at a publisher in Berlin. One of his very first projects was a new German-language edition of *The Sun Also Rises*. He'd texted me constantly during those weeks, referencing passages he had questions about or had found a new appreciation for. I reveled in his happiness, so much so that I couldn't bring myself to tell him I'd moved past the novel. I didn't need Hemingway's Spain anymore; vicarious living was behind me for good.

My six Spanish months would always be a part of me, though, and I often found myself asking if I were more Barcelona or Madrid. Certainly, there was a healthy pinch of Pamplona thrown in; I'd only spent a week in that city, but I was pretty sure every moment I'd experienced on its famed streets counted for double. I'd run as fast as I could with the bulls, and even though they would always outpace me, I'd surpass them in my own way. No one—not myself, not my nightmares, not human or beast—could hold me back anymore. My destiny was open now.

I sipped my wine, helping it along. The balcony door clicked open behind me. Toni scurried out, springing into my lap—a fuzzy, black blur. She was making herself comfortable when Teddy, only an instant behind his sister, began curling at my feet.

"Kauhlie, I must say you were right. There are many financial opportunities in this city." He smiled and leaned down, pecking me on the lips. "I visited the most amazing start-up today. My father will gladly invest, of this I am sure."

"Of course, I was right, dear," I replied, laughing. "I told you as much back in Madrid. Remember?" I lifted the bottle and introduced a generous pour to the empty glass in his hand.

"I know, but you were so very right," Claudio said, seating himself in the matching chair and sipping his freshly poured wine. "Much more right than I could have anticipated."

We'd started a small life together in San Francisco, creating our own world with our own traditions. We cooked together after work at least one night a week, no matter how busy we were. On the weekends, we often went for long walks—we'd created a standard route. Claudio and I would stroll down the hill, through the park, and past the cutest adobe church, before circling back and heading up the hill. Whenever we could, we explored the city's art scene, taking in galleries and auctions; the living room was already running short on display space. No matter how we spent our time together, Toni and Teddy were always happy to see us when we returned home.

"You were right too, Claudio. You were right to drop everything that day and catch the next flight to San Francisco."

"My Kauhlie, what choice did I have?! When I watched you fly away, I knew I had made the gravest mistake of my life. No time for packing. I did not even take a toothbrush!"

I smiled at him. "We have plenty of toothbrushes here, you know."

"I did not come to San Francisco for the toothbrushes. I came for you." From his chair, he grasped my hand with an impassioned squeeze. Ah, *el duende*.

"I knew this would be the right life for us, Claudio." I hadn't known he would fly nearly six thousand miles to embrace me, but the moment I'd found him at my door, I welcomed him and his embrace with all I had.

"Yes, you were right, Kauhlie. There could be no other life for us."

Of course I was right, my dear Spanish lover, of course I was right. I'm Callie McGraw.

ACKNOWLEDGMENTS

I first want to thank my wife Jennie, whose love and support made finishing this novel possible. Jennie, you totally got it. I also want to thank my parents for their support and devotion through the years and the inspiration they offered me. Thank you to my children who absorbed the idea of their father writing a novel with the rugged malleability so particular to youth. A huge thank you goes out to Erika DeSimone of Erika's Editing, whose patient editing and coaching elevated this book to beyond where I hoped it could go. I also want to thank Fidel Louis, also of Erika's Editing, for his proofreading of the same. Thanks go to Beth Burrell at Elizabeth Lane Designs for her wonderful cover art. I send a big thank you to Marissa DeCuir and her teams at Books Fluent and Books Forward for their publishing and marketing support; their cooperation was vital to making this novel a reality. Finally, I want to thank all the people who asked over the years, "How's the book going?" Writing a book is like farming—both take a long time, and both are ultimately binary: a book is either finished or it isn't; the crops are either harvested or they aren't. Your inquiries helped drive me forward until I finished the harvest.

ABOUT THE AUTHOR

Ken Dortzbach is a native of Madison, Wisconsin. As a graduate of Princeton University and the Northwestern University School of Law, he practiced law internationally for almost twenty years, including living abroad and working in countries across the globe. During that time, he found a special appreciation for Spain's history and culture; when it came time to pen his first novel, the country became the perfect backdrop for his book. In combining his passion for Spain with his longstanding interest in Ernest Hemingway and his works, *Finding Hemingway* was born.

Ken likes to pretend he can cook like Claudio and is keenly aware he dances like Trevor. The leftovers in his refrigerator are nothing like Jean-Francois', although he did run with the bulls in Pamplona like Callie. He does not bake fresh bread, but he does have two kittens—along with two grown children. Ken and his wife now live in Wisconsin and divide their time between Milwaukee and Madison; they enjoy traveling far and wide together.

Made in the USA
Monee, IL
27 October 2020